ACCLAIM FOR ONCE UPON A PRINCE

"I didn't just love this story, I wanted to dive in and live in it . . . If you are looking for a book to get lost within, this is it!"

—USAToday.com

"Hauck has created an enchanting novel featuring a charming hero and heroine."

—*Booklist*, STARRED REVIEW

"Well-developed secondary characters are entertaining in their own right, adding a quirky touch (as do cameo-style appearances by real-life royals). Hauck fans will find a gem of a tale."

—*Publishers Weekly*, STARRED REVIEW

"*Once Upon a Prince* is a modern-day fairy tale that's a delightful page turner full of fun, faith, and barbeque."

—*CBA Retailers + Resources*

PRINCESS
Ever After

Also by Rachel Hauck

The Royal Wedding Series
Once Upon a Prince

Lowcountry Romance novels
Love Starts with Elle
Sweet Caroline
Dining with Joy

Diva Nashvegas
Lost in Nashvegas

With Sara Evans

Sweet By and By
Softly and Tenderly
Love Lifted Me

PRINCESS
Ever After

RACHEL HAUCK

THE ROYAL WEDDING SERIES

ZONDERVAN

Princess Ever After

© 2014 by Rachel Hayes Hauck

This title is also available as a Zondervan ebook. Visit www.zondervan.com/ebooks.

Requests for information should be addressed to:

Zondervan, *Grand Rapids, Michigan 49530*

Library of Congress Cataloging-in-Publication Data

Hauck, Rachel, 1960-

  Princess ever after : a Royal Wedding novel / Rachel Hauck.

    pages cm. -- (The Royal Wedding novel ; #2)

  ISBN 978-0-310-31550-6 (trade paper)

  1. Weddings--Fiction. I. Title.

  PS3608.A866P75 2014

  813'.6--dc23

                    2013037377

Any Internet addresses (websites, blogs, etc.) and telephone numbers in this book are offered as a resource. They are not intended in any way to be or imply an endorsement by Zondervan, nor does Zondervan vouch for the content of these sites and numbers for the life of this book.

Printed in the United States of America

14 15 16 17 18 19 20 /RRD/ 20 19 18 17 16 15 14 13 12 11 10 9 8 7 6 5 4 3 2 1

In loving memory of my aunt,
Betty Jane Burnside Hayes
June 9, 1925–October 16, 2012
See you soon!

ONE

S he'd found bliss. Perhaps even true love. Behind the wheel of a '71 Dodge Challenger restored to Slant-6 perfection.

Fishtailing into turn two of a west side Tallahassee dirt track, Reggie shifted into fourth gear and pushed the car to its max, the thrill of the race electrifying her entire being.

The engine rumbled with authority as the tires hummed over the track, churning up dust as if to truly bury yesterday. Firing down the straightaway toward pinkish-gold remains of twilight leaking through the tall pines, the last thread of Reggie's lingering doubt flitted away on the cool September breeze.

This was what she'd been born to do—restore junked-up, forgotten old cars to their original, classic beauty. And it only took her twenty-nine years to figure that out.

Ha-ha. Come on, baby. Show me what you can do.

The boys at the finish line—Al, Rafe, and Wally—flagged her home with their hats in hand.

This was amazing. Simply amazing. She should've done this years ago. Jump from the corporate CPA ship onto the barely floating life raft of "pipe dreams."

In the last six months, she'd endured more than her share of sleepless nights since she traded her business suits for coveralls and entered into the car restoration business with Al, who was like a second father to her.

Restoring the Challenger was their first big job. And their first test.

Reggie checked the speedometer. The needle shimmied right at one hundred.

"Wa*hoo*!"

She sped past the finish line. An air horn sounded. Male voices rose with hoots and hollers. She'd done it. *They'd* done it. And without leaving a trail of car parts littering the racetrack.

Downshifting, Reggie aimed for center field, whipping the car in a series of donuts, mashing on the horn, gunning the engine, letting the 440 breathe and have its say.

Oh mercy, building and installing this engine had given them fits. Those days were the ones most filled with doubt, when Reggie considered dialing her old firm, Backlund & Backlund, and begging for her job back.

One last spin around the infield and Reggie stopped the car and hopped out, letting the engine idle. Rafe swooped her up, whirling her around. "We did it!"

When he set her down, Al embraced her in his dark, teddy bear arms. "I'm so stinking proud of you, girl."

"No, *you*, Al. It was your idea."

"But you were willing to take the leap." Al, a retired Marine master sergeant, and her daddy's best friend all the way back in the '60s at Sullivan Elementary School, was the brains and brawn behind opening the shop.

When Al had approached Reggie with the idea six months ago, she had nothing to say but "Where do I sign?"

Then he hired Rafe, a Marine who served with Al right before he retired. Rafe left the Marines after three tours in Afghanistan and hitchhiked from North Carolina to Tallahassee in search of "Sergeant Al."

Ole Wally arrived at the idling car last. "I do believe she's plum beautiful. Reg, you drive better than Danica."

She threw her arms around the wizened old redneck with thin wisps of white hair sticking out from under his Jeff Gordon 24 cap.

"Wally, your engine work is the best in the business, and I'd bet my firstborn on it."

"Reg,"—Wally spit, an old habit left over from his Red Man chew days—"don't go banking money on an account you don't have. Got to find a man, go on a date, get married so's you can have a firstborn." Wally sauntered around the car. "Rafe, did you hear something pinging with the engine? Thought I heard it long about the eight cylinder."

Wally—the car whisperer.

"Let's listen for it on the ride back to the shop," Rafe said, leaning over the hood, listening for the ping.

The shop was an old red barn Al had found way out Blountstown Highway. It worked because it was big and airy with a solid roof. But mostly, because it was cheap.

"Say! Reg,"—a loud bass voice boomed across the infield with irritation—"what happened to seven o'clock?"

Reggie squinted through the long angles of light and shadow as Mark, her date for the evening, made his way toward her.

"Mark . . . hey . . ." Reggie tugged her phone from the pocket in her coveralls. Was it seven already? No, it wasn't seven. It was seven thirty. Seven thirty-one, to be exact. She was late. "I'm so sorry." She met Mark on the other side of the car, glancing back at Wally and shooting him a goofy look. "We had to run the car one last time. Wally heard a ping in the engine." *Well, he did.* "Danny Hayes is picking her up in the morning, and we have to be sure she's running at one hundred percent."

"Wally and Al can manage a *ping*, Reg." Mark swiped his finger across the dusty hood and made a grand gesture of checking his watch. "Because you and I are late." He stared at her coveralls. "Is that what you're wearing?"

"Yes, it's all the rage in women's fashion this season in New York, Mark. Grease-stained coveralls." Reggie raised her foot. "But I am changing into a pair of fancy boots. Won't that look smart?"

"That-a-way to give it to him, Reg." Rafe nudged her in solidarity as he came around to slip into the driver's seat.

"Drive careful, Rafe. Get the car back to the barn and cleaned up, okay?" She unzipped her coveralls and stepped out. Underneath she wore jeans and a black, pleated V-neck top—perfect attire for a Wakulla County fish fry. Even if the guy hosting it was crazy rich.

Handing her wadded-up coveralls to Rafe through the window, she winced at the worrisome sound of "overbearing mother" in her words. Nevertheless . . . "White-glove the interior, the exterior, even the wheel wells."

"Gotcha, boss." Rafe grinned and gunned the gas while Wally hovered over the engine, ear cocked to the sound of the mysterious ping.

Al motioned for Reggie to step aside with him. "Reg—" His voice broke, and when he looked up, a dewy sheen slipped across his brown eyes. He sniffed, raised his chin, and drew a deep breath. "We done good, girl."

"Yeah, we did." A well of tears filled her own eyes. "I owe you, Al. Big. Now we just have to figure out where our next job is coming from. I was thinking—"

"Have a good night, Reg." Al grabbed her shoulders and turned her around. "I just wanted to tell you I was proud of you. Now, go. Have fun. Laugh. Enjoy your success."

"We are a success, aren't we?" She smiled.

"A one-car success, but yes, so far, so good."

"Al, say, what if we—"

"Girl, go have fun with your beau."

"He's not my beau."

"Fine. Just go. Enjoy. Miriam is waiting for me at home with the grandkids. It's popcorn and Disney movie night for me." Al's bold laugh rang out. He was having the time of his life.

"Well, okay." She patted her hands against her legs. "Off I go."

"Good. Off you go," Al echoed her intent.

"Look, now, if you need anything, call me."

"Reg, what could we need at seven thirty on a Tuesday evening?" Al grabbed her shoulders and turned her toward Mark. "Have fun. That's an order."

"Yes, Master Sergeant Love."

Walking with Mark toward his car, she exhaled, pressing her hand over her middle. She'd done it. They'd done it. Restored a whole car.

"We were down to the chassis when we started working on that Challenger," she said to herself more than to Mark.

"Old Mr. McCandless is going to wonder where I've been." Mark aimed his remote at the late-model Porsche sitting at the entrance of the track. "What about seven was so hard to do, Reg?"

"I was working." She ran ahead of him, waving and cheering, chasing the Challenger as Rafe, Wally, and Al exited the track and headed for the shop.

"Let's go," Mark called.

Reggie met him at the Porsche and slipped into the passenger seat with confidence in her belly that she'd finally found her destiny.

❧

A mellow Hunter Hayes melody played over Mark's speakers, his Porsche buzzing toward the Gulf Coast.

Reggie nestled against the Italian leather and followed the brilliant red plume streaking the western horizon. Was it possible for life to be perfect? Or almost? For the first time since Mama died when she was just a kid, life made sense. Didn't it? Sure it did.

Working on the Challenger, going into business with Al, steadied her, harnessed her restlessness. Her heart stopped wondering, "Is there something more?"

"I played golf with Eric Backlund yesterday." At thirty, Mark was one of the top real estate developers in Florida. He ate lunch with congressmen and played golf with CEOs, moving farther and farther away from the skinny, sad-eyed, latchkey kid living in a rusted-out trailer.

"Does he still have a seven handicap?" she asked. Her former boss took every occasion to let the office know how well he could hit a little white ball with a thin wooden club.

"He asked about you. Wants to know when you're coming back."

"When a blizzard buries Tallahassee." She powered down her window. The dewy air swept past her face and cooled the heat rising from the conversation.

"Reg, come on. You've got to be smart, think ahead. So, bravo, you restored a classic car." He raised his hands from the wheel for a short round of applause. "Proved to yourself and everyone else you could run with the big dogs. Now it's time to consider your future."

"Not quite with the big dogs yet. We restored one car, and I don't care for your sarcasm." Did he mean to exhort and deflate her in one single breath?

Reggie ignored the knock-knock of guilt, of wanting to please, to acquiesce. But doing what others expected and asked of her was what got her into the CPA business in the first place. Daddy thought it would be a good career for her. He was right. For a season. But she'd learned her lesson. Now was her time. To do what she wanted.

"A little sarcasm goes a long way in opening blind eyes," Mark said.

"Gee, it's a wonder Jesus never used it as he went about doing good and healing. Look, Mark,"—she turned to him—"I'm not going back to Backlund & Backlund, even if restoring cars doesn't work out. So get that out of your head. Or anyone else's. I'd rather sling groceries at Publix." She sat back and faced forward, her gaze fixed on how the headlights were cutting through the darkness, her comfort and sense of well-being evaporating.

"Fine, forget accounting," Mark said, his voice gearing up for Plan B. She'd known Mark for almost twenty years, and he always had a Plan A and a Plan B, C, D, and E.

"But, Reg, for crying out loud, cars? Old cars at that? You're too intelligent and talented, too gorgeous to be wearing coveralls all day and sticking your head in a smelly engine." He slowed the car, leaning to see a blue rural street sign hidden behind a tree.

"You're good with people," he went on. "They walk right up to you and tell you their stories. Remember that woman at my office Christmas party last year? She downloaded her whole life story to you in the buffet line. She still talks about you." He shook his head and hit the gas, craning for the next street marker. "What about being a politician?"

"Ha! Politics? I'd rather work for Backlund & Backlund, *Criminal* Public Accountants."

"Har-har. Backlund is reputable and you know it."

"Even if they weren't, I'd rather work for them than be in politics." She turned to Mark. "Do you *not* know me? After all these years?"

"I *do* know you. Maybe better than you know yourself. Reg, you'd be a good politician. You'd care more about people than your own power or wealth." He slowed at the next street sign, then jerked the car left, leaving the road and hitting a soft, sandy driveway. He downshifted with a low growl. "McCandless develops million-dollar complexes. You'd think he'd pave his own drive."

But he spoke too soon. The car broke into a clearing, easing onto a curved, pebble drive that circled under a high portico to the front door.

Reggie peered out the windshield toward the second floor and the high-pitched eaves. "A palace out here in the middle of Wakulla County." She laughed. "I think I've seen it all."

"McCandless is a bit of an eccentric, but he knows real estate development."

"Let me guess. You want him to back you in something you're doing."

"A development over on St. George." Mark put the car in neutral as a red-vested valet scurried down the front steps. A second valet opened Reggie's door. Her stomach rumbled as she stepped into the potent aroma of frying fish.

"Valets," she said as Mark came around to her side, watching the man drive off with his car. "Hoity-toity. That's definitely not Wakulla County."

Wakulla County was rednecks, good ole boys and girls, her kind of folks. Not valets running down carved stone steps from the doorway of a... palace.

"All this?" Mark slipped his arm around her waist. "This is going to be me one day, babe."

Babe?

"Well, not me." Reggie shrugged out of his embrace and moved ahead of him up an illuminated path. Maybe she was being paranoid, but more and more it seemed Mark was painting her into his rich landscape. One in which she didn't belong. What was up with him? When did the air between them change? They'd been friends forever. *Just friends.*

Though they did have a "date" pact. If one or the other needed an escort to a wedding, Christmas party, work or family event, and couldn't scrounge up anyone else, the other would go. But Mark had a slew of girlfriends. The dating trail behind him was littered with gorgeous women.

"Ever hear from Monica?" Reggie said with a casual air when he caught up to her. Mark had met the dark-skinned beauty at a congressional luncheon, and Reggie didn't see him for four months. "I thought maybe she was the one."

"She went home and got engaged to her college boyfriend."

"Already? That was fast."

"I was her rebound and, frankly, I didn't see a future with us." Mark touched her elbow, lightly steering her down the path toward a white-haired, Colonel-Sanders-looking character—McCandless.

Reggie, on the other hand, had never been in love. Not that she didn't want to be, but, well, she'd not met *him*. *The one.* The love of her life.

Besides, she didn't feel she needed a man to carry on a happy life. She rather liked going to parties or weddings alone, meeting up with friends and family. If she really needed a date, she drafted her best friend, Carrie Mitchell, instead of Mark, because it always gave Carrie an excuse to buy a new pair of shoes.

"Before we get too deep into this party . . ." Mark slipped his hand into hers and suddenly tugged her off the path. A wash of dread caused her to shiver.

Mark, don't . . .

"We've been—"

Reggie's phone jingled from her jeans hip pocket. *Thank goodness.* She jerked her hand from his, reaching back for her phone. Saved by the ringtone. She never loved the Florida State University fight song more.

"It's Al," she said, turning the screen for him to see. "Hey, is everything all right?" Reggie laughed low, relieved to be away from Mark, shaking the heat of his hand from hers. "Please don't tell me you wrecked the Challenger."

"Reg, please . . . The Challenger is fine. Rafe has it spit polished and gleaming. I'm calling 'cause I thought you'd like to know we just might have our next job."

"What? Who?" Her heart pummeled her ribs. *This is great!* "A Starfire #89?" She laughed. "I'll walk on air all the way home if you say yes."

"A Starfire #89? Girl, are you out of sound mind?" Al's laugh boomed. "Now, how do you suppose the rarest car on planet Earth would make its way to Dixie? And to our little shop no less?"

"A girl can dream, can't she?" Why not? Dreaming, with some unction, was what freed her from Backlund & Backlund.

Dreaming inspired her first car restoration. Al might have dreamed up the shop, but Reggie was the one who talked Danny Hayes into giving them a chance with his Challenger.

So there was nothing wrong with a little dreaming. She'd get her a Starfire #89 one of these days. Okay, maybe not, but she'd at least sit behind the wheel of one. Someday.

"There's dreaming and then there's ridiculous, Reg. If ever a Starfire #89 comes across my path, I won't call you but walk on air to tell you in person. And you'll know what I have to say before I open my mouth because my beautiful black face will be as white as a ghost."

She laughed. "I'll look forward to it. So what car *do* we have?"

Al was right. Best be realistic if they were going to be in the restoration business. Only seven Starfire #89s—one of the world's first race cars commissioned by the Grand Duke of Hessenberg in 1904—had ever been made. Six were known to exist. Four were in museums. Two were owned by billionaires. One, the original, was lost in time. Perhaps destroyed by wars, or rain and snow, or someone looking for scrap metal. Who knew? Or maybe the car was waiting somewhere for someone to rescue it.

"I got the next best thing to a Starfire, Reg. A Duesenberg."

She exhaled every ounce of breath. "Al, no . . . come on . . . you can't be . . . a Duesy?" The air around her swirled, swift and cool, scented with fried fish, and for a moment Reggie thought she was floating. "You're kidding. No, you're not. You wouldn't kid about a Duesenberg!" She trembled. "H–how? Wh–who? When?"

"A Marine buddy—"

"God bless the Marines."

"—retired sometime back, went on to make good with a second career, and bought himself a 1933 Duesenberg Touring Car. He called to ask if I knew anyone who might be qualified to restore it."

"We. Me. You. Us." Reggie slapped her hand to her chest. "Did you tell him we could, Al?"

Mark tugged on her sleeve. "Reg, you're on my time. Call Al later. McCandless is on the move and I want to introduce you."

She shushed him, waving him off.

"Yeah, but this is a pretty special car. Our credentials might be a bit shallow, but we're friends and he trusts me. He's going to think about it."

Reggie snapped her shoulders back. "What? You call me with a think-about-it Duesy? Get on the phone. Tell him *we* are the ones for the job."

"Let's not look overeager, Reg. Let's give him a day to think about it. He's just dropped six million dollars on a car. He's not going to rush. We push him, he'll lose confidence."

"Right, right . . ." Six million dollars. Reggie's CPA brain calculated the weight of a six-million-dollar investment and her excitement iced a bit. "W-we can do it, right?"

"Yes, but very carefully. We'll have to do a lot of research and work to get all the right materials and parts, fabricating to exact specifications what we can't find or buy. But yeah, Reg, we can do it. One day at a time. One piece at a time."

When Reggie ended the call, she saw Mark still waiting for her on the edge of the lighted path.

"It's not going away, is it? You and this car business?"

"No, it's not." She stood next to him, tucking her phone into her hip pocket, replaying Al's call in her head, reviving her excitement. "Al's friend bought a Duesenberg. He's looking for someone to restore it."

Mark whistled, then, after a pause, said, "Reg, just so you know, I'm not going away either."

She looked at him through the glow of the golden, flickering finger-flames of the party torches. Mark was handsome and sweet, if arrogant. His man's-man confidence was tempered only by the remnants of the lonely little boy who waited under the bare porch light of a broken-down, cold trailer for his mama to come home. In many ways, that's how Reggie still saw him. The kid who needed a friend. Who needed to belong. And she loved him. But only as a friend.

"I mean it," he said, stroking her jaw gently with the tips of his fingers.

"Mark,"—she lowered his hand away from her face—"you are one of my best friends—"

"Stop." He flashed his palm past her gaze. "I'm hungry. Let's eat. My mouth's been watering for some of that fish since before we got here." He grabbed her hand. "Let's say hello to McCandless."

"Not letting me say it doesn't change anything, you know."

He stopped midstride and faced her. "We're alike . . . you and me. Wounded in some way by life. Me with my dad walking out and Mom working two, three jobs to keep food on the table. You with your mom being killed when you were twelve. Yet we've made something of ourselves. At least you did for a while. Until this car business. I count it as some kind of young life crisis—"

"I'm not in a crisis. Mark, you don't listen. This is the life I want. I followed Daddy's advice for my education and training, but that season is over. Now I'm following my heart."

"Old cars? Are you kidding me?" He reached for her. "We'd be a power couple, Reg. Your knack for numbers and dealing with people, my gift for sniffing out good investments and deals."

"Does love factor into your equation at all?" She brushed past him, heading for the food table. He could greet McCandless on his own. Not with her in tow as part of his future power couple.

She was right earlier this evening. She'd found bliss, even a bit of love, behind the wheel of a '71 Dodge Challenger. And for now, that's where she'd keep her heart.

March 2, 1914

Meadowbluff Palace

It's been a year since Father's untimely and sad death. Mamá, Esmé, and I are still lost without his large, comforting presence, but we have some joy and laughter again.

Mamá keeps busy with her duties as does Uncle Francis, the reluctant duke, as Mamá calls him.

He is rather fond of me as I am his heir apparent. Mamá worries his affection and desire for me to be Grand Duchess has kept him from choosing a bride and siring children. But I believe he never married because he still loves Lady Rosamond.

Uncle never speaks of it, but I believe she crushed his heart, turning down his marriage proposal the way she did, then dying so soon after. Poor Uncle!

So he dotes on me, as well as Esmé. He's done so ever since I can remember, long before he was the Grand Duke of Hessenberg.

I do believe he's missing Papá and Grandfather as of late. He seems quite troubled after his goodwill tour to Russia and Germany to visit Cousin Nicholas and Cousin Wilhelm. Since his return, I sense his heavy heart. He walks the halls with his head down, his hands locked behind his back. He used to be so merry, full of gaiety, coming around for Esmé and me to listen to his beloved ragtime on the Victrola.

He's retained a new scribe, a young university chap, Otto Pritchard.

Not being able to read and write troubles Uncle more than Lady Rosamond's rebuff, I do believe. Though he never speaks of either.

This morning he sailed to Brighton to meet Cousin Nathaniel, then on to London to see Cousin George.

Mamá whispered to me over tea that Lord Chamberlain believes war is brewing. She's been rising early and taking a carriage to St. John's Chapel. In the afternoons, before tea, she sits by the parlor fire with her Bible in her lap, rocking, her lips moving in silent prayer. Uncle believes faith is for the weak. Mamá says faith is for the strong because it takes a hearty heart to believe what is unseen. The eyes of our hearts tell our minds what the Spirit is saying.

As for me, I'm burdened by the load Uncle and Mamá carry, but I continue in my studies at Scarborough. Uncle insists Esmé and I have our education so we can "run with the lads," as he likes to say. Mamá thinks him too progressive, but I rather like scholastics and am doing quite well in Mathematics.

I suppose I'll end writing in my journal here. The aroma of Berta's fresh cakes reaches my room, and now I'm famished. After all, it is teatime.

Then I must study. French is giving me such a bother!

Alice

TWO

*T*anner Burkhardt rather enjoyed when September's white-gray clouds and soft drizzling rain descended upon Strauberg, Hessenberg's capital city. And this rainy Wednesday was no exception.

With a small box under his arm, he walked from his car toward the side entrance of Wettin Manor, the former city home of what had been Hessenberg's royal family. Now it was the capital's government center.

The chill in the wet air reminded him of his boyhood. Of dashing through the parish front door into the aroma of Mum's simmering beef stew and baking biscuits.

But those days were long gone, and he only allowed himself an occasional reminiscent journey into the past when fall first rolled round. Otherwise, he avoided looking back. The days and years were too painful, littered with the debris of his foolishness.

Tanner entered the manor, his heels tapping on the sparkling marble floors, and bounded up the stairs to his fourth-floor office. Navigating the ancient and hallowed halls, passing under the lancet arches, he shook the rain from his overcoat and brushed the drops from his long hair.

He considered again that perhaps his dad was right—as much

as it pained him to admit it—the time for his long locks ended when he played his last rugby match.

But the look fared well for him when he was a young barrister, and Tanner's style became a symbol of his success, rather than a reminder of his failure.

Long hair was one luxury he could afford after the incident with Trude. After leaving seminary.

And now, as Hessenberg's Minister of Culture, he'd succeeded in putting all of his failures behind him. Had he not?

Tanner caught his thin reflection in the glass of a corridor picture frame.

Perhaps someday he'd cut his hair. But not today. Or tomorrow. His hair reminded him to be diligent and focused lest he forget the depths of his depravity.

Back to his external tasks . . .

His morning at the museum had gone well. He was rather pleased with the Saxon Museum curator's organization of the Augustine-Saxon royals in the main hall. As the newly appointed Minister of Culture, Tanner lent the exhibit his seal of approval. Save one: the Renoir of Princess Alice.

Tanner requested that her painting be hung at Meadowbluff Palace. After all, the palace was the princess's last home before her uncle, the Grand Duke, surrendered Hessenberg to Brighton at the beginning of World War I without a shot being fired, then fled the country with his family members in the dark of night.

It felt right, returning the princess, the last heir to the throne, to her palace.

And with the end of Hessenberg's entailment with Brighton approaching, the hunt for Princess Alice's heir would produce a living, breathing person and return the House of Augustine-Saxon to the palace's hallowed grounds.

Rounding the corner toward his office, Tanner met his assistant, Louis, in the corridor.

"There you are." Louis fell in step with Tanner, his ever-present mini e-tablet in hand. "I've been ringing you."

"I left my phone in the car while in the museum." Tanner reached inside his breast pocket for his mobile as he crossed into his office, slipping from his overcoat and draping it and his suit jacket over the coatrack, and set down the box. "What's so urgent?"

Tanner lifted the lid of the box, taking out one half of a torn photo. Princess Alice, young, smiling, emanating her classic beauty, her left arm—or what Tanner could make of her arm—linked to another. By the edge of the sleeve, he guessed the princess's partner to be a young man.

He flipped the image over. The writing was faded. And also torn.

—edrich

—14

—alace

"Are you listening to me?" Louis bent over the desk. "What have you there?"

"Nothing. A box I found in one of the palace suites."

"Rather boring box, don't you think?" Louis angled for a closer look at the smooth brown wood.

"Yes, rather boring." Lonely, actually. Tanner felt sorry for the old box, abandoned at the palace. He thought it belonged to one of the cleaning crew until he opened it.

Then he knew. It belonged to the princess.

"Are you ready to go over your diary?" Louis said, holding up his iPad calendar for Tanner to see.

"Go on." Sitting at his desk, with one eye on Louis and one on his computer screen, Tanner listened to his daily schedule—as read by Louis Batten.

Meeting with the university cultural department.

Review of the art festival sponsors and vendors.

Assign speechwriter for his address to the Center of European Art Preservation.

As Tanner listened, a disturbance rumbled in his soul, rocking his sense of harmony and balance. But what? So far, all seemed well. Perfectly typical.

Maybe it was the box. Maybe it was his fixation the last few months on the former royal family of Hessenberg.

Six months ago, the newly crowned His Majesty, King Nathaniel II of Brighton, appointed Tanner Minister of Culture with the primary goal of preparing the Grand Duchy of Hessenberg to be an independent, sovereign nation again as the one-hundred-year entail between Brighton and Hessenberg was coming to an end.

The king was determined to find a solution to the entail's ardent, ironclad stipulation. There must be an heir to Hessenberg's Augustine-Saxon throne for the island duchy to be free from Brighton.

If not, the Grand Duchy of Hessenberg would become a permanent province of Brighton and cease to be its own nation.

Just thinking of it gave Tanner heart palpitations—a yearning to see his country remain ... a country. He wanted his beloved Hessenberg to go on for another thousand years. A sapphire gem in the North Sea.

"—and I pushed off the meeting with the Young Artists until next week." With that, Louis perched on the side of Tanner's desk, smiling, pleased with himself. "Tally ho, as my old uncle would say. On with the day."

"Right, tally ho."

"So what did the curator do with the Renoir of Princess Alice?" The aide had fallen in love with the painting of the last Princess of Hessenberg every bit as much as Tanner.

No more than sixteen at the time of the painting, the princess posed in a spring meadow, wearing a white summer gown.

Wisps of her brilliant red hair feathered across her cheeks

and her blue eyes were eager and innocent, *hopeful.* Most likely she had no knowledge that war loomed or that her uncle, Prince Francis, was ill prepared to fight.

Tanner liked the painting because it touched him in the hidden place of his heart. It made him ... *feel.*

"I sent it to the palace. Where it belongs."

Louis let out a low whistle. "I bet the curator didn't care for that decision. The only bright and beautiful painting of someone in the royal family sent off, leaving him with dark, somber ancient dukes and duchesses whose expressions have all the merriment of sitting on a straight pin or drinking bitter dregs."

Tanner laughed. "He said much the same, but the princess's portrait is not big enough for a museum wall. The others are eight to ten feet. Hers is no more than five. She belongs in the palace. Maybe in the suite we've set up for the coming princess."

Tanner sat back and began to roll up his shirtsleeves, his heart's eye still viewing the painting of Alice stored in his memory.

Feel. Like he must protect her. Like he must protect Hessenberg.

He'd failed miserably at his last call to be a protector, when it mattered most. Now that he had a chance to do something for his country, perhaps even for the memory of Princess Alice and her scattered generation, he'd do it. And with his whole heart.

"Speaking of the palace,"—Louis tapped on the tablet's screen—"the house manager you hired, Jarvis, made his recommendations for the rest of the staff. Shall I set up interviews?"

"Let's wait. We've no idea where we are in the search for Princess Alice's heir." The king kept him apprised since he'd launched an investigation, but so far all they knew was that the heir was most likely an American. All other avenues and leads had been dead ends.

"Fine. I'll let him know, but he is anxious to move forward. Anything else?"

Louis peered at Tanner. Barely out of university, he was the poster boy for the next generation. Good-looking and hip, a decent chap. In fact, Tanner used his face for his first cultural campaign, plastering Louis's image all over the duchy.

The End of the 1914 Entail. Do You Know How It Impacts You?
Visit www.hessenberg.co.gd.

"Louis," Tanner said, "what do your mates say about Hessenberg becoming a sovereign nation again—self-ruling, becoming a voice, no matter how small among the nations of the earth?"

"As long as their Euros still spend in the pub,"—he grinned—"I don't suppose any of us see much difference between being ruled by Brighton or being independent again. We've never known anything else."

"What if being independent means your Euros buy more?" Tanner motioned to Louis's suit. "More pints, more holidays, more custom-tailored skinny suits?"

Louis's sense of fashion was the point of office ribbing on a weekly basis. In fact, Marissa, Tanner's office manager, found it personally offensive that Louis owned more shoes than she did.

"Pardon me,"—Louis feigned a frown and smoothed his tie—"but I say long live an independent Hessenberg if that be the case."

"Your consideration of our political and economic future, and that of our children, is profound, Louis. Thank you." Tanner crossed the corner office space to a tea cart. Beyond the arched windows, the drizzle had become a full-on rain shower.

"Why were you ringing me?" Tanner lifted the lid of the teapot and sniffed. Strong and bitter. Just as he liked it. But the tea was cold and he had no taste for that at all. He returned the pot to the cart. He'd get a hot cup at lunch. "You said something about calling me in the corridor."

"Yes, right." Louis stood, tucking his tablet under his arm. "The king and his aide are on their way with Brighton's prime minister."

"Here?" Panic forged a canyon in Tanner's chest. "Louis, might you have led off our meeting with this information? What does he want?" Tanner turned a small, stunted circle, surveying the room, jerking down his shirt sleeves. Why had the fashion gods decreed all buttonholes must be smaller than their corresponding buttons?

His office walls . . . He'd not yet decorated them with trendy paintings or classical art or sophisticated decorative accessories. No, he'd only brought his rugby trophies from home and a framed Hessenberg Union poster signed by the team.

More than that, debris and dust flecked the thick blue carpet, and the walnut shelving most likely would not pass a dust inspection. And the remains of last night's dinner were still in the rubbish bin.

Tanner walked around the center circle of leather and wood chairs, then kicked his rucksack full of sports gear into the small water closet and slapped the door shut.

"Jonathan just said they were on their way. Boarding Royal Air One when he called."

"He'll be here straightaway then." The flight from Brighton to Hessenberg took less than thirty minutes. "Does the governor know the king is coming?" Governor Fitzsimmons' office and staff occupied the entire second floor of Wettin Manor. He would want to know the king was on his way.

"Yes, and I've put security on alert."

"Are you sure he's coming to see me and not the governor?"

"Jonathan specifically said you."

"Get housekeeping up here," Tanner said, squaring away his desk, stacking his notes and papers, shoving them into a bottom desk drawer. "And have a fresh pot of tea brought round. Ask Marissa to arrange for some fresh biscuits from Loudermilk's Bakery. She's to tell them they are for His Majesty. I believe puffs are his favorite."

Louis was already on his phone. "They are. I read that same article in the *Liberty Press*. Manfred, this is Louis. We need house-keeping up here—" Louis made his way out of the office. "Yes, I'm aware, but the king is coming to the Minister of Culture's office."

Tanner slipped on his suit jacket, wondering for the hundredth time in the last sixty seconds, *What does the king want with me?*

Louis reappeared, still on the phone, offering Tanner a thin linen envelope. "This came for you while you were out," he said, still listening to Manfred on the other end of the line. "Listen, do you want the king to see rubbish all over Tanner's carpet? Who do you think will get the blame?" Louis's voice faded as he walked out. "See you in two minutes. Thank you."

Tanner frowned at the envelope. His name was printed across the front in a fancy machine-pressed script. But who was it from? Flipping it over, he read the return address while dropping into his desk chair.

Estes Estate
2 Horsely Hill Road
Strauberg, Hessenberg 93-E15

The name, the address, awakened all those yesterdays he'd fought to put away and forget. Awakened his failure.

His throat constricted with his thickening pulse as he smoothed his hair with his stiff, icy hand. Why in the world would Barbara "Babs" Estes send him a letter? Actually, an invitation? He'd not been to their hilltop mansion since that fateful night eight years ago. But he didn't have to invoke his lawyer-trained mind to surmise the contents of the envelope. Some details and memories refused to sink into the recesses of forgetfulness.

The twins were turning ten in a few weeks. On five October to be exact.

Tapping the envelope against his palm, Tanner reached for his letter opener, debating the merits of looking inside or just tossing the blasted thing in the rubbish.

He was in a good place, far away from the evidence of his failures and shortcomings. He'd rebounded. Made law review. Joined the governor's staff before catching the king's eye for Minister of Culture.

Then he proved his worth by remembering a former professor, ole Yardley Pritchard, who might have a link to a long-lost heir to the Hessenberg throne.

And if Tanner's instincts proved correct about the professor's knowledge of the heiress, Hessenberg would be on her way to being a sovereign independent state once again.

So why today of all days—when the king was actually on his way to this very office—did Tanner receive an invitation from Trude's mum? Did he have so bold a past it could march in on his present whenever it willed? Well, he'd see that it did not.

Jerking open the middle desk drawer, Tanner tossed the envelope inside, shoving it toward the back. There. Out of sight, out of mind.

A technique he had quite perfected.

THREE

*V*oices sounded beyond his door and Louis's deep tone announced the king's presence.

"Good afternoon, Your Majesty."

Tanner greeted the king, Nathaniel II, and his aide, Jonathan, at the door and invited them to sit for a spot of tea. Governor Seamus Fitzsimmons, Tanner's old boss, trailed into the office behind them, the buttons of his silk vest straining.

The conversation was light, casual, with talk of sports and the weather. Twenty minutes passed just sipping tea and eating biscuits.

Perched on the edge of a wingback chair adjacent to the king, Tanner's nerves were on their last, frayed edge.

What does the king want?

Next to Tanner, Governor Fitzsimmons prattled on about his accomplishments, preening his political feathers without shame.

"Your Majesty, did you see our report? We've funneled more public funds toward education. And with parliament's new tax initiative, the economy is likely to rebound."

Enough. Tanner didn't care if Seamus got mad. He was rescuing the king from this continual campaign-trail drivel. He knew full well what the governor was up to—bolstering his political future with the king should Hessenberg not gain her independence and find herself a permanent part of Brighton.

Tanner took command of the conversation.

"How are your wedding plans coming on, Your Majesty?"

Since Nathaniel's engagement to American Susanna Truitt, the media saturated the public with royal wedding news, comparing the pretty, blonde, athletic Susanna to Duchess Kate, wondering if she will adjust as well as Britain's new darling to royal life. After all, America hadn't had a royal ruler in nearly two hundred and forty years.

"Very well, Tanner. Thank you for asking." Nathaniel smiled, and something beyond gratitude lit his eyes. *Ah, 'tis the look of love.* Tanner hadn't experienced such a feeling, but he'd seen it in others. And envied them.

"Her mother arrived to help with the initial wedding preparations, and I say, you've not lived until you've watched the Dowager Queen of Brighton spar with the Queen of Georgia Barbecue." He laughed. "I'm afraid poor Susanna is more referee on occasion than blushing bride."

"Don't be fooled." Jonathan moved toward the tea cart. "Susanna can well handle her own. Give it out too."

"Never a dull moment then?" Tanner rose himself for another spot of tea, but Louis, who'd finished refilling Jonathan's cup, stepped in for Tanner's and refilled it without a word.

"Throw in my brother, Prince Stephen, and we've a three-ring circus." Nathaniel dusted his fingers with his napkin, giving a conferring look to Jonathan, who dipped his hand inside an attaché case for a thin brown folder, and handed it to the king. "But we didn't come to talk about my wedding." The king passed the folder to Tanner. "We came to talk about the entail."

"What news have you?" Seamus huffed and puffed, pulling a pipe from his vest pocket.

"Tanner," Nathaniel said, cutting Seamus a short glance.

"You were spot-on when you introduced us to Yardley Pritchard. His older brother, Otto, did exchange a few letters with Princess Alice for some years after she left Hessenberg."

"Professor Pritchard never said for certain he knew of the princess or her whereabouts," Tanner said, "but he mentioned many times in his courses about how his older brother served as the prince's reader before he fled the country. So I guessed that some correspondence had gone on."

"You guessed right, Tanner. Yardley said his big brother rarely talked about his service to the prince and the royal family until his latter years," the king said. "He'd been convinced by the old duke that if the prince's enemies found out Otto knew any-thing about the entail or the royal family, *his* family would be in danger. Or worse, Otto might have been shot as a traitor."

"Poor brother Otto," Seamus said. "He was a good bit older than old Yardley, I do believe."

"Seventeen years," Nathaniel said. "Times were turbulent after the prince signed the entail, and then came the war. Otto was right to keep his mouth shut."

"But fortunately the old man Otto had the wherewithal to tell Yardley where he'd stashed his letters from the princess," Jonathan said.

"Are they in here?" Tanner flipped open the folder for evidence of any letters, thinking he could put them on display in the museum.

"Turns out he had only one," Nathaniel said. "If there were others, they got lost, displaced, we've no idea. But we put a copy of the one in the report for you."

"We're not destined to know much about Prince Francis and his family," Tanner said, scanning the brief letter, wishing he had a quiet, alone moment to read and think.

The illiterate prince kept little to no records of his life. Had television or talking movies, even the radio, been around in his day, he might have had something to say, to leave behind. But instead, they had one photocopied, water-stained letter. From Princess Alice to Otto. On the eve of her crossing to America.

Tanner looked up. "So it's most certain the heir to the throne is an American?"

"That will never do." Seamus leaned over Tanner's shoulder, tainting the thin air between them with his lavish aftershave. "An American?"

"It will *do*, Governor, because she is the legal and rightful heir. A Miss Regina Alice Beswick. The investigators had a bully of a time tracing Princess Alice's journey from Hessenberg to Brighton to London and finally to America. Turns out our first Alice was not the *Princess* Alice."

"Records were a bit shoddy after the war," Tanner said, skimming the report.

"All of Europe was shoddy after the war." Nathaniel leaned forward, resting his arms on his legs. "The investigators finally found an Alice Stephanie Regina who married an RAF pilot in London in 1922. She's our princess. They had a daughter, Eloise, in '24. Alice's husband was killed in the second war and she immigrated to America with Eloise in '46 and eventually married again. Well, you'll see the information in the dossier. At any rate, Alice's heir, her great-granddaughter, lives in Tallahassee, Florida." The king stood. "She's twenty-nine and—"

"I expected someone older," Tanner said. "A daughter or granddaughter."

"As did we all. Alice's daughter and granddaughter died young. In fact, she outlived them both. Regina is an only child, though she had an older brother who died shortly after birth."

Tanner finished reading the pages and started to pass the folder to King Nathaniel. But the king refused to take it.

"Tanner, as Hessenberg's Minister of Culture, a man who knows the entail law, I'm commissioning you to be our ambassador to the new princess. Travel to America and bring her home."

"Me, sir?" He was barely Minister of Culture. Just six months. Surely there was someone more qualified. "I'm honored." Tanner jumped to his feet, meeting his king eye to eye. "But might you be the proper one to tell her?" Tanner sensed the tension rise in the room, fueled by the governor's indignation. He bet if he glanced down, he'd see the carpet quivering beneath the man's big, scheming feet. "Or perhaps,"—Tanner motioned to the long-time governor—"Seamus might be the proper one."

"Indeed, I quite agree with Tanner." Seamus stepped forward. Tanner expected no less. "I might be better suited, having been governor these fifteen years now."

But the king remained unmoved. "You're too busy and needed here, Seamus. And I'm not the one to go. My diary is much too full. Tanner, you are the perfect candidate." Nathaniel nodded once as if satisfied with his decision. "Not only do you know the entail, you're the most current on the House of Augustine-Saxon history. You're Miss Beswick's age. Besides, we don't know how long it will take to convince her to come, to step into her rightful place. It could take weeks, and since you're new to your position, you're the most flexible." Nathaniel pointed at Tanner. "A convenient fact only, mind you. So I can't leave for any length of time. Dare I say, neither can Seamus. Wouldn't you agree, Governor?"

Nathaniel's tone seemed to soothe the elder statesman. "Quite right, I say," Seamus blustered about. "Quite right."

"I know you're just getting your feet under you on this job," Nathaniel said. "But I believe you are the right man for fetching the princess."

"Sir, I'll do whatever you ask." Tanner released his emotional and mental grip on his heart. On his schedule. For the king he could forgo his own plans, could he not, and move farther from his past failures? "If you feel I am the one to travel to America, to bring round the princess—"

"I do." Nathaniel smiled as if it were all settled. "We've

reserved Royal Air Force One for your travels. I'd like you to leave tomorrow, if you've no objection." The king regarded him, waiting, the casual air about him solidifying into something regal and commanding.

So Tanner was traveling tomorrow...

"I'll be ready, Your Majesty." He'd be all night clearing his diary. Did he have enough clean laundry? Three of his suits were at the dry cleaners. They closed at half-five. "Shall I go alone or take someone along?"

"Go alone, if you're willing. The more discreet, the better. We want no press on this. Not one word." Nathaniel glanced about the room, gathering visual agreement. "Let's get her here, get organized, then we can alert the media, and I daresay the whole world. Tanner, you're our sharpshooter, as it were. You have the full backing of the government. The King's Office has prepared all the formal documentation along with what you have there." He motioned to the folder. "It'll be waiting for you on Royal Air Force One."

"Your Majesty," Seamus said, "is there really all this need for a rush?"

Nathaniel turned to the governor, calm, steady. Jonathan reared back with surprise in his eyes.

"The entail ends in a month, Governor," Tanner said. *Seamus, old chap, don't be a fool.*

"What would you suggest, Seamus?" Nathaniel said. "If she doesn't know she's the heir, the news will take time to settle in, even more to convince her we need her. If perchance she does know of her heritage, it will most likely take time for her to negotiate her way here, I'm quite sure."

"Posh." Seamus jammed his unlit pipe between his lips, mumbling. "What girl doesn't want to find out she's a princess?"

"This is not a movie, Governor," Jonathan said. "Miss Beswick has a life, friends, family..."

"What if she refuses?" Tanner went straight to the bottom line. "Rejects the whole lot? Royal princess needed to save the future of a small country and all."

"You convince her." Nathaniel squared off in front of Tanner. "Don't come home without her."

Tanner's pulse tapped out his fear. *Can't fail, can't fail.*

"I'll do my best—"

"Let's have no illusions that this is going to be easy." Nathaniel continued to offer wise, calm counsel. "We can all pray that in some way, large or small, she's prepared to hear the news. Perhaps all our concerns are for nothing. Princess Alice may well have told Regina who she was before she died."

"But we really don't know what Alice knew when she fled Hessenberg in 1914. So we don't know what she might have told Regina." Jonathan glanced at his watch. "Your Majesty, we've got to go."

"I'm sorry to rush off, but I've a state reception at the palace." Nathaniel moved with his aide to the door. "But I wanted to ask you in person to take on this task, Tanner. It's of the utmost importance to us. Jonathan will be in touch with further details."

"I'll have Louis notify you when I'm ready to go." Tanner walked with Jonathan to the door. "Plan on the morning. Around ten."

"Tanner,"—Nathaniel paused in the doorway and offered his hand—"your king and your country thank you."

Tanner clasped his hand with the king's, the significance of this moment a weighty mantle around his soul.

The last one hundred years of Hessenberg's history had been traveling toward this moment. First with the speed of a ship adrift at sea, then as the decades passed, with the steady force of a motorcar. But now, as the Brighton-Hessenberg Entailment neared its end, the weeks passed with the power of a rocket ship.

And Tanner was the lone pilot who must not fail.

June 13, 1914

Meadowbluff Palace

I've my final sitting today in the meadow by the thicket for Mr. Renoir. He claims I am a great beauty and must be painted to perfection. Though he must be weary of me sitting before him day after day. Nevertheless, we are having the most beautiful Hessenberg summer, so I don't mind being out of doors.

Uncle is quite pleased with Mr. Renoir's work and has declared we'll have a great unveiling when the portrait is complete. So, it's off to the thicket as the light is perfect there midday. It's quite magical. I feel peace when I cross the lawn to the meadow and the edge of the thicket.

It's there I say my prayers with the most faith that God is listening. I'm not ashamed to say I've asked him for a husband. I rather fancy Rein Friedrich, as does Mamá, but he's not called at the palace since the spring. Nor have I seen him in attendance at the summer socials.

Lady Sharon says she heard rumor that Rein joined the army. Though which army I don't know. Hessenberg has not one to speak of. I know because it's vexing Uncle as his prime minister is insisting he rebuild our armed forces.

I'm not sure what Uncle is thinking, but while in the meadow the other day, waiting for Mr. Renoir, I noticed Uncle moving his beloved Starfire #89 into the stable. I thought it rather odd, but when I asked him about it at dinner, he said he stored it there for safekeeping.

My own art lessons will advance next month. Mamá has invited renowned artist Rose Maynard Barton to spend July at the palace. She accepted and graciously offered to tutor Esmé and me. But Esmé would rather play sports than paint, so I'll have this talented woman all to myself. I'm delighted.

Alice

FOUR

On Friday nights, Reggie held court. At least that's what Al called it. Reggie's Court. And he dubbed the crowd of friends and family who gathered at the barn the courtesans.

But Reggie was no queen. Just an ordinary girl sharing her life with the people she loved. The weekly "court" happened rather spontaneously one week right after she and Al opened the shop. A few of Reggie's colleagues from Backlund & Backlund happened by to see if her blind leap into the car restoration business was worth sacrificing her future as a well-paid CPA.

They had their doubts, but Reggie had a feeling the success of the Challenger restoration would bring them around. Then friends started coming by to watch the transformation of the car. And perhaps Reggie. *Could she do it?*

Rafe mounted speakers outside the barn, under the eaves, and around five o'clock on a Friday night, Reggie turned up the music—a blend of country and soul—and ordered a dozen pizzas.

Six months later, it wasn't just her court anymore. Al's friends and family came by. Wally's grandkids. Lately, car enthusiasts and friends of friends joined the Friday night throng.

Tonight Reggie walked out of the barn with a cold bottle of

root beer in her hand. She'd ordered the pizzas and looked forward to an evening of music and laughter.

And maybe, just one or two "I told you so's" when she recounted the Challenger's success. Maybe she'd talk Al into dropping a few hints to the courtesans about the Duesenberg.

Perching on the picnic table, Reggie took a swig of her drink and grinned at Carrie, her best friend since forever, trying to teach Rafe a line dance. He moved with the grace of a lumberjack after a long hard day. He went left when he should've moved right. He was a soldier, not a dancer.

"Give it up, Carrie," Reggie called.

"Never," she called back, grabbing Rafe around the waist and steering him along.

He laughed and glanced down at the petite, dark-haired Carrie. Well, well, lookey here. Something more than friendship was developing between those two.

Good for you, Car-bear. Good for you. Rafe is one of the good guys.

Reggie shifted her gaze to Al as he came out of the shop with an armload of folding chairs. Wally followed with a wicker basket of chips and, hopefully, his famous onion and horseradish dip.

"Great night for holding *court*, Reg," Al said, leaning the chairs against a tree.

"Don't start with the court business, Al."

"Why not? I find it rather fitting."

"You'll get everyone saying it."

But it was a great night for *court*. If court meant being with people she loved. This evening was the first night of fall and the equinox had graced the Florida panhandle with a crisp, thin breeze.

"Hey." Mark hopped onto the table next to her, causing the boards to pop. The scent of his Obsession soaked the air between them. "Clear your decks. We're going sailing tomorrow."

"*Sailing?* Mark, I get seasick if the bathtub is too full." Reggie scooted away from him. Because he sat too close. Because she didn't want him getting too cozy. She'd kept him within their friendship bounds the other night, but his "I'm not going away" sounded all of her alarm bells.

"You've never really tried *sailing*, Reg."

"What? I've gone deep-sea fishing twice." What was she thinking when she did a repeat of that disaster? She hung over the side of the boat the first time, puking, trying for six hours not to inhale the smell of cut-up squid bait. "And three times Backlund's Christmas party was on a yacht. I spent the entire time dancing with the toilet. Don't tell me I've not tried it."

"Not like this, with the wind in the sails and—"

"Mark, I'm not stepping on a watercraft just to puke over the side all day with nary a piece of land in sight." Really, did he not know her? See her? "I'm sleeping in tomorrow, eating pancakes,"—it was a spur-of-the-moment idea, but she liked it—"and working on the books."

As a CPA, it went without saying that Reggie would handle the shop's finances when she and Al hung out their shingle.

"All work and no play makes Reggie a dull girl." His voice rose up and down, in a silly singsong, as he hooked his arm around her shoulders. "Come on, live a little. Devin Swain and his girlfriend invited us to St. George. You remember them from the fish fry. Kate really liked you."

"What about being queasy and sick, wishing I were dead, is 'living a little'?" Reggie snapped her fingers by his ear, then leaned closer, whispering, "I'm not going sailing."

"All right. Sheesh, Reg." Mark moved off the table. "Say, I'll be back in time for dinner tomorrow night. I can pick up Chinese and meet you at your place . . . eight o'clock?" He regarded her, brows raised.

But what she saw in his expression wasn't a successful, well-groomed businessman but a skinny kid longing for attention.

"Mark, I, um . . ." Her mercy toward him was not sanctified. Her faux compassion allowed him to foster romantic hopes. Saying they were *just* friends, holding up the physical barriers to keep him from stealing her first kiss. The one she was reserving for her very own Prince Charming.

But Mark needed real, truthful words. A clear, distinct expression from her heart about their relationship. Trying to spare his feelings would only hurt him more in the end.

"Eight then?" He backed away, pointing at her. "I see Bob Boynton over there, and I've not talked to him in a month of Sundays."

"Eight it is." She smiled. Tomorrow she'd sleep in, work the books, and then pray, asking God to help her find the words to convince Mark of the truth.

Rafe fired up the outdoor lights, and Reggie made the rounds among the courtesans, checking in to see how their workweek went and asking if anyone had fun weekend plans. One of the newer courtesans, a legislative aide, had Wally cornered in an intense conversation about an antique Mercedes he'd found online.

A cheer erupted with bottles and cans raised in the air when the pizza delivery car turned down the drive. Reggie pulled a fresh root beer from the cooler and leaned against the side of the barn, watching the pizza huddle, listening to the conversations, loving the bursts of laughter.

"Happy?" Carrie joined her against the wall.

Reggie thought for a moment, then nodded. "Very."

"I'm proud of you, Reg. For taking a leap, going into the car restoration business." Carrie was the opposite of Reggie. An FSU sorority girl turned political lobbyist with her eye on politics, she went to spas for a whole day, flew to New York in the spring and fall to shop, and took yoga vacations. "You made believers out of us all, Regina Beswick, quitting your job and following your heart."

"You dare doubt me?"

Carrie laughed. "Foolish, I know, but even the strong falter once in a while."

Reggie shot her a sideways glance. "I see you and Rafe are getting a bit cozy." Rafe was way outside Carrie's usual taste in men. She dated legislative aides. Fellow lobbyists. Fund-raisers. Men who wore designer suits and had standing manicure appointments.

But the last boyfriend? A narcissistic zombie. Truly.

"Rafe and me? Naw . . ." But even the approaching cloak of night couldn't hide the pink tint on the woman's cheeks. "He wanted to learn to line dance. That's all. He's not my type."

"What type is that? Human?"

"Har-har. Very funny." Carrie shifted her lean body against the wall, one foot propped behind her. "I admitted you were right about zombie man."

"I'm right about Rafe too. Give him a chance."

"You assume he wants a chance."

"Are you telling me he doesn't?"

Carrie's blush deepened, sweetening her smile. "We're going to dinner and a movie tomorrow night." She pushed off the wall, her finger pointed at Reggie. "Not a word. Not a word." Carrie fell against the barn again, then hollered to Rafe to bring her and Reggie some pizza.

"Remember how Mama and I used to sit out on the back porch at night, watching the stars?" Reggie said, sentiment waxing over her heart. "She'd ask me what I wanted to be when I grew up, told me to dream big."

"I wonder if she's looking down over the edge of heaven, busting her proverbial gold buttons with pride." Carrie glanced at her. "Do you think they have that kind of pride in heaven?"

Reggie shook her head. "I don't know, but I kind of think God says to all of heaven, 'Hey, look at what my kids are doing. Aren't they cool?' But this,"—she knocked on the side of the barn—"is far from what I claimed I wanted to be."

"No kidding." Carrie laughed. "You were going to be a princess."

"I blame Great-Gram Alice for that wild idea."

Gram used to make a game of it with Reggie and Carrie, creating construction paper crowns and decorating them with glitter.

"I still have one of the crowns I made with her," Carrie said.

"Even at ninety-seven, when she could barely see, she still loved to play pretend." Reggie wove her arm through Carrie's. Besides Daddy and stepmom, Sadie, Carrie was her only link to those childhood memories, the only other person on earth she could reminisce with about Gram and Mama.

Rafe showed up with two paper plates of pizza, flirting with Carrie who ... *giggled*. A twenty-nine-year-old giggler? Definitely, love was blooming.

Reggie made her way back to the picnic table where the courtesans always reserved a space for her. As she stepped over the bench, something between the shrouding oak branches and the top of the barn caught her eye. Made her heart flutter.

What was that? Reggie settled her pizza on the table and scanned the fading twilight patches visible through the tree.

There. A blue flash. Something in the clouds. Reggie squinted, trying to see between the light. What was that? It made her pulse pound.

"Reg, you got enough room?"

She placed her hand on Seth Davis's shoulder. "Yeah, yeah, you're fine. I just thought I saw something." But she didn't, did she? Surely her imagination was playing tricks on her. With a final glance at the dimming sky, Reggie sat down, pressing her hand over her heart, shivering. Call her crazy, but for a split second, she could've sworn Gram's gentle blue eyes were peering down at her.

FIVE

*T*anner's departure for America was derailed by a media firestorm.

An informant had alerted every print and online paper of the newfound princess.

The details were exaggerated and, in some places, downright wrong. But nonetheless, the stories exploded all over the media.

The Princess Has Been Found! So Long, Brighton Rule!

An Independent Hessenberg Cannot Stand. We'll Fail.

Old Laws to Kick In Once We Break from the Entail. We'll Go Backwards 100 Years!

The *Liberty Press*, the supposed newspaper of record, ran an irreverent political cartoon with a ghostlike image of old Prince Francis giving King Nathaniel II and the royal family a swift kick with a jackboot, including the king's newly arrived fiancée, Susanna.

So Tanner spent his departure morning putting out fires and holding an impromptu press conference. All of which delayed his mission.

"What do we know of the new princess?"

"Is she a loon?"

"What if she's undesirable? Unappealing? Unattractive?"

"How can we trust a foreigner to lead Hessenberg?"

The questions were bold, unrefined, from the gut. Tanner did his best to field the questions with gentle answers, but in truth, he wondered much of the same himself.

He'd spent the evening before going over the details of the princess's dossier. She seemed nice. Her driver's license photo was pleasant enough. But more than that . . .

He did not know. It seemed she worked at a motor car garage but she was college educated. How did he decipher those facts?

While he dealt with the press, Louis collected intel from the Wettin Manor staff and suspected the media leak came from the governor's office.

What are you up to, Seamus?

The man had not been happy with the king selecting Tanner to meet with the princess. But surely he'd not stoop so low as to undermine the security of the mission.

No matter, he mustn't dwell on it. None of yesterday's shenanigans altered the king's edict. "Bring back the princess."

Tanner had landed in Florida in the early hours of Friday morning and checked into his hotel, collecting himself, trying to adjust to America's time zone.

Along about evening, he decided to drive out to Miss Beswick's garage.

Stepping out of his hotel into what seemed like a cloud fallen to earth—how did they endure this humidity?—he motored west, according to the rental car's GPS. The investigator's report indicated Miss Beswick spent Friday evenings at the shop where she worked.

Easing through downtown and weekend traffic, he passed the university, Florida State, where flags and banners waved from windows and walls bearing the likeness of a Native American.

It was American football season, and Tanner felt the exuberance of the city in his chest. He recognized the sensation from his nearly two decades in the rugby leagues.

His emotional memory stirred, lifting its head. He wondered…
might he pop in on the game? Maybe Miss Beswick—

An icy chill froze his musings. Hours on his own in America,
and already he was mentally straying off course.

Stay on task! Focus.

This was how he failed so miserably before, how he ruined his
life's calling. Ten years later, after being given a second chance,
being shown grace, he found he was no more mature than he was
at twenty-two.

Look, something shiny. And off he'd go.

What had the last ten years been about if not disciplining his
emotions and thoughts, his body to be in control?

To be *worthy*.

Tanner cut the SUV through the dark swags descending on
the city. Along the curb, the streetlamps began to glow with a
low burn.

He practiced his introduction again. On the flight over, he'd
written it out a dozen times and read it aloud while pacing the
customized fuselage, envisioning himself repeating the words to
Miss Beswick, who may or may not be aware of her destiny.

Assuming she knew nothing, Tanner attempted to front-load
his speech with backstory, which took entirely too long. She'd
think him crazy long before he got to, "Are you the true great-
granddaughter of Alice Edmunds, born December 10, 1897?"

He possessed a good memory and had memorized the dossier
and the details of his future princess. Now to relay them to Miss
Beswick in an appealing manner.

Regina Alice Beswick. Born March 21, 1985. Only child of
Noble and Bettin Beswick. Bettin was killed in an auto accident
in 1997.

Great-grandmother, Alice Edmunds, died a year later in
February 1998. Age one hundred and two months.

Education. Graduated Florida State University. BA Finance.

CPA accredited. Senior associate, Backlund & Backlund. Resigned six months ago. New occupation. A motorcar garage owner.

Father, Noble, owned plumbing company. Stepmum, Sadie, bank president.

His mind's eye studied Miss Beswick's driver's license and graduation photo. Pleasant enough. Lots of red hair and blue eyes, like Princess Alice.

As he continued driving west, the city sights and sounds began to fade into a rural area with houses set back off the road, guarded by trees and all sorts of brush. Was this right? Had he not been paying attention? He glanced at the GPS. The direction arrow remained on course.

Exhaling, he released his taut grip on the wheel. It wouldn't be the first time he missed his mark because he'd been mentally reading a document or rereading a book he'd memorized.

The mechanical GPS voice spoke. "Turn right in half a mile."

Tanner closed his mental dossier. His mission was about to begin.

Focus.

He inhaled long and slow, filling his lungs to capacity. *Can. Not. Fail.* A single word dropped from his lips. *Wisdom.* He needed wisdom. His request was not a prayer, exactly. Because Tanner had an arrangement with God. They'd leave one another alone. Stay in their mutual corners. However, his subtle petition today was for the princess. For Hessenberg.

Tanner's thoughts and energy converged on his heart. *Miss Beswick, prepare yourself for the truth.*

The GPS directed, "Turn right in five hundred feet."

Scanning the landscape, Tanner spotted a circle of lights above a wide square of yellow light. An open door of some kind. People were moving in and out.

He turned right when the GPS commanded and bounced down a gravelly driveway, parking beside the farthest car out.

A slow, investigative approach to the facility would serve him best, allowing him to observe the crowd, even Miss Beswick. He hoped she'd not left already.

The atmosphere was lively, bouncing with music and the fragrance of American pizza. Tanner had it once and rather fancied it.

Just find the redhead. Please, let there be only one . . .

To his left, under a cold, bare light swinging from a narrow light pole, a crowd gathered around what appeared to be an old Corvette.

There was a bit of excitement about it, voices rising and falling. Curious, Tanner moved closer. He fancied classic cars as a youth, but preferred newer models these days.

Casually moving into the crowd, Tanner stood shoulder to shoulder with a black gentleman who wore his cap backward and studied the car.

The old Corvette needed work, but was a rare beauty.

"What year is it?" he whispered to the man.

"'Fifty-three. One of the originals. Handcrafted."

Tanner whistled. "Lovely."

The man peered up at him. "Not from around here?"

"No, sir."

"Name's Al." He offered his hand.

"Tanner Burkhardt," he said, clasping his hand with Al's rough, firm grip. "I just arrived from the Grand Duchy of Hessenberg."

"Hessenberg?" The man's brown eyes widened. "That's a far piece to come for an evening in Reggie's Court." He laughed, a smooth sound that made Tanner think of jazz. "But Reg swears folk'll do just about anything, go anywhere, for a slice of pizza."

"Reggie's Court, did you say?"

"Ah, we like to rib her, call the Friday night gatherings 'Reggie's Court.' But it's just folks getting together to talk cars and such. Which is why you showed up, I reckon. Do you have friends here?"

"Actually—" Tanner hesitated. Should he obfuscate the situation? Agree with Al that he came to talk about motorcars? Carve out more time to observe? No, best get on with it. "Actually, I'm looking for Miss Regina Beswick."

The man reared back. "Miss Regina Beswick?" His chuckle rumbled in his chest. "I'm not sure she'll answer to that, but you can try." He pointed to the Corvette. "She's under there."

"Under the car?" Tanner bent to see through the shadows, finding a thin light beam and a body crawling along.

"Urban,"—a strong, Southern-accented voice fired from underneath the chassis—"did you check the oil before you drove this across town?"

From among the men gathered around, one stooped to respond. He looked like a professional with his trimmed hair and fine-weave slacks.

"Of course I did."

A barrister. Unless Tanner missed his guess, which he was confident he hadn't. He'd worked with men like . . . this . . . *Urban.* That's what she called him, correct? Tanner recognized the lawyer kind, his kind, even in America.

"He's the car's owner," Al said. "Just bought it off his brother-in-law and drove it over to show us."

"And Miss Beswick is . . . inspecting it?"

"Urban thinks he can restore it himself. Reg is convincing him he needs to let us do it."

"I see." So, she restores cars. Fascinating. And how serendipitous—perhaps even divine—to find an open spot next to Al.

Miss Beswick scooted out from under the car. One of the men standing around jumped forward to help her up. Dried grass and leaves clung to her mussed burnished hair while a wide river of motor oil sleeked down her face and neck.

"Rafe," Al said in a low voice, "run get Reg a towel."

"Reg, what'd you do to my Vet?" Urban dropped to his knees and peered under the car.

"I touched the oil plug and it shattered." Miss Beswick wiped the oil from her face with the edge of her top. "Did you put new oil in on top of the old, Urban?"

The man jumped to his feet. "The dipstick said the oil was low, so I added a quart."

Definitely a barrister.

"The dipstick? Urban,"—Miss Beswick laughed, her white smile breaking up the dark smears of motor grease on her cheeks and around her mouth—"*you're* the dipstick. The oil was low because it's old and tacky. Probably been in there for years. You're lucky you didn't blow the engine on your way over here."

She walked around the car with a casual survey of the group, her gaze landing and lingering on Tanner.

Their eyes met, and for a moment he thought she might speak to him. "Who are you?" Or "Can I help you?" Was he ready to respond?

Would the truth spill out, right here and now, like the oil on the ground? Like the oil on her face?

Tanner inhaled. Exhaled. Waiting. Braced and at the ready, his nerves pinging. A fluttery and funny sensation tickled down his ribs. Anticipation. Was he about to meet Miss Beswick, the heir to the Hessenberg throne?

The wind whispered between them, stirring up the fragrance of the sun-baked earth. Miss Beswick smiled, sparking a light in her eyes. They matched the same brilliant blue Renoir painted of Princess Alice.

Miss Beswick was beautiful. Much more than Tanner imagined, and the flutter in his chest confirmed what his eyes beheld.

When she moved on, he exhaled. Thank goodness. He needed to collect himself and meet her in a tamer setting. Perhaps without grease on her face. Without the thunder of his own blood pulsing through his ears. Yet the fluttering burn in his middle lingered. Tanner pressed his fingers to his breastbone. He wasn't given to nerves, really. Or heartburn. Must be his body was out of sorts from the travel and time change.

Or it might just be that he found her striking and sublime. Even covered in motor oil.

"Urban,"—she patted the barrister on the shoulder—"tell me this. If you bought a Rembrandt, would you let a kindergartner with crayons restore it?" The man, Rafe, showed up with the towel, tossing it to Miss Beswick.

"Not the same, Reg. I don't know anything about art."

"You don't know anything about restoring cars either." A thin laughter rippled through the crowd.

"I can learn. Get help."

"From who? Us? Not for free."

The man scoffed. "Fine, I'll pay for the help." He motioned to the car. "This is my midlife crisis because my wife won't let me trade her in for a younger model."

Tanner's laughter fed the fluttery feeling in his gut. How fortunate to happen upon this scene and a chance to observe Miss Beswick.

This Urban was a straight shooter. As was Miss Beswick. She got down to business. Mustered no dancing about. He best take note.

"Urban, how old are you? Sixty, sixty-one?" Miss Beswick folded her arms, the oil-stained towel dangling from her hand.

"Urban,"—Al cupped his hands about his mouth—"give it up. She's going in for the kill."

"I'm not scared, Al. This isn't my first rodeo."

Al nudged Tanner. "Urban prosecuted a serial killer early in his law career. It was a big deal, very salacious, lots of media hoopla. Took the jury less than two hours to come back with a guilty verdict. He's been on top ever since."

"Can she convince him?" Tanner said. "Will she win?"

"Urban knows the law. He don't know squat about restoring cars, and he knows it. Reggie knows it. And he *knows* she knows."

As the evening light faded to a deeper shade of midnight blue, the barrister finally dropped the car keys into the palm of her hand.

The crowd cheered and swirled around Miss Beswick, congratulating her.

Shoulders bumped Tanner's, and he was shoved along toward the red barn with the rest of them.

When he saw a break in the crowd, he sidestepped out of the fray and caught the trail of Miss Beswick as she hurried toward the open barn doors where gold light spilled from the wide lamps.

Urban walked on one side, Al on the other.

Tanner veiled himself in the shadows of a large tree, watching, deciding how to approach. Observing was one quality of his nature he rather liked. It gave him an advantage on the rugby field, in the courtroom, and now in the Minister of Culture's office.

Urban and Al exited after a few moments, heading toward a truck. Others in the party began to clump in smaller groups, then make their way toward their parked motorcars.

Tanner urged himself forward. *Now or never, chum.*

In the barn, he found Miss Beswick in a long, narrow room, some sort of makeshift office, working on a computer. She looked around when he rapped lightly on the door frame.

"Hey," she said. "Come in." She stood, offering her hand. "Have we met? I saw you out there, with the Corvette. Friend of Urban's?"

"No, I'm not. And we've not met previously. I'm . . ." The moment his hand touched hers, he lost sense of self. The floor beneath him seemed to turn to putty, making it impossible to stand without wavering. "Tanner Burkhardt." He jerked his hand away, stepping back, looking for solid ground.

"Reggie Beswick," she said. "Do I detect an accent? British?"

"Hessen. I'm from the Grand Duchy of Hessenberg."

"Wow, really? What can I do for you? Have a seat." She motioned to the chair behind Tanner as she kicked out the desk chair for herself.

Tanner sat, calming his nerves. What was it about this woman that unsettled him? This wasn't the first time he'd met a royal. Or a beautiful woman.

"My great-grandma was born in Hessenberg," she said.

"Indeed. Did she tell you much about it?" Tanner collected his professional decorum, trying to remain focused on his mission but feeling as if he were sinking in her presence. Every time she smiled, he lost a piece of his mettle.

She shrugged with a glance back at the computer, moving the mouse, then typing. "Just that it was a beautiful place."

"As it remains so to this day."

She turned to him, smiling, which ignited a buzzing thrill around his heart. Tanner swallowed, reaching for his attaché case. *Guard your wits.*

"I'm sure. Gram didn't talk about it much, at least not that I can remember. I was twelve when she died and didn't care that much about our family history."

"Miss Beswick—"

"Hey, you seem like a nice man, but please call me Reggie or Reg. This Miss Beswick business has to go."

"Right, well, you see . . ." Tanner retrieved the king's letter along with the carefully preserved original entail. Let the eloquence and power of the original document speak. "I'm here on urgent, official business. Are you aware of the 1914 Entailment between Brighton and Hessenberg?"

"Sure, from history class. But it's been awhile. Why do you ask?" She rolled her chair backward, reaching for a small refrigerator. "Want something to drink?"

He was parched, but he wanted to tend to business first. "No, thank you."

"What kind of urgent, *official* business?" She retrieved a water bottle and scooted toward him, leaning to see the documents, sprinkling the air with the slightest scent of lilacs.

"You recall that Hessenberg became a part of Brighton in 1914 when our Grand Duke, Prince Francis, signed over his land, which was the whole of Hessenberg, to the King of Brighton."

"Okay." She sat back, taking a swig of her water. "Duke's own land, right? The duchy was his to do with as he pleased."

"Yes, exactly. Brilliant." She was making his job a mite easier. "Prince Francis feared the coming war and was ill prepared to build a worthy military, so he aligned with King Nathaniel I of Brighton."

"What did you say your name was again?" Regina wiped one hand on her jeans and reached for the papers. "May I?"

Tanner hesitated, but released the documents. "Tanner. Tanner Burkhardt."

"Well, Tanner Burkhardt, what does any of this have to do with me?" She drank some more water, her eyes on the king's letter. "Why is it addressed to me?" Drawing closer, she pointed to the king's cipher. "From the King of Brighton?"

"Because he wrote it to you."

She laughed. "The King of Brighton wrote me a letter?"

This wasn't how Tanner planned to tell her, but so far this approach was working. "Go on. Read it for yourself."

She set down her water with an unsure glance at Tanner then regarded the letter.

"Dear Miss Beswick, on behalf of Brighton Kingdom... receive my servant Mr. Tanner Burkhardt . . . my official ambassador . . . inform you . . ."

She stopped reading and the light in her countenance dimmed.

"What? This is crazy. No way . . . no way." She gave Tanner the letter, her arm stiff. "Is this a joke? Who hired you?"

As if on cue, a dark-haired chap, one of the professionals who'd been by the Corvette, stuck his head through the doorway. "Reg, some of us are going to a movie—" He drew back when he saw Tanner.

"Mark, did you do this? Hire this guy?" Miss Beswick snatched the letter back from Tanner and waved it about. "What kind of joke is this? A princess? Please, come on. It's not my birthday and it's not April Fools', so what gives?"

"Hi." The chap offered his hand. "Mark Harper. Please pardon the insane woman ranting in front of you."

"Tanner Burkhardt." He shook his hand. "It's a pleasure, Mr. Harper."

"Mark. Please call me Mark. Mr. Harper is my deadbeat ole man."

"You didn't do this?" Miss Beswick said with more letter-waving.

Mark patted Tanner on the shoulder. "Have you ever seen me before in your life?"

"Yes—"

"Aha!" She waved her finger at Mark.

"Out by the Corvette a few minutes ago."

"Aha yourself, Reg." Mark jabbed his finger at her. "Let me see this letter."

"Nothing doing." Miss Beswick jumped up onto her desk chair, balancing precariously. "This sounds exactly like something you'd write, Mark." She glared down at Tanner, then read the letter with an exaggerated Hessen accent. "On behalf of our two nations, we implore you to take your rightful place as heir to the Grand Duchy of Hessenberg and her throne."

Miss Beswick slapped her thigh, laughing, angling down at Mr. Harper. "We *implore* you . . ."

"When was the last time you ever heard me use the word *implore*?" Mark folded his arms, smiling in a told-you-so manner.

"Never, but for a good gag, you'd pull out a word like *implore*." Miss Beswick hopped off the chair, causing it to fire back against the wall. Tanner jumped to his feet, reaching for her. But she landed steady, facing Mr. Harper.

"Okay, yeah. But I didn't do this, Reg."

"So if you didn't do this, then who did?"

"Miss Beswick,"—Tanner snatched the letter from her in one quick move, thanks to his rugby muscle memory—"perhaps we can discuss this tomorrow. When you've cleaned up and I can have your full attention."

"Wait, wait—"

A pretty brunette peered round the door. "Mark, Reg, are we going to the movies or what?"

"I'll ring you tomorrow, Miss Beswick." Tanner escaped the office, heading for the barn doors. He'd not count this as a failure. He'd count it as a false start.

Tomorrow was another day.

He felt a slight tug on his arm. "Mr. Burkhardt, wait. Come back."

He turned to Miss Beswick with a narrowed gaze. "Only if you are serious. I'll not waste my time on folderol and jesting about. I've a job to do for His Majesty, and I intend to do it."

"His Majesty?" Mr. Harper interjected.

"Never mind," she said, shoving him toward the wide doorway. "Have fun at the movies."

"Reg, you going to be okay?" This question from the lass wanting to go to the movies. She furrowed her brow at Tanner. "We don't have to go to the movies. Rafe will be happy to wait around."

"I assure you Miss Beswick is in the securest of hands."

"Miss Beswick?" Mr. Harper grinned. "The securest of hands?"

"Mark, hush. Go. Carrie, I'm fine." Miss Beswick hugged the woman. "Call you tomorrow."

"Reg, dinner tomorrow night," Mr. Harper hollered. "Around eight."

Back in the office, Tanner remained standing. "Let's just get to the bottom line, shall we?"

"Let's." She folded her arms, waiting. "Now, what's this all about?"

"Your great-grandmother Alice was born December 10, 1897, as Her Royal Highness, Princess Alice Stephanie Regina, heir to the royal throne of the House of Augustine-Saxon."

"I've never heard any of this except her birthday."

"Her uncle, her mother's brother, was Prince Francis, Grand Duke of Hessenberg. He had no children, making his eldest niece his heir."

"Gram? A princess? An heir?" She narrowed her gaze at him. "How come she never said a word—" Beneath the motor oil, her face paled and she paced again, her hand to her forehead. "No, no, no . . ."

"What is it?"

"We used to play princess. When I was a kid. But she never, ever said a word about being a *real* princess. Did you ever meet her? No, I guess not. Gram was the sweetest, most down-to-earth woman you'd ever want to meet. She worked at church, on every committee known to man. Visited the sick and infirm. She wore the same pair of shoes until they wore out. Drove the same car for fifteen years and then lamented when she had to trade it in. She drove her last car until she was ninety-two." Miss Beswick stopped in front of him. "This is crazy. Gram? A princess?"

Her words were music to his heart. "Miss Beswick, the woman you just described sounds very much like the princess she would've been trained to be. Very much indeed."

"Even the bit about the shoes? And driving herself around?"

Tanner laughed. "Perhaps not. But all the rest." He set his attaché case on the desk. "Shall we start from the beginning?"

Miss Beswick sat down slowly. "Please. From the beginning."
She made a face. "She was really a princess?"

"Yes." Tanner handed her the royal dossier. "As are you,
Miss Beswick. The Hereditary Princess, the Grand Duchess of
Hessenberg."

SIX

At the kitchen table, Daddy read the official document signed by King Nathaniel II. He was too quiet. Too calm.

"Daddy?"

"Hmm," he said with a grunt. "I'm reading."

"You've been reading for the past ten minutes."

Reggie looked at her stepmom, Sadie, sitting next to Daddy, her expression somber. Over her shoulder, in the corner of the family room, a cop show was paused, frozen in mid-action, on the television screen.

Still reeling with the news, Reggie had left the shop with Mr. Burkhardt and headed straight to Daddy and Sadie's. The only thing she craved more than a shower to wash the oil from her face was the truth.

She'd anticipated shock and surprise from Daddy and Sadie when she barged in on their Friday night programs with Mr. Burkhardt in tow, announcing Gram was a princess. Which made *Mama* a princess, rest her soul. And now Reggie.

"Daddy,"—Reggie tapped the table in front of him—"did you know about this?"

Sadie slapped her palm down and scooted back her chair. "I'm in the mood for baking." Sadie jumped up from the table.

"Who's up for chocolate chip cookies?" She baked when things got tense.

"Bake?" Reggie peered at Daddy, then Sadie. "Daddy, what are you not telling me?"

"I'm off to the store." Sadie snatched her purse from the small, inset kitchen desk. Yep, she was a bank president by day and a stress-relief baker by night.

"Sadie," Daddy said, stopping her with the tone of his voice. "I need your help here."

"Help?" Reggie glanced between her father and Sadie. At the end of the table, Mr. Burkhardt watched and listened. "What kind of—"

"I told you this would happen, Noble."

"We didn't know for sure." Daddy set the king's letter on the table and looked at Sadie. "But when I wanted to tell her, you fought me, Sadie. Said she'd get all bigheaded and run off."

"Bigheaded?" Reggie echoed. "When was this?"

Sadie dropped her bag to the counter with a huff. "Oh, when you were seventeen and going through that rebellious patch. Your dad wanted to tell you, thought it might make you feel special, help you deal with the stress of your senior year, but I said to wait because, really, we didn't know if any of it was true—"

"What rebellious patch?" Reggie demanded. "I came home late a few times and wanted to study abroad for the second half my senior year."

"We"—Sadie motioned to Daddy—"thought it best to wait." She clasped her hands at her waist, her cupid face pinched with thought.

Sadie had been one of Mama's best friends. A career woman, not a wife or mother. But when Mama died, Sadie stepped up and devoted herself to serving Daddy and Reggie. A year after Mama's funeral, Daddy proposed.

"To wait for what?" Reggie said.

"I really need to bake." Sadie started opening cabinets. "Mr. Burkhardt, do you like sugar cookies?"

Tanner stood, buttoning his suit coat, hemming himself in all proper and stiff. "Ma'am, there's no need—"

"Oh, but there is a need. And a simple 'Yes, I love sugar cookies' will do." Sadie pulled out the flour tin.

He cast a glance at Reggie. "You heard her. Just say yes," she said.

"Yes, ma'am, I love sugar cookies."

"Wonderful." Sadie continued to inventory her cupboards. "Oh look, I've found leftover sprinkles from the Fourth of July."

For a moment, the only sounds were the ones Sadie made setting up to bake cookies, then Reggie reached for the letter.

"So this is true?" She read aloud. "At the end of the hundred-year entail, Prince Francis intended for his heir, whoever he or she be, to return to Hessenberg and reestablish the monarchy ..."

She read with the intent of understanding each word, but the reality of being heir to this throne—this House of Augustine-Saxon—seemed about as likely as flying to the moon.

Gram was a princess? Alice of Hessenberg? It felt more like she was Alice in Wonderland. Reggie's heart could not comprehend what her head strained to grasp.

"I've got everything I need to bake sugar cookies. No Publix run. How about that, Noble?"

"Not surprised, Sadie-bun." Daddy's deep voice resonated through the kitchen. "And, yes, Reg, I guess it's true."

"Mr. Beswick," Mr. Burkhardt began, "did your wife give you a clue? Or perhaps Princess Alice told you the history of Hessenberg and the entail?"

"Well, first, right before Reggie's mama died, she whispered something to me about Gram's secret. But she was fading in and out. When I pressed her for an answer, she didn't seem to know what I was asking. I thought she might have been thinking of when Gram played princess with Reg, you know." He shook his head. "She died about an hour later and I, well, I had bigger fish to fry than some murmur about a princess."

"I'm sorry, Mr. Beswick, of course."

"Don't be sorry. You weren't the son of a gun who ran the light and T-boned her car." In the seventeen years since her death, an ever-present pain darkened Daddy when he spoke of Mama's accident. And in those moments, a fresh wave of missing her crashed the shores of Reggie's heart.

"So, then, you asked Gram?" Otherwise, why would he consider telling her during her rebel years?

Reggie shot a glance toward Sadie, busy in the kitchen. *Rebellion . . .* What was she talking about? Reggie no more rebelled than Sadie Beswick missed a Christmas baking season.

"As a matter of fact, I got around to it. A few months later." Daddy's voice drew in Reggie's heart and attention. "One night after supper, I was sitting by her bed and, well, you know"— Daddy chuckled as if it all seemed so silly now—"I said, 'Gram, before Bettin died, she said something about being a princess.'"

"What did she say?" Reggie hooked her hand over Daddy's arm.

He shrugged. "She said since Bettin had died, Regina was the princess." Daddy scratched his head and peered at Mr. Burkhardt. "Gram always called Reggie by her full name. Anyway, I asked her what she meant and her eyes kind of clouded over. Then she muttered something about Reg being 'my princess' and I thought, 'Well, there you go, she's gone to her soft place, remembering the past when she played dress-up with Reg. Same as Bettin.' Or maybe she was telling me Reg was *my* princess." Daddy patted his chest. "My girl, treat her like a princess."

"Her soft place?" Mr. Burkhardt leaned toward Daddy.

"Here." Daddy tapped his temple. "Those moments when— we thought—she'd slipped from reality. The older she got, the more she talked about her past, her girlhood in Hessenberg, an old stable, someone named Rein." Daddy ran his hand over his chin. "Her Mamá, her uncle. Her sister, Esmé. Folks I'd never met. They'd all gone on, passed to the other side.

"We couldn't make heads or tails of it. Guess we should've paid her more mind. But she had so much heartache in her life, being a widow, losing her daughter, then her granddaughter. After Bettin died, Gram seemed to go to her soft place a good bit. Sadie and I figured escaping to her childhood gave her peace, helped her mourn. Shoot, all of her blood kin were dead except Reg. You live to be a hundred, you outlive most of your people. So we just let Gram go on, live in her own brand of dignity. Wasn't any use in correcting her."

"What about telling me?" Reggie demanded. "Was there any use in telling me?"

"To be honest, Reg, it didn't make much sense to me. A princess? For real? I thought about telling you when you were seventeen, like Sadie said, but we talked it out and, well, it sounded kind of silly. Maybe we had no proof, no way of really knowing." Daddy shook his head, shoving away from the table, and walked into the family room for some peppermints.

When he returned, he offered one to Mr. Burkhardt, who refused with a kind, "No, thank you."

"She said something else to you that day, Noble, didn't she?" Sadie stood nearby, a bowl in her arm, stirring a mixture with a big silver spoon.

"What? What did she say?" The need to know, to understand, pressed against Reggie's ribs.

"More of the same." Daddy popped a peppermint in his mouth and reached for another one. He was lean and wiry from working hard his whole life. His dark hair was thick and black with only a subtle hint of gray. And when he laughed, his blue eyes twinkled. "She was a good woman, your gram." His eyes glistened. "I miss her. Anyway, just as I was leaving her room that night, she said, 'Nobel, you let her go when the time comes, hear me? She'll restore the kingdom.' Then she muttered again about you being her princess."

"Restore the kingdom?" Reggie's voice rose with wonder. "What does that mean?"

"Exactly. I dismissed it," Daddy said. "Thought maybe she was quoting lines from *Star Wars*. We'd just finished a marathon weekend with Sadie's nephews." He glanced back at his wife. "Remember that, Sadie?"

"Daddy, you didn't at least look into it?" Reggie ran her fingers through her hair. She really wanted a shower with slick, warm water running down her face, washing away the remains of motor oil. The remains of this conversation and she needed to think.

Gram . . . Hessenberg . . . the entail thing . . .

"No, Reg, I'm sorry, I didn't. Connecting Gram and you to a royal house in Europe was like assuming a man could build a ladder to the stars. Impossible. I knew Alice Edmunds for fifteen years and she never, ever hinted at being a royal other than what I just told you. Nor did your mama."

"The truth is, Alice Edmunds *was* a royal." Mr. Burkhardt peered at Reggie. "And your daughter is her heir. Alice was right. Your daughter is the one who can restore Hessenberg to its sovereign status. Return us to our own kingdom, as it were."

In silence, Daddy fixed his attention on unwrapping his next peppermint. "Are you telling me that time is now, Mr. Burkhardt?"

"Yes, sir, I am." Mr. Burkhardt motioned to the documents on the table. "It's all there. The agreement between Brighton and Hessenberg ends October twenty-second at midnight. If there is no heir to the Hessenberg throne, Hessenberg will be absorbed entirely by Brighton as a province, much like Normandy into France, and Tuscany into Italy, and lose her status as a sovereign nation. Forever. Unless Hessenberg is willing to go to war and spill blood for her independence. Which at this point is not an option."

Reggie stood to pace around the table. "I should hope not, Mr.

Burkhardt." She wearied of addressing him so formally, but as long as he called her Miss Beswick, she was going to call him Mr. Burkhardt. "Why can't you just void up the entail? The men who made the agreement are dead."

"This is not a school-yard, spit-in-your-hand agreement, Miss Beswick. It's legal. Binding. With all the rights and restrictions of any law and upheld by a European court. We cannot just void the entail. America has not voided your constitution because the men who penned it are dead."

"I don't understand why this is so important. You've been ruled by Brighton for a hundred years. What's wrong with Hessenberg becoming a permanent part of Brighton?"

"If it's all the same to you,"—Mr. Burkhardt's countenance steeled—"we'd like to remain a nation. Determine our own destiny. Hessens are a patriotic and proud people. In a more practical word, our two economies are sinking one another. It's the desire of both nations for Hessenberg to be independent, a sovereign nation again, at the end of the entail."

"All right, then exactly how does Reg fit into all of this?" Daddy tossed his peppermint wrapper toward the kitchen trash. Sadie commented that he missed. "And really, how do we know you're legit? How do we know these formal-looking documents aren't forged?"

"Those are solid, fine questions." Mr. Burkhardt examined the documents on the table, selecting one to show to Daddy. "You see here, this is the king's cipher and his seal."

Reggie listened on the edge, using the moment to examine the Hessenberg visitor with her heart's eyes. What was in this for him? Just a job? Doing the king's bidding? Yet, if Hessenberg separated from Brighton, he'd no longer be Mr. Burkhardt's king.

Was Mr. Burkhardt seeking promotion, position, or just being a loyal servant? A fastball revelation smacked Reggie's heart . . .

"If I do this, will I be your boss?"

He glanced over at her, his expression, the strong cut of his jaw, reflecting nothing of his feelings. Nothing beneath his surface. He was handsome, built like an athlete with a corporate-guy demeanor.

"You will be my sovereign, yes."

"And you'd be fine with that? Me? A car enthusiast who cares little about politics other than my right to vote telling you what to do?"

He straightened. "If I say yes, will you come to Hessenberg?" Deep-toned, matter-of-fact, extremely serious.

"Do you ever smile?" Reggie said.

A very soft, faint smile flirted with his lips. "If I say yes, will you come to Hessenberg?"

"Depends." She crossed her arms. "You saw that Corvette in the yard tonight?"

"What Corvette?" Daddy said.

"Oh, Daddy." Excitement bubbled in her chest. "Did you meet Urban Jessup? He's one of Mark's friends."

"That big-time lawyer from the serial killer trial?"

"Yeah, that's the guy. Anyway, he bought a '53 Vet. One of the originals."

"Ho, ho, ho, Reg." Delight sparked in Daddy's eyes. "One of your dream cars. God is smiling on you."

"I couldn't believe it when he drove up. And you know he wanted to restore it himself?"

"But you convinced him otherwise."

"Yes, I did." Daddy slapped Reggie a high five.

"Miss Beswick." Mr. Burkhardt exhaled what sounded like his last breath. "We need you in Hessenberg immediately." Nothing remained of his slight smile.

"For how long? What will I have to do?" Reggie turned back to him. Al and the boys could start on the Vet. She'd hate to make Urban wait. Either way, she'd be back in time for the good stuff.

Besides, it might be kind of cool to visit Gram's birthplace, get a taste of her own heritage and roots.

"You will have to . . ." Mr. Burkhardt shuffled the papers, displaying the first nervous break in his steel visage. "This is rather awkward, Miss Beswick."

"It wasn't awkward a few minutes ago."

He met her gaze, his confidence returned. "This will sound unusual to you, an American, but you will prepare to take the Oath of the Throne. Then take your place as head of state, and move toward a full royal coronation."

"Oath? Head of state?" Reggie, Daddy, and Sadie spoke together, in harmonious surprise.

"Once you take the oath, you will be the official heir and enabled by law to sign the end of the entail and inherit, if you will, the duchy and return her to full nation status once more. Thus you'll be our leader under which our government can be established." Mr. Burkhardt offered her a document. "We've prepared a summary of events that must take place."

Reggie hesitated, then reached for the paper. She skimmed the bulleted lines. Return to Hessenberg. Become familiar with the capital city, Strauberg, and the palace, Meadowbluff. Prepare to take the Oath of the Throne. Meet with government leaders.

All to return a small duchy to full nation status? Her heart pinged with increasing alarm. The paper shimmied and wavered in her cold, trembling hands. A second later she couldn't concentrate enough to read.

"Mr. Burkhardt,"—she let the paper drift down to the table— "I–I don't understand. How is it possible I can do any of these things?"

"Because you are Princess Alice's great-granddaughter." He pointed to a line of the summary. "She's the direct descendant of one Oscar Augustine, who freed the duchy from Prussian rule in 1602. He asserted himself as the Grand Duke of Hessenberg, a jewel floating on the surface of the ore-enriched North Sea. The people were serfs in the beginning, but he organized the land into farms and mines, established a constitution and parliament. The people prospered.

"But in the end, Hessenberg was owned by the House of Augustine-Saxon. When the Grand Duke Prince Francis, your great-grandmother's uncle, gave her up to Brighton, he abdicated his throne and legal rights to the land for one hundred years."

The picture was becoming clear. "Then the House of Augustine-Saxon gets to come roaring back."

"If the proper heir was found."

"And that proper heir is me."

"Yes, miss, 'tis you."

"Okay, I'll see you later." Reggie headed for the front door without offering a by-your-leave or kiss-my-grits.

From the kitchen, Sadie made a racket wrenching her cookie sheets from the bottom cupboard. Reggie never could figure how the woman managed to bury the baking tools she used the most. But that was her stepmama.

"Reg?" Daddy called.

"Miss Beswick, please, wait." Mr. Burkhardt hurried after her.

Reggie moved faster. A dog with a bone, that man. "I've got to go."

A princess? An oath? A coronation? It was laughable. If Mr. Burkhardt wasn't so darn serious, she'd swear someone was punking her.

No woman Reggie ever knew dreamed of being a princess after the age of twelve. Well, except for Mable Torres, who wanted to be Miss Springtime Tallahassee. And Christi Selby, who was crowned Miss Florida. But they were temporary princesses with no authority. Burkhardt was asking her to establish a country.

A country!

Down the front porch steps, Reggie made a beeline for her old '78 Datsun, fumbling for the keys.

"It's overwhelming, isn't it?" A bit of kindness, of empathy, tenderized Mr. Burkhardt's words.

"Look, Mr. Burkhardt—" Reggie tossed her bag into the passenger seat. "And, please, can I call you Tanner?"

"Certainly." He stopped next to her, hands locked behind his back.

"I wouldn't have a clue what to do with your country." She regarded him in the bright white of Daddy's driveway luminaries.

"You won't be alone, Miss Beswick."

"Please. Reggie. Call me Reggie."

"You'll have advisors. We've functioned under a constitutional monarchy for hundreds of years, and we can do it again. On our own. We've a core of stellar leaders to assist you. King Nathaniel II and his prime minister will advise and aid you in every way. As well as our own governor."

Daddy's dark silhouette appeared on the porch. Watching. Waiting. Probably praying.

"After the oath, then what?"

"Sign the end of the entail."

"Then what?"

He hesitated. "That would be up to you, Miss Beswick. Stay in Hessenberg as a reigning royal, reestablishing the House of Augustine-Saxon, helping to form our new government. Or abdicate and return home, leaving us to find our way without a royal house for the first time in our history. But we will be independent again, and most grateful."

"Abdicate? You mean quit? Sign me up to be a princess, then make me resign in order to return home to *my* life?" She jerked open the car door and the rusty hinges creaked and moaned. Yes, her sentiments exactly.

"If you'll just—"

"Look, Mr. Burkhardt—Tanner—this is who I am." She spread her arms, turning a small circle. "A Tallahassee lassie, born and bred. I love my job, don't you see? I love my life. Save a certain Mark Harper who's expecting too much, which I do intend to address, I want for nothing. I have my freedom, my friends and family, my faith."

She'd just made her case for a firm refusal. "I can't." She turned back for the car. "And I won't. This is crazy. I can't even comprehend what you are telling me. And frankly, I don't want to comprehend it."

"Will you take this? Read it all carefully?" Tanner approached with the attaché case, his subtle scent cleansing the air between them. "Take this. Review the papers. You'll see you are the true and only heir." When she didn't reach for the case, he took another step toward her. "Please. There's something in there you'll want to read."

"Like what?"

"Just read . . ." He offered the case once more. "I'm staying at the Duval downtown. My card is in the side pocket with my mobile number. Call. Please. If you have any questions."

"Breathe, sweet pea," Daddy called from the porch. "Take the papers. Read them. Think on it. Pray. Can't hurt."

Reggie stepped around Tanner toward the porch. "Daddy, whose side are you on? Do you want me to move away? Far away?" She turned to Tanner. "How many miles to Hessenberg?"

"Four thousand two hundred and twelve miles."

"Four thou—holy cow. Daddy, do you want me to move four thousand miles away?"

"You know I don't." He took one step down, then two. "But I don't want you to say no to this princess thing without considering the evidence, weighing your options."

"You mean like you wanted me to go to FSU for accounting because it was a nice, safe career?"

"Was I wrong?"

"But I hated it." She squinted, shielding her eyes with her hand, trying to see Daddy through the backlight of the porch lamps.

"I think you *came* to hate it eventually. You were restless. Still are, I imagine. But that CPA job was the highway to do what you wanted, Reg. You couldn't have started that shop without the money you saved reconciling other folks' accounts. Same might be the case here. You might find you like being a princess."

She groaned. "Like restoring cars is a highway to being a princess?"

"Maybe."

Ha! "Daddy, my life is not a Disney movie." She waved him off, turning back to the car. If she didn't know him to be a teetotaler, she'd swear he'd been nipping at the cooking sherry.

"You liked playing princess with Gram," he called. Relentless, her daddy. More of a dog with a bone than Mr. Burkhardt.

"I was six. And she made the best construction paper tiaras."

"Miss Beswick—"

"Reggie. For crying out loud, call me Reggie." She'd hit the wall. Tired, frustrated, and confused. There was nowhere to go but straight to irritated.

"Take this." He reached for her hand and settled the case on her palm. "You'll want to read it, I promise."

"Fine." She grabbed it to her chest, her mind firing thoughts out of rhythm with the beat of her heart. *Read the documents. No! Read them. No!* "I'll read the papers, but I'm pretty sure I'll never be getting on an airplane to Hessenberg with you."

"That's my girl," Daddy said. "Way to keep an open mind."

"Miss Beswick . . . Regina," Tanner said with a slight bow, "thank you. Hessenberg thanks you."

She shifted her stance. "What happens if I say no?"

"Simple," he said, locking his hands behind his back.

"Hessenberg, the nation of your gram's birth, disappears from the face of the earth. Removed from the world's maps. A nation with history dating back to ancient Rome will cease to be."

The last straw had been laid, and Reggie felt she might crumble to the ground. "And all of that falls on me? It's crazy." She spoke to her own soul, to the night, as she stared across the street at the shards of light slicing through the neighbor's shrouding trees and shrubs.

"It's also true—"

Reggie whirled to face Mr. Burkhardt. "Are you always this confident?"

"No, but—"

"Good, because it's a bit grating." She settled the attaché case in the passenger seat. "How long do I have to decide?"

"Technically, until the entail ends. Midnight, October twenty-second. But in truth, we'll need time, a few weeks, to get you and the people ready."

"October twenty-second? That's a month away. So, basically, we'd have to leave ... now."

"If possible. In a few days, yes."

"Y'all had a hundred years to keep track of the royal heirs to this August-Saxon-whatever house, but you lost them. So you come crying to my doorstep giving me a few days to decide. How's that fair?"

"It's not, Miss Beswick, I agree. But your uncle Prince Francis abdicated and scattered the family on purpose. To keep them safe, for one. And to honor his part of the entail with Brighton Kingdom. Had we known about you, we'd have stopped by sooner. But alas, your great-gram was difficult to track down."

Hearing the recap of her royal heritage boiled the confusion in her chest to anger. Her breath burned in her lungs. "I've got to go."

Reggie climbed into the Datsun and fired up the forty-year-old engine, which rattled and knocked, threatening to stall. Easing down on the gas, Reggie fed the carburetor and shifted into reverse.

Tanner leaned his arm on the door and peered at her through the open window. "Sooner is better than later, Miss Beswick."

"And you're leaving when?" She inched the car back down the driveway.

"When you agree to go with me." He exhaled and stood back. "Or when the Grand Duchy of Hessenberg ceases to be a nation."

SEVEN

The cold air of his hotel suite felt good on his hot, sticky skin. Had he known Florida nights came with such a concrete wall of humidity, Tanner might have reconsidered his late-night run.

But he had to move, stride, work out the kinks in his weary muscles and tired mind.

Down the elevator and out the front doors of the Duval, he hit the pavement, his legs refusing to coordinate at first, leaving him to trip down the city streets like an old man.

About ten minutes into the run, he found his strength as he forced his body to move and kicked up his heels, cutting in and out of the bar parties spilling into the streets. Seemed the whole town was lit for this football match tomorrow.

For forty-five minutes he ran and thought of nothing—*nothing*—but striding, breathing, and maintaining a steady pace.

Back in his suite, he stripped off his sweaty shirt and lifted a bottle of water from the mini-fridge. Finding a hand towel, he wiped his face and arms, then ordered a late-night dinner. Salad? No, dessert. A slice of chocolate cake à la mode.

Collapsing into the chair by the window, he fixed on the burst of amber-hued city lights flickering above the city. And like a rising moon, way off in the distance, the arching white glow of the university campus.

Tanner pressed the cold water bottle to his forehead, then took a drink. He liked this town, humidity aside. Tallahassee was a blend of government, higher education, and what Americans called rednecks.

He knew a few rednecks back home, except they were called *ringers*—an old term, given to the coal and ore miners when they came up out of the belly of the earth after a long day's work with a ring of coal dust or dark clay about their necks.

The national rugby team went by Ringers until the 1914 entail. After World War I the Hessenberg and Brighton rugby unions merged and the Ringers simply became the Hessenberg Union.

Another swig of water and Tanner tipped his head back and closed his eyes. A thread of sleepy peace drew him toward slumber. *So much history gone by . . . so much time past . . . never to be undone . . .*

He jerked awake, sitting forward, when Miss Beswick's face flashed across the palette of his drifting thoughts. He stood, taking another gulp of water, and moved closer to the window.

She'd gotten to him. Slipped under his skin. He'd been curious about his reaction to meeting his future monarch. Would he have feelings of respect? Admiration? Relief? Or perhaps disdain and loathing?

Any number of feelings were possible, but not the fluttery ones, not the sensation of infatuation tickling across his chest, making his stomach sink to his toes.

Blast! She was rattling him with her womanly charms.

But it was more than her fine features and mass of golden-red hair that tapped his soul. It was her determination. Her commitment to the life she'd made for herself. Her ability to stare at conflict and ask, "Why?"

He, on the other hand, surrendered the moment conflict reared its ugly head. Tanner had his demanding yet devoted father to thank for his shrinking from confrontation. The man demanded obedience, to live a life of honor, and set aside his ambitions.

Somewhere along the way, Tanner chose his own way and took a wrong step. A very wrong step. Then another. And another.

Ah, never mind. You're beyond your past mistakes. Are you not?

Back to Miss Beswick. Tanner liked that she had a mind of her own. Pushovers and people pleasers didn't make good leaders. Or legendary royalty. Prince Francis proved how fear of man could destroy a family dynasty. Indeed, a whole nation.

He also loved how Miss Beswick bore a strong, almost eerie resemblance to the Renoir of Princess Alice. Almost as if the former heir to the throne had stepped out of the 1914 portrait and into the twenty-first century.

Perhaps she had.

All that aside, would Miss Beswick travel with him to Hessenberg? Tanner had no idea. Would the investigator's report and the entail edicts in the attaché case have any bearing on her heart?

One must hope. He must hope.

Turning back to the room, Tanner downed the last of his water and fired up his laptop.

Had he overplayed his hand? Put too much on her? If someone informed him the future of a nation rested on his shoulders, would he step up?

He hoped so. Especially after his past mistakes. He wanted to make good. Help others. And if possible, forget that he had dau—

Don't awaken the pain, chap.

He shoved the almost-thought from his mind, leaving his heart reaching and yearning. What was done was done. If he'd been a wiser young man, he'd have paid closer attention to his actions and their effects on his life. But he'd been foolish and it cost him his future.

Which was how he came to owe a debt of thanks to old Seamus Fitzsimmons. Tanner had been offered a new path and a new beginning.

Launching e-mail, Tanner also reached for the telly remote and surfed to a sports channel, looking for some American football. He'd watched a few exhibition matches in Hessenberg when the Dallas Cowboys and Indianapolis Colts came to play. He fancied it a fascinating sport.

Finding a game, Tanner set down the remote and fixed on his messages. He had several, rather a lot, from Louis and one from the King's Office requesting an update as soon as possible.

He was about to wade into work when a new e-mail popped in from Louis. He was awake early, tackling e-mail on a Hessenberg Saturday.

The subject line disturbed Tanner's peace: Envelope in Your Desk.

Oh, bother. Louis, what have you done? Tanner ran his hand through his damp hair and exhaled.

His stellar memory aside, Tanner could compartmentalize his thoughts and emotions. If he chose to forget an envelope in his desk, he did. But now Louis reminded him of what he wanted to forget.

He clicked on the e-mail and read his aide's brief note.

Looking for your office key . . . found it in the middle drawer . . . saw the envelope . . . thought it might be something for your diary . . . a personal invitation . . . tenth birthday party . . . Britta and Bella . . . Sunday the 5th. Shall I schedule . . . apologies for entering your personal mail.

Tanner stared at the message, reading it once more. Birthday party . . . and *he* was invited? He imagined an invitation inside the fine linen envelope but he didn't believe they'd really *invite* him.

It didn't make sense. Not in light of the past eight years. Britta and Bella were the two "things" in his past he could not compartmentalize, shove aside, and forget. Though he'd thoroughly tried. For their sake. For his.

But he'd not forgotten the twins were turning ten on five October. He was just prepared to ignore their birthday. Like every other year.

Tanner took another water from the fridge and strolled around the suite. He was finally cooling off when this business with the twins sparked a flame in his heart.

On the telly screen, a player ran down the field, ball tucked under his arm, the crowd cheering.

Tanner read the e-mail again.

Shall I schedule?

Setting down his water, he clicked a reply.

No.

He wasn't even sure if he'd be home with Miss Beswick by the fifth. And even if he was home ...

Tanner snapped up his mobile. Why did Trude even invite him to the girls' party? Did Mum know about this? She was the only one who had kept in touch with Trude over the years, even if it was only at Christmas.

He started to dial home when he realized it was five in the morning Hessenberg time. On a Saturday. His parents would be sleeping.

Tanner tossed the phone back to the desk and stripped for a shower.

Just when he had life managed, contained, all roots to his past severed and the ground well covered, a force like Trude

Estes Cadwallader came wheeling by with her rotary tiller and reminded him he was not the man he pretended to be.

Just inside her back door, Reggie hit the light switch, igniting a floor lamp and kitchen track lights. She was home where finally her world would settle down and make sense again.

She had driven home with the wind whipping through the old Datsun's windows, feeling knotted and irritated. Mad. Frustrated.

And challenged to the core of her being.

What was a girl to do when someone came along and told her she was not who she believed herself to be?

The idea sliced through her heart into her soul and dissected everything she believed about herself. Her life.

The force of it all toppled her truths and turned her convictions at right angles.

Setting her purse on the kitchen counter and Tanner's attaché on the table, Reggie stared at the smooth brown leather of the case for a long moment. He seemed convinced something among the documents would convince her she belonged in Hessenberg. At least long enough to deal with this entail business.

Dumping out the contents of the attaché, she spread them on the table, scanning each one.

A letter from King Nathaniel II. She sighed. Okay, that was cool even if the rest of this was *craaaazy*!

Shuffling through the papers, she noticed the oil stains still on her hands, and pressed her thumb against the black streaks. She'd need a hot shower and good scrubbing.

But she'd also need time to understand these events that had suddenly burst into her life. What in these papers could convince her to leave everything behind and go for the unknown?

See, when Regina Beswick woke up every morning, she knew

who she was, where she was going, why, and how. And she liked it. Change was not necessary or required.

With a resolve to dig in to the attaché contents, Reggie pulled out a chair and sat down.

That Tanner was something, wasn't he? Strong. Assertive. Yet charming and polished. Sincere. Not smarmy and pushy like Mark. Despite his suit-and-tie formality, he was kind of sexy, and that hair... long, coiffed blond hair. He wore it well. *Very.*

Reggie fingered over the documents, separating them one from another, willing herself to find nothing interesting among the state and legal documents.

She'd shuffle through the papers one last time and call it a night.

Near the bottom of the pile, however, she discovered a chart with names and dates. Lifting the page, her hands trembled with a surge of adrenaline.

Compiled by Lieberman Investigators LLC.

Reggie spied Gram's name. Alice. Married Harry Pierce, Captain, Royal Air Force, England. Her first husband, a flyer killed in action.

Gram immigrated to America in July 1946 with daughter Eloise, Reggie's grandmother. Attached was a photocopy of their entrance through Ellis Island. *Alice Pierce. Eloise Pierce.*

Gram married William Edmunds in October 1947. He died before Reggie was born but she remembered Gram telling stories about him.

Eloise married Charles Hiebert in June 1948, giving birth to Mama two years later in 1950.

Reggie's memories of her grandparents, Eloise and Charles, were short and sweet since both of them died when she was young. Seeing their names stirred a certain longing for them.

Grandma Eloise was a Pierce, not an Edmunds, who became a Hiebert. Did Reggie know this family tree had so many short branches? Did anyone ever tell her?

She tossed the chart to the table, familiar with the rest of the details. Mama married Daddy, Noble Beswick, in January 1979.

Reggie's older brother was born in 1981. But he died six months later. Then, in March 1985, she came silently into the world. Actually, that was a fact she did remember. Mama said Reggie came into the world so peacefully, without one sound, as if to say . . . How'd Mama put it?

Hello, world, aren't you happy I'm here?

Tears of missing Mama burned in her eyes. Back to the chart, Reggie regarded the names, trying to see the people, trying to remember a history she never knew.

Scanning the death dates, the short life spans, a tightness formed in her chest. All except Gram and, of course, Daddy died before the age of seventy. Reggie smiled. *Gram, you defied death more than once, didn't you?*

Yet what did this prove? None of this information specifically declared Gram to be Princess Alice. Certainly it didn't name Reggie as heir. The contents of the attaché case only confused Reggie more. Why didn't Gram ever speak of this life?

Tanner seemed to think there was something in this case that would convince her she was the long-lost princess. But so far, all Reggie found was a well-documented family tree.

With a sigh, Reggie sifted through the last few documents, spying the edge of a photocopied letter. Pulling it free, she recognized Gram's sprawling handwriting.

May 1946

London

Dear Otto,

It's been so long since we've corresponded. But this war has taken it out of me. Eloise and I lost Harry in '45, and we cannot seem to get away from the pain of missing him.

Esmé, my dear sister, invited us to stay with her in America, and we are setting sail tomorrow. I pray there is a new life, a new joy for us there. London is so ravaged from the war. I fear we will never laugh again. I so desire to put this all behind me. Hessenberg. Brighton. The wars. Death. I must begin again if I wish to survive this life.

Uncle has died, as you may know, in Sweden, in early '44. Mamá will remain in London. She is happy and comfortable in the king's circle. George VI has embraced her as a sister more than a cousin.

So much death in life, dear Otto.

I hope this letter finds you well. I'll write when I arrive in America and get settled.

Lovingly yours,
Alice Pierce

Reggie read the letter a few more times, then set it aside. Her tired mind couldn't comprehend any more. She shoved away from the table, desperate to think, desperate for a shower. The oil would adhere permanently to her pores if she didn't wash soon.

Standing, stretching, she'd taken one step toward her room when her cell buzzed from her purse. When she saw it was Mark, she let the call go to voice mail.

Then, as she passed the back door, a soft tap-tap resounded. Daddy.

"Isn't it past your bedtime?" she said, opening the door wide, letting him pass. He looked dressed for bed, wearing his FSU sweatshirt, sleeping pants, and worn-out old slippers. He'd tried to train the dog to retrieve them about fifteen years ago, but Buster misunderstood and used them as chew toys.

"Yes, and I got a big job starting in the morning up in Thomasville. But this business with Hessenberg and your gram got me all worked up." He shoved a square, nondescript box at her. "I brought you something."

A box? "This couldn't have waited until morning?"

"Maybe." He stared at the box, hands on his hips. "I'm not sure. But when Sadie reminded me about the box after you left, I couldn't shake the notion. Someone was nudging me to bring it to you tonight."

Reggie set it on the table by Tanner's leather case. "What is it?"

"Besides a box? I've no idea. Gram left it to you." Daddy walked toward the dark front of the house. "I put it away, figuring I'd give it to you when you were older, when you could appreciate it. I stuck it in the attic and time got away from me. Next thing I know you're rounding the bases to thirty and I'd forgotten all about the box. Then this Hessenberg dude shows up . . ." Daddy paused along the farthest reach of the kitchen light and peered toward the unlit, unused living room. "Reg, you still only living in three rooms?"

"I've been busy." She cut through the kitchen and leaned against the doorway facing the *un-living* room.

"Doing what?" Daddy flipped a light switch, powering up an austere ceiling lamp that made the white walls and white brick fireplace feel like a cold waiting room.

"Working. Starting a new business." The only color in the room was on a Tiffany lamp shade by the front window.

"How long you lived here?" Daddy stooped, picking up the Tiffany cord. "It ain't even plugged in, Reg." He snooped under the shade. "And there's no bulb."

"I meant to get a bulb." She'd bought the house two years ago with the money Daddy set aside from Mama's insurance policy. "And I'm going to use the lamp. I just need to find a good place for it."

"How many barbecues have you had?" He walked to the darkened bedroom hallway. "Those rooms empty too?"

"Is there a point to all of this?" She snatched up the Tiffany lamp and carried it to the family room.

"The point is . . ." Daddy's voice clouded with emotion. "I never saw it until now. Reg, you're not living. You're existing."

"You been watching Dr. Phil on YouTube again, haven't you?" Reggie set the lamp by a chair. "What do you think Al & Reg's Classic Car Restore is about? It's about me living, as you say. When I worked for Backlund, I was existing. But now I'm doing what I want to do. My passion."

"How long have you had that old Datsun?"

She shrugged. "About a year, I guess." A bit of fast math and she nailed the exact month. "I got it last July. Right after I sold the '70 Nova." Which she'd intended to fix up but never found the time. *That's* why she went all in with Al.

And where was Daddy going with his questions? She didn't remember him being so lawyer-like.

"That yellow Corvair still in the garage?"

"Well, I didn't sell it." After all, it had once belonged to Great Gram.

"But you've not worked on it either."

"In case you missed the news, I've spent the last six months restoring a '71 Challenger to Slant-6 perfection. We have a very happy customer in Danny Hayes. Before that, I was working sixty-five hours a week at Backlund. I was lucky to fix me up once in a while, let alone a car."

"Know what I think?"

"I'm sure you'll tell me." She leaned against the front wall and shoved her toe into the plush frieze carpet.

"I did you wrong, Reg."

She glanced up. "What? Daddy, no way. How did you do me wrong? You raised me. Gave up your nights and weekends to be both father and mother. You took care of Gram too." A sentiment of truth whispered across her heart and tapped on the locked doors of her dark, inner rooms. "We'd go out back and toss the football, talking. You'd set up Gram on the porch with a blanket around her legs." Reggie shook her head. "You saved both of us, Daddy."

"You and Gram saved me. But I let you down. I closed off parts of the house," he said as he motioned to the dark rooms. "Closed off a bit of myself."

"You were grieving."

"Yeah, but I had a job to do in raising you right."

"Raising me right? Daddy, you were there for me. Every day. Every night. You'd lost your wife. I'd lost my mama. And you were the one who circled the wagons."

"I taught you that when things get painful, you just shut yourself down. I didn't let you in your mama's sewing and craft room because I was afraid your fragrance would replace hers. Remember that? You wanted to study in there, listen to her music."

"But I understood." Even at the tender age of twelve. Death caused a girl to grow up fast.

"We stopped having holiday dinners and barbecues. Bettin wanted that big ole house on three acres so we could have parties. Invite the world. Instead, we lived just like you do here, Reg, in two rooms and a bedroom. Shoot, half the time we slept in the recliners or on the sofa."

"Getting up and going to bed felt so lonely." Even now she still slept on the sofa half the time.

"Me too." Daddy sighed, running his hand over his face. "Like father, like daughter. Reg, I'm proud of you, but I taught you to cordon off part of your heart and I'm sorry. I think it's kept you from really living."

His words sliced. Offended. "I am living. Doing what I want to do. So don't go feeling all sorry for yourself with the woe-is-me parent routine. Are you saying if I open up the whole house, buy some furniture, hold a party or two, you'll consider me living?"

He shook his head. "It took Sadie for me to realize how shut down I was, Reg. When we got married, it took some time, but I started to move on." Daddy squinted at Reggie, looking as if he was weighing his next thought. "But it never occurred to me that I might have left you behind."

"I'm not cordoned off. I'm not left behind."

"Still, it won't hurt to hop on over and give Hessenberg a look-see, Reg. Sadie called her friend who's got a contact in the FBI. We're looking up Tanner Burkhardt, but I think he's all right."

"Dad, I'm not going to Hessenberg—to be a princess, by the way—because two bedrooms and a living room aren't furnished. That's crazy logic."

"It's not about logic, Reg. It's about—"

"Or because the Corvair and Datsun haven't been restored yet." She was really convincing herself, not Daddy.

If Mr. Burkhardt's, er, Tanner's, news made her topsy-turvy, this conversation with Daddy turned her on her head, inside out and spinning around.

"It's that you haven't met your Sadie yet. The one thing, that makes you long to open up your whole heart."

"Isn't Jesus that *one*? That thing?" She'd walked the aisle of Community Christian when she was eight. Gave her heart to Jesus. She meant it then and she meant it now. Even when Mama died, she believed he was good. And she often felt his presence like a hand on her head, walking beside her.

"He is, but I've a feeling this is all part of his plan."

"Then why didn't he tell me or have Gram say something? All those times we played princess and she never once coughed up the truth?" Daddy followed her back to the kitchen and Reggie shuffled the official papers into a pile. "Neither did you, for that matter. I'm in the car business now."

"Yet you've never ventured farther than Georgia for a car show, and I don't recall you flying up to the Detroit car museum to see the Starfire #89."

"You are really starting to grate on my nerves."

"Sorry, sweet pea, but I need you to see the truth before you shut the door to what this Tanner fella is saying."

"You know what really bugs me in all of this?" She jammed

the documents into the attaché case, taking extra care with the copy of Gram's letter. "That I was settled, knew who I was and wanted to be. Then this bubba Tanner comes along and tells me I am someone else."

"No." Daddy twisted the knob on the back door and eased it open. "He's telling you who you really are."

In the shower, hot, cleansing water slicked down Reggie's head and back, then swirled at her feet before slipping down the drain.

Lord, what are you calling me to do?

The first tears were gentle, but they opened her soul's cellar door and the deep sobs came rolling out. Pressing her forehead against the shower wall, she released every buried missing-Mama emotion, then spoke to God in a short, cauterized dialog asking "why" and "what am I supposed to do now?"

Peace came about the time the hot water ran cold, so she toweled off, inspected her face and hair for greasy remains, and slipped into her pajamas.

If Tanner's appearance was merely a challenge to start really living, then yeah, his surprise visit was worth it. But in her heart of hearts, she couldn't shake the weight of his words, "You're heir to Hessenberg's throne."

Was he telling the truth? After examining the items in the attaché case and reading the letter, how could she continue to doubt? Yet how could she believe?

Walking the house, turning off the kitchen lights, Reggie noticed the box. Daddy's box. She reached for it, then drew back. Tomorrow. She'd deal with it tomorrow.

Shoot, she wouldn't be able to sleep wondering what was in that box. So she snatched it up and carried it to her bedroom.

And, mental note, put a lightbulb in the Tiffany. And . . . and . . .

throw a party. Get with Carrie and plan the largest, most whoppingest Oktoberfest ever.

She'd start living. Right now. By looking inside this box.

Sitting on her bed against a plump of pillows, Reggie examined the plain, ordinary box before unlocking the brass clasp and raising the lid.

The perfume of history—a thick, spicy, and floral oil undergirded by the scent of ancient paper—changed the aura of the room.

Changed the texture of Reggie's heart.

The contents of the box were few. Reggie's gaze fell on an old black-and-white photo, torn in two. A young man with trimmed, pale hair, dressed in an everyday suit, smiled at her, his expression brash and jaunty, his chin raised with pride. Reggie studied his posture. He seemed quite pleased with himself. With life. And he was in Gram's box.

She leaned toward the end table light. Was that the tip of a woman's sleeve on his arm? Reggie flipped the picture over, hoping to see a name. Sure enough, someone had written on the back, but the ink had faded with time. And what she could read was cut off by the tear line.

Rein Fri—

Spring 19—

Meadowbluff P—

And who was Rein F-r-i, Gram?

A friend? A boyfriend? Maybe a cousin or something? Did Gram have brothers she never told her about?

Questions with no answers made Reggie regret the permanent silence of death.

But there was more to explore. Maybe some of the answers were among the fragrances and personal items in the box. Setting Rein aside, Reggie took out a small jewel box and discovered a stunning sapphire ring mounted in a filigree shank with sparkling, clear diamonds resting on a bed of blue velvet.

"Oh my word." Reggie rose to her knees, holding up the ring. The diamonds captured the lamplight, then splashed it against the wall in a glorious prism. The beauty of its design made her a bit giddy. Like the first time she saw a classic car. Like the first time she saw a Starfire #89.

But this ring . . .

It was spectacular. A work of art. Reggie slipped the shank down her finger, surprised and delighted to find it fit perfectly.

What else was in this mystery box? Another jewel case contained a pendant on a gold chain. It was delicate and beautiful, but cut in half, and engraved with something Reggie couldn't make out.

That was it, except for a small artist notepad that barely fit the bottom of the box. And Reggie recognized it instantly.

The fairy tale. *Her* fairy tale, penned and illustrated by Gram for Reggie's sixth birthday. With trembling fingers, she worked the book out of the box, careful not to bend the sides more than necessary.

She'd all but forgotten about the fairy tale. Thought it'd been lost along life's way or ruined during the great rains of '00 when the attic leaked.

Reggie smoothed her hand over the first page. *Regina's Fairy Tale.* The words leaned a bit too much and the press of a calligrapher's pen spread the ink outside the bounds of the letters. But it was Gram's writing. And a good job too, at ninety-four, painting a story for Reggie. Turning the page, she read out loud.

Once upon a time, you see, there was a princess, a duchess-in-waiting, because her uncle was the Grand Duke.

Reggie stopped, her pulse fluttering in her throat. This fairy tale was about *Gram.*

The thin watercolor image was of the duke and the young

princess. She was dressed in royal array, her mass of red hair piled high on her head.

> The princess lived in a beautiful land surrounded by the sea. Her palace of gleaming floors and flickering lamps sat on the meadow of Braelon Bay and the Cliffs of White. When the spring winds came, the salty breeze moved through the peaks and into the palace's open windows, bringing the music of the waves.

The painting depicted a turreted stone palace with high gabled peaks and multiple smoking chimneys across two pages. Gram added a paving stone walkway and a carpet of green grass dotted with yellow daffodils.

In the background were the tall, rather ominous-looking white-tipped cliffs and a hint of the blue-green North Sea.

Reggie hopped up for her laptop and googled Braelon Bay and Cliffs of White. Chills gripped her scalp and trickled down her neck and arms when the images popped on the screen looking exactly as Gram had painted them. Had she painted them from memory. Or from a photograph.

Back on the bed, Reggie returned to the story, her resolve, her "no" waning. But she could not let a booklet painted by an old woman direct her life.

On the next page, the princess sat on a settee under a bay window in a luminous room with swirls and swirls of sunlight falling through the window.

> The princess was most happy with her mamá and sister, living with her uncle in the palace of the magical kingdom. But as she grew older, she fell in love.

Reggie glanced at Rein. "Was it you?"

But all was not well in the land.

Turning the page, Reggie's heart sank to see the swirls of golden light now swirls of dark, ominous clouds. The princess ran through some kind of forest, a possessed one if Reggie ever saw one, with craggy limbs and twig fingers snatching at the girl's hair and clothes.

Evil came to the kingdom, and the princess and her family had to flee.

Evil? *Gram, what evil?* Did she mean the war? The entail?

The princess clutched a brown bag to her chest, peering back over her shoulder, her red hair streaming over her eyes.

In the next scene, the princess found safety in a red stable nestled in a light-washed thicket clearing, thin brambles and vines growing about the structure as if to protect it from outside intrusion. Sitting under an arch of white light, the stable image was ethereal. Surreal. Reggie could almost see the light beams dancing in the air.

Reggie flipped the page and walked with the watercolor princess through the stable door, her lantern raised high.

With only moments to spare, the princess stowed away her treasures, believing that one day, when salvation came, they would be found and loved again.

Hmm . . . *Gram, what do you mean?* When salvation came? Was she referencing the entail? The war? The future heir? Was she even aware of the entail's consequences? While fascinating and reminiscent, Reggie found none of the fairy tale compelling enough to leave her home, her job, her security, her friends and family to...

How did Daddy say it? *Hop on over and give Hessenberg a look-see.*

Turning the page, Reggie read to the end of the story, still unmoved to travel four thousand miles for the sake of some old piece of political paper. Or the whims of a dead uncle she'd never met.

However, the last page torpedoed all her resolve. Bombarded all of her walls of reason.

In the depths of the stable, darkness all around save the lone lantern, the princess knelt by a sparkling red Starfire #89.

Scrambling off the bed, her pulse surging and every nerve firing, Reggie collected the contents of the box and stuffed her legs into a clean pair of jeans without bothering to remove her pajama bottoms. Pulling on a top and jamming her feet into boots, she grabbed her purse and the attaché case and headed out the door, barely caring that the clocks were striking midnight.

EIGHT

𝒯he pounding on his suite door was a little too aggressive for late-night room service, but it mattered not to Tanner. He'd waited forty-five minutes for his chocolate cake à la mode, and his mouth was buzzing. His stomach was rumbling. The server could bust down the door for all he cared. Just let him eat cake.

"Finally." Tanner swung the door wide, but Miss Beswick, not a server with a tray of cake, stood in the hallway.

"Finally? You were expecting me?"

"No, but please come in." Tanner leaned to see down the hall. No cake in sight. But oh, it was far better to see Miss Beswick. His vacant stomach would have to wait.

"Look, I know it's late but—" She stood in the middle of the suite, a box in her hands, the attaché case swinging from her shoulder, staring at the floor. "Can you put a shirt on?"

"Begging your pardon. I wasn't expecting you." He reached for the dress shirt he'd left on a chair. "I was working on e-mails . . . waiting for cake. What are you doing here?"

A light knock peppered the room.

"There's your cake."

"*Now* he comes." Tanner opened the door and the server entered, a tray balanced on his palm.

He signed for the dessert, feeling awkward for crossing lines of impropriety by standing in front of his future sovereign half naked.

"Is everything all right?" he asked when they were alone.

The server had left the cake and ice cream on the bar, but Tanner shoved it out of his mind, composed himself for king and country, and focused on Miss Beswick.

"It's true, isn't it? This princess business." She trembled, a wild look in her eyes.

"Yes, it's true." He motioned for her to sit in one of the twin club chairs while he brought up the recessed lighting with the dimmer switch.

She cradled the box in her lap, a concerned expression bruising her beauty. She'd showered so the grease was gone, and her likeness was all the more like Princess Alice in the painting.

"My father brought me this box." She leaned forward, handing it over, her hair flowing free, framing her face. Tanner ignored the airy sensation in his chest and focused on the box. "Gram left it for me. He was going to give it to me when I got older but . . . forgot . . . until now." She smiled softly. "And technically, I am older."

"Then the timing of the delivery must be spot-on." The box was made of dark wood, plain, except for the brass hardware. He opened the lock and started to raise the lid, but when he glanced at Miss Beswick, tears gleamed in her eyes.

"Aren't you going to eat your dessert?" She glanced back at the bar. "I don't mind."

"But perhaps I do." Tanner scooted to the edge of his seat, setting the box on the coffee table. "Unless you care to share. I've extra spoons at the bar."

She hesitated. "What kind of cake?"

"Chocolate . . . à la mode."

She smiled with a wave of her hand. "Bring it. Can't resist chocolate when I'm mulling over a problem."

Tanner brought the cake to the table, offering Miss Beswick a spoon. For the first few bites, they ate in silence save for the "mms" and exclamations of, "This is so good."

Then Miss Beswick set her spoon aside. "You can have the rest. I'm good."

"Are you sure?" Tanner eyed her, eyed the cake. He was still quite famished and had to control himself from hoarding the whole thing.

"I'm sure."

Tanner cut another bite of cake, the rich edges soaked in melting ice cream, allowing himself to relax while maintaining his guard in her presence. "Can I ask a question?"

"Depends."

"How did your grandma die? Eloise, was it?"

"Cancer at sixty-six. She'd been a heavy smoker her whole life."

"And your grandfather?"

"Heart failure, diabetes. Died just before seventy. I have some memories of them but they died when I was pretty young. They were Depression babies and wartime adults. Hardworking, honorable people but food and smoking moderation were not qualities they embraced."

"What about your father's parents?"

"Still alive. They live on a farm in Live Oak."

Tanner raised his brow, spooning up another round of sweet ice cream and cake goodness. "Farmers."

"You do realize you're getting a country girl in me, don't you?"

He stopped motion, spoon in midair, a drop of ice cream hitting his bare foot. Shoving his spoon in his mouth, Tanner snatched up a cloth napkin. "Are you saying you'll come to Hessenberg?"

He peeked sideways at Miss Beswick. But she stared blankly toward the window, distracted with the questions Tanner knew rattled her heart.

"I don't know," she said after a moment. "I'm just reminding you I'm nothing fancy. Just a simple north Florida girl."

Tanner tossed the wadded-up napkin to the table and set his spoon in his dish. "Who said we were looking for fancy? You appear to be a woman of substance to me, and I do believe that will service us more."

"The very definition of princess is fancy." She shook her head.

"Only in movies or cartoons."

"I don't know . . ." She sighed. "This morning I woke up sure of my day, my future . . . Then you walked into the barn and told me I was someone completely different."

"Did I?" Tanner attempted one more bite, but he was done. He carried the tray with the remains of their snack to the door and set it in the hall. "Seems to me I only filled in some missing information."

"Which yanked me around,"—she mimed a jerking move—"in a completely different direction."

"I'm sorry the news came as a surprise. But I can't think of any other way to inform you of your true heritage. Of Hessenberg's need for you."

She laughed with irony. "A country needs me. Do you know how strange that sounds? How strange it feels? My heart feels like a rock and my thoughts are running around, bumping into each other."

"Did the contents of the box help or hurt?" Tanner pointed to the box.

"Both." She exuded a confident innocence that fascinated him, made him want to spend the night talking to her, learning about her, watching her face, and memorizing her unique nuances. "Go on. Take a look." She motioned to the box.

"All right." Tanner raised the lid to see a spiral artist notebook on top, barely fitting.

"Gram wrote and illustrated a fairy tale for my sixth birthday."

He tugged it free and turned the pages. "Your gram did this?"

"When she was ninety-four."

She'd painted a beautiful replica of Meadowbluff Palace. "This is where she grew up. It used to be the country palace until the capital city, Strauberg, expanded into the countryside. In the winter and social season, the royal family lived in the city, at Wettin Manor." He looked up at her. "It's a government office now, but you will have discretion to—"

"Hey, don't look at me. I'm not even sure who I am anymore." Miss Beswick slipped from her chair, pointing to the next page. "What's this scene about?"

"I don't know." Tanner studied the image of a young woman fleeing through an angry forest. "There were no woods behind the palace in 1914 when the princess lived there."

"What was it when she lived there?"

"A meadow." He offered her a smile. "Thus, Meadowbluff Palace. The royal mews, stables, would be about here somewhere." Tanner pointed to the top of the page. "The prince, her uncle, kept a couple of race horses there along with his automobiles." He waved his hand over the forest scene. "All of this used to be a meadow. But after two wars and a depression, the extended grounds around the mews were not maintained. They grew wild and left to become whatever. The mews were torn down in the twenties, I believe. This whole area is actually woodlands now. It's funny your gram would know that."

"Maybe she saw a picture?" Miss Beswick left her chair, perched on the edge of the coffee table, and leaned over the book, leaned into Tanner's personal space with her air of sweetness.

He exhaled, tilting away from her, quite sure his veins were visibly pulsing in his neck. "Did you find the letter? In the attaché?"

"Yes, to an Otto."

"He was your uncle's scribe."

"Scribe?"

"The Grand Duke was illiterate. Probably due to dyslexia. He employed a lad to read and write for him. Otto Pritchard. His younger brother, Yardley, was a law professor of mine—"

"You're a lawyer?"

"I am. Rather was. Now I serve Hessenberg as the Minister of Culture."

"Right." She rested her chin on her clasped hands. "You did tell me that." Then she sat back, sweeping her hands through her hair. "It feels like eons since we first met."

"Yes, eons." This would never do, her every move fanning the small flame she ignited in his soul.

"You were saying . . ."

Yes, he was saying . . . What was he saying? "Yardley recalled his brother saying Princess Alice moved to London in the twenties, after the war, and married an RAF officer."

"She never said a word, at least to me, about her life in London. I was four and five when my grandparents died. As I got older, Gram talked a lot about Hessenberg and her childhood love of painting . . . She had mild dementia in her early nineties so stories were interwoven with truth and fable and I didn't pay much attention. The older I got, the older she got. I loved sitting with her, holding her hand. But by then, she was in her late nineties, hard of hearing, and sleepy." She smiled softly. "Very sleepy." Miss Beswick shifted her gaze to him and Tanner felt a bit like he was drowning in pools of blue. "She was the sleepy princess."

"Leaving Hessenberg, two world wars, living in Brighton, then London, losing her husband . . . all painful seasons in her life. Maybe she tried to forget."

"The letter to Otto said as much. That she wanted to forget her past and all of its death."

Tanner turned to the fairy tale's last page, his gaze landing on the Starfire #89. "Miss Beswick—"

"Okay, Tanner, please. Call me Reggie. Or Regina. Miss Beswick makes me sound like a spinster."

"She painted a Starfire #89. Did you know her uncle—your uncle—commissioned the original Starfire #89? He paid for its engineering and production. He put it in its first race. Against Henry Ford's #999."

His brief time as Minister of Culture had so far centered on Augustine-Saxon history. It served him well now.

"I knew about the car but never that my great-great-great-uncle commissioned it to be made. I didn't know about him at all." Miss Beswick, rather, Regina studied the picture. "The princess is putting a bag of something in the trunk. Wonder what that means?"

"I've no idea. But this stable and the car are long gone by now, Miss Besw—Regina." Her name felt good on his lips. "The Nazis occupied some of the island during the second war. If the Starfire was still there, they'd have found it and shipped it to Germany."

"But there's only one Starfire #89 in a German museum, and it's documented as number seven, the last one made, and sold by the owner at an auction."

"I can't tell you." He closed the book. "I'm your entail chap, your royal family and Hessenberg historian, but the whereabouts of an ancient auto, I've no idea."

She sighed, taking the notebook and flipping through the pages. Her shoulders rounded forward with weariness.

"This stinks. How can I go back to being just Reggie, have-tools-will-restore-your-car, Beswick while the idea of being a real princess floats around in the back of my head? What am I supposed to do with this?" She waved the fairy tale at him. "I feel like half my life is a lie."

"Not a lie, Regina. Just incomplete."

She collapsed back into the chair. "None of this makes sense. Why didn't she tell me?"

Tanner held up the fairy tale. "What do you think this is, Regina?"

She made a face. "Tanner, I'm too tired, too confused—"

"Regina, look. A book. An offering, an avenue of communication. Fairy tale, parable, letter, novel, e-mail, blog, whatever. Words communicate. Your gram was communicating truth to you through this story."

"If she wanted me to know the truth, why didn't she just come out and say it? Why hide it in a fairy tale? And the bigger question is, what did Mama know? Because when Gram painted this, Mama was alive and well and the true heir."

"There are some mysteries we may never know the answer to, Regina." A passion fueled his thoughts, and Tanner slipped down to one knee next to her. "But this book is for you, about you . . . You *are* the princess in the story, more or less. Your gram is telling you who you are. Look at the last line. 'Believing that one day they would be found when salvation came.' She means you. The one who can save Hessenberg, save your gram's legacy. You are her treasure, her heritage. There's your truth."

Regina pressed the heels of her hands to her forehead with a deep sigh. "What truth ever started with 'Once upon a time,' Tanner?"

He laughed low and rose to his feet. "Resist all you want, but you know I'm right." He retrieved two waters from the mini-fridge. "You are the princess, the heir to the Hessenberg throne. No doubt, fear, or once-upon-a-time can change the truth."

"I keep waiting for someone to show up with an, 'Aha, we got you!'" She reached for the water bottle he offered and twisted off the cap.

"If they do, I'm as goosed as you, Regina." Tanner sat, picking up the notebook again. Something he saw on the back of the car suddenly registered with him. Yes, there on the license plate. Princess Alice was a clever woman. "See this? RAB. Your initials if I'm not mistaken. And this." He pointed to the emblem in the top right corner of the plate. "Princess Alice's cipher with the Augustine-Saxon crown above her initials. She's speaking to you loud and clear. She used to mark her cipher with a sapphire ring—"

"What did you say?"

"She'd mark her cipher with the shank of a sapphire ring. I know that—"

"Like this?" Regina retrieved a small jewel box from the larger box and opened it.

"Yes, like this." Tanner examined the ring, raising it to the light of the lamp next to him. The sapphire stone surrounded by diamonds was set in an intricate filigree setting. "The Grand Duchess ring," he whispered. "We thought it'd been lost. Grand Duke Earnest Wilhelm fashioned this ring for his wife in 1833. The sapphire came from Hessenberg's own mines when they were producing some of the world's best."

"Then take it. It belongs to Hessenberg," Regina said.

"No, the ring belongs to the royal family, Regina. It belongs to you."

"But I'm not a royal, Tanner." Her protests about her true heritage were weakening. "Besides, what would I do with that here?"

"Mark your seal on . . ."—he shrugged, grinning—"a new paint job for one of your autos."

She laughed, and he loved hearing the melody of her heart. She reached for the ring as he passed it back. "What's this thing worth anyway? Or do I want to know?"

"A quarter of a million pounds. Roughly. See the princess—"

"A quarter of a mill—shoot, Tanner, that's like . . ." She held up the ring, calculating. "Three hundred and fifty thousand in dollars. Roughly."

"The old Grand Duke spared no expense. The sapphire is over two karats and cut with the rare jeweler's cut. Same with the diamonds, all flawless with the jeweler's cut," Tanner said.

Regina leaned toward the lamp behind her, offering the ring to the triangle of light falling from under the shade. "What's so rare about the cut?"

"No one knows how to fashion it anymore. It was developed by a Jewish family in Germany. All very skilled and talented artisans. All killed, every one of them, in Dachau and Auschwitz."

The words *Dachau* and *Auschwitz* raised the blinders on history's dark past and the sins of men.

"Then the ring is priceless," Regina said, low and tender. Thoughtful. "So much talent and knowledge was lost in the war. You can't kill six million people—"

"Murder."

"Murder six million people and preserve knowledge or hold on to culture."

Tanner regarded her. Did she hear herself? Such an observation. And spoken like a true princess. "You're making an argument for why we need you, Regina. To regain our heritage, our culture."

"But I know nothing of your heritage or culture."

"You carry the blood of your gram, your uncle, within you."

Regina regarded the ring, shaking her head. "I'm sorry, but I am not anyone's hope of restoration." She held the ring at arm's length, one eye closed. "The filigree is so detailed. Like it's trying to say something."

"It is. It's your gram's cipher." Tanner moved behind her and leaned over her shoulder. Soft wisps of her fiery hair burned his cheeks. "The shank was restyled for her when she became the Hereditary Duchess. See here? The *P* for Princess. Half of an *A* for Alice. And half of a crown. On the other side of the ring is the rest of the *A* and crown."

"That's extraordinary. And amazingly clever. I should come

up with some kind of cipher for the cars we restore." She laughed. "A brand. Sear it on the undercarriage."

"Yes, it's quite clever. It's the ingenuity of Earnest Wilhelm, passed on from Grand Duchess to Grand Duchess. It was a secret. Only the royal jeweler knew the cipher was embedded in the ring. When the Duchess sealed a letter or marked an official document with her seal, she added the cipher, usually in private, so no aides or staff discovered the secret."

"So, the royal life is fraught with secrets and intrigue."

"More than you know." He could lean over her shoulder all night and never tire. His lips were inches from hers and his heart was alerting his whole body to her beauty.

"Really, you should take it home with you." Regina returned the ring to its jewel case, shoving it to Tanner's side of the coffee table. "What do you know about this?" She reached inside the box, bringing out a rather tattered, torn photograph. "Do you know him? He doesn't seem connected to anything we've talked about so far."

Tanner pinched the end of the photo between his thumb and finger. So this was the other half of the photo he found in *his* box.

"Your gram loved boxes, Regina," Tanner said, walking into the bedroom and from his suitcase dug out the box he'd found at the palace, in one of the suites. The one he had carried to the office the other day, wondering how he'd discover the mystery of the box's unusual contents.

He set it on the table next to Regina's box, opened the lid, and retrieved the other half of the picture.

"Oh my gosh, she tore it in half. Put them in two different boxes." Regina sighed, but with a smile. "Gram, were you a little upset at this boy?"

"Maybe she meant to give one half to the young man," Tanner offered, tapping his half of the photo. "And keep one for herself."

"Maybe. Or she was brokenhearted. Otherwise, why keep it

all those years? When she had two husbands?" Regina reached for the two halves, piecing them together, studying them, her questions defining her fine features.

"Perhaps it was love unrequited," Tanner said. "There, turn over the photos. What does the writing tell us?"

"Let's see." When Regina bent to the light again to read the back of the photograph, her thick, sun-kissed bangs streamed over her eyes. At once she was both worldly and innocent, a tomboy with a feminine flair. Tanner breathed in and breathed out. *Steady, ole boy.* "Rein Friedrich . . ." She looked to Tanner. "Ring any bells? This was the spring of 1914."

Tanner studied the man's face while his private thoughts urged his heart to shut up about love and desire. *Focus on the task at hand.* "There was a Rein Friedrich who fought for the Kaiser in the first war. Jumped sides, he did, which was what the Grand Duke, Prince Francis, feared all along with Hessenberg's young men."

"Didn't he fear the Germans? The Kaiser? Seems I remember something about that in a history class."

"He did, but moreover, he feared the men of fighting age would join ranks with his cousin, the Kaiser, his rival. Francis wanted to fight with his Anglo cousins in England and Brighton. But Hessenberg's strong Germanic influence divided the country in 1914."

"So he abandoned ship."

"Something like that, yes. But he wasn't ready to lead in wartime anyway. Rein Friedrich, if this is the same chap, joined the German army, rose through the ranks until he eventually found himself in Hitler's inner circle."

"Gram saved a picture of a Nazi?" She moved the photo pieces apart, making a face, disgust sharpening her tone.

"He wasn't a Nazi when this was taken," Tanner said. "He was most likely a jolly university chap with the world at his beckoning."

"Cocky and full of himself."

"Aren't all young men? Rein's life ended with him swinging from a rope. He was sentenced to death at the Nuremberg trials."

Regina dropped the photo into the box. "What about this pendant?" She rested the piece in his palm.

"Looks like it's been cut in half. And"—Tanner dug in his box—"like the picture, I have the other half here." Tanner matched his half of the pendant to Regina's. "It's engraved with her initials. It's a cipher pendant."

"Do you think she wanted him to have the other half?" She held up her palm and Tanner settled his half of the pendant against her skin.

"Very well could," Tanner said. "The picture was taken in 1914 before the war. She might have fallen for Rein. Maybe she tore the picture before the family fled, leaving it behind for him."

"Do you think that's what the fairy tale is about? Gram leaving things behind for him?"

"I don't think Rein would never be the 'salvation' of Hessenberg. Besides, he obviously didn't go off with the box, the picture, or the pendant. I found the box in the princess suite of the palace."

She sighed, packing up the box. "More questions. Fewer answers." Regina stood, collecting her box. "Gram, *grrr*, why didn't you say something?"

"Regina, she did."

"If you say to me the fairy tale is her 'saying something' . . ." She pointed her finger at him, her chin lowered, her eyes narrowed. "I might have to punch you."

He laughed. "Have I rattled you that much?"

"Yes . . . no . . . It's not you . . . I don't know, Tanner. I don't know. I can't think."

"You're tired. Go home. Sleep."

But she didn't move past the chairs. "What . . . what would I have to do again? And for how long?"

Tanner started down this road tenderly. Slowly. "Go to

Hessenberg, of course. Meet with the king and other leaders, the prime minister and governor, go through the formalities—"

"Become the actual princess."

"Yes, by reinstating the House of Augustine-Saxon. You'll be the heir and princess, Hereditary Duchess—"

"Grand Pooh-bah and Chief Potentate?"

"If you'd like." He wanted to laugh, wrap her against him, kiss the worry lines from her forehead, and promise her all would be well. She moved his heart in a way no woman ever had. Not even Trude.

He'd chide himself later about the inappropriateness of his affection, but he was tired, still famished, and on the cusp of winning her over. So he gave his heart permission to feel.

"Then what? You said something about an oath."

"Oath of the Throne. To be the proper heir, the proper princess. You'll pledge to protect and defend Hessenberg. I don't think you'll find any of it objectionable."

"Tanner, I'm an American."

"Yes, well—"

"I have to give up my citizenship?"

"You will be a sovereign of Hessenberg, Miss Beswick . . . Regina." Could she hear what he whispered to her?

"Oh no, no—"

"Not even for your gram? For her people?"

"But she left Hessenberg. She left Europe. Came to America and lived like an American."

"And you'll return, to do what your gram couldn't do. Return to her royal house and her people. Establish the Augustine-Saxon throne once again."

Regina made tracks for the door. "Be sure to text me when you leave, okay?"

"You're not coming with me?" He must not let her make her decision so quickly. "Regina, give it another day."

She turned back and grasped the front of his shirt with light-ning speed.

"Look me in the eye."

"Steady on."

"This is real? All of it? For real?" Determination flared in her eyes, poured forth in her words.

"You're the one with the box, Regina. With the ring, with your gram's fairy tale message. I'll ring His Royal Highness, King Nathaniel II, if you'd like—"

"No." She released him, stepping back. "I believe you."

"Th–then you'll come?" He adjusted his shirt, moving around to see her face. Her eyes. He was already becoming familiar with her visual messages.

"Maybe." She went to the door and jerked it open. "I would need a couple of days to get ready."

"Regina?"

"What?" she said, one foot in the hall, her back to the room.

"Thank you. All of Hessenberg thanks you."

"I said maybe, Tanner. Maybe."

And she was gone.

August 10, 1914

Meadowbluff Palace

From the Grand Ballroom and through the open windows, I can hear the orchestra tuning. The music is so lovely. And the breeze is rising up from the bay, cooling off the August heat and bringing the scent of the sea mixed with honeysuckle.

It's nearly eight in the evening and the sun is setting, leaving a beautiful but curious white glow over Uncle's stable. Almost like a beacon. Oh for my Brownie camera! How could I have left it behind at Wettin Manor? Must ask Mamá if Lark can take me into the city tomorrow to retrieve it.

If I cannot have a paintbrush in my hand, I should like to have my camera. There is so much beauty and wonder to capture in life.

I taught Esmé to use the camera. For a picture of Rein Friedrich and me when he came to call. But that was before . . . Oh, he's so rude and mean toward Uncle.

Mr. Elliott brought the picture development round last evening and I had half a mind to tear up the photograph of Rein and me. Right in half, I tell you.

Though I must say, having a ball when the talk of war escalates and burdens us all does seem untimely.

But Mamá is so looking forward to tonight's festivities. It's been a year since Papá's death and she longs to wear a colorful gown.

Uncle and Mamá want to present me as the official Hereditary Grand Duchess of Hessenberg during the ball as well. Though I'm a bit young yet, only sixteen.

I've mixed feelings about it all. About so many things.

War.

Love.

Men.

Rein.

He insists he and the other lads are restless, wanting to go to war. They are congregating in the afternoons and evenings in Wisteria Park, in the avenues, and on the university campus demanding Uncle and Prime Minister Fortier enter the fight. They ask why the grand isle of Hessenberg should sit by while our brethren in Brighton and Britain—yes, even Germany—spill their blood on the battlefields.

Uncle's advisors, Lord Raeburn and Lord Strathem, have already joined the Brighton navy, serving as officers for His Majesty, King Nathaniel I.

I do believe Uncle's pride is wounded, but even more he is afraid. He will not enter the war because he cannot lead Hessenberg through.

He has said so to Mamá and me many times over. He claims he has no mind for military strategy..

Let the Kaiser and Tsar fight their own battles. What has it to do with Hessenberg?

But I can tell Uncle regards this as his worst failure. He fears, as do I, our English and German heritage will divide rather than unite us. We are literally cousins to them all.

So Uncle continues the summer social season as if Germany, Russia, Austria, Serbia, the United Kingdom, and Brighton have not chosen up sides and are preparing, perhaps this very hour, to fire upon one another.

It seems impossible to think our young men may fight against one another. Some decry, "Fight for the Kaiser." While others are fighting for the king of Brighton and sporting about in their brown-and-navy uniforms.

Last week when Rein came to call, he criticized Uncle for not joining in with Kaiser Wilhelm. When I defended Uncle, Rein insisted, to my face, that Uncle was arrogant and selfish, caring only for his royal ways with no care toward the bourgeois.

Uncle has every care toward the bourgeois. He's built three schools for the mine workers, the "ringers," and for the poor. He charges nothing for their children to attend. He's even begun a special program for children who cannot read well. Something about the letters flipping about on the page, or dancing around. He's never said aloud but I do believe he suffers from such a malady. 'Tis why he employs Otto to do his reading and writing.

I suppose he does appear self-righteous regarding war, but his fears and inability to read leave him no choice.

The sun is moving farther west and elongated shadows fall on the lawn, taking my heart with it. I am remembering my friends and our days at the summer shore. Was it only a month ago we walked along the beach, kicking at the waves, holding hands, us all, singing the evening song, reminiscing of our school days? Laughing and laughing and laughing.

"La-da-da. Moonlight, sunshine, waves upon the shore—"

I think it's my favorite evening song.

Rein asked permission to call on me tonight. I told him yes, but he must face the duke first.

"I shall make the arrangements," he said.

Now I wonder. He was so hard on Uncle, on all of us. We shall see tonight.

Alice

NINE

*H*e prayed it wasn't too late. In the inner sanctum of his office in Wettin Manor, Seamus Fitzsimmons poured himself a shot of whiskey from the decanter he kept hidden away behind a panel in the wall. He wasn't sure what possessed the ancients to build palaces and manses with hidden corridors and secret panels, but he appreciated them all at the moment.

After tossing down the shot, letting the liquid burn down his throat, Seamus set his glass down. How had he not acted sooner? He'd let familiarity and gentle politics dull his senses.

He'd become too enamored with his position and ease of life. And because he'd been mates with King Nathaniel's father, King Leopold, at Bryn Academy and Knoxton University.

When King Leo appointed Seamus to the governorship of Hessenberg, Seamus pledged his loyalty and devotion to the king and kingdom.

Now the security of his political future rested solely in his willingness to lead Hessenberg toward her future. If this so-called heir to Hessenberg's throne proved solid, then what chance did he have to survive this new wave of government? He must assert himself. Take the bull by the horns, as it were.

Who in blazes ever imagined a long-lost princess being found? Five months ago, not a soul in Brighton Kingdom or Hessenberg. Now Seamus felt he'd tarried too long in taking action.

He couldn't delay to see if this *heir*, Regina Beswick, embraced her inheritance and assumed the Hessenberg throne.

He must seize his opportunity now. Besides, kowtowing to King Leo was one thing. Seamus could even tolerate it for his son, King Nathaniel II. But bowing and scraping to an uncouth American? He'd not do it. It was beneath him. Even his wife said as much at dinner last night. With, mind you, their guests agreeing quite heartily.

Do something, Seamus. Don't sit idly by.

He reached for the decanter and poured another shot of whiskey.

Then an idea came to him after the guests departed. A clever way around the need for a royal heir.

Seamus downed his drink as his vice governor, Courtland Hamish, entered.

"It took all morning to go through the entail, comparing it with old laws, new laws, and court rulings. But you were right. Hessenberg never filed a petition with the European court to be a sovereign state on behalf of the people. The petition always came from Brighton on behalf of the government, but not the people themselves. Very clever twist, Seamus. Anyway, the court always upheld the entail as ironclad based on the state-to-state law."

"Precisely. But we've found a way round," Seamus said. "What about the other issue?"

Courtland exhaled, shuffling the papers in his hand. "We can do it, though I'm not as confident with this move, Seamus. There is legal precedent, but let me warn you on behalf of the duchy's legal counsel, this could wreak havoc."

"Of course it will. But suing Germany for financial restitution dating back to 1914 is our bargaining chip. Our throwaway argument. Once they agree to back our case with the European court, we drop the suit."

"You do realize if the EU court decides to hear our people's case and rules in our favor, that we can be a sovereign nation without a monarchy? But we will immediately be without a government. Every anarchist and communist, conservative, liberal, you-name-it political faction will fire out of the woodwork and wharf-side pubs, from the universities and Market Avenue, decrying their right to form the new government of the new Hessenberg state."

"Precisely, and that's where I come in. Papá Fitzsimmons. 'Let me lead you through these turbulent waters.'"

Courtland grinned with a shake of his head and took a seat in the wingback chair adjacent to the desk. "I've known you for twenty years, Seamus, but I never saw your devious side before."

"Devious? My dear fellow, I take offense." Seamus smoothed his tie beneath the folds of his jacket and walked over to the window where he could see the glorious afternoon sun streaming over Strauberg through white pillars of clouds. "I've found my purpose."

"To rule Hessenberg?"

"Do you disagree?" Seamus returned to his desk and leaned toward his colleague, his friend. "Now we just need the court to decide on hearing the case. Preferably before Tanner returns with the princess..."

"*If* he returns with her." Courtland cleared his throat and nodded toward the decanter. "You might want to pour another glass. There's more to this tap dance."

Seamus rose up, the implication of Courtland's words darkening his mood. He'd been feeling spry and fine just a moment ago, basking in his brilliance.

"Tell me."

"If and when Tanner returns with the princess, King Nathaniel II can style her as a royal princess and have her take the Oath of the

Throne, making her officially Hessenberg's royal. We will have our monarchy as the entail requires and you will be hard pressed to get her out of the way. Especially if she earns public favor."

"Well, let's just see to it that she doesn't." Once Seamus inhaled the heady nectar of power, of steering Hessenberg toward a new horizon in history, nothing less than being the duchy's leader would do. He'd destroy the monarchy or himself in the process of power, but Seamus Fitzsimmons would not so much as bow or nod to this American interloper.

"Seamus, be careful here. We don't mean to harm the very country we love. And the innocent people along the way."

"We will do our best to protect and defend Hessenberg." Seamus decided another shot of whiskey was indeed in order. "And let it be known, Tanner Burkhardt is not one of the innocent."

Courtland nodded when Seamus raised the whiskey bottle toward him. "Your protégé is on your naughty list?"

"We'd not be in this mess were it not for him and his affection for Yardley Pritchard. I daresay Pritchard was an old coot when I was in the law review."

"Give the boy the benefit of doubt, Seamus. Tanner was merely looking for a way to help Hessenberg."

"Without a glance toward me, I'll say. After all I've done for him. He owes me, that lad."

"Owes you? For what?"

Seamus passed Courtland his glass. "Let's just say I gave him an opportunity when he most needed it. Saved him and his father humiliation."

"His father? The archbishop?" Courtland raised his brow, tipping his head toward Seamus. "Care to tell me more?"

Seamus hammered back his shot and thirsted for more. "Have you dinner plans, Courtland? I've a standing Monday evening reservation at the club."

"I could ring Penelope. Make sure she's not far in her dinner."

He reached for his phone. "Are you going to tell the king of your plans to file a new petition with the EU court?"

Seamus shook his head. "And alert him of my plans so he can make his own? No. He'll find out with the rest of the lot when he reads his morning papers."

"Careful not to burn your bridges. I believe the king respects you."

"Only because of his father."

"Still, there is a third option in all of this, Seamus. The princess refuses to come. The court denies our petition and at midnight on 22 October, we become a permanent province of Brighton Kingdom. One which will *still* need a governor."

Seamus shook his head. He'd considered and weighed all options. "Nathaniel will replace me with someone else. All sons replace their father's appointments."

"Eventually, perhaps. But not right away."

"I'm fifty-nine years old, Courtland. If I ever wanted to make my mark on the world, this is my hour."

Tanner sat straight up from a dead sleep, shoving his hair from his face. Wh–what time was it? Where was he? Had he overslept? Blimey, he'd overslept.

Scrambling from bed, Tanner found his bearings by focusing on the slivers of fresh, warm light haloing the edges of the drawn curtains.

Tallahassee. The princess. Hotel Duval. Right, right . . . His heartbeat slowed as he dropped to the edge of the bed. He was fine. Not late for work at all.

Besides, his flat back home didn't have curtains. The windows had shades. And he rarely drew them because the downtown Strauberg lights didn't disturb him.

Flopping back to the bed, Tanner closed his eyes, breathing deep, gathering his thoughts, letting his heart and mind wake up and surface.

After Regina left Friday night, he worked all Saturday, e-mailing back and forth with Louis about his schedule, working through details for a Music Festival request and a proposal by university film students to develop a multimedia documentary about the duchy.

So much history and information had been lost in the last one hundred years. And Tanner was eager to get back to their roots.

While he liked the film students' idea, he knew in his heart of hearts Hessenberg's history began with the redheaded princess-in-waiting he'd not heard from all weekend.

If she didn't return to Hessenberg with him, Tanner wasn't sure how to engage the heart of a people trying to find their way home again.

On Sunday morning, he roamed the Capital campus and explored the quiet downtown streets. Something about the old southern city reminded him of Strauberg. Minus the heat and humidity. Mercy and the saints, it was hot in the South. Especially for fall.

In the afternoon he did something he'd not done in twenty-eight years. Napped.

But when he awoke, the sun was banking west, turning the day toward night, and anxiety snapped in his chest.

What was *she* doing? What was she thinking?

He spent a restless Sunday evening watching a Tom Cruise movie, eating in, hoping she'd call, willing himself to be patient, to wait to hear from her.

Either way, he'd resolved not to let another day go by without seeing her. Somewhere in the last moments of the weekend, he became restless, eager to see Regina, wanting to know her more than as his future sovereign but as a fascinating, lovely woman.

A desire he could share with no one.

Now it was Monday and he must forge ahead.

Tanner's phone pinged from the desk and he bolted out of bed to answer it.

"Burkhardt."

"Tanner, it's Nathaniel."

"Your Majesty." Tanner squared his shoulders, glancing about the room for a shirt or something. Four thousand miles away and the king's voice demanded all due respect. "What can I do for you this morning?"

"Morning? It's afternoon, mate." The subtle merriment in his tone did not soothe the Tanner's wakening, driving senses.

"Yes, afternoon." In Brighton surely, not Tallahassee. Tanner scanned the room for his watch. There, on the dresser. He glanced at the white-faced dial. Drat it all. One o'clock? He'd slept until one o'clock Tallahassee time? He felt a burn of embarrassment. He'd been a runny-nosed chap the last time he slept so late.

He cleared his throat, trying to sound more awake.

"How's it going with Miss Beswick? Any news since your last update?"

"No, sir. She asked for a few days, so I stayed clear the weekend. Am on my way to see her now." Tanner walked into the living area, jerked a bottle of water from the mini-fridge, and dumped it over his head, shivering as the first drops splashed on his warm, sleepy skin. *Wake up, chap.*

"I hate to do this to you, but we need you to bring her home now."

"Now? As in today? What's happened?" Tanner drank the last ounce of water, soaking his parched throat.

"Seamus Fitzsimmons happened. Jolly ole Fitzsimmons."

Tanner made his way to the bathroom for a towel. "The one who could play St. Nicholas for the department stores every Christmas?"

"He filed a petition with the European Court today for

Hessenberg to be a sovereign state outside of the conditions of the 1914 entail!"

"Blimey. Haven't we all been through this? Several times?" Tanner snapped the towel over his shoulder. "The EU court has upheld the entail."

"Seamus found a way round, or through, however you choose to call it. He filed on behalf of the Hessenberg *people*. Not the government."

Tanner returned to the living area and sat in one of the club chairs. "What? That was tried in 1992 by Lord Kilroy. The court threw it out." Tanner could still see the details in his mind, the reasoning and writing in his law book. Top of page 581, right-hand side.

"Yes, because Lord Kilroy wasn't actually an official of the people. Just a titled nobleman. But Seamus is an official representative of the people. I believe the court may see the merit of his case."

"That's brilliant." Tanner slightly chided himself, rising to pace. How did he not predict this? "He may have found the one and only way to break the entail."

"It was a masterful move. Seamus seems to have all the i's dotted and t's crossed on this one. That's why I called you."

"Yes, sir. What do you need me to do?"

"Well, first of all, Tanner, I must ask. Are you my man? Do I need to replace you? I've heard Seamus has meant a lot to you over the years. He was somewhat of a mentor. So, are you with me or Seamus?"

"You don't need to even ask, Your Majesty. I'm in America on a mission for the King of Brighton and Hessenberg." Tanner shoved open the curtains so the sunlight flooded his suite, flooded his soul. "I am your loyal servant."

"And should Seamus call you? Demanding loyalty to him? I'm sorry to grill you on this but I do need to know who are my allies. This could get politically ugly."

"I understand, sir. If Seamus should call, I'll inform him that I serve a higher authority, with all due respect, and must complete the king's task." Tanner exhaled, dropping down to the nearest chair, wondering if he should confess his past sins and secrets to Nathaniel. Just in case Darth Vader—Seamus Fitzsimmons— decided to use his force against him.

"There's more," Nathaniel said.

"More?"

"Seamus filed suit against Germany asking for compensation and restitution for the Hessenberg bank accounts seized by the Kaiser at the beginning of World War I."

The man had gone mad. But Tanner understood Seamus's bold move. "It's a red herring, Your Majesty," he said. "Germany will squawk. Seamus and his lawyers will barter. Drop the claim on Germany if they back Hessenberg's petition for independent, sovereign state status."

Why else would he poke the giant bear known as Germany? But wanting everyone to know it? Tanner believed he'd overplayed his hand.

"We've concluded the same thing, Tanner. But if Germany pressures the court to review and rule on the case before we get the princess back and set in—"

"Hessenberg will be thrown into political turmoil, anarchy, and civil unrest. Innocent people will be hurt." He didn't mean to interrupt the king but his thoughts raced miles ahead.

Seamus, fool man . . .

"Precisely. Tanner, you need to return to Hessenberg immediately. With the princess. We have to prepare her to take the Oath of the Throne and establish the royal house as soon as possible. Our guess here is we have a week. Or less. We've enlisted the aid of Britain to help influence the court to uphold the entail, as it has in the past, but even in the past ten years the political landscape of the court, of our countries, has changed. Seamus may find favor this time and, I fear, set up Hessenberg for chaos and disorder."

"And Regina will be a princess without a country."

"Yes, and make no mistake, Seamus is masterfully working the press as well as the youth. Some university students held an anti-royal rally this very morning."

Tanner exhaled, burdened with the new pressure and severity of his task. "I'll see her right away, sir."

"Tanner, don't just see her. Collect her. Be on the plane. Tonight."

TEN

*R*eggie loved Mondays. They were like mini New Years four times a month. A chance for a fresh start, a do-over from last week's failures. Or even success. Monday was the day to renew personal pledges, reset goals, and charge at them wholeheartedly.

So this Monday, after a fitful weekend wrestling with the arrival of Tanner Burkhardt and his disturbing news, she arrived at the shop early, ready to "get 'er done."

By afternoon, she'd finished payroll and paid the bills with only pennies to spare, started researching materials for the '53 Vet, and contacted her parts suppliers.

She'd already alerted Urban that finding the pearl white paint was going to be difficult. And when she found it, expensive. But if she located the base color and the blend recipe, Rafe could take it from there. Mixing and creating extraordinary paint was his super power.

Around one o'clock, Al came whistling into the office from running errands with a fresh box of donuts and a gallon of chocolate milk.

"Reg, strap in, 'cause I got some news."

She swiveled her chair around to see him. "Good news? You

bought more donuts. It *has* to be good news." Donuts and chocolate milk were Al's morning routine and on occasion, his good news celebration treat.

"Oh, yeah, well, partial good news, on its way to being great news." Al poured a tall glass of chocolate milk and took a donut from the box. "First, you doing all right? I didn't get to talk to you this morning, but you looked a bit preoccupied."

"I'm good." She smiled. *See?* "It's Monday. I love it. Hey, I went shopping this weekend."

"You? Now I'm really worried. What's up, Reg?"

"Ha. Very funny. I went furniture shopping. Found a living room set, and I think I'm going to actually order it."

"Furniture? Well now, good for you. I've been waiting for you to really move into that big ole house. Either move in or move out." With his gaze still on her, Al took a long drink of his milk.

"Move out?" Reggie turned to the desk and gathered the scattered invoices. "Wh–why would I move out?"

He shrugged. "I don't know … move on with life … maybe—"

"Move on with my life?" She stood, gesturing to the long narrow office, a set of invoices crumpled in her hand. "What do you call this?"

Al bit into the donut and chewed, regarding her. "Who was that fella who showed up looking for you? The one with the accent?"

"Just some dude." Reggie jerked open a file drawer. Now, why did Al want to rain on her sunny Monday?

"You're clamming up. Must be an old flame?"

"Old flame? There must be more than chocolate in your milk if you're accusing me of having an old flame." She slammed the drawer shut. "When have you ever known me to have *any* flame?"

"Never, but I was hoping you had a secret."

Oh, she had a secret all right. Just not the kind Al expected. In fact, her whole family had a secret. Of the royal princess kind.

For two days Reggie had immersed heart and mind into *her* life, balancing Tanner's announcement with an ordinary, everyday routine.

She did the shop's books on Saturday morning, then helped her neighbor Mrs. Shaw rake the leaves from her fall flower garden.

On a whim, she drove to the furniture store and *almost* bought furniture.

That evening, Mark came over as promised with a big bag of Chinese food. He was tan and cheery from sailing, with an extra jolt of charm.

When Reggie suggested a romantic comedy for movie night, he agreed instantly instead of protesting and rattling off the merits of the latest blow-'em-up thriller.

He stayed on his side of the friendship line, so she pushed off having a serious conversation with him about their relationship. Hey, maybe he'd finally heard her.

Sunday morning, Reggie sat in church all but convinced she'd have to pass on Mr. Tanner Burkhardt's offer. Hessenberg would have to weather the end of the entail without her. Her life was here. In Florida. With Daddy and Sadie, close to Mama and Great Gram's graves, to her friends, her family.

She was born to restore classic cars, not an ancient country.

Besides, if God decided to wait twenty-nine years to tell her she was a princess, Reggie knew darn well he'd not expect her to go "all in" over a weekend. He just didn't roll that way. Did he?

She'd determined to tell Tanner no until Pastor Stuart closed his message with a line that speared her right between the eyes.

"What are you giving your life and energy to achieving? Your purposes or God's?"

God's, of course.

Pastor leaned over the edge of the stage toward the congregation. Leaned toward *her.* Did his piercing gaze really land on her or did she just imagine it?

"If God is calling, why are you refusing?"

Who's refusing! He's not calling.

"Reg, hey, Reg." Al snapped his fingers. "What's going on behind your faraway stare?"

"What's going on? I'll tell you what's going on. You ... asking me all these questions." She walked out of the office into the shop and started organizing the tools on the peg board.

Al came after her, set his chocolate milk on the workbench, and grabbed her hands. "Whatever it is, it's going to be all right. Hear me?"

Tears sprouted in her eyes. "You have no idea, Al."

"Not unless you want to tell me. But I do know this. God never misses."

"*Au contraire,* he missed big this time." She moved a torque wrench from one side of the peg board to the other. There. Perfect. How could she have let that be out of place all this time? "What's your news anyway? Come on, I could use some donut-chocolate-milk kind of good news."

"Oliver Claremont is coming to see us."

Reggie jerked toward him. "The Duesenberg owner?"

Al sipped his milk like a fine wine. "One and the same."

"I knew it. I knew it." She banged the workbench with her hand. "Yes, yes, yes!" Arms raised, head back, she spun in a circle. "Thank you, thank you." She blew heaven a kiss. "See, I knew this was where I belonged." Okay, so God had her back after all. He didn't miss. She was to stay put, right here in Tally.

Poor Tanner. She hoped it went well for him when he returned to Hessenberg without her.

"Reg, hold on. He's just coming to check us out, but—"

"Shush, Al, no doubts." She wrapped him in a big hug, rocked side to side, and turned her thoughts into a song. "We have a Cor-ve-ette ... and a Du-du-duesy."

"Reg, listen to me." Al walked to the middle of the shop, one hand motioning to the work space, the other sporting his treasured milk. "Look around. You think Claremont is going to feel safe leaving his car in this old barn?"

Reggie frowned, joining him in the middle of the bay. "Urban did." She peered up at the ceiling, then around the walls. A few of the boards were splintered near the roofline, and on the west side, the walls got wet if the wind slanted the rain at the right angle.

"It's dusty in here," Al said. "And the old doors don't close all the way."

"We padlock them." Reggie walked toward the doors, examining the old locks. "Danny Hayes trusted his car here."

"Danny didn't have a rare, million-dollar car. And to be honest, I'm not so sure Urban should leave that Vet in here. He paid three hundred grand for that thing and, Reg, a lot of people saw him park it here Friday night."

"Shh, Al." Reggie scooted over to him, holding up her finger to his lips. "Don't go declaring bad things over us."

"I'm taking a realistic look at our setup, Reg." He shoved her hand away. "And don't point that thing at me. I'm your elder, girl."

"Okay, fine." Reggie stuffed her hands in her coverall pockets. "Then we have to find a better shop. Think outside the box."

Wasn't this the beauty of Mondays? Finding a new lease on life? Living instead of merely existing?

"Well, look for a box that's got some money in it," Al said. "Reg, shug, we've had some luck come our way with these cars, but I need to confess that when we opened up this shop I was really just—"

The low, power rumble of a Porsche downshifting interrupted and punctuated Al's sentence.

"Sounds like Mark." Reggie walked to the open barn doors and called to Mark as he stepped out of his car. "What are you doing here on a Monday afternoon?"

"Coming to see you two," Mark said, pointing at her and Al with his signature smile, wearing his trademark khakis and a starched, button-down shirt. He hooked his arm around Reggie as he entered the barn. "I've got an idea."

"What kind of idea?" Al finished off his milk. "Donuts are in the office, Mark."

"Great, thanks. Listen, Al, Reg, let me run this by you." Mark stood in the middle of the workshop, facing Reggie and Al. "I don't know why I didn't think of this sooner, but I've got a huge warehouse on the north side of town that's been empty for a year. I can't find a tenant I like or trust."

"That big place on Meridian?" Reggie said with a glance at Al. "It's three times the size of this place."

"Secure?" Al said.

"Steel construction with overhead door locks, alarm system, barred windows, and a barrier fence."

"Square footage?"

"Three thousand. All under air with a separate unit for the office. There's a break room with a full kitchen." Mark grinned. "You can have a desk without donut dust on it, Reg."

Reggie studied him through narrowed eyes. "What's the catch? How much?" This was Mark's MO. Get people salivating over his idea or project, get them believing they can't live without it, and then lower the money boom. "This sounds a little too good to be true."

"I was thinking the same thing," Al said.

"Ah, friends, it's me, Mark." He slapped his hand over his heart. "I can't believe you don't trust me." Holding his arms wide, he grinned, seemingly very pleased with himself. "There's no catch. The warehouse is free." He settled his hands on his hips and leaned toward Reg, then Al. "How about them apples?"

"Free?" Al said, with Reggie echoing, "Free?"

"Free," Mark said. "Look, I'm paying the insurance and taxes now. Why not put it to use? You guys move in, pay the utilities, and I'll cover the rest."

"No way." Reggie shook her head, hands on her hips. "Don't believe him, Al. There's always a catch."

"Mark," Al said, low and sergeant-like. "Is this your way of getting Reg to marry you?" he asked without hesitation.

"What? No." Mark paced off a few steps. "You think I'm so desperate I'd manipulate her like this? Al, come on."

In that moment, Reg saw the young Mark hungry for approval. Wanting to belong. "I believe you, Mark. But are you sure you don't want some kind of rent or payment?"

"Look, I'll admit when Reg decided to leave her job I thought she was nuts. Toss over a great position at a top CPA firm to rat around with smelly old cars? What kind of career is that for someone like her? But then I realized we all have to do what we love, and if she stood a chance of succeeding—"

"We, Mark. We. Al and me. It was his idea. He is the expert. I'm still learning."

"Fine. Whatever. If y'all stood a chance of succeeding." He made a face at her. "What's that car Al called you about? The one you might get to restore. Had you all hyped up the other night."

"The Duesenberg."

"Right, a Duesenberg. Really? A Duesy? How'd I miss that? Anyway, you got Urban's Vet in here, and I'm pretty sure if someone really wanted to break in they could. You need a secure place. I have a secure place. Empty and waiting."

"You're serious, son?" Al said, arms folded over his lean, muscled chest, the empty milk glass still in his hand. "A new, secure facility would help Oliver swing his decision our way."

"Then it's a deal?" He glanced between Reggie and Al.

"Well, Reg, what do you—"

"Mark, in the office." She grabbed his arm and dragged him off, leaving Al to wait. Closing the door behind her, she faced Mark, arms folded.

"Last week you were asking me to be a power couple with you. You thought opening the shop was some kind of crisis for me. Now you're all on board?" She queried him with her gaze. "If we do this, it's strictly business." She'd not hold back her feelings. The weekend taught her that secrets and silence hurt innocent people. "No funny business on the side."

"Reg, I heard you, and I'm down with us just being friends. But can't a friend lend another friend the use of his property? Lots of people helped me out when I needed it." He finally spied the donuts and went for one. "I never will forget your dad coming to the trailer, getting Mom to sign me up for baseball. Changed my life. Now it's my turn to lend a helping hand."

"No strings. All business. We'll sign a lease and everything."

"Absolutely. All business." He offered his free hand. "Deal?"

She hesitated, but the smile in her heart tugged on her lips. "Deal." She took his hand, but he pulled her into a one-armed embrace and whispered in her ear, "I had fun Saturday night."

"Mark—" She pushed away.

"Relax, Reg." He laughed and headed out. "Al, I'll have the papers drawn up and the keys sent over. See y'all later. Thanks for the donut." White powder floated above Mark's head as he waved the donut in the air.

Reggie turned to Al. "What do you think?"

"I think we got us a place, Reg." He swept her up in a sweet hug. "I was about to tell you I didn't . . ." He set her down and flagged off his comment. "Never mind. Nothing negative, right?" His smile lit his eyes. "We just might make a go of this thing yet."

"Now you're talking."

"I'm going to call Oliver. Convince him we can handle his

Duesenberg." Al started for the office. "Listen, let's make a moving plan. Might as well move the Vet as soon as we get the keys."

"Sounds good. Can't wait to tell Rafe and Wally." Reggie walked back to the open barn doors and stared toward the quiet road.

As much as she knew they needed the space and security of the warehouse, she was sure going to miss this sweet ole place.

But now, as the afternoon breeze snapped around the side of the barn, stirring up the dry leaves, awakening the fragrance of fall, a fresh yearning twisted in Reggie's soul.

Three days ago, Mark's offer would have been the most glorious news. A sign from God. *You go, Al and Reg.*

Today it felt ... wrong.

What happened to yesterday's confidence? To Tallahassee being her home. Classic cars her life.

"Reg," Al called from the office. "Phone for you."

She glanced over her shoulder at him. "Be right there."

Pausing one more second as the leaves skirted past her feet, Reggie returned to her Sunday morning confidence about *this* being her life. Al. The shop. The cars.

Yet everywhere her mental eye roamed Tanner Burkhardt shadowed her thoughts and whispered to her heart that she was the Princess of Hessenberg.

ELEVEN

etermined, focused, Tanner entered the barn, keen on speaking with Regina.

He'd not be deterred. He had a mission. Be on the plane tonight. With the princess.

The car bay was peaceful, empty, except for the '53 Vet and an older man with tufts of white hair sticking out from under his cap, huffing and grunting as he lifted a red-leather seat from behind the wheel.

"Might I assist you?" Tanner stepped lively to steady the man who tripped sideways, then backward, balancing the seat in his arms.

He glanced at Tanner and righted himself. "Thanks, son. But I got a method to my madness."

Tanner smiled. "I gather you do."

"You looking for Reg?" he said, settling the seat against the wall.

"Indeed, I am. How did you know?"

"Spotted you hanging around Friday night." The chap faced him, panting for a bit of wind, hands on his hips. "You keen on Reg?"

"Keen? No, I'm—"

"Get in line. I think every man from here to kingdom come has a crush on her. Including me." He moved to the passenger side of the car. "In the purest sense, mind you. But she's holding to herself. Not like some dames running off after every guy who winks at her." He leaned toward Tanner with an outstretched hand. "Name's Wally. And you are . . . ?"

"Tanner Burkhardt." He slapped his hand into Wally's.

"Reg is in the office with Al." Wally pulled a wrench from his hip pocket. "Making plans to move. Seems we got us a new shop."

A new shop? Hmm . . . she'd not mentioned this Friday night. Tanner made his way to the office and peered inside, knocking lightly on the metal door frame.

Regina glanced up, recognition in her eyes. Perhaps even a bit of a welcome. "Tanner, hey. Come on in." Dressed in coveralls with her hair wrapped into a loose ponytail, she still managed to spark his heart. "You remember Al?"

"Indeed I do." Tanner shook the man's hand, then turned to Regina. "Miss Bes . . . Regina . . . might I have a word?"

"Um, yeah. Sure." She exchanged a look with Al, then motioned for Tanner to lead the way outside. "We're all pretty excited around here. Mark—you remember him—is giving us a warehouse. Rent free. It's three times the size of this place."

She hopped up on the picnic table and Tanner perched next to her. "This is a good thing for your business."

"It's an *amazing* thing for our business."

He nodded, a twist of dread between his ribs. Her change of circumstances didn't change his mission. It just made it more difficult.

"I've a bit of news as well." He leaned forward, rubbing his hands together as if the action might form the perfect words out of thin air. "Since we talked, circumstances have changed for Hessenberg. And me."

"Wh–what do you mean?" Was that concern in her tone? "How so? Good or bad?"

"Depends on how you choose to look at things. The situation

has become more urgent." Tanner bullet-pointed the facts as King Nathaniel relayed them. Of the petition filed by Seamus with the EU court on behalf of the Hessen people. "The king and prime minister fear unrest and violence among the people. They ask for you to return with me now, take the Oath of the Throne, and establish the royal house. The sooner you are in your rightful place, the less likely we are in for political chaos and anarchy. If you are in Hessenberg, the court might reject even reviewing the petition."

"And you want me to walk into this mess?" She stared off, away from him, her composure tight and guarded. "I can't fix this . . . no . . . no way. Did I tell you I hate politics?"

"You mentioned it."

She gazed at him. "I'm the last person you want leading the charge in Hessenberg, Tanner. I know nothing about your rule of law, your people, or even how to govern."

"You won't be alone," he said, thinking it best not to mention that Seamus, Hessenberg's governor, was behind this quasi coup. "You'll have advisors."

"Like who? People I do not know? How can I trust them?"

He smiled. "Exactly. 'Tis why I think you will do quite well as our sovereign. You will try and test everything and everyone. From what little I've seen, you don't seem keen on merely pleasing people."

"But isn't it best if Hessenberg becomes a sovereign state without a monarchy? They can be a republic like America, right?"

"Aha, the question of the ages. The source of political, university think-tank, pundits' debates."

"Forget think-tanks. What do *you* think, Tanner?" She faced him. "Not what you're being told—I get you have a job to do—but if you could wave a magic wand and *poof,* create the ideal country, what would you do?"

"Honest?"

"The preferred thing. Honesty over lying, yes."

"I'd be on the plane tonight"—he swallowed, feeling lost for a moment in her intensity—"with you."

She jerked around, facing forward with such force her ponytail slipped free. "I'm moving to a new shop." Jumping off the table, she started for the barn, then whipped right and aimed for the road, then backtracked to the table. "Don't you see? A shop... a new and bigger shop. Why would Mark suddenly offer his warehouse the same time you show up offering me a country?"

"I've no idea, I'm sure."

"I—I have to think on this..."

"I'd expect nothing less. But, Regina, I'm not offering you a country in the same way Mark is offering you the warehouse. I'm offering your true inheritance."

She paced around the picnic table. "I—I can't, Tanner. I can't leave Al and the business. I mean, things are looking up. We went into this venture together in good faith."

"Regina, I understand you have a life. Have plans." A watery sheen glistened in her blue eyes. "I do. And I'm sorry my mission is disturbing it."

She glanced away again, touching her fingers to the corners of her eyes. "This is just too ... crazy." Regina cruised down the gravel and grass driveway toward the road, talking to herself. Tanner watched her until she disappeared from view between the light and the shadows, bolstering his heart that he'd not failed. Yet.

Removing his phone from his pocket, he tapped the king's aide, Jonathan, a brief message.

No return 2night

TWELVE

*T*he bluish-red hues of Monday evening's dusk settled over Reggie's house as she sat in the garage behind the wheel of Gram's old Corvair, eating McDonald's and listening to an oldies station on the push-button radio.

Comfort all around. She'd not deny it. French fries, chocolate shake, the Beach Boys, and Gram's Corvair.

It's where she came when she needed to think, pray, find harmony in her soul.

Drawing a long drink of cold chocolate richness from her straw, the sweetness cooling her turbulent emotions, she stared out the windshield through the open garage door toward the purple end of day and the amber rise of the streetlamp.

Who would help Mrs. Shaw with her flower beds if she went to Hessenberg?

"Care for some company?" Tanner peered through the passenger window.

Startled, Reggie steadied her racing heart with a deep breath. "Where did you come from?"

"Through the house . . . you didn't answer the bell and the front door was unlocked." He slipped into the passenger seat. "This is a fun old motorcar."

"It's was Gram's. She bought it in '68. Drove it for twenty years. Have you had dinner?"

"No, I—"

"They're still hot." Reggie passed him the fries.

Tanner reached for a few sticks off the top. "So this is what you do? Eat fast food in an old car?"

"Sometimes. When I need to go back to ground, figure stuff out."

"Such an admirable quality, Regina. You take time to ponder a matter."

"Heaven help the girl who didn't ponder *this* matter. The one you dumped in my lap."

Tanner took a few more fries. "May I ask you something? Why do you like old cars so much?"

Reggie set her milk shake on the console and reached for a napkin, wiping a bit of cold dew from her fingers. "After Mama died, Al had just retired and his wife, Miriam, had us over to dinner just about every night. Daddy loaded up Gram and me and off we went. Miriam was—and is—very kind to me. Motherly. Al had just purchased an old GTO to restore, so after dinner Daddy and Al went out to work on the car. I started tagging along to watch, helped if they let me. Miriam played gin rummy with Gram or watched TV."

The words flowed easy and smooth, surprising Reggie because for the first time in seventeen years, she was vocalizing her memories. "The sounds of the garage, the clank of tools, the murmur of Daddy's and Al's voices, the gunning of an engine . . . it became home to me."

"Home base."

"After Gram died, I'd go out to the garage and sit in her car. For hours. Just thinking and listening to the radio, running down the battery." She laughed softly. "Don't you know I learned to use jumper cables early on."

"I'm sure it was a difficult time for you, being so young, without a mum."

"Then my dog died."

"Then your dog died? I say . . ."

Reggie shook her head and gazed out the windshield. "Bonnie. A Sheltie. She was going on fifteen, so she had a good life. Just the timing was rotten."

"Sounds like the makings of an American country song."

"I'm saying . . ." she said, glancing at Tanner. "But no country song I ever heard ended with the girl being a real princess."

"There's a first time for everything. You should give it a go." He seemed more relaxed than earlier. She liked this Tanner better than the formal, stiff, all-business one. He grabbed a few more French fries. It was as if he couldn't quite decide who he was or what kind of man he needed to be.

"What's your story, Tanner? Why did they send *you*?" Reggie reached for the volume knob as the announcer introduced Van Morrison and "Brown Eyed Girl."

"My story . . . pretty boring. Parents. One brother. Boarding school. University. The law college—"

"You know, listing your life in bullet points isn't telling me who you really are, Tanner."

"—four years as a barrister, three as a staffer in the governor's office, six months as Minister of Culture."

"And yet I still don't know why they sent you?"

"I know the entail." He looked in the McDonald's bag and took out a napkin, his tone back to a clipped, formal sound. "And I'm Minister of Culture." He looked over at her, his face half in shadow, half in the light. "*You*, in essence, are our culture, Regina. The king needed an ambassador and he thought I fit the bill."

"Are y'all friends?"

"We knew each other a bit . . . at university. Friends? I'd say not."

"Do you, like, get fired if I refuse to go?"

"Lose my position?" He wadded the napkin into his palm. "No, but it won't look smart on my record."

"Then I'm sorry for putting you between a rock and a hard place."

"As I am sorry for doing the same to you." His expression sparked her heart with a strange new sensation. "You're determined not to return with me?" he said.

No, not *so* determined. "Still thinking." Would she return for Hessenberg's sake or because she *liked him?*

Oh no, please, Reg.

See, Carrie was right. Reggie should've been boy crazy in junior high and killed all the juvenile love flutters. But no, she'd refused. So here she sat at twenty-nine infatuated with a man determined to ruin her life.

Ruin? No, he isn't here to ruin anything. Reggie peered at Tanner to discover he was peering at her. She flushed with a blend of embarrassment and desire.

"What of your father's advice?" Tanner said after a moment. "Have you spoken any more to him of this situation?"

"He says I should go."

"Brown Eyed Girl" faded and "Love Me Tender" drifted from the speakers into the car.

"Ah, the king of rock and roll," Tanner said with a slight bow toward the radio.

Elvis's smooth, velvet voice swirled around Reggie, making her mellow and nostalgic.

Love me tender, love me true . . .

The intimate melody, along with Tanner's presence, made her melancholy. Then her eyes met his and . . . *Oh boy.* She hit the chocolate milk shake hard.

"Regina, is there anything I can say or do—"

"How long would I have to stay?" She cranked the engine to

charge up the battery. The old motor grunted and hissed, then settled down to a smooth idle. "We just got that huge warehouse, rent free."

"Stay? In Hessenberg? Several weeks. A month. Maybe more. Until the entail is executed and you've taken the oath and accepted your inheritance."

Anxiety burned under her skin. "What exactly is my inheritance?" Was this who she really was to be? "And this is all imminent, right?"

"Yes, and there are other details . . . the business of government. As I said, you'll be Head of State and therefore required to call for a government to be formed. As for your inheritance, it is the throne and the Grand Duchy of Hessenberg."

Each detail layered her anxiety with panic. "I inherit a country?"

"That's what dukes and duchesses are, Regina. Owners of lands, regions. In your case, a whole island nation."

"But I can leave?"

"We pray you won't, but yes, you can abdicate."

"Abdicate. I couldn't have cared less about that word a few days ago. Now it sounds ominous, full of failure."

"But it's how you can return home."

"Then what? What happens to Hessenberg? Anarchy again?" The weight of Tanner's request, of the nation's need, rested on her heart, growing heavier with each breath.

"Your government will take over."

"My government? Even when I'm not there?"

"The one you established after signing the entail will carry on. And yes, there will be turmoil."

Reggie pressed the heels of her hands to her temples, shivering, trying to imagine the impossible. "When I was a kid, there was a big dirt pile at the end of the road. A bunch of us would run down there and play King of the Hill. It's the only ground I ever wanted to rule."

"And did you?"

She laughed softly, remembering. "I was the reigning champ."

"I rest my case," Tanner said.

"Beating other kids to the top of a dirt pile is not the same as running, or helping to run, a country." She had a wild thought and voiced it. "By the way, how do I know you're not some international criminal making all this up?"

He stared at her for a moment. "You've the documentation to prove I'm not, but I suppose you don't know for sure. However, rest assured, if I were, as you say, an international criminal, my target would not be a garage owner in Tallahassee, Florida."

His tone, his inflection, his voice all smacked her funny bone. "Touché."

"Regina, don't misunderstand. I know this is not easy for you."

The bass thump of "My Girl" buzzed the speakers. *I've got sunshine . . .*

"Not easy? Tanner, I don't want to go forward, but bubba, I'm not sure I can just stay in place. Certainly not go backwards." The core question of her heart surfaced and confronted him. "No matter what I choose, I know the truth and my life is forever changed. Go or stay, I'll always know I am . . . was . . ." She swallowed, the word stuck in her throat.

"A princess?"

"Yes, a princess ever after."

"Will you come with me to Hessenberg? Please?"

She peered at him, his question drilling into her heart, deeper and deeper, scoring her very foundation. She must go see. She had to try. For Gram.

With this new truth and revelation rattling around in her heart, how would she ever be satisfied with anything less?

133

At half past midnight, Tanner rode in the back of a Mercedes limo through the quiet city streets of Strauberg, bluish-white streetlamps tinting the rain-soaked night.

He'd made it home. With the princess. Once she decided to go, she charged through her world, leaving no doubt in her wake. Perhaps a set of confused friends and coworkers, but seemingly no doubt. She claimed she was visiting Hessenberg for a few weeks to "check this thing out."

Watching her prepare for the trip, Tanner gained perspective on his charge. Regina processed things, the largeness of her destiny, one mental bite at a time.

Now she sat across from him, crushed into the soft leather seat, her eyes at half-mast. He wasn't sure what turmoil churned in her heart and mind, but she appeared peaceful.

"Did you sleep at all on the flight?" he asked when she looked at him.

"Who can sleep at forty thousand feet over the Atlantic?" She sat forward, tucking her hands under her legs and peering out the rain-dotted window. "It looks so quiet out there."

"This is Market Avenue, the business district of the city. There's little activity after nine. Two streets over is where the nightlife happens. Restaurants and pubs."

"The city has an old feel." She moved to power down the window. A gust of cold, wet air swooped into the limo.

"If you think four hundred years is old, then so it is."

She laughed and stuck her arm out the window, cutting the breeze with her hand. After a moment, she pulled inside, shivering, and raised the window.

"Are you glad to be home?"

"I don't know . . . I rather enjoyed Tallahassee. I'd have liked to see a football game."

"They are fun. My friends and I never missed one in college.

Maybe next time you're in town, in the fall, we can get in a game."

"It's a deal." He warmed with the notion he might be in her future falls. "I played rugby myself in university."

"Rugby." She smiled with surprise. "Hmm, somehow I can't see you in the middle of a scrum."

"Yes, well . . . there you go." He refrained from saying more, guarded against crossing the line between personal and professional. Too many times in the past twenty-four hours he had found himself bumping up against propriety. She made it too easy to talk, open up his heart, be her friend. It started the night she barged into his hotel with the fairy tale and the signet ring. Her wild-eyed wonderment and confusion about what was happening endeared her to him.

The limo slowed for a caution light, and the edge of the blue streetlamp lit the shadows in the back of the limo.

He liked her. *There, heart, are you happy?* He'd admitted something romance-related to his emotions. But make no mistake, he'd erected safety walls long ago, and they must be maintained. For personal security and professional decorum.

"Are you married?" she asked.

He focused on her as the car moved on, away from the city and toward the palace on the hill. "Pardon?"

"Are you married?" She pointed to her ring finger. "No ring, but that doesn't mean anything these days."

"I'm not. Married. No."

"Divorced? Kids—"

"So many questions so late in the evening?" He tried to make light of it, deter her attention, but his words felt forced. He didn't want to lie to her. But he could not confess his deepest and darkest sorrow. No matter how much he loved talking to her.

"Regina, I'll have my assistant print out a schedule and

information for you, including my phone number. But for now, I'll come around in the morning after breakfast to collect you. We've a ten o'clock meeting with the king, Brighton's prime minister, and the governor of Hessenberg in my office."

"Wow . . . so many important people. And me." She pressed her hand to her middle and blew out a low, slow breath. "Is it too late to change my mind?"

"Until you take the oath and are set in officially as Princess of Hessenberg by the king and archbishop, you can leave at any time without consequences."

"Welcome to Hotel California."

He laughed. "Hardly. You can check out, *leave*, and return home. But you're here now, so you might as well give it a go. As you say, now that you know the truth, how can you return to who you were?"

The limo climbed and maneuvered through narrow country lanes, winding up a hillside.

"We're almost to Meadowbluff Palace." Tanner opened the window to the driver. "Please open the roof, Dickenson."

The top panel over Regina's head slid back and the moon peeked inside.

Regina drew a deep breath. "I smell the ocean." She stood on the seat and stretched to see above the car. "Oh, we're so high. The lights below are so beautiful."

Tanner hesitated, then squeezed in next to her, watching as Meadowbluff loomed on the pearly horizon. He'd made it. Brought the princess home.

"What's the name of the bay again?"

"Braeleon."

"Braeleon Bay," Regina repeated. "What does it mean?"

"I have no idea."

"Fine Minister of Culture you are." She bumped him with her elbow, rattling the stones in his emotional walls, then stretched farther over the top of the car to peer down. "It's a straight drop."

"We're going up a mountain," Tanner said. "From where the palace sits, a watchman can see the southern ports and all exposed roads. On the other side of that ridge"—he pointed to the dark line behind the palace—"there's a watchman post for the northern ports and roads."

"So the palace is a safe place."

"Yes, guarded by the watchmen."

The limo dipped with the road, shoving Regina against him. He wrapped his arm about her waist to steady her, then found he didn't want to let go.

"We're nearly there. Let me ring ahead to make sure everyone is ready." He ducked inside the car, quite sure Regina could hear every boisterous beat of his heart.

The place around her waist where Tanner held on to her was still warm after he ducked inside the car.

She'd registered and tucked away how different Tanner's touch felt from Mark's, but for now her energy, her emotions, her thoughts were not on romance but on the palace and the night-scape ahead of her.

Meadowbluff, with its gables and turrets, was framed perfectly by the towering Cliffs of White just like in Gram's fairy tale.

Reggie followed the straight line of the cliffs down to the water. A ghostly stream of moonlight draped across the surface of the bay and lapped against the shoreline, which was buttoned to the earth with a row of pearly-diamond lights.

Reggie ducked inside the car. "It's beautiful."

"Yes, quite." Tanner read his iPhone without looking up.

"Is everything all right?"

He set his phone aside, popping on a smile. "Indeed."

"What's down at the bottom of the mountain? By the bay?"

"Docks. Restaurants. Hotels."

Reggie settled back in her seat. "Thank you . . . for having him open the roof. The view truly is breathtaking."

"Welcome to Hessenberg and Meadowbluff Palace, the childhood home of your gram, and your inheritance."

Gram. Palace. Princess. All so surreal. Reggie was Mary Poppins, jumping into a watercolor painting with the power of one word. *Inheritance.*

The limo paused at the gate and Reggie peeked out the top again, watching the high, ornate wrought-iron bars swing wide.

Down the paved pebble drive, Reggie propped on her elbows, the breeze in her face. The palace windows were lit and bright, every one of them, spilling light onto the manicured grounds and flower gardens. Floodlights splashed illumination on a high, arching front portico and round columns.

When the limo pulled up, Reggie reached for her bag and slung the strap over her head. Treat this as an adventure. One moment, one day at a time. Sooner or later, she'd pop out of the fairy tale painting and back to real life.

Reggie stepped under the palace portico, feeling minuscule in the presence of the grand structure. "I could fix a lot of cars in this place."

"You could," Tanner said, urging her toward the broad stone steps with a light touch on her elbow. "But know that the marble floors are four hundred years old."

"We can throw down a tarp." He didn't laugh. And after she heard her words, she agreed. They weren't funny.

Following him up the steps, turning, observing, she wished she knew as much about European architecture as she did about cars and accounting.

At the door, Tanner pushed a button. "Most of the living is done on the second floor. But the dining hall is on the main floor. Jarvis should be able to get you squared away."

"And who is Jarvis?" Her legs quivered, suddenly a bit weak from the length of her journey.

"Your butler and house manager." Tanner glanced back at the driver coming up the steps with her one little roller board suitcase. "Dickenson is your driver."

"Pardon? Driver?" She glanced at the older man with round cheeks coming up the steps. She twitched with the urge to step back and help him by reaching for her suitcase. "It rolls," she said when he got to the top. "Tanner," she said, leaning toward him. "I can drive myself."

"Dickenson will drive you until you get familiar with the city." Matter-of-fact, no debate. "You have other staff as well. Two ladies-in-waiting, four maids, two chefs, and two footmen. For now."

"I'm one person. I don't need a staff. I can feed myself. And I'm not even sure what a lady-in-waiting does. Or a footman."

Tanner angled toward her as the door, twice the width and height of any ole door she'd ever seen before, glided open, exposing a grand, glowing foyer and peeling back the first mystery of life inside a palace.

"Regina, you're not in Tallahassee anymore, working in an old red barn. You're in Hessenberg as our Princess and future Grand Duchess. Welcome to your life as a royal heir."

THIRTEEN

September 16, 1914

Meadowbluff Palace

    I write tonight with a heavy heart, pouring out words to understand what is happening in our world.

    Everything is changing. The world is at war. Brothers have taken up arms against brothers. I find I am at a loss on how to pray. On what to believe.

    The worst is Rein. Word is he has abandoned Hessenberg and Uncle's declaration of neutrality and enlisted in the Kaiser's army.

    Uncle and Cousin Wilhelm are quite at odds with one another, and I see Rein's choice, if it's true, as a betrayal of Hessenberg, of Uncle, and of me.

    He messaged me this afternoon, asking me to meet him at the stand of trees on the edge of the meadow, eight o'clock sharp. I should have asked Mama's permission, but I felt sure she would deny me. And rightfully so.

    Yet I have to see him. My heart must know Rein did not join sides with Germany. If by chance Uncle does enter the war, it most certainly will not be with the Axis. Others may fight against their country, their brothers, but how can Rein?

It's unthinkable that he'd raise arms against Uncle's army, or Brighton's, and spill his countrymen's blood.

So tonight I slipped out of the palace unnoticed and arrived at our meeting place, searching the shadows and the open meadow for him. I love him so much. And I am quite certain he loves me. I held hope that all would be well. Everything would sort out.

"Rein, I'm here." Uncle's ragtime melodies drifted across the lawn, playing through the open music parlor windows.

"Rein," I called again, a bit louder. If he stood me up, I thought, he'd rue the next time we were together. I was just about to leave when strong, powerful arms snatched me from behind. "Miss me?"

My heart leapt to my throat. I pounded his chest with my fist. "You frightened me, you silly boy. And yes, I missed you."

"Sorry, darling. I was trying to surprise you." He kissed my cheek and I felt utterly warm all over, as if I might swoon.

"Well, be more tender about it in the future." That's when I noticed his attire.

"Rein, you're wearing a German uniform." My legs quivered. I felt positively ill.

"Alice," he said, stepping fully into the moonlight so I could see his lean, handsome face, his eyes intense like a hawk's. "I've joined with the German hussars."

"Rein, how can you enlist against Hessenberg? Against Uncle?"

"Your uncle is a coward. He'll not fight. Mark my words, before it's all said and done, Hessenberg will be in this war. The Kaiser will see to it."

"But he doesn't want to fight. Especially with the Kaiser. Why did you not join Brighton's army, or England's?"

"Ha. Brighton? Those traitors. Right in there with your cowardly uncle. No, I'd not fight for the likes of them. I followed my German heritage. Of my father and grandfather." He gripped my arms and fear quelled my feelings of love.

"Rein, you are on royal Hessenberg soil. Uncle could arrest you for treason against the crown if you're found out."

"Treason? No, Alice, he is the treasonous one, betraying all of Hessenberg. Betraying you. He's throwing away your very way of life."

"Are you mad? Uncle would never betray me! His own heir? You're full of propaganda, Rein!" How I despised arguing with him, but I could not let his words go unchallenged.

"Am I? Then why won't he fight?" His laugh chilled the last warm sentiments I ever felt for him. "He's no leader, Alice." Rein snatched my arm again, his fingers digging into it. "Come with me. You won't be safe in Hessenberg."

"I most certainly will be safe. This is my home."

"Marry me, Alice. After the war, we can return to Hessenberg."

"Marry you? Uncle would never allow it."

He released me at last, and I stumbled back, catching myself against a tree. How could I have been so blind and deceived?

"The world is changing, Alice. There won't be kings and princes, grand dukes or ruling royal families when we finish the fight. All men will be equal. The revolution is happening."

"You're a fool, Rein Friedrich. The House of Augustine-Saxon has stood for four hundred and fifty years. We were not toppled by other revolutions and wars. We will not be toppled by this one."

"This is the war to end all wars, Alice. No more kings sending troops into battle to save their precious throne."

Everything became clear. So very clear. "You say you love me, but yet you mock my very existence."

"Mock? No. I'm offering you a place in the new order." He looked down at me, speaking in a secretive tone, giving me gooseflesh. "New leaders will emerge. Come with me, Alice. You'll be the wife of a military officer for the most powerful nation on earth. A noblewoman among the superior race."

"A noblewoman? When I am already the rank of a royal princess?"

"You won't be a royal princess when this is all over, Alice. The royal houses will fall."

"My dear Rein." I dusted him from my hands, from my heart,

displaying more courage than I really had. "No war can erase my birth nor my title. I am now and always will be Her Royal Highness, Princess Alice of Hessenberg. A princess is defined not by her title alone but how she lives her life. Never, ever speak to me again with such disrespect. I am not your bar wench or lower-wharf whore whom you can beg to run off with you in the night. You want my hand? Discard this horrid uniform, stand before my uncle like a man and ask. Not that I would say yes, mind you."

"I'll ask him for nothing but his royal scepter."

"Get out!" I shoved him into the shadows. "Get out of my meadow."

"You'll regret this, Alice." He snatched at my arm and shoved his half of my cipher pendant into my hand. My gift to him. Cut in half to show we shared our hearts.

"I most assuredly do." I clutched the pendant to my chest and willed myself not to weep. My love, my Rein, is a traitor.

'Tis where we ended our short love affair. With angry words and broken dreams. But oh, my heart.

I didn't cry until I returned to my suite where I tore our picture, our one and only picture, and threw it to the ground. Then I had immediate determination to save the photo as a reminder of this day, of love's foolishness. To never let my heart be deceived again.

My cipher pendant will serve as the same.

Yet as I slipped into bed, Rein's words about Uncle and some entail with Brighton lingered in my thoughts. I felt grieved, as if something happened that neither Uncle nor I will never be able to undo.

Alice

FOURTEEN

"W"ell, what did you find in those law books?"
Seamus's wife, Beth Ann, joined him for breakfast looking smart and fashionable in a pale blue suit. He could always count on her to showcase his governorship with style. "I daresay you were up all night."

"I slept in the library." Seamus kissed her cheek as he stood, reaching to hold out her chair. "But I found something, yes, thanks to your wisdom and keen memory, my dear."

"Next time you grouse about the little trivia tidbits I like to share"—the maid came around with tea and muffins—"thank you, Vivian . . . I'll remind you of this moment."

"Please do, but know that I'm far more interested in recalling Hessenberg's *Vox Vocis Canonicus* than I am about some old lord's fascination with the color blue." Seamus chuckled, returning to the business section of the *Liberty Press*.

Beth Ann tapped the top of her three-minute egg with her fork, breaking the shell. "Lord Traybourne wore nothing but blue. You don't find that intriguing? Everything, down to his underdrawers, was cut from blue cotton."

"Shall I be worried you are gob smacked over the color of an old lord's underwear?"

"Seamus, please." She chortled. "Eat your toast."

The *Vox Vocis Canonicus.* The authority canon. Pure brilliance on Beth Ann's part. Why he'd not thought of it tempted Seamus to doubt his political and legal prowess.

He'd spent half the night reviewing *The Grand Duchy of Hessenberg Law & Constitution* and the *Vox Vocis Canonicus* accord of 1715.

The authority canon sealed his race to rule Hessenberg. He could challenge the authority and rights of this new princess based on her lack of experience and leadership, never mind she was not born Hessen. She was an American. In summary, she was not fit to be their royal. To be their de facto Head of State.

Seamus need not wait on the European court to back his claims. Old Hessenberg law already did.

"Governor." The butler stood in the dining room archway. "Your aide has arrived. Shall I usher him in?"

"No, Carson, I'm finished here." He kissed Beth Ann once more and reached for his coat draped over a chair. "Have a good day, my dear."

"You as well, Seamus. Good luck and all that."

Outside, Seamus met Brogan by the car. "Well?" he said in a low tone, pausing on the steps, out of hearing of the house and the car. He never allowed for unforeseen witnesses. Unless the witnesses were the ones he'd planted.

"Germany has agreed to back our petition to be a self-governing state without a monarchy. We, in turn, drop this business of restitution for seized bank accounts."

"Splendid." Seamus patted him on the shoulder. "Most splendid."

"I must say,"—Brogan drew up his coat collar when the wind cut sharp around the side of the governor's manse—"I thought Germany would laugh in our faces when we approached them with a law suit or to be our ally. What do they need with a small island duchy in the North Sea?"

"There's nothing *small* about an ally, Brogan. Especially one with the earning potential of Hessenberg. Once we free ourselves from Brighton's noose and taxes, we'll have an economic boom. Think of all the money we spend supporting *their* country, their government, their monarchy."

"My hat is off to you, sir."

"On to our next phase." Seamus grinned and moved toward the car. "Alert the proper media."

"About?"

"The princess. She's here."

"But the Minister of Culture ordered a complete media blackout. At the king's request."

"And since when did we take our orders from the wet-nosed Minister of Culture? And the king is on his way out, one way or another. Brogan, it's a new day in Hessenberg. Now, the Governor of Hessenberg is ordering you to alert the media that the new Princess of Hessenberg will arrive at Wettin Manor for a meeting, ten o'clock sharp."

Tanner rose early and went to the office. By nine o'clock, he'd nearly polished off a whole pot of tea while clearing his desk, finalizing Regina's schedule for the day, and reviewing the short film festival proposal from Knoxton University film students.

Clever chaps, using their own medium, film, to present their case. The budget they suggested would have to be trimmed, but Tanner embraced the idea at its core. In fact, he had in mind a team that could submit a short film on the princess. Should she agree.

She. He woke up this morning thinking about her. At first, wondering how her night went, curious if she slept in peace or trepidation.

How might he have responded should a foreigner arrive at

his home announcing he was someone completely other than who he thought? "You're not Archbishop Burkhardt's son, the one with the dark stain of moral failure, but you're ... a prince!"

Tanner took up his empty teacup and filled it with the last of the brew. He would have responded like Regina—only more so—and not believed a word of the stranger's message.

As a lad in Sunday school, he struggled with the idea of God becoming a man, dying on a cruel cross for his sins, and lovingly inviting him to receive the gift of redemption. It wracked his brain and rattled his heart. Took him years to embrace the truth. Then only a few months to let it go.

But he had no time for spiritual musings. Regina would be here shortly. And that was another thing. Rising at six, he found himself counting the hours until he'd see her.

Four. Three and a half. Three.

He was developing feelings for her. Such foolishness. Thank goodness His Majesty would assign her an aide or tutor this morning and Miss Regina Beswick would be out of his life.

Tanner mimed removing an invisible hook from his heart. Be gone. Then he gulped his tea.

Ah, that's the ticket. Hot and bitter, the way he liked it.

He was about to slip on his suit coat and check his tie in the loo when he noticed the linen envelope sticking out from under the base of the desk phone. The invitation. Louis must have put it there for him to see when he returned. *Note to self: Remind Louis to leave personal matters where I store them.*

Tanner jerked the envelope free and read the invitation again.

Bella and Britta are turning 10!
You're invited!

He was invited? No, this had to be some mistake, the work of a bumbling party planner. If he arrived at Estes Estates, Trude would laugh at him, remind him of his pledge, and ask him to leave.

Louis popped in around the door. "Jonathan and His Majesty are here with the prime minister. The archbishop is on his way."

"What of the governor?" Despite Seamus's shenanigans, he was required for this meeting.

"Haven't heard, but I'll ring his office again."

"And Regina?"

"Dickenson is ready at the palace, waiting."

Tanner held the invitation over the rubbish bin, but then opened the middle desk drawer and tossed the envelope inside. "And the media blackout holds?"

"As far as I know. Haven't seen one photographer or had one press inquiry."

"Excellent. Everything is going to plan."

September 30, 1914

Meadowbluff Palace

There was a grand argument in the great hall just now. Shouting and swearing. Lord Fitzsimmons arrived shortly after dinner, flustered and bothered, demanding Uncle do something about the Germans. Chancellor Bismarck seized Hessenberg's accounts in German banks! Will they stop at nothing to draw Uncle into the war to fight for their side?

Uncle insists Hessenberg will remain neutral in this war and I cheer him on. Stay your course, Uncle. What is a man, a prince, if he has no convictions?

Mamá fears Lord Fitzsimmons will gather a majority among the other lords and depose Uncle, putting him to disgrace, putting all of us to disgrace. She wants Uncle to banish Lord Fitzsimmons from the

Court, but Uncle refuses, claiming Lord Fitzsimmons is a servant and lord of the people, and a voice of wisdom.

They are all a bunch of Reins in my book, and we've no need of them. Lord Fitzsimmons called Uncle a coward. Well, it's a coward who wants to join a war simply to free his bank account.

My heart is sick over the war, over Uncle. He's so thin and so troubled. I'm not sure how much of this he can bear. He is a kind, loving man, but Father in heaven, it is my opinion you did not build him for war but for peace.

Alice

Someone call a doctor because she must have been crazy when she decided to hop on that plane with Tanner and explore the world of a royal princess.

Last night, she slept in a palace suite the size of her house back home. It consisted of large, windowed rooms—a bedroom, a bath and a half, a sitting room, a media room with the widest flat screen she'd ever seen, a library, and a kitchen.

Reggie stepped out of bed onto a two-inch pile carpet that felt like silk against the soles of her feet. She'd curled her toes into the blue-and-white patterned weave and considered crawling back into bed and getting out once more just to experience the *carpet*.

But the light of day burned through her windows, showcasing the luxury and beauty of her living quarters.

And the portrait of Gram above her bed was breathtaking. The image carried Reggie to another time and another place. *Oh, Gram, so young and very beautiful.* At least through the eyes of the artist...

Reggie stepped closer to read the artist's signature. *Renoir.* Renoir?

She angled back, exhaling, shaking out her hands as she

scoped the height and breadth of the painting. Mercy a-mighty, Gram sat for Renoir.

Truly, every second of this adventure felt like a fairy tale. Like Reggie would wake up any moment, find herself at home, rousing from the most vivid dream of her life.

Reaching up, she barely touched the hard dried oils that gelled together and created the image of Gram. The ridges and grooves of the artist's brush beneath her fingertip were all very, very real.

Reggie closed her eyes, trying to imagine the gram she knew— stooped and slow with a raspy voice and white hair—as the same woman peering out of the yellow, orange, green, and blue of the painting, so happy and full of hope, with the wind twisting her hair and snapping at the blue scarf around her shoulders.

Gram, I'm here. I'm here.

After a moment of waiting, praying, Reggie lowered to the bed, gathering her knees to her chest, tipping back her head and offering her fears and pain to the One who loved her.

He'd been there for her when Mama died. She had to believe he'd not abandon her now.

Another heartbeat or two and she slid off the bed, heading for the shower, remembering she had something with Tanner this morning, every step, every movement stiff and difficult, as if she was somehow peeling away the old, dried, dead skin of winter.

She dressed in her favorite boot-cut jeans, white blouse, and boots—the cockroach kickers with the pointed toes and ornate stitching—and headed down the broad front staircase.

Jarvis met her in the foyer, bowed, and said, "Breakfast is this way, Your Majesty."

"Please, call me Reggie."

He seated her alone in a formal dining room half the size of a football field with a highly polished table that seated seventy-five. Reggie knew because she counted. Seventy-five chairs. And she bet if they added a leaf or two, they could easily seat one hundred.

She ate her eggs and toast with the best sweet blackberry jam, alone. Quiet.

Serena, her lady's maid, came in, curtseyed, and asked, "Do you need anything, Your Majesty?"

"For you to call me Reggie."

"Yes, miss." But she didn't sound convinced.

At twenty till ten, Dickenson came to drive her to Wettin Manor. "Mr. Burkhardt will meet us there, Your Majesty."

"Reggie, call me Reggie."

"Yes, miss." But he didn't sound convinced.

Yeah, this is going to take some time.

Reggie insisted on riding up front, in the passenger seat, which made Dickenson all kinds of nervous.

"Wouldn't you prefer the back, Your Majesty?"

"How will I keep you from speeding if I'm sitting back there?" She laughed. He did not. "And it's Reggie, okay?"

"Yes, miss."

The car was not the limo from last night but a brand-new Mercedes. If one could not have a classic car, then a new Mercedes would do. Reggie loved the new car smell. It was second only to the fragrance of humanity lingering in the leather and vinyl of a well-used classic car.

Down the hillside, a cluster of trees sporting brilliant orange-red foliage captured her attention. "Those leaves are gorgeous. I've never seen that color before."

A breeze whisked through the treetops, shifting the leaves, exposing their orange underbellies, then their radiant red tops. A gauzy white hue hovered around the hillside with a light trimmed from the cloud-muted sun.

"They are Princess Alice Oaks, Your Majesty. Named for your great-grandmother by her uncle, the Grand Duke."

"Gram had trees named after her?"

"The story goes that the duke ordered the royal gardener to

plant a tree with fall leaves the color of Princess Alice's hair in honor of her sixteenth birthday." Dickenson slowed the car to take a hairpin turn. "I see you have the same color tresses."

"She was completely white when I knew her . . . The gardener planted all of these trees?"

Reggie brushed aside her bangs. They were too long, but she'd actually fired up the old straight iron and did something with her hair this morning. She'd had no time for a salon appointment when a nation called.

"Only one tree was planted, over a hundred years ago," Dickenson said.

As they moved toward the bottom of the hill, Reggie peered back over her right shoulder to find the entire hillside engulfed in the flames of Princess Alice trees. Chills scooted down her arms, sinking beneath the skin into her muscles, her sinews, her very core.

Gram, even the trees remember you.

Tears surprised her eyes and watered her soul. So many glorious secrets about Gram. It made Reggie yearn to speak to her. So many questions. So many whys.

The Mercedes hit the bottom of the hill and, within the span of a city block, left the countryside behind and pressed full-on into a busy, bustling Strauberg.

Reggie tipped her head to see the height of cut-stone buildings, polished to a gleaming gray surface. Pedestrians flooded the streets, moving from corner to corner, hurrying about their day. Men in white shirts and ties clustered around one of the iron streetlamps with a Victorian-style lamp. When they laughed, Reggie smiled.

"This is the financial district, ma'am." Dickenson slowed for a red light. "Two streets over is Market Avenue with the shops."

She glanced at him. He'd yet to do the same to her. "Are you married, Dickenson?"

His round cheeks flushed. "No, miss. My wife died some years back. And we didn't have children, so I found myself in the employ of His Majesty, King Leopold, King Nathaniel II's father."

"I'm sorry about your wife, Dickenson."

"She was a lovely, generous soul."

"And you miss her."

"Every day, miss."

"And how did you come to drive for me?"

"The King's Office selected me because I am Hessenberg born and raised. I've lived in Brighton nearly ten years but I was happy to return home, miss." He spoke looking straight ahead, harnessing his words as if he didn't want to say too much. "To drive for you. To be with my old mates again. I can visit me brothers more often now."

"Well, I'm happy to know you. Glad you're working . . . for me . . ." The words felt awkward. But they shouldn't. Rafe worked for her. And Wally. Why did this feel different?

"Happy to serve you, miss." Finally, the man gave her a wide, genuine smile.

Serve. Ah, that's why it felt different. "Dickenson, do you think Hessenberg people want a princess again?"

"I reckon they do. Better than the alternative, becoming Brightonians for the rest of our lives and our children's." Dickenson stopped for a red light, clearing his throat. He still refused to look at her.

"It's okay to look at me."

"I'd rather keep my eyes ahead, on me job, miss." But he cut her a quick glance. "You should really be sitting in the back."

"Because?"

"Because you are the princess. Just speak to Mr. Burkhardt. He'll explain." Dickenson white-knuckled the steering wheel and pressed his lips taut, gentling down on the gas when the light turned green.

Reggie let the subject drop. Dickenson wasn't the only one who'd kept his gaze downcast this morning. Jarvis and Serena both avoided direct eye contact, though Jarvis addressed her more directly than the others.

She'd ask Tanner about this *straightaway*, as he would say. Speaking of the man with the long golden hair and ice blue eyes ...

She kind of missed that rascal when she woke up this morning. He'd been nothing but a pain in her backside since they met, but somewhere along the way, she'd grown attached to him.

Dickenson steered the Mercedes through a roundabout, past a center-city park, and down a wide avenue lined with thick-trunked trees dropping colorful leaves onto the avenue.

Maybe she felt this tug toward Tanner because he was her only friend in Hessenberg and it was easy to anchor her emotions with him. In the meantime, she needed to get ahold of her heart, her thoughts, and figure out this strange mission.

Was it a permanent call? Temporary? Did she even belong in this tiny sea duchy? With these people? What was expected of her and, good grief, what in the world would those people on the street, waiting at corners to cross or leaning against lampposts, think of her? Demand of her?

A sediment of anxiety rose from the bottom of her soul and clouded her reasoning.

Oh Lord, a princess. I can't ... Forget discussing protocol when she saw Sir Blue Eyes. She needed to have a heart-to-heart with him and figure a true way out.

Her phone pinged and she dug it out of her bag. A text from Al.

Oliver coming next week. Lking gud. Hv fun there.

She was about to respond *Yea!* when a text from Mark came through.

Ur in Hessenberg??! WT—A princess? Hahaha. Wht's the bit?
Call me!

Reggie groaned. Mark lived in the world he created in his
own mind. Did he not hear the letter she read aloud at the garage?

"Miss, you best duck down," Dickenson said, pulling into the
curved drive of a flat-front, golden-brick building. "Looks like
the press is waiting for you." He blasted the horn, steering the
car through a throng of cameramen and reporters waiting under
an arched, stone entrance, casting their large, leering shadows
against the car windows.

FIFTEEN

anner shoved his way through the crowd of photographers and reporters toward the Mercedes as Dickenson pulled around.

One guess. The same leak as the first wave. Seamus Fitzsimmons. Tanner would have to organize security straightaway.

"Stand aside, please. Stand aside."

But the press swarmed like bees to honey. Cameras flashed, videoed, robbing Tanner, Hessenberg, and the rest of the world from a formal, organized introduction of the princess.

Blasted, loose-lipped, tongue-wagging insider. Seriously, if he found out who specifically leaked her arrival . . .

"Pardon me." Tanner reached for the back door, then noticed Regina was sitting up front, next to Dickenson. Why was he not surprised?

Louis trailed behind him, along with another bloke, Elton, the front lobby man, trying to clear a path for Regina to the door.

"Stand aside, the lot of you. Move back." Elton had a commanding presence, for which Tanner was grateful.

When Regina stepped out, it was all over. The shouting commenced as cameras flashed and bodies crushed against bodies.

"Are you the princess?"

"Look here, Princess."

"What's your name?"

"Can I get a look this way, Princess?"

"Burkhardt, let us talk to her. We've a right to know."

Tanner ignored the demand and all but shoved Regina through the manor door. Taking her hand, he raced her up the stairs, the mob stalled a few moments by Louis and Elton. But they were no match for that frenzy.

"Here. This way." Tanner shot down a second-floor corridor, the rhythm of his heels against the marble in harmony with Regina's.

He found a room at the end of the hall, ducked inside, and slammed the door.

"Oh my gosh, that was scary." Regina collapsed onto a long wooden pew, its old joints creaking in protest. "I'm shaking." She held up her hand and in the soft, colored light filtering through the round, stained-glass window in the front of the room, Tanner could see her tremors.

"I'm so sorry." Tanner paced down the center aisle, raking back his hair, not caring if he messed up his morning gel job. "Someone . . . someone leaked you were here. There are limited options as to who."

"It's okay. You didn't know." Under her mop of red hair, she narrowed her gaze at him. "Did you?"

"Of course not." Tanner pulled out his phone, reading the screen. "The king is here, along with the prime minister and the archbishop." He pressed the phone to his ear. "Louis, we're on the second floor—" Tanner glanced around, engaging the room for the first time. "In the chapel. What's going on with the press? Still here. Arrange for the meeting to be here, in the chapel. The press won't look for us here."

Ha!

"And call Seamus's office. Let him know."

He rang off and sat in the pew in front of Regina. "How are you?"

"Other than being chased by a mob? I'm shaking. You?"

"Other than nearly getting my princess,"—the words left his mouth and settled in his heart in a strange yet comfortable way—"crushed by a mob, I'm shaking."

She smiled and swooped her bangs out of her eyes. "What's this about the king and everyone?" Her expression, her gesture, coated the feelings stirring in his chest, beckoning his emotional doors to swing open.

"I told you last night. You're meeting the king this morning, along with the prime minister, governor of Hessenberg, and the archbishop."

"Excuse me, you never said anything like that to me."

"Regina, I did, in the limo, when we were driving up to Meadowbluff."

"Did I respond? Did I say, 'Oh, the king? Wow, I've never met a king before! Do I curtsy?'" She smacked his arm. "'Cause that's what I would've said."

"No, you don't curtsy. *He's* coming to see *you*. He will bow to you."

"To me?" Now she paced down the center aisle, her hands tucked into the hip pockets of her jeans.

Tanner glanced away, walking to the door, searching for the light panel, anything to get his mind off her . . . well, various assets and charms. He came to work this morning determined to hold his heart and affections at a professional distance.

But the moment he saw her, he wanted to escape his duties and spend the day with her, alone, discovering her, pondering how well she fit a pair of jeans.

Give a poor chap a chance.

"What is this room?" She stood by the altar, inhaling. "It has a sweet presence and aroma."

"It's the chapel. The royal family held services here when they were in the city. As a matter of fact,"—Tanner walked toward her—"this is the Oath of the Throne chapel. Every ascending royal took their oath here upon the death of their predecessor."

He'd not thought of that when he randomly directed her down the second-floor corridor.

"Are services still held here?"

"It's a government building." Tanner shook his head. "So no. Maybe at Christmas there might be a service but—"

"It feels 'full' in here. Does that make sense?" Regina studied the high, flat ceiling with its carved inlays.

"Oddly, it does." Tanner grew up with that feeling. In his father's parish. As if God himself filled the room.

"This is incredible. I see all of this and think, 'This was my family.'"

She was winning him. Over and over again. Her willingness to investigate with an open heart. But he would remain guarded.

If Regina knew the real Tanner Burkhardt—which she never would—she'd not want him. No woman would want him and, frankly, half the time he wasn't sure he wanted himself.

The sooner the king assigned her a more appropriate mentor, the better. Off he'd go back to his safe, albeit stark world.

"So, Tanner, what's this meeting about?" Regina made her way back to him, her voice low, concern in her countenance.

"As I said, you're meeting with King Nathaniel II, the prime minister, the governor of Hessenberg, and the archbishop." At last he found a switch panel by the door and powered up the lights. "We'll discuss our next steps."

A patterned, gentle glow spilled down the side walls from the iron and glass sconces. Working another switch turned on the light fixtures above the altar.

"I don't know, Tanner." Regina squeezed her fingers in her hand and walked the length of the aisle. "I–I feel . . . like . . ."— she shook out her hands, then gathered her hair away from her face—"like a cow trying to run with thoroughbreds."

He made his way toward her. "You're far from a cow, trust me. I'm sorry If I miscommunicated about this meeting, but, Regina, you must start thinking of yourself as worthy. The Princess of Hessenberg."

"Easy for you to say, Tanner." She mimicked his accent, trying to smile and lighten the tension in the room.

He debated. Should he tell her Seamus was the one who filed the petition? She was already so nervous. On the other hand, being armed with the truth would serve her well. "Regina, you should know—"

"Hello, Tanner?" The chapel door creaked open and Louis entered, leading the king, prime minister, and archbishop into the room.

Tanner bowed to Nathaniel, then introduced Regina. The king shook her hand, bowing slightly, so very real yet so elegantly proper. "It's an honor to meet you."

"You too." Her voice wavered a little and she offered the king a tender curtsy.

Tanner smiled. She was going to be a stellar princess. Next he introduced Regina to the prime minister, Henry Montgomery. Then the archbishop, Miles Burkhardt.

"It's a pleasure to meet you." Regina glanced at Tanner, then at the archbishop. "Burkhardt? Any relation or just a coincidence?"

"Some believe there are no coincidences." Dad shook her hand and Tanner formed his hand into a fist, tensing. *Why does he have to be so . . . obtuse?* "It's an honor to greet you face-to-face, Your Majesty. Welcome to Hessenberg."

"Please, call me Reggie. Or Regina." She smiled as she shook his hand. "I feel very welcomed." Then she shot Tanner a look. *Whaaat?*

Oh, blimey. Out with it. "The archbishop is my father, Regina."

Dad locked his hands behind his back with a nod at Tanner. "Quite right."

And the man wondered why Tanner never came round. Or why during the toughest years of his life, he sailed the turbulent sea alone.

Regina twisted her hands together, holding on to her smile, clearly unsure where to go with Dad's curt, formal "Quite right."

"Gentlemen, Your Majesty,"—he nodded to the king—"I apologize for moving the meeting to the chapel, but the media frenzy caught us off guard."

"Do you know how they found out she was here?" Nathaniel asked. "Another leak about the princess in less than a week?"

"I do not, sir." Tanner hated the defeated sound of his answer. "But I will investigate. Only the five of us plus the governor knew she was coming."

"And our aides." Nathaniel unbuttoned his suit coat and took a seat in the nearest pew. "I suspect a pretty pound could be earned by the one who alerted the press of the princess's arrival and whereabouts."

"It's a sad day, Nathaniel," Henry said, "when we have to suspect our staff."

"Wouldn't be the first time. Speaking of, will the governor be joining us?"

"Yes, sir," Tanner said. "Louis is contacting his office."

"Regina," Nathaniel said as he turned to her, "welcome. I do apologize for the mess with the press." The king leaned back, putting everyone in the room at ease. "We thought a formal presser later in the week or early next would be the best course to introduce you to the people, but, well, welcome to *that* side of your new world." He smiled.

"It's all . . ." She remained standing, shifting from side to side, slipping her hands in her hip pockets, then folding her arms over her chest, and generally looking as if she might make for the exit. When she met Tanner's gaze, he smiled encouragement and nodded for her to sit. "It is mildly overwhelming."

"I understand. My fiancée, Susanna, is new to the royal life and also finds it very overwhelming. She sends her regards, by the way, and offers to do all she can to assist you."

"How nice. Thank her for me." Regina swiped her hands down the sides of her jeans and sat in the pew ahead of Nathaniel, one foot tucked under her. "So, what do you all need from me?"

Straight to the point. No mussing about. If Tanner knew anything about Regina Beswick, she waded right into every situation, sorting it out as she went.

He could learn from her.

"We'd like to talk about the entail. Has Tanner explained our situation?"

"Yes. It's all a bit unbelievable. My gram never said a word to me about any of this."

"She did of sorts." Tanner moved to stand beside Reggie. "Seems she painted a fairy tale and told the story of a princess who needed to return home."

"A fairy tale?" Nathaniel said.

"She . . . she wrote and illustrated a fairy tale about a princess," Regina said, "and gave it to me for my sixth birthday."

"Fascinating," Henry said. "But she never openly spoke to you of your heritage?"

Reggie shook her head. "And I wish I knew why."

"The key question we must sort out now is, are you willing to take the Oath of the Throne? Be the true princess and receive your inheritance as granted by the entail?" Nathaniel spoke in a low, soft voice, asking gentle, probing questions. "How do you view living four thousand miles from home? Of being a government official? Of being a royal? Of your life being onstage for all to see? To a life devoted to serving the kingdom and its people?"

Gentle, yes, but honest. Uncloaked.

Regina answered with equal honesty. "I find it unsettling, a bit terrifying, and a little bit like a movie I want to watch to the end to see how it turns out." She looked up at Tanner. *Is that right?* He smiled and nodded. *Be your true self.*

"A week ago I was a simple Southern girl dealing in cars, eating pizza on Friday nights with the car heads. Now I'm heir to a kingdom? A royal?" She stood, pressing her hand to her forehead. The men stood with her. "And I know you're under the gun with this entail and now, I hear, a lawsuit, but I'm not sure what I want to do. I'm sorry . . ." She peered at the king with a straight, steady gaze. "I can't promise you more than here I am, checking out the country and people, testing the waters."

"Regina, please, we understand. Yes, we are under the gun, as you say, and we requested you come to Hessenberg as quickly as possible. But the EU court has not yet agreed to hear the case. You have a few extra days to ponder your future."

"I'm not sure I can decide my future in a few extra days." She stood stock still, trembling. "Politics and me . . . not so much."

Nathaniel laughed. "I'm not sure any of us really love it."

"Hold on there, Your Majesty." Henry stepped forward. "Some of us find it quite rewarding." He bowed toward Regina. "Miss Beswick, we will do all in our power to help you. You won't be alone. But I find the best part of me, of life, often reveals itself when I'm faced with severe complications and trials and am forced to leave my own comforts."

"Well, y'all shot my comforts to pieces. I've no grid for this. I wouldn't even know where to begin to find normalcy or comfort." She articulated her concern with passion. "I really appreciate that y'all will support me and I believe you . . . but, wow. I mean, maybe this EU court petition will end all of our questions, right? I won't have to sign the entail, be the princess, and, you know . . . own a country."

"Regina, let's square away two things," Nathaniel said. "You are the Princess of Hessenberg no matter what transpires with the court petition, which we believe will fail, as have all the others. We'd like you to take the Oath of the Throne, set you in officially as the ruling princess with all full and legal rights. And yes, as the Grand Duchess you'll own the land. In Hessenberg, the land is administered by the government."

"What will the people say? I mean, I feel like I'm sneaking in behind their backs. Won't they resent this foreign chick moving into the palace? 'Hey, y'all, what's up?'"

Regina's exaggerated Southern accent made them all chuckle.

"Might I offer advice?" Dad said, tall and straight in his tailored suit and priest collar. Tanner cleared his throat and stepped aside as his dad faced Regina. "It's not what man thinks or believes, Regina. Whether in Florida working on cars or in Hessenberg working from the royal palace, it's what God believes. 'As for me and my house,' said the warrior Joshua, 'we will serve the Lord.'"

Come on, Dad, save your sermon for Sunday. You're making her nervous. Would he ever understand how he intimidated people?

"That's just it." Her eyes glistened and emotion threaded her words. "I don't know what God is saying."

"Then keep seeking him, but do not fear the people. Fear the Lord. King Saul feared the people and ruined his reign and his name. But David, he—"

"Found strength in the Lord."

Dad nodded. "Ah, you know the Scriptures."

"Born and raised in a house of faith."

Dad smiled. "Then trust the one you've heard about all those years, Regina. We are nearest to him when we are in the wilderness."

"Ho boy." Regina exhaled, giving Dad, the archbishop, a weak smile. "That's what I'm afraid of, sir."

"You have our support and prayers." He took a card from his pocket. "If you need to, ring me. Anytime."

Tanner turned his back, pressing his fist to his lips, containing a brutish response. Where was this kind of tenderness when he had required it?

From the back of the chapel, the door swung open and Seamus Fitzsimmons waltzed in with his chin high and his chest puffed out.

"You're late," Henry said. It wasn't a secret that Brighton's prime minister didn't care for the Hessenberg governor, but he was an appointment by Nathaniel's father, King Leopold, so Henry honored Seamus out of respect for the deceased king.

"Quite right, Henry, and my apologies to the king for being tardy." He came around the last pew with an arrogant air that unsettled Tanner, then stopped in front of Regina. "You must be our American princess." He bowed, clapping his heels together and offering his hand. "Governor Seamus Fitzsimmons, at your service."

Tanner exhaled, hands on her hips, and pinched her words against her lips. Seamus mocked her with the exaggerated bow and heel clap. This was not his old mentor, the man who offered him a way out of his mess with Trude and coached him along. This was a man seized by the prospect of power.

"Nice to meet you." Regina shook his hand, then withdrew, tucking her fingers into her hip pockets again. By now Tanner realized it was her go-to stance when she was nervous.

"Have you been informed?" Seamus postured and strutted, smoothing his mustache while retrieving his pipe—his hand-crafted briarwood binky. "Nothing personal, Regina. You seem to be a sweet girl, but I must do what's best for my country."

"See here, Seamus," Nathaniel said. "We're not here—"

"Pardone, Your Majesty?" Seamus pulled a folded document from his breast pocket. "Miss Beswick, you may well know I've filed a petition for Hessenberg to be granted sovereign state status without, well, a sovereign. I'm most sincere when I say I do not believe a descendant of His Royal Highness, Prince Francis, Grand Duke of Hessenberg, is worthy of inheriting the kingdom. He was a coward and traitor. We should be able to forge ahead as a nation without Brighton and, my dear, without you."

"For all that's sacred, Seamus," Henry said, "don't put this on her now."

"I'm afraid the entail has already done that for me."

"You know as well as any of us, Prince Francis was trying to save a country ill prepared for war. Hessenberg had no military to speak of in 1914. If it weren't for Francis's foresight, Hessenberg might not have existed at all after the first war."

"It's one thing, Prime Minister, to find a solution to a war one is not prepared to fight, but it's another thing entirely to surrender one nation to another without having a single shot fired or one drop of blood spilled."

"I find that rather optimal, don't you?" Henry removed his mask of cordiality, revealing his inner disdain for the governor.

"I find it treasonous. Francis refused the counsel of his lords, and when he signed over his lands and the government to King Nathaniel I, he signed over the lands of his lords. He betrayed us all."

"Enough, Seamus." Nathaniel reached for the document waving from the governor's hand. "You've obviously come here to say something. Out with it."

"Quite right, Your Majesty. I came here to enact *Vox Vocis Canonicus*."

Tanner made a face. "The authority canon?"

Henry moved around Dad to read the document Seamus handed Nathaniel. "Seamus, what are you plotting, my man?"

Tanner stepped closer to Regina, who seemed to be shrinking into herself by the moment. "Quite the show Seamus puts on, eh?" he said with a low laugh for her ears only.

"Why's he doing this?" she asked, eyes wide, her heart in her words. "Plotting against me."

"I've no doubt he'll tell us." Tanner tucked in a bit closer, enough for her to feel his warmth but not touch her.

Seamus's aura darkened as he ended all pretense. "It's all in the document, but in summation, if this lass signs the entail, Hessenberg law reverts back to the constitution and laws held in this land in 1914. Our old constitution. Which contains an authority canon. After all, it's what Francis wanted, wasn't it? For Hessenberg to go back to her old ways and once again be a land of lords, of which his heir would reign supreme."

"I see." Henry tapped Seamus in the chest with his finger. "How do you plan to enact the lord's authority canon? There are no lords in Hessenberg. Their houses have died out. Lands sold to the highest bidder."

"Just as there is one descendant from the prince, there is one descendant from the House of Lords. I am that man. My great-grandfather was Patrick Fitzsimmons, Earl of Estes. The land was sold during the Great Depression before World War II. I think you're familiar with Estes Estates, are you not, Tanner? Anyway, I am the great-grandson of the Earl of Estes."

He shot Regina an exacting, slicing stare.

"If you are the legitimate heir of Prince Francis, then I, as the legitimate heir of the Earl of Estes, as well as the governor of Hessenberg, enact the authority canon and ask that you stand down as Hereditary Duchess due to your lack of leadership and experience, and your foreign birth. You've no right here. I will file a motion declaring you incompetent and inept on behalf of the Hessen people, and once Hessenberg is freed from Brighton, by the entail or the courts, I'll have you charged as an enemy of the state if you remain on Hessenberg soil."

Pandemonium erupted, everyone talking at once, as the men rushed forward in one accord.

"Enemy of the state? Now see here, Seamus—"

"What's the meaning of this? You can't stand here and accuse her . . . charging her as an enemy of the state."

Tanner argued right alongside the king and prime minister. Even Dad brought up several good points. Their voices blended, rising and falling in a medley of anger, determination, and reason.

A shrill whistle pierced the room. The men turned at once to see Regina standing on a pew, her fingers on her lips. She regarded each one while slowly lowering her arms.

"Let me get this straight. If I sign the entail, Seamus here will charge me as an unfit ruler. Got to tell you, I agree with you on that one. But an enemy of the state? Yet if I don't sign the entail, then what? Hessenberg ceases to be a nation?"

"But the court will rule in our favor," Seamus said, sure and pompous. "Granting us the right to become our own sovereign state without you, dear princess. Either way, as Prince Francis's heir, you are an enemy of the state."

The voices roared again. Seamus had lost his proper mind.

"Seamus," Henry said, "you have no precedent for any of this."

The tension among the men settled in Tanner's gut, and he wondered how he had ever admired Seamus Fitzsimmons.

"Let's just say I've gained a few allies myself. Germany is backing our petition in exchange for forgiving their debt to us . . . for seizing our bank accounts in 1914."

"This is outlandish," Henry said. "You cannot negotiate with Germany outside my authority. I'll have *you* arrested for treason and insubordination."

"I refer you to Brighton law PR-859—"

Tanner stepped back. This confrontation did not need him. He needed to get Regina out of here.

But when he turned to get her, the place where she'd stood was vacant, and the chapel door stood wide open.

SIXTEEN

eggie exploded out the door and into the pack of waiting press. The chilled air reached for her, and she longed for Tallahassee's late September heat.

"Princess, over here."

"What do you think of Hessenberg?"

"Are you really the great-granddaughter of Princess Alice?"

"Are you going to sign the entail?"

Cameras clicked and buzzed in her ears and her forward motion stopped when she sank into the mud of media.

"Please, let me go. Please." She spun in one direction, then another. But she was surrounded by people with cameras and questions. A shove from behind crashed her into the Mercedes and she tried to open the back door, but it was locked.

"Pardon me." She shoved forward and knocked one odious photographer into another. "Stand back."

She worked her way around the back of the car and found Dickenson reaching for her, his eyes popping, his expression grim. "Your Majesty, I didn't know you were coming." He wrapped his arm about her shoulder, shielding her from the press.

"Dickenson, give me the keys." She hovered by the driver's side door.

"I–I can drive you, miss. Please, let me . . ." He reached around her to open the door. "I'll unlock the back . . . Stand down, man, give the princess room." Dickenson put his shoulder down and rammed a man twice his size in the chest.

"Dickenson, please." Reggie raised her head long enough to look him in the eye. "Give me the keys." She held up her palm.

"I–I . . . miss . . . please . . ." He sighed and dropped the keys in her palm. "Unlock the ignition with the key, then press the starter button on the panel."

"Thank you." She'd kiss him if she wasn't in such a hurry to get out of Dodge. Oh poor, sweet Dickenson. He wore the most bamboozled expression.

In the driver's seat, Reggie exhaled her anxiety and inhaled confidence. She knew nothing about being a royal or how to handle the media, but she sure as heck knew how to handle a car. The engine roared to life when she engaged the push button ignition. She gunned the gas as a warning to the photographers hovering about her window and the front of the car.

"Move, bubbas," she muttered with another rev of the engine. "I'm going whether you're standing there or not."

She mashed the horn, giving it a good long blast, then shifted into gear and was about to take off when Tanner knocked on the passenger door window.

"Regina, let me in."

"Stand back, Tanner." She inched the car forward, motioning for the photographer aiming his camera through the windshield to *mooove*!

"Open the door." He banged his fist against the glass, then raised up to peek over the hood. "Dickenson, how could you—"

His voice faded, lost in the rest of the crowd noise.

Reggie powered down the passenger window. "Hey, don't yell

at Dickenson. I demanded the keys. And by the way, did you set me up? Did you know he could charge me with all of that? Did you know he was the one who filed the petition?"

"Open the door." Tanner bent over the door, looking for the lock button.

Reggie inched the car forward. She'd waited too long to get out of here. "Tanner, back up, because I'm going."

"Open the door, you insane girl."

"Insane girl! Is that how you speak to your princess?" She powered forward, scattering the last lingering, daredevil photographers.

"Yes, when she acts like she's lost her last marble." Panic infused his words. "Open the door, Regina."

"I need to think." She gunned the car forward, laying on the horn again. A photographer with a death wish had stepped in front of her. "Maybe I have lost my last marble."

"I'm coming with you. We can search for the lost marble together." Tanner skipped along the side of the car as Reggie rolled out from under the covered portico. "Regina, oh, you are a stubborn one."

With that, she hit a clear path and pressed the pedal to the metal. Tanner lunged through the window as she whipped the car around toward the entrance, fishtailing the back end, planting his face in the passenger seat, his legs flailing, his feet kicking at the wind.

"Tanner, I suggest you buckle up."

He moaned and contorted, twisting around, catching himself as Reggie fired out of the manor driveway, hitting the street ahead in front of a wall of oncoming cars.

"Do you aim to kill us?" Finally upright, Tanner dropped down in the seat and fastened his seat belt.

"Sorry, but I need to drive."

"Do you know where you're going?"

"No." In every sense of the word.

"Turn left at the next avenue." Tanner gripped the dash as she sped around the corner before the light flashed red. "He can't do it, Regina."

"Arrest me? He sure seems to think he can." She checked the side mirror and threaded in and out of traffic. "Didn't anyone else in your government figure this out?"

"A lorrie, Regina. Truck, truck—" Tanner planted his hand on the dash and leaned right as she skirted around a truck exiting a narrow side street. "Next left . . ." He pointed.

Reggie barely slowed, cutting the Mercedes hard and making the corner. "He's right, Tanner. I'm not fit to lead. Who am I?"

"You think just because he's got years of experience and the title governor *he's* fit to lead? What kind of leader pulls a stunt like this?"

"One who thinks he's doing it for the good of the people."

"For the good of himself." Tanner seemed to relax, just a bit, but she was still booking it through midmorning traffic. "At the light, take another left."

At last she was leaving the city behind and finding good, open road. She slipped the Mercedes between a small, two-seater car and another truck and aimed for the hills. The feel of the wheel beneath her hands, the song of the engine, the power of speed soothed her anxiety. The sense of being overwhelmed subsided as she steered up the hillside.

Coming here may well have been the worst decision of her life. Even more than the seven precious years she lost to Backlund & Backlund. Did she really think she'd waltz in and be a princess without opposition?

"Remember what my father said, Reggie." She glanced at him. He stared ahead, his right hand gripping the door handle. "Do you fear God or man?"

"At the moment, I fear being arrested. In a foreign country."

"You won't be arrested." He sounded *not* confident at all.

"Exactly. I'll go home first. Forget this mess."

Reggie let the Mercedes hug the side of the narrow lanes, feeling the tires grip as the road dipped and turned.

"Regina, we'll get this sorted out."

"Sorted out? Tanner, this is not who is coming to dinner on Sunday. Shoot fire, how did y'all not see this coming?"

"Regina, curve . . . around this hill . . . it's a tight—"

She braked and cut the Mercedes right, urging the vehicle to cling to the inside of the road, skidding around tail end toward the barrier rail and a sharp hillside drop.

"Sweet heaven . . ." Tanner flattened one hand against his door and another on the dash. The car fishtailed out of the turn and Reggie drove on, straightening the car's path with a bit of speed.

"*Wahoooo* . . . Ha-ha!" She powered down her window and stuck her arm into the air, palming the stiff breeze, waving to the blazing Princess Alice trees. "Now we're talking."

Tanner swore beneath his breath. "You're a madwoman. I should think the threat of arrest is preferable to death. And remember, I'm in this car and I choose life. No matter my pitiful existence."

"What? Pitiful?" She cut him a quick look just as the straightaway bent into another hairpin curve. Reggie fixed her eyes on the road and gripped the wheel.

"Eyes ahead . . ."

Out of the turn, the road shot out of the mountains into a straight stretch, fields on either side. She'd told Tanner she wanted to think but what she really wanted was to feel. To get her heart around this whole mess. And driving did that for her. Then she could think. Sort things out, as it were.

Ahead, Meadowbluff Palace rose, majestic and graceful on the horizon. A fortress. A safe harbor. Her adrenaline ebbed, leaving her legs and arms trembling. And she just wanted to go *home*.

"Meadowbluff is a beautiful place." She turned down the palace drive, stopping just shy of the heavy wrought iron gate. "What's the security code?"

"One, nine, six, zero." Each number came with an exasperated exhale. "I do believe I had a mini heart attack back there."

"Dang, Tanner, could you be any more dramatic?" Reggie gentled the car forward as the gate opened and slowly made her way to the palace steps. "What was with the pitiful life remark?"

"Must have been the heart attack talking." The car eased to a stop in front of the palace and Tanner popped open his door. "And you're one to talk of dramatics. You didn't even give us a chance to deal with Seamus before you ran off. Now we'll have to gather again." He slammed his door shut and walked around to Reggie's side of the car. "Nathaniel is a kind man, but he's also a busy one."

Tanner opened her door as Reggie slouched forward, dropping her forehead against the steering wheel. Now that she was still, the tension, the anxiety, the questions came rushing to the surface, demanding audience with her emotions and her thoughts.

"Regina?" Tanner crouched down next to her. "Please, we can manage Seamus. But I understand it's a bit much, all at once."

Tears, slow and warm, slipped down her cheeks. "I'm not sure you do."

"Come on." He hooked his arm through hers. "Gentle off your worries. Let's go inside for a spot of tea. Jarvis tells me the chef makes extraordinary cakes. We'll sort this out, Regina. We will."

Maybe it wasn't proper or the princess thing to do, but Reggie leaned into Tanner, wrapped her arms about his waist, and wept against his chest.

After tea, when her nerves had settled, Reggie dialed Daddy. She needed to hear his voice. Needed his counsel about what she faced.

But she had to admit, the peace she felt in the midst of her mental turmoil was beyond her human capacity.

"Daddy, hey, it's me. Thought I'd give you a call but you're probably out ... hmm ... I just wanted to hear your voice. Feels like forever since I left Tally. Doing good, I guess. Found out I have an enemy. The governor said I was an enemy of the state! Said I'm inept to lead, and I gotta give him props on that one. Tanner says it's just a bunch of hooey but ... I ... feel ... really overwhelmed. Call me, okay?"

Al, any news on the Duesy?

Mark, har-har, yes in Hessenberg. Call Daddy 4 the latest. Thx agn 4 the warehouse.

Carrie, sup? U & Rafe in luv? Miss U big!

SEVENTEEN

anner let himself into his flat shortly after eight o'clock, tossed his keys to the table by the door, reached for the remote, and powered up the telly.

In the kitchen, he flicked on a light and sorted through his mail. Rubbish, all of it. Why did the cable company keep soliciting his business when he already subscribed? He held up the shiny, fancy advertisement. Bet this cost a pretty tuppence. If they'd stop sending these things out, they could reduce their monthly cable fee. What was it now? A hundred quid? And all he watched was sports.

The rubbish bin needed to be carried out, but he didn't feel like it. What an exhausting wild day.

The media. Seamus's stunt. The media again. The wild car drive.

Regina's tears. Tanner brushed his hand over his chest where her tears had soaked through his shirt. Soaked through his pores and seeped all the way to his dry, thirsty heart.

Facing the stark, barren kitchen, he ran his hands through his hair, corralling his feelings for Regina, mildly considering cutting his long locks. He secretly kept his hair long as a way to annoy the archbishop. But that didn't sound very mature for a thirty-two-year-old Minister of Culture, now, did it?

But his restless thoughts wandered back toward Regina and the feel of her body leaning against him, his arms wrapped about her.

Must. Think. Of. Something. Else. Tanner marched into the living room, snatched up the remote, and raised the telly's volume.

He'd compartmentalize. Keep his feelings a secret with the best of the world's wounded, pitiful blokes.

On the telly, the presenters ran down last week's rugby scores and predicted the winners of the upcoming matches. Tanner collapsed in the reclining chair, the only furniture in the room besides a table and the television.

Here he had a lovely downtown Strauberg flat with windows overlooking the city and part of the south bay, but all he could manage was a lazy chair, a telly, and a table he rescued from a church rummage sale.

What was it Regina said about existing and not living?

Tanner shifted forward in his chair, uncomfortable, trying to migrate away from the fragmented images, thoughts, and emotions of the day.

—Regina in those jeans with her hair sweeping over her eyes. A young, redheaded Marilyn Monroe.

—Her nervous humility while meeting the king, Henry, and Dad. What was the idea behind Dad's cloaked answer when Regina asked if he and Tanner shared a last name for a reason? *"Some believe there are no coincidences."*

—Seamus barging in with his arrogant plan to oust Regina.

Tanner had studied the entail law at university and explored the consequences of reverting back to 1914 law. The scholars believed the old law to be sound and able to hold the nation steady, if need be, in time of transition. But no one really knew how the people would respond to even one day with no legal government. Would the old laws tarry? Would anarchy ensue?

If Regina wasn't the princess, and the court mysteriously decided Hessenberg could ignore the law of the entail, it would be open season for every political faction.

But the real truth? No one thought an heir would be found. All believed the Grand Duchy would become a province of Brighton.

Then there was the press firestorm. And Regina driving off with him face-first in the seat.

Tanner laughed aloud. What a sight he must have been. No doubt he'd be in the papers tomorrow, bottoms up.

Poor Dickenson, left behind in the city to spend the evening swapping stories with his mates at the Fence & Anchor until Tanner returned with the Mercedes.

And oh, he must organize security straightaway. Tanner wasn't sure if it was his duty or not, but now that the press had caught wind, Regina would not find a moment's peace unless she hid inside Meadowbluff.

Patting his pockets for his phone, Tanner composed a mental e-mail to Louis about security, ignoring that back-of-the-mind tug to explore his earlier thought.

Existing but not living.

Pulling his phone from his right front pocket, he found he'd missed a call.

Trude Cadwallader.

Tanner stared at her name. Why was she calling him? He listened to her voice message, walking to the window and peering out over the twinkling nighttime city.

"Surprise, love, it's me. Did you get the invitation? Please say you'll come. It would be grand. The girls . . . well . . . they're . . . Oh listen, we'll talk Sunday, when I see you. I will see you, right? Grand. Ta-ta."

He regarded the screen before deleting the message. A week ago he was a happy, single, solitary chap trying his wings at a new minister position, forging a new career path. Then suddenly the king appears, sending him on a journey designed to change one person's life, yet oddly enough, it was Tanner who found his life, his heart, changing.

Returning to his chair, he typed his message to Louis, then sat back, closing his eyes. Could it be he wanted to go to the party? He wanted what he'd given up, what he'd been resisting for so long? At every level? Love.

He moaned and sat up. *Time for bed, chap.*

Maybe someday he could muster the courage for romance. With someone. Not Regina. She was beyond his league in more ways than one.

But driving up to Estes Estate on a Sunday afternoon? No. That part of his life was over. Opening up that locked and guarded door of his heart would require more courage than he could gather in a lifetime.

October 19, 1914

Meadowbluff Palace

While Hessenberg has not joined the war, the war has come to us. Several missiles have been launched at our shores. Uncle is sure it's the Kaiser and Chancellor Bismarck behind the attacks, but all of his inquiries met a dead end.

Wettin Manor was struck just before dawn the day before, and Uncle's quarters were burned. He swears it was done on purpose, not a random firing, and it makes him so despondent, which makes us all despondent.

Uncle has ordered a blackout on the palace, so we sit in darkness after the sun goes down, which is quite early these fall days.

There's no music. No laughter. I almost feel anything would be better than this.

Uncle says we must hold together. But he's near his own breaking, I fear.

I've seen none of my friends. Many more of the lads have joined the war by fighting for Brighton and Britain. This makes Uncle even more despondent. He says he's failed the youth of Hessenberg. For the sake of his past, he's ruined their future.

Mercy, I wish I could write about more pleasant things. Oh, I stored the two halves of the pendant and picture in my box. Mamá would be so disappointed to know I let Rein cut my cipher pendant in two. I, however, am all too glad to have it back in my possession! What might he have done with my cipher had he thought to keep it and use it for his own gain!

Mamá still prays faithfully by the small fire allowed in the parlor, rocking, her Bible open in her hands, her lips moving in prayer. It is the one constant that brings me peace and hope.

God alone can save our spirits. But only he knows how or when.

Alice

She woke early, before dawn drifted past her window, with a sense of resolve. As Sadie would say, "It is what it is. No use fussing over it."

Maybe she needed to stop bemoaning how her life got bulldozed and start digging around in the rubble to find the gems. Pending arrest or not, she was here, the princess, and she might as well discover the truths and realities lurking beneath the surface.

Digging in and facing the truth was how Daddy got her through Mama's death. How she got through college and how she rose up the ranks at Backlund & Backlund, on her way to becoming their youngest partner. How she found the courage to face Backlund, Daddy, and her friends when she decided to go into business with Al.

And how, have mercy, she got on the plane with Tanner Monday night and flew to Hessenberg.

Reaching to switch on the bedside lamp, Reggie crawled out from under the covers and stood in the middle of the bed and greeted young Gram, Princess Alice.

"Hey, Gram, I'm still here, in your watercolor fairy tale. Any words of advice for me today?"

But Gram's innocent, hopeful expression remained unchanged.

Was that a message in and of itself? Closing her eyes, Reggie inhaled the essence of the image and exhaled her trepidation.

Wasn't that faith? Believing what the heart knew to be true even if the head raged with doubts?

Opening her eyes, she whispered a prayer for guidance and wisdom, tried to invoke the hope of the portrait, and jumped off the bed.

A princess is defined not by her title alone but by how she lives her life.

The words came with a whisper and swirled around her heart, settling deeper and deeper, and Reggie decided those words were a good place to start her day.

Showered and dressed in jeans, she smoothed up her bed covers, organized her suitcase, then unzipped her backpack to retrieve Gram's fairy tale. Maybe by studying this book—Gram's message to her, as Tanner declared—along with a bit more talking to God, she might understand this journey she was on.

Jogging down the wide front staircase with gilded banisters and a royal red carpet, Reggie cut through the foyer, passed by the big formal dining room, and headed for the kitchen. As she came around the corner, Jarvis met her in the back hall in his uniform of a dark suit and dark tie.

"Your Majesty, good morning." He bowed slightly. He was not much taller than Reggie but he carried himself with confidence and stature. "Serena was just about to see if you cared for breakfast."

"I'm starved. But I'd rather eat in the kitchen. With everyone else."

"In the kitchen? With everyone else?" He locked his hands behind his back and rocked up on his heels. "If you wish, miss. But it might make the staff feel a bit uncomfortable."

"Really?" She leaned to see around him. The chef and a maid were chatting over a plate of what looked like scones. "I'm just like them. A regular gal."

"Perhaps in some ways, yes. But in many ways, you are not. If I may be so bold, you must remember your station, Your Majesty. And while cordial terms with the staff are welcomed and encouraged, the moment you become 'one of us,' you compromise your authority. And your station. You are the heir to the Hessenberg throne. We are not. I'm sure similar standards are employed by American households with service staff."

"Right. Okay. I see your point. I've been to the Governor's Mansion and the gov doesn't eat in the kitchen with the help."

"Precisely. You'll get used to the routine. Now, how about breakfast in the parlor? You can see the sunrise over the forest."

"Sounds perfect." Reggie followed Jarvis down the back corridor, through the back-of-house foyer—yes, there was one, and it was quite elegant—to a cozy room with a fireplace and bank of windows overlooking the grounds and the forest.

"Will this do?"

"Very much." She tipped her head to him. "Thank you, Jarvis."

"Miss, I hope you realize what an honor it is for me and the staff to be in your service. Don't be shy about asking for our assistance."

"O–okay . . . and, Jarvis, thank you for sharing with me . . . about . . . you know. The rules of engagement."

"Not at all, miss." He started for the door. "What shall you have for breakfast?"

"Diet Coke and a couple of those scones. Heated. With butter."

He smiled. "I've no Diet Coke, but I'll arrange for some to be delivered. Will tea do this morning?"

"As long as it's cold and sweet."

"Very well." He started for the door. "Will there be anything else?"

"As a matter of fact . . . What do you know about the old constitution? And the authority canon?"

"Nothing specific. Just that they were the laws of the land before the entail hitched our wagon to Brighton's. Why do you ask?"

"I'd like to read them. Catch up with the history. Do you know how I could get my hands on some old law books or the actual documents themselves?" Seamus had access to them, so she hoped the constitution and authority canon were accessible to her as well.

"I'm quite sure Mr. Burkhardt would be happy to provide you with the information."

"I'd like to do this on my own. Surely there's a university library laden with dusty old law books."

"Quite right." He laughed with a skip in his step and turned for the exit. "Let me see what I can arrange. Shall I keep this between us?"

"Ah, I can see we're going to get along great. Thank you, Jarvis."

"My pleasure."

"Oh!" She snapped her fingers. "I need a coat. Is it possible to do some shopping?"

"Miss, this you must discuss with Mr. Burkhardt. The media is keen about you now and how you dress, and Mr. Burkhardt can advise you."

"Right." She'd not fully considered the ramifications of yesterday's frenzy. "Am I in the morning paper?"

"You are."

"Can I see it?"

"There are three papers, miss. The *Informant*, the *Liberty Press*, and the *Sun Tattler.*"

"Three, huh? I'm in all of them?"

"I'm afraid so." He made a slight face.

"That bad?" Was this venture to make her a princess really going to work? For any of them? "What'd they say?"

"I didn't read the articles, but one referred to you as 'Our Redneck Royal.'"

"Redneck royal?" She made a face and anchored her hands on her hips. "It could've been worse."

Jarvis popped a wide smile. "Well done, miss. The attitude of a princess."

When he finally clicked the door closed behind him, Reggie collapsed into the nearest chair and turned it toward the window. *Redneck royal . . .*

Clutching Gram's fairy tale to her chest, she watched the last trails of the sunrise over the trees.

A princess is defined not by her title alone but by how she lives her life.

184

EIGHTEEN

*T*anner paused on the second-floor landing of Wettin Manor, the morning papers tucked under his arm, and peered down the hall that led to the governor's suite of offices.

The press surpassed themselves with the morning's stories. The papers ran front-page, full-page photos of Regina shoving a photographer. Even the paper of record, the *Liberty Press*, went tabloid with the headline, *Hessenberg Braces for American Invasion.*

The *Informant* went cheeky: *Meet Our Redneck Royal.*

But the *Sun Tattler* was Tanner's favorite. They ran a full-page photo of his derrière as he dove into the car with his legs flailing, before Regina could leave without him.

The cutline read, *Minister of Culture Displays His Better Side.*

What bothered him more was the media leak in the first place. He had half a mind to walk straight up to Seamus and demand an explanation.

But was it his place to do so? Seamus answered to the prime minister and the king, not to the Minister of Culture. In their ten years of friendship—mentor and mentee—Tanner had never resisted the formidable man in any way.

He'd listened and learned. Followed his counsel. Until yesterday, Tanner never had reason to doubt the old boy's integrity.

At the core of it, he owed Seamus, and shy of violating the Ten Commandments, he'd do just about anything for the man.

Tanner squared his shoulders, cleared his throat, and started for the governor's quarters.

Seamus, I say, what's this business all about? Arrest? Enemy of the state? And did you alert the media?

Tanner's heart thudded with determination to the same rhythm of his click-clacking heels, but as he rounded the corner, he stopped. Seamus knew things about him only a few others knew. Was it wise to risk making this press leak personal? Which was exactly how Seamus would see Tanner's confrontation.

He turned round. *Keep your nose where it belongs, chap.* In the business of Hessenberg's culture. Leave the media business to Henry and His Majesty, King Nathaniel II.

For a soft moment, he felt a coward. But truly, *this* was not his fight. If it became his, then he'd like to think he'd boldly enter the fray.

Louis met him at his office, falling in step, reading from his tablet. "The king is on his way with the prime minister. The archbishop will be along momentarily and Dickenson is driving in with Regina."

"Splendid. We need a plan for moving forward." Tanner shifted his thinking, his emotions, compartmentalizing, putting his disappointment in Seamus in one corner of his mind, his feelings for Regina in another, and the reality that he had a decision to make about Sunday's party in another. "Do we know of anyone who might take my place as Regina's mentor? Preferably a woman. We can give her name to the king."

Tanner needed to get back to normal. His life before Regina. Before the party invitation. Before this business with the press.

"What of Sibella Glenn, one of the museum curators? She's keen on culture and often appears on the talk programs discussing the Brighton and British royals."

"You're a genius, Louis." Tanner dropped the papers to his desk and headed for the tea cart. "She's perfect." A cup of hot, bitter tea ought to help sort out the things swirling in his heart.

"So you saw the papers?" When Tanner glanced up, Louis was leaning over his desk, reading the *Sun Tattler.* "Do I want to know how you got yourself in this pickle? Hanging out of the car, your legs flailing?"

"She wouldn't open the door." Tanner sipped his tea. Perfection. "When she rolled down the window, I plunged. She was about to leave without me."

Louis perched against the side of the desk, arms folded. "What do you make of her? The princess? Does she have the stuff?"

"Yes, I believe she does." Tanner took another hearty drink of his bitter tea as a light knock sounded on the door.

King Nathaniel and Henry arrived with the archbishop, Tanner's dad, in tow.

Louis went down to meet Dickenson and Regina. When she arrived in Tanner's office, they gathered round and King Nathaniel went straightaway to business.

"First, our apologies about the press frenzy yesterday, Regina." She shrugged. "No worry."

"You are most gracious. But I'd like to organize a plan to care for you the next few days while the barristers sort out this authority canon business along with Seamus's petition to the EU court. Tanner, I must return to Brighton this morning. Mum is introducing Susanna to several charities, and I'm told in no uncertain terms that I am to be there."

"Welcome to married life, Your Majesty," Henry said with a discreet chuckle.

"Your Majesty, can the governor really have her arrested?" Dad asked with a kind glance at Regina. The men remained standing as they talked and none had poured tea except for Tanner. Regina stood among them, withdrawn and shy.

"He can charge her, certainly. Then the police and the courts go to work. Seamus will have to build a case. But . . ."—Nathaniel looked them all in the eye—"he has the political persuasion and clout with the people to do it."

"But he can't build a solid case," Tanner said with confidence. "So he's waging his war in the press. I'm almost certain he's our leak."

"My guess as well, Tanner. None of us predicted this assault from the governor," Nathaniel said.

"Shall we go forward and organize a presser for Regina?" Tanner glanced around the circle, waiting for advice.

"Oh, I don't know, Tanner." Regina spoke for the first time. "I'm not prepared."

He regarded her, and for a flash moment he felt the warm wetness of her tears on his skin. And he changed his mind about Sibella Glenn. He'd be her mentor, and protector, as long as the king saw fit.

"We're going about this all wrong." The king moved around the room, lost in his own thoughts. "No presser. Regina is right. She's not ready for the questions they'll ask. Nor their fervor. But the key here is not the press, our actions as leaders, nor what Seamus does. The key is Regina."

"Me? What can I do? I'm so new . . . so unsure . . . of everything."

"Quite right," Nathaniel said. "Nevertheless, you are the princess minus the official formalities. Tanner,"—the king's countenance changed as he formed an idea—"let's slow things down just a bit. The EU court has not yet agreed to hear the case. We might be fretting for nothing, but we have the princess here, so let's get her out and about in the city." The king turned to Regina. "You shall see the sights. Listen to the people. Forget the petition and Seamus's threats. Take the weekend to tour around. Have fun! Embrace the beauty of Hessenberg."

"Quite right," Henry added. "Let her meet the people one on one."

"The press will be all over us, sir." Tanner held up his hands in quiet objection. "We're organizing security this morning, but if we go out in the streets . . . and people get word . . . it will be a madhouse."

"I see your point." Nathaniel pressed his fingers to his chin, thinking. "Susanna and I went out in disguise recently. You could always—"

"Let's do it." Regina moved to the middle of the convocation. "Let's get out in the city, among the people." She looked toward Tanner. "I came here to see what Hessenberg was all about, so let's do this. Embrace the good, the bad, and the ugly." She raised her chin, squared her shoulders. But Tanner could see her trembling beneath the surface.

"Take her to Wisteria Park," Dad said. "There's always something going on there."

"But first"—she jabbed the air with her finger—"I need a coat."

"A splendid idea," Nathaniel said. "Take her to the shops. Melinda House will be more than eager to clothe the princess, the future Grand Duchess of Hessenberg."

"How about the pubs, like the Fence & Anchor?" Henry offered.

"The Fence & Anchor . . . stellar idea, Henry." The king patted his prime minister on the back.

"Treat her like the princess she is, Tanner. Woo her, and she'll woo the people."

Woo her? Shops and pubs? The park? She was his sovereign. His royal charge. Not his girlfriend. Or even his friend.

Did the king and prime minister, his dad, see they were fashioning for them a first-rate *date?*

Tanner peeked at Regina. Her cheeks were a bit rosier than they had been a second ago. And he knew one thing. He wanted to spend time with her more than he'd wanted anything in a long, long time.

"Tanner, I'm confident you can handle this well. Regina, I have full faith in you." Nathaniel glanced at his watch. "I hate to lay a plan and be off, but I must." He shook Tanner's hand. "Let's reconvene on Monday. Miles"—he turned to the archbishop— "perhaps we can begin preparing the oath ceremony. Regina, if you're willing, we'll proceed with the official ceremony next week."

"Wow. O–okay. I guess we'll see."

"You've got the weekend. Think it over. Pray." Nathaniel lightly gripped her arms. "Prayer makes all the difference in my life and decision making."

"I'm familiar with the power of prayer."

"Good. Then use it." He started for the door. "Miles, you'll gather the ceremony script and sacraments."

"Will do, Your Majesty."

With the king and prime minister gone, Tanner retreated to his desk, waiting for his dad to leave. But he lingered by the office door. "Is there anything else, sir?"

"Your mother was curious to know if you'd received an invitation from Trude for the twins' birthday." Dad took a few steps farther into the office.

"I did, yes." Tanner folded the newspapers in half and stuffed them in the rubbish bin. He did not want to discuss this in front of Regina.

"Your mother talks of nothing else." Dad laughed softly, scratching his head. At fifty-eight, his hair was still thick and blond. "She's been shopping at least three times, buying presents. And of course, nothing in her closet is good enough to wear. She must have four new dresses. I warn her they probably won't remember her, but I'm not sure she really cares. She wants to see them."

Dad locked his hands behind his back as if waiting for Tanner to join in the conversation. This private, personal exchange in front of Regina was highly inappropriate. Besides, when had his father ever approached something so personal so . . . openly?

Tanner cut a glance at Regina who was at the window, surveying the city. It was her. She had this odd effect on people that made them want to open their hearts.

"Dad, is there anything else?" Tanner reached around for his chair, his gaze averted. "I need to get this day organized with Regina."

"No, no, nothing else. I'll be off then." At the door he paused and started to say something, but then simply bid good-bye to Regina.

"Tanner?" Dad cleared his throat. "We're here if you need us, son."

"Have a good day, sir." Tanner fussed with the items on his desk, surprised and unnerved by a soft blur of tears leaking from his eyes to the dry, hollow wells of his soul.

In all her days, Reggie never imagined she'd hear the words "I'd like to introduce you to your security detail, Clarence and Todd."

"How do you do?" Reggie curled her arms against her torso, guarding against the cold, making her way down the manor's steps. The sun sat high in the sky, but its warmth had not yet reached the shadows lurking between Wettin Manor's stone columns.

"Regina,"—Tanner followed her, offering her a large navy-blue cardigan with a big KU crest on the breast pocket—"wear this until we purchase your coat."

She took the sweater, and the very action of Tanner giving it to her wrapped her with warmth. "Do we really need two security guards?"

"Do you not remember yesterday? The media mess?"

"I remember you riding around town with your face planted

in the passenger seat and your feet flailing in the air." She slipped her arms through the fine-wool sleeves. "Whose is this?" When she lowered her arms, the sleeves slinked past her hands and dangled near her knees.

"Mine. From university. I keep it in my office."

"So ... are we ... like ... going steady now?" She grinned, rolling up the sleeves, liking the feel of the words on her heart. She'd never gone steady and, well, it was on her bucket list.

"Har-har. You're quite chipper today." He started down the rest of the steps toward the black SUV and the two serious, Navy Seal–looking dudes waiting by an open passenger side door. "Did you see the papers?"

"I did, and the one with the shot of you in all your glory got me laughing—"

"If you'd have opened the door like I asked ..."

"You didn't say please." Reggie walked toward the waiting SUV, the click of her boot heels resounding.

Something about this morning—sitting in the parlor ... staring out over the lawn toward the forest ... talking with Jarvis ... looking at Gram's portrait ... reading the fairy tale with a whole new view of things ... talking to Jesus ... talking to the king and his men—gave her peace. Gave her a bit of confidence.

She'd heard about faith and trust in God her whole life. But not once had she lifted her wings and tried to catch a current knowing nothing was beneath her but the invisible hand of God.

College? Safe because Daddy and Sadie were across town.

CPA degree? Safe because she was good with numbers.

The shop? Safe because Al was there.

Even hanging around Mark. Safe. Because she had known him her whole life.

But princess of a small North Sea nation? Terrifying, and there was only one Man who could see to her success. Jesus himself. If he could hang on a cross for her, she could scope out a princess gig for him. If, of course, this whole journey was his idea in the first place. She wouldn't know for sure unless she lifted her wings.

Tanner stepped around her to hold open the back door of the SUV. She slipped inside and Tanner went around, joining her from the other side. The security goons sat up front, Clarence behind the wheel.

Reggie rode down to Strauberg and through the city streets in peaceful silence, the clear day beginning to fill the streets with a warm light.

"This is Market Avenue," Tanner said when Clarence turned right at the light. It was a broad street with thin, tall shade trees and Victorian lamps dividing the lanes. "Three hundred years ago, this was where all commerce happened." He tapped his window and lightly touched her arm. "See through those buildings? The bay, South Port. The ships from Germany and Italy, all southern countries, dock here."

Reggie leaned into the fresh burst of wind as Tanner powered down his window, and the clean, subtle fragrance that she'd come to know as "Tanner." He intrigued her. He was a puzzle. She could see most of the pieces but not how they all fit together.

Beyond the window, however, the sun created a golden stream in the middle of all the blue-green water, and Reggie drew a deep breath.

"Beautiful, isn't it?" Tanner said just over her shoulder.

"It is, yes. Very."

But when Reggie glanced at him, he wasn't watching the bay but her. With his very intense blue eyes. *Sir Blue Eyes.*

She jerked back into her seat, her heart snapping and popping, a funny, disturbing sensation burning up her middle.

"Sir." Clarence peered at them through the rearview mirror. "Turning down the lane for Melinda House. Please close your window."

The SUV ambled down a narrow, cobblestone lane nestled

between two tall buildings and thick with shadows. Clarence stopped by a small, lean door.

"Wait here, please." Todd stepped out and disappeared beyond the door.

Reggie turned to Tanner. "For real? Security? This is crazy."

"Recall yesterday."

"I know, but that was at Wettin Manor. Someone leaked I was there, right? This is some dark back alley. Who's going to know we're here?"

"Regina, a photograph of you is probably worth thousands if not hundreds of thousands of dollars. You're the new royal on a very old royal front. You saw what happened to the British royal family when Kate officially came on the scene? Even before she was official . . . men will stalk you, haunt you." He gently held her chin. "Hear me, please. Never, ever let your guard down."

Todd emerged from the door a few minutes later and opened Reggie's door. "Go straight in, miss. Up the stairs to the second floor."

"Wait for me." Tanner exited his side of the SUV and met her at the alleyway door, leading her inside.

"This cloak-and-dagger stuff feels so over the top."

"Yes, love, but this cloak-and-dagger stuff will keep you safe."

Love? He stumbled over the word, but kept rising up the stairs, talking, without peeking back at her. But, ho boy, the word landed on her heart sweet and tender.

Good grief, she *was* crushing on Tanner Burkhardt.

They landed on the second floor and stepped into an open loft area with brick walls and hardwood floors. To her right, the loft looked out over a gleaming showroom through a steel railing. From the exposed ceiling, white lanterns hung suspended from thin black pipes, and soft music sweetened the air.

Up front, floor-to-ceiling mirrors were anchored into the brick, and the glass gleamed, catching the lights and twinkling them back into the room.

"Your Majesty, welcome, welcome." A lean, platinum-haired woman in a tightly tailored chartreuse suit was striding her way. "This is most exciting. I'm Melinda." She curtseyed. "We are thrilled you chose Melinda House as your first designer."

"Melinda,"—Tanner pressed his hand lightly against Reggie's back—"thank you for this special appointment. After yesterday's media mess, I thought we should take every precaution and come in the back door."

"Agreed! Think nothing of it. We do value privacy and confidentiality for all of our clients." She clasped her hands at her waist, smiling all the while, eyes glued to Reggie.

She was starting to feel self-conscious. What was this fashion guru thinking? Hubba, but we got our hands full with this one. Mack, bring out the industrial-strength girdle and push-up bra.

"Well, shall we get started?" Melinda moved toward the mirrors in quick, short steps, hindered by the tight hem of her long skirt. "We've selected several coats for you to try, Your Majesty. We also took the liberty of choosing a few of our newest dresses we'd be delighted for you to debut."

"Reggie. Please, just call me Reggie." She grabbed Tanner's arm as he started to move, letting Melinda walk toward the coats without them. "You've got to be kidding me. Designer coats. *Debut?* Don't you have a Target or Burlington Coat Factory around here? All I need is a simple coat."

"Melinda, hold on, please." His eyes glanced past Reggie's and she stepped back, surprised at what she saw beneath those blues. Discouragement. As if he was letting her down, that his effort did not please her and it . . . *hurt* him.

She pressed her palm to her forehead. "Never mind, it's okay. Let's look at the coats." When would she learn everything wasn't about her? Tanner was trying his darnedest to do his job.

"Are you sure?"

"I'm sorry, Tanner. It's just that . . . Shew, this is all so thrilling yet terrifying. Last week I was a wrench jockey. This week I'm a royal princess . . . kind of gives a girl whiplash."

"Right, I'm sorry, I didn't think—"

"No, no, it's okay. Just, zoom,"—she sliced her hand through the air—"zero to sixty." She linked her arm through his, wondering for the first time if this wacky journey was every bit as much about Tanner as it was about her.

"Help me pick out something that will go well with jail wear."

"Regina,"—he held her back—"you're not going to jail. Seamus can huff and puff all he likes, that arrogant bloke and his binky pipe, but he cannot make it stick. He'd have to buy off the entire European court, and I daresay he's not got enough reputation or financial wherewithal to do so."

"Even so . . . what sway does the court have?"

"More than they should, I'll say, but not enough to throw you in the tower."

"There's a tower?" She made a face.

"Metaphorically speaking. Listen, love,"—there was *that* word again—"they can rule in favor of his petition on behalf of the Hessenberg people, but that will only be the beginning. Then it's a fight for government control." Tanner paced off, the reflective light highlighting his thick blond hair. "You can bet that's what Seamus is about . . . making himself some sort of supreme leader. Perhaps even the Grand Duke. He doesn't mind a royal house. He just wants it to be his." He circled back to Reggie. "I daresay he's bitten off more than he can stuff in his blooming pipe."

"What's with you and his pipe?"

"Oh, it just annoys me." He reached for her hand. "No more talk of Seamus or lawsuits or arrests." He walked backward, peering down at her. "I think we both need some giggles . . . a spot of fun. And the king ordered a day of frolicking, so let's obey him and enjoy the day."

"Frolicking?" Reggie laughed, quickening her pace to keep

up, not wanting her hand to slip from his. "He never said frolicking. I was listening. But you, however, said frolicking." The word rolled off her tongue and tickled her ears. Teased her spirit. Made her laugh.

"I do believe you're mocking me," Tanner said, feigning a weak frown. But his eyes were bright with humor.

"No, just loving the sound of frolicking." Reggie tried for a Hessen accent, failing miserably, which made Tanner laugh. "After shopping, can we take the Mercedes out and race up the hill again? Now that's a frolicking good time."

Tanner slapped his hand to his chest. "Be kind to my weak heart, dear Regina." He swooped his arm wide and took an exaggerated bow, but oh, his words . . . anything but teasing.

She released his hand, trembling from the feelings he stirred in her, and faced the waiting, ever-smiling Melinda. Reggie didn't know about Tanner's weak heart, but hers was weakening by the second.

Just a crush. A schoolgirl crush. Don't overthink this, Reg.

But mercy, he was charming and confident with a James Dean kind of smolder. Something dark lurked beneath the surface, longing to come out. She just knew it.

Besides all of that, he was handsome. Poster-on-her-wall, heartthrob handsome.

"Your Majesty—"

"Call me Reggie, or Regina. Please."

"All right." Melinda gave her a curt nod, her perfected smile faltering.

"Or miss. Miss is good." The woman seemed reluctant to call her by her first name.

"Well, *miss*, here we go . . . Melinda reset her smile and slipped a coat from a silk-wrapped hanger.

Tanner, meanwhile, took a seat behind Reggie, choosing an oval-shaped, white leather ottoman.

"This is our latest." Melinda held up a long, creamy beige coat, exchanging it for Tanner's college sweater. "In fact, after Mr. Burkhardt's call last night, we rushed it from the factory."

When Reggie had slipped on the coat, Melinda situated it on her shoulders, belted it closed, and stood back with a complete look of wonder.

"Marvelous," she said with a glance at Tanner. "We are so proud of this coat. Doesn't it accent her gorgeous red hair so well? Stunning. Just stunning."

Reggie could see Tanner angling to catch her reflection in the mirror. "The coat is beautiful. Regina?"

She made a face. Glanced at Melinda, then Tanner through the mirror, and smoothed down the coarse material with her hand. "Well—"

"It's mohair. All the rage this season."

"I–I don't think I've ever owned mohair."

"So what do you think, miss?" Melinda walked around Reggie, her chin in her hand, inspecting. "We've had a lot of interest in this design, and we really wanted to make a splash with it at the spring show. But, Your Majesty, we'd be honored for you to wear it this fall. It'd be the only one like it in the world."

Ho boy. No pressure.

"Regina, be honest," Tanner said.

"All right . . ." She faced her audience of two. "I look like a lit match. Red hair, tight beige coat that goes past my knees. If the press sees me in this, I'll go from redneck royal to Princess Match-on-Fire."

Tanner snort-coughed into his fist while Melinda frowned, a solid steel glint in her glare.

"I completely disagree, but if you're not comfortable,"—she moved to help Reggie out of the coat—"we've other styles."

"Look, let's just save some time here," Reggie said as Melinda returned the coat to the rack. "I need something simple and serviceable, every day, you know? I like blue and black, maybe green if it's the right green. Otherwise, I look like some kind of rose."

Tanner's laugh popped once, then faded with his cough and throat-clearing. Reggie winked at him through the mirror while Melinda sorted through the coats. She liked making him laugh because it sounded good on him.

"May I suggest you start thinking more like a princess rather than, well, whatever it was you did before?"

"Restored classic cars. Before that I was a CPA."

Melinda cast her a dark, hooded gaze, her expression tight with frustration and confusion. "Your Majesty—"

"Reggie."

"Or Regina," Tanner tagged on.

"R–Regina," Melinda began, slow and deliberate, "women around the world will write blogs about what you wear and how you wear it, *when* you wear it. The copycat designers will scurry to knock off our originals. Don't you want to make a bold, brilliant statement with your first royal coat, as it were?"

"I appreciate your insight, Melinda. I do. All of these coats look . . . lovely. But let's face it, I may not be the princess of anything for very long, so for now, let's keep it simple. How about a car coat or something? My mom used to have one." A sudden missing-mama splashed Reggie's heart and seeped into her voice. "In fact, if she were alive, she'd be the one standing here with you now instead of me."

Melinda regarded her for a moment, her lips forming a question she did not verbalize, her fashion designer demeanor giving way to one of a woman talking to another about the loss of her mom.

"Then a car coat it is. Navy blue? You won't look like a match or a human rose." She allowed herself a soft laugh. "Lost me own mum a year back. I still miss her."

"Oh, I'm so sorry. Were you close?"

"Talked by phone every morning and every night." Melinda

offered up a simple but beautiful coat. "Were you close to your mum?"

"She was killed in a car crash when I was twelve. So yes and no. I didn't get to know her as an adult because some guy ran a light and took her from us."

"Oh, that's rubbish. Pure rubbish. I'm so sorry, Princess. Rotten thing for a girl to lose her mum at twelve, just when she needs her most."

"I had Gram for a while, but she was ninety-nine and not always keen on what was going on. My dad, though, he was ..." Her heart yearned for her daddy. "Amazing."

Her voice mail to him had yet to be answered. But that was his way. Reggie pictured him sitting up to the table with Sadie ...

"Reg called. Says she's doing all right. Ah, dinner looks good, Sadie. Don't you know that crew on the south side had me straightening out their mess all day? I never did get to lunch."

Then sometime in the next day or two, he'd remember and call her back.

"Me own dad was a louse, but I'm glad for you girls with good ones. There." Melinda patted Reggie's shoulders and stood back. "What do you think?"

Reggie examined her reflection front and back, then checked with Tanner. He had the same look on his face as when he showed her the bay. Heat burst beneath her skin and sank into her soul, lighting the dark, cold regions where love had not yet shone its light.

"Perfect," he said, shifting his gaze, resituating his sweater over his leg.

"I'll take it. How much?" Reggie fixed her thoughts on the coat, on Melinda. Not on the way Tanner made her feel. She'd best get ahold of herself. Falling for Tanner in any way, shape, or form would taint her decision-making process.

"No charge. It's our gift to you. Welcome to Hessenberg, Princess Regina." Melinda clapped her hands together, then held them at her waist.

"I'm sorry, I can't do that." Reggie worked the buttons to remove the coat.

"Wh–why not, miss? It's our gift . . . to you."

"One thing Daddy taught me a long time ago. There's no such thing as free. If I take this coat now, I'll be obliged to you. Then sometime down the road, an issue of some kind will crop up and I'll find myself compromised because I accepted a free coat. I don't know squat about politics, being a princess, or being a fashion designer, but in the CPA and the car business, the 'I'll scratch-your-back-if-you-scratch-mine' thing usually leaves some poor knucklehead bleeding and in trouble."

"I see." Melinda. Stiff and solemn. Insulted.

"Melinda, it's not you. Please hear me. I don't think you'd hold a car coat over my head, but if I take this from you, then I have to take gifts from other designers and on and on. Besides, my daddy also taught me, 'A laborer is worthy of her hire.'"

"Melinda," Tanner said, standing behind Reggie, "send the bill to my office."

"Hey, no, wait." Reggie pressed her hand to Tanner's chest. "I don't want to owe you either. I can pay." How much could a car coat cost? Couple hundred?

"This particular coat is two thousand pounds, miss."

Reggie spun toward Melinda. "For a car coat?" She itched to remove the thing and make do with Tanner's sweater, but the look on Melinda's face said, *"Don't do it."*

"Send the bill to my office." Tanner.

Reggie sighed. "Yes, send the bill to his office." She wagged her finger at the Minister of Culture. "But I'm paying you back."

He made a wry face, making her laugh. "I'm sure you will. One way or another."

Their banter was smooth. Light. Flirty. Reggie already liked the coat ten times more because it would forever remind her of today. Of Tanner.

Melinda suggested trying on a few dresses, but Reggie was done with shopping.

"Maybe next week?" She checked with Tanner. "Do I need a dress?"

"You didn't bring one?"

"No . . . I packed so fast . . . I didn't think . . . just grabbed my usual jeans and T-shirts."

"Melinda," Tanner said, "select a few of your favorites with Her Majesty in mind and send them to the palace. Her lady's maid can help her choose a dress."

"What of accessories? Shoes? Handbags?"

"Send those as well."

Reggie shot him a look. "What kind of budget does your office have?"

"Never mind." He tried to sound stern, but his twitching lips gave him away. "Melinda, thank you. We appreciate your kindness and discretion."

Tanner backed toward the stairs, motioning for Reggie to follow.

"Thank you, Melinda." Reggie offered Melinda her hand, but when the designer reached for her, Reggie drew her into a hug. "Sorry I'm not a good shopper. And . . . sorry about your mum. It does get easier."

Melinda's stiff posture relaxed and she returned Reggie's hug. "You don't know how much that means to me, Your Majesty."

With glistening eyes, Melinda escorted them to the door, asking about the rest of their day, agreeing that showing Reggie the city and taking tea at the Fence & Anchor, a favorite pub of the locals, was a splendid way to get a feel for Hessenberg. Reggie was about to start down the stairs when Melinda snapped her fingers, her eyes bright with an idea.

"Want to have some real fun, Mr. Burkhardt? Walk about the city unhindered?"

He narrowed his gaze. "What do you have in mind?"

Melinda turned to Reggie. "Your Majesty, are you game?"

She liked the woman's enthusiasm. "Sure, I'm game. Tanner?"

He hesitated. Then, "Y–yeah, I–I guess."

"Oh, this is marvelous. I'll be right back." And Melinda ran off.

Tanner emerged from the loft's side door with Regina's laughter ringing in his ears. She'd laughed when Melinda came out of her storage room. Laughed while the designer presented her idea. And while wholeheartedly agreeing to the entire scheme, completely ignoring his protests.

"Regina, I can't do this." Tanner peered down the sidewalk, praying no one saw him.

"Yes you can. This is hilarious."

Clarence and Todd exited the SUV, smirks on their broad faces.

"Excuse me, but we were waiting for the Minister of Culture and the Princess of Hessenberg," Clarence said, walking around the back of the vehicle and stepping up on the curb. "We're going to need to see some ID."

"But it's obvious, Clarence." Todd crossed his arms, his feet in a wide stance. "It's Sonny and Cher."

Regina started to sing "I Got You, Babe," but lost the melody in her laughter.

Next to her, Tanner growled and frowned, his straight, bad-bangs wig twisting in the soft breeze. "We are going to look more conspicuous than if we didn't have on this getup." He shook the fringe of his suede vest.

"Don't be a rotten egg." Reggie flipped the long, silky black ends of her Cher wig. "What do you think? Do I make a good brunette?"

"No, your red hair is marvelous." Tanner turned back to the door, holding up the bags with their real clothes. "I'm going to change."

"No you're not." Reggie motioned to Clarence with a flip of her hand. "Grab him and let's go."

So *now* she steps into her authority. Fine. But this was a foul way to do it. Mumbling to himself, Tanner walked around to his side of the SUV. How could Melinda do this to him? Just last month he'd given her first go at organizing Hessenberg's first fashion show in decades.

"So," Reggie said, continuing to explain to Clarence and Todd, "Melinda had this '60s thing in the spring and kept the costumes, thinking she'd need them again. So here we are, Sonny and Cher."

"Not really, we just look like a couple of ill-dressed hippies with bad hair." Tanner peered down at Reggie, who was doing no wrong in that bodysuit and striped, multicolored hip-huggers.

"You don't have to wear the wig if you don't want to, Tanner." She curled her lip at him. "You're such a fusspot."

"Drive on, Clarence." Tanner was sure the big man was snickering, but he didn't care.

He wanted to move, get into motion, and leave his creeping, yearning thoughts behind. Every molecule in his formerly rugby-trained body wanted to grab that Cher imposter and kiss her until one of them couldn't breathe.

No mistake, she could be as annoying as a rain drip on a steel pipe. And she made it very hard to play by his own rules. To *not* get his heart involved.

"Where to, sir?"

"City center. Wisteria Park."

Regina peered out her window as Clarence steered the motorcar through the midday traffic. Tanner exhaled, easing the grip on his heart.

His king sent him on a precarious mission and he'd found . . . her. And maybe a little piece of himself.

"What's that building?" Regina tapped her window. "It's gorgeous."

"St. John's Chapel." Tanner knocked on the back of the driver's seat. "Clarence, can we park, walk a bit?"

It took a few passes for Clarence to choose a parking situation, but once he did, Tanner stepped with Regina out of the dark SUV and into the blue, crisp day.

Clarence took point while Todd watched the rear. Tanner walked beside Regina, negotiating the bustling sidewalk. Their strides hit the same rhythm, and everything he hated about his costume evaporated because he was walking with her.

"What's the population of Hessenberg?" Regina sidestepped a hustling lass in a yellow coat.

"Five hundred thousand in Strauberg. Four million on the duchy."

"What's the GDP?"

"GDP?" Impressive.

"You can take the girl out of accounting but you can't always take the accounting out of the girl."

"Last report of our gross domestic product was around three hundred billion."

She stopped. "And the country has financial woes?"

"Ah, clever, you understand what so few do."

"Well, I paid attention in a few of my finance and econ classes."

"Our financial relationship with Brighton has not been handled wisely. We're like codependent sisters, taking each other down. We've lived beyond our means, as well. Much like America."

"Touché. That is a problem." And she walked on.

Around the corner, St. John's Chapel came into view again. Regina pressed toward the gothic-styled columns, jumping into the street nearly ahead of Clarence.

"Can we go inside?"

"I believe we can." Tanner started down another narrow side street.

"What's the story of this place?" Regina skipped along beside him.

"St. John's?" Tanner knew the history from the time his father served here. "It was founded by a Dutch missionary who came to the island in 1682. He had a vision of Jesus telling him to start a church that prays." They stopped at the short, thin chapel steps leading to the narthex. "He built a thatched dwelling where we now stand, and three hundred some odd years later here we are, with this grand structure built late in the nineteenth century."

"The real question is, do they still hold prayer meetings? Let's go inside and see." Regina dashed up the steps, and her excitement charged him to see his city, his country, his life with fresh eyes.

The narthex was a simple, pure area with a red marble floor and white walls. No paintings or religious symbols.

Tanner tiptoed toward the sanctuary doors. But Regina held back.

"Can you feel it?" She breathed deep, eyes closed.

"Feel what?"

"The millions of prayers. The peace. The presence."

Tanner closed his eyes, trying to *feel* what she described. But nothing. All he got was a blast of hot air from the overhead vent for his trouble.

"This was the official church of the royal family," he said, reaching for the sanctuary doors.

Regina stepped in with a "Wow" and awe, her white go-go boots a stark contrast to the deep-red carpet. "Tanner, this is incredible."

As he followed her, his shoes, which were his own because he refused the horrid ankle boots Melinda offered him, sank into the plush floor covering.

Hands tucked in her coat pockets, Regina walked the red-carpeted aisle, gazing up at the ribbed trumpet beams of the nave's arching ceiling.

"Look at that." She pointed overhead. "It's like the architect had in mind that they'd blast a sound to the heavens." She slipped her hand over the top of the pews. "Stained glass. How old do you reckon these windows are?"

"Not awfully. St. John's was hit with bombs during both wars." Tanner trailed after her. "Most of the windows were blown out except that one right there." He gestured to the image of a resurrected Christ at the end of the nave, behind the pulpit.

When Dad served here, Tanner used to stare at the image the whole service, imagining the return of Jesus, seeing him in the clouds, and Tanner nearly scared himself out of the faith.

What if he wasn't worthy ... well, he wasn't now, was he? Not that God couldn't or wouldn't forgive him. Tanner just didn't see how he had the right to ask.

"What are these?" Regina bent next to the gold plates on the sides of the front pews. "Ciphers? Here's one like the one in Gram's fairy tale. GD PF I R."

"Grand Duke, Prince Francis the First, Regent. St. John's is the coronation abbey."

"Gram's coronation would've been held here?"

"Most likely."

A forceful whisper came from the back of the sanctuary. "Might I help you?"

"Begging your pardon, we're just looking." No way was Tanner going to introduce himself to the bishop as the Minister of Culture wearing a bad wig and psychedelic bell-bottoms.

"Yes, you can." Regina skirted around Tanner and toward the bishop. "Do you still have prayer meetings here?"

"We do, yes. Every morning at six and seven. Every evening at nine and ten."

"Good." Regina nodded with a sigh, hands back in her coat pockets. "That makes me feel good."

Tanner couldn't confirm it—he wasn't even sure Regina knew—but he had a subtle feeling some part of her heart had just made a decision about her future as Hessenberg's regent.

NINETEEN

long about sunset, Reggie sat on a knoll in Wisteria Park, still dressed as Cher, watching a serious rugby pickup game with a bunch of college dudes. The breeze through the trees was cold on her face, but the setting sun on her back warmed her heart.

It had been a fun day. Touring the city, seeing the business and shopping districts. Eating something called puffs at a bakery not far from here.

"What was the name of the bakery? Where we got the puffs?"

"Loudermilk's Bakery." Tanner, still dressed as Sonny, jumped up, hands cupped around his mouth. "Pass, you blooming ox, pass." Then he moaned and sat down. "Everyone wants to be a star."

"Do you?"

"Do I what?"

"Want to be a star?"

"I want to go for supper. I'm famished." Up on his feet again, shouting instructions to the team with the ball. "Call a ruck! Call a ruck!"

Regina laughed, reaching up and tugging him back toward the ground. "You're like Dad when he watches the Seminoles play."

"I used to be out there with the lads. But now all I do is mostly watch on the telly or from the sidelines of a park. Most depressing is that I get to spend all day cooped up in an office wearing a suit and tie." Tanner returned to his seat on the knoll. "I really need to get in a city league. Play on the weekends," he murmured. More to himself than to Reggie.

"Tanner, what's with you and your dad?"

"What do you mean, what's with me and Dad?"

She thought he might not like her asking, but she couldn't help herself. "You know, the archbishop? Burkhardt. The one with the same last name as you. The one who tried to talk to you in your office this morning and you were all like"—she lowered her voice, trying to sound masculine—"'Anything else, sir?'"

"I'm sorry, but such questions are not allowed."

"Not allowed? May I ask why not?" She leaned to see his face, but he focused on the rugby game.

"That-a-way, lads. That's how to score." Tanner applauded the scoring team.

"Tanner?"

"You hungry?" He stood, reaching for her hand, helping her up. "The Fence & Anchor has the best stew and warm sourdough bread. Just a few blocks this way." He led her down the knoll and across the park.

From the corner of her eye, Reggie spotted Clarence moving in front of them, and when she glanced back, Todd was only a few feet behind her.

"What happened? Did he misunderstand your youth? Was he a mean father? What?"

Tanner stopped short, causing Reggie to bump into him. "Don't go analyzing my relationship with my dad from a sixty-second exchange."

"He was trying to talk to you in your office and you all but ignored him."

"He was prying."

"No, he was asking you about a party that your mum is super excited to attend. Is this a family event or something?"

"Regina, let's just say I have a different relationship with my father than you have with yours." Tanner headed around the side of the park toward another tree-lined avenue.

"One where you are rude when he's being kind?"

"I know my father. Don't try to second-guess me. He wasn't being nice."

"Wow, really. Then I'd hate to see what you consider cruel."

"Change the subject. I don't care to bother with this conversation. We are supposed to be having fun and all that."

"Sometimes it's fun to, you know,"—she mimed pulling something from her heart—"let go of stuff, air it out, get free."

"And you are an expert on this?" A certain edge sharpened his words.

"No, but, boy howdy, I've had to do my share of letting go. Can't hang on to stuff when your mama is there in the morning and gone that night."

"Then let me ask you . . . What's with the chap, the one with the dark hair and capped teeth? Mark Harper, was it?" Tanner moved out of the park, stopping at the corner light.

"What about him?" He noticed the thing between her and Mark? "Nothing. Well, not much. Just an old friend. And his teeth aren't capped. I know. Crazy. Those are his real choppers."

The light changed, and Tanner charged into the street with his Sonny wig flopping about his angular jaw. Reggie scurried to keep in stride.

"Tanner, why do you ask about Mark?"

"Are you honest with him? He's into you, Regina, in case you didn't know."

She laughed. "I know, but the question is, how did you know?"

"I've got eyes."

"Are you jealous?"

"Certainly not," he barked.

"Hallo, Sonny and Cher," a male voice boomed from the direction of the waiting cars. "I got you, babe."

Tanner sprinted to the curb while Reggie swung around to see an older man hanging out of his car window, waving. She smiled and waved back. But Clarence and Todd closed ranks fast and escorted her out of the street.

"Regina, don't draw attention to yourself," Tanner clipped.

"I wasn't. I was drawing attention to Cher. I'm sure she'd thank me."

Tanner muttered under his breath. "I'll get Melinda for talking me into this."

Reggie stopped. Smack in the middle of the sidewalk. "If you're going to be grumpy, let's just forget this."

Grumpy faced the street, hands on his hips, his jaw tense. "My apologies." He fixed his blue gaze on her. "Nothing but frolicking fun from this moment on. Frown gone." He forced a smile while adjusting his attitude. "Grumpy to happy."

"Just like that?" She grinned and started down the walk with him. "You're a zero-to-sixty kind of bloke, aren't you?"

He sighed with a slight shake of his head, adding in a light laugh. "Regina, I do believe you've solved a mystery I've been trying to unravel for thirty-two years. Yes, I'm zero to sixty."

The Fence & Anchor sat on the corner of Gilden Avenue and Fleet Street. The exterior was of hewn stone and stained wood with multi-paned windows shaded by a green awning. When Tanner opened the door for her, the wind kicked up around the corner and skirted in ahead of her, causing the place mats on vacant tables to flutter to the floor.

A male voice commanded, "Close the door, you bloomers."

Reggie squinted through the dim, yellow light toward the sound of the voice. A wiry-haired man at the bar was flagging them in with his hand.

"Let's sit back there." Tanner lightly touched her elbow, leading her to a corner booth.

Scanning the room, Reggie felt she'd been here before, the same sense she'd had in the chapel sanctuary. Like a home. Warm and cozy. As if she'd been invited into some inner club or sanctum.

Scooting into the booth, Reggie removed her coat. "I love this place already." Up front, Clarence and Todd had taken a table by the door and were already engaged with the server.

"Wait until a match comes on. The place will fill up and you won't be able to hear your own thoughts." Tanner hung his coat and hers on the rack behind the booth. "And I'm losing this thing." He slipped off his wig. "Good-bye, Sonny Bono. No more American hippie for me."

"Can't say the costumes didn't do the job, Tanner. We walked around all day without being harassed."

She watched him as he took his seat across from her, combed his fingers through his hair, then removed the faux suede, fringed vest. He was so controlled on the outside, but something untamed boiled beneath, trying to be free.

He caught her staring and she glanced away. His eyes, so blue, so intense, disturbed her. "Do you want tea?" he said.

"No . . ." she croaked, removing her wig. "Um, yes, tea. Hot for a change. Sweet."

"Welcome to the Fence & Anchor." The server stepped up to the table. "My name's Gemma." She was short and round, wearing a lifetime supply of blue eye shadow and pink lipstick. She squinted at Reggie, wagging a pencil at her. "I know you, right? But from where?"

Reggie shifted in her seat, shooting Tanner a look. *What do I do?*

"She's from the telly . . . *Talent Factor* . . . the American dancing juggler." Tanner spoke without even a hint of a smile. "I'm her, or rather *his*"—he chuckled and winked—"talent agent, Malcolm Jabberwaller."

"You don't say?" Her blue-lidded eyes widened. "You're that dancing juggler? I loved your act. Can I have your autograph?"

Reggie made a face. *What now, genius?*

"Actually, we're . . . . shh,"—Tanner touched his finger to his lips—"on the down low. We'd appreciate it if you'd keep this to yourself."

"Oh, right-o, naturally." Gemma lowered her voice and leaned toward Reggie. "I thought you were really good."

She smiled, trying not to laugh. "Thank you."

"Gemma, bring us two pots of tea, one sweet, one bitter, a basket of your freshest, warmest, sourdough rolls, and two steamy bowls of lamb stew."

When she scooted off, Reggie gaped at Tanner, then snorted behind her hand. "A dancing juggler? For real?"

"There actually was a redheaded dancing juggler on *Talent Factor*, whom I believe was not a *she* but a *he* and his act was horrid. You can't make this stuff up, Regina. And he-she was American."

"And you think I can pass as a horrid he-she juggling act?"

"Oh, and lower your voice a bit when you speak." He grinned, scratching his throat, the lingering somberness fading from his eyes. "And try for raspy."

Reggie hammered the table with her fist. "You beat all." She flicked her gaze at him. "This is payback for making you dress like Sonny, isn't it?"

"You betcha." He was so adorable when his confidence rode high.

Voices rose from the bar where a cluster of men wearing the same color jerseys gathered, talking and gesturing at the televisions mounted in the corners and behind the bar. At the tables, several men in work shirts and matching trousers sat with their hands clasped around their beer glasses, eating chips.

She sighed.

"What?"

She peered at Tanner. "Nothing."

"You sighed."

"I like this place." From her coat pocket, Reggie's phone pinged. She retrieved it and smiled at the name on the screen. "It's Al. He says 'Going to miss u @ court 2morrow night.'"

She replied.

Just thinkn same thing. @ a pub drinkn hot sweet tea.

"Where did this court thing start again?"

"Al. He dubbed the Friday night gathering my court. When I left the corporate world, my friends wanted to see what I was up to and started coming to the shop Fridays after work. We ordered pizza the first night and next thing I knew, a tradition was born."

"Maybe Al was seeing something of the future."

She shook her head. "Ha! I doubt it. Daddy never told him about Gram, or me, being a possible princess." His inflection and quick gaze awakened unfamiliar flutters in her heart.

Gemma arrived with their tea and basket of bread. "Stew's a-coming."

Reggie reached to pour her tea, looking up when the front door opened and a cluster of young-looking professionals entered. Men in suits with their ties loosened. Women with handbags swinging, smoothing their wind-bounced hair. Gathering in the center of the pub, they shoved three tables together, talking all the while, casting the broad shadow of youth over the older, tired-looking workmen.

Tanner filled his cup, taking a long sip. "Everyone comes here. The union blokes, the professionals, mums, dads—"

"Ministers of Culture."

He scoffed, reaching for a roll. "Yes, even the mighty Minister of Culture. And the Princess of Hessenberg, don't forget."

"Why do you do that?" Reggie raised her tea to her lips. *Hmm, might need more sugar.*

"Do what?" He sat back, defensive, leaving his roll abandoned on his plate.

"Make fun of yourself."

"I don't—"

"You do."

"Haven't you heard it's best not to take oneself too seriously?" He reached for his knife and the butter.

"Not taking yourself seriously doesn't mean you mock yourself."

His jaw tensed again and he focused on buttering his bread. "Try the bread while it's hot. It's fabulous."

Reggie selected a roll, noticed Clarence and Todd were enjoying the same rolls and a big plate of meat, and watched the front door again as the rugby boys from the park entered, their voices loud, their faces ruddy, their hair sticking out in all directions.

So this was the core of Hessenberg. Her people. Her life and blood.

She'd just taken a bite of bread when Gemma came with the stew. Reggie thanked her with a smile, sensing a change in the room.

The table of workers was staring at her.

"Tanner—"

"What?" He dipped his bread in his stew.

One of the men pointed at her. "I think we've been found out. Or that table of men really believes I'm the dancing juggler."

He jerked around just as the gentleman with the wiry hair got up and came to their booth, dragging a chair behind him.

"You're her, ain'tcha?" A man in his late sixties, maybe older, with miner's wrinkles on his brow and coal stains on his fingers, straddled the chair and propped his arms on the back. His hazel eyes demanded the truth. "The heir."

She didn't check with Tanner. Just spoke. From her heart. "I am."

"Well, I'll be." His chin quivered as a glossy sheen covered his eyes. "I–I never thought I'd live to see it . . . the heir returned home."

Reggie offered her hand. "Reggie Beswick."

The man started to take her hand, but stood instead, giving her a short bow. "Keeton Lombard III, at your service." When he looked up, tears had gathered under his eyes. "Me own grand-pappy was in service to His Majesty, the Grand Duke. Broke his heart the day the duke surrendered Hessenberg to Brighton Kingdom."

"I'm so sorry. Did he think the prince was a traitor?"

Keeton returned to his seat. "My grandpappy told me he was a good man but a frightened one. They say he couldn't read so he trusted almost no one."

Reggie leaned toward him. "I guess it had to be hard. For all."

"Have you come to restore the kingdom? My grandpappy used to tell me since I was a little lad, oh, about yea high,"— Keeton held his hand at waist level—"look for the kingdom to be restored, Keet, my boy. Pray for it. And, well, here you are." He wiped his eyes. "As I live and breathe, the answer to my prayers."

"Keeton, you'll be wanting to keep this quiet, please," Tanner said. "We want to give Regina, rather, Her Majesty, time to adjust, get to know the people without a media frenzy."

"Quiet, lad? Didn't you see the papers? Catch the talkies? And who, may I ask, are you?"

"Keeton, this is the Minister of Culture. The guy with his backside, legs, and feet flailing out of the car," Reggie said.

"Ah, that was you? Nice to meet you, Mr. Legs and Feet." Keeton shook Tanner's hand with vigor and a laugh before turn-ing to his friends and waving them over. "I was right, lads. It's who I said. It's her."

The remaining gentlemen at Keeton's table dragged over

their chairs, alerting the younger crowd that something was going on. They regarded Reggie's booth over the rim of their raised pints.

"Your Majesty, it's a pleasure. I'm Archibald Littleton." The man bowed with a sweeping arm gesture. Like Keeton, he was in his late sixties, early seventies, with work-hardened hands.

"I'm Carlton Borling." Another man bowed before straddling his seat and glancing at Regina with both sorrow and wisdom in his eyes. "I'm seventy-eight years old. My grandfather was an earl in 1914. When Germany seized Hessenberg accounts, he lost a good deal of the family fortune, but when the duke signed over the land, he lost his title, his dignity, and his will to live. He was humiliated. Had to find a regular man's job. Me father had to go to work for the shipping lines as a boy. Never finished his education. First Borling son in three hundred years who didn't go to university. My brothers and I, along with our sons, work in the mines or out on the oil rigs. What your uncle did . . ."

"See here, now," Tanner started.

"I'm sorry, Carlton," Regina said, feeling his words. Feeling the pain of his ancestors.

"How ironic Prince Francis gets his wish—from the grave, mind you—to have his heir show up and restore what he destroyed. For him. But for the rest of us, it's bully-me-down, blokes."

"Carlton,"—Keeton tapped the man on the shoulder—"we can't go blaming the princess here for ole Francis's cowardice. Let's be thankful he saved us from the Kaiser." He hammered the back of his chair with a "harrumph." "Don't be trusting that mulligan, Seamus Fitzsimmons, Your Majesty. You might just find yourself worse off for your troubles."

"I do blame her." Carlton rose from his chair. "Nothing personal, miss, but if you get to inherit your dear ole uncle's station and position, one he abdicated long ago, then you ought to bear the burdens of his sin. Where's my inheritance? My fortune? I'm with the governor. Bully to the lot of you. No more royals. We've a chance to get free from them."

Clarence appeared over Tanner's shoulder and whispered in his ear. Concern marred his expression. "Pardon me." He walked over to the TV bank with the somber security officer.

Reggie peeked over the old gents' heads to see the governor's broad face on every screen.

Tanner returned with a strong stride. Reggie knew they were leaving. And she didn't even get a bite of her stew.

"Pardon, chaps." Tanner urged Archibald to scoot aside. "The princess has had a long day." He drew her into him, his arm protective about her waist, urging her toward the door.

"Tanner, my purse is back there."

"Todd's getting it. Clarence went for the SUV. Don't look at anyone."

They stepped outside into a frenzy of waiting photographers. "It's the redheaded dancing juggler!" Cameras flashed and hummed. Voices rose. Bodies pressed against bodies.

"Look over here . . . Are you a woman or a man?"

Tanner pressed his hand to the side of Reggie's head. "Keep walking."

"A woman," she hollered, trying to raise her head.

"Can you juggle for us? Do a dance?"

"Sure."

"Regina, do not taunt them. Get in the SUV." Tanner, tense and stiff. She laughed into his chest.

"Whoa now," a voice boomed from among the photographers, "'tis not the redheaded dancing juggler. It's the princess." The photographers pressed in closer, harder, and the air between them evaporated.

Clarence was behind the wheel, firing up the motor.

"It's the princess."

"Princess, this way."

The car was surrounded by photographers pressing their camera lenses against the window, trying for a picture.

"Go, go, go." Tanner slapped the back of the driver's seat.

When the SUV broke clear of the photographers, Reggie doubled forward and laughed the entire drive to the palace.

"I'm doing what's right for Hessenberg, boldly, proudly. My thirty years in public service has honed my understanding of what the citizens of this small but mighty duchy need. I cannot sit idly by and watch our future be dictated by a hundred-year-old entail."

Seamus turned the page of his speech with a purposeful glance at the reporters standing before him on the steps of Wettin Manor. He timed his press conference for the slow, Thursday-at-five hour, gearing up to make weekend news waves where the hardcore reporters would leak his message.

Soaking the press and the people with his message was the way to go. Convince everyone he was the leader for their future.

By the time the court decided on his sovereign, independent state petition, he'd have enough political backwater flowing that he'd be able to manage all outcomes in his favor.

"Governor—"

Seamus recognized the *LibP* reporter. "Christopher, yes."

"It's rumored you plan to have the princess arrested as an enemy of the state." A snicker waved through the reporters. "Is that your intention? And on what grounds?"

"On the grounds it's the law." He chuckled and plied his charm. "Go home, my boy. Do your homework. Once the entail is signed, or the court grants the people's petition to be free of an aristocratic monarchy, the constitution and authority canon of 1720 come into order and a royal can be considered an enemy of the state."

"But did you not just say Hessenberg must move forward, away from our old laws?"

Ignorant troll. Seamus fashioned a serious, concerned expression. "Fine point. Fine point, indeed. Hessenberg must move away from a four-hundred-year-old way of *life*, you see. A monarchy is an institution of the past."

"Might we say the same of governorships?"

Blast! Ban Christopher Mullins from future pressers. "The office of the governorship, no, lad. But we allow the people to decide who leads them. The democratic way."

"Calling the princess an enemy seems a mite extreme, Governor."

"You speak correctly, Christopher." Seamus came from around the governor's podium, hands grasping his jacket lapels. "It is a serious crime. Need we all be reminded of how Prince Francis betrayed his country? Yet now we are considering his heir as our Head of State, a leader among the nations?" He grumbled, shook his head, and moved back behind the podium.

"Shall we let his crime continue? What right has he to demand our land be given back to the House of Augustine-Saxon? None, I say." He pounded the podium. "We, the people, will determine Hessenberg's future, not Prince Francis from the grave. Not King Nathaniel II, long may he live, nor Regina Beswick of Tallahassee, Florida."

Heads bobbed as a rousing "Hear, hear!" rose from the reporters.

Then Deanna Robertson from the *Informant* fired a question without waiting to be called upon. "If you want the people to decide, then let us meet the princess. Have a go at her."

"I'm not the one keeping her from you, Deanna. Ring the Minister of Culture's office."

Several hands shot up in the air.

"Lord Governor..."

"Lord Governor..."

Seamus called up a BCC telly reporter. "Jordan Sloan."

"Who do you see leading us into this new way of life, new form of government?"

"I'm glad you asked. I say with all humility, I consider myself the best and most experienced candidate."

October 26, 1914

Meadowbluff Palace

Mamá just entered my room tonight by candlelight, grim and grieving. I am to pack my things and prepare to leave, rather flee our beloved Hessenberg. How can this be?

My maid, Priscilla, will not be traveling with us, and I am to take only what I can carry. Mamá's instructing Esmé the same.

The palace is dark and I was admonished not to turn on my lamp or light a candle.

Uncle has signed over all rights and rule to Cousin Nathaniel. He surrendered to Brighton. I'm so confused. Wasn't he strong and courageous to make a stand for neutrality? Now we surrender without a shot fired?

I can only imagine what the likes of Rein Friedrich are saying, and Lord Fitzsimmons, walking the gallery in the House of Lords.

"Treason!"

I pray this sin does not fall on me and mine. Help us, dear Father.

I've only a few moments, and I'm not sure why I'm writing. But I reached for my journal the moment Mamá left the room.

My hands are trembling. I can barely read my own writing for my tears.

Mamá said to dress warm, in my finest wool, and to wear as many layers as I can along with my winter boots.

The words of Jesus fill my heart. "But pray ye that your flight be not in the winter, neither on the sabbath day." It is neither winter nor the Sabbath, and I should be thankful. But I am not. I'm frightened. and angry.

Will I see Hessenberg again? What of my friends? My heart . . . we are a disgraced, fallen family.

Uncle just came to my room, admonishing me to hurry. Then he said with no emotion, "The House of Augustine-Saxon has fallen."

My heart nearly stopped beating. Surely after the war, when all is settled, we can return. I said as much to Uncle.

"It's over, Ali. We've lost." But he was most grave and so very sad I could not remain angry with him.

"I don't understand."

"No, I suspect you would not. I'm not sure I understand it all myself."

"Why can we not stay? Why must we flee?"

"I've abdicated the throne, Alice. The earls and lords will come for us tonight. If caught, I'll be tried. Most likely hanged. We might all be hanged."

Then as if some punctuation to Uncle's declaration, the windows rattled as a cannon fired. Sovereign Lord, be near us.

"Will we ever be able to return?" I didn't bother to hide my tears.

"At the end of the entail."

"When will that be?"

"Long after you and I are gone."

"Then how can we return? What are the conditions of the entail?" I felt in that moment we were not uncle and niece, but peers sharing a common burden.

"One hundred years."

"One hundred years!" I could not help but gasp. "None of us will be left. How can we return home?"

"Find your courage, Alice. The future of Hessenberg and the restoration of the House of Augustine-Saxon are within you and your children." He handed me an envelope. "Keep this in a safe place."

"What for? What is it?"

"For Hessenberg." I peered inside the envelope. "Bonds? Uncle, what good are bonds when I am leaving, being forced out? By you, I daresay."

"They will pay out, love. Trust me." Then he seemed to lose all breath and strength as he turned to go, leaving me there with my mouth gaping. "Pack. Be ready to go."

Pack. That's exactly what I plan to do. Pack for my eventual return to Hessenberg. Yes, I will return. One way or another.

Alice

TWENTY

O n Sunday afternoon, the clock on Tanner's wall seemed to tick-tock louder and louder by the moment.

One-o-one. One-o-two. One-o-three.

He closed the book he was reading and turned on the telly. He was tired. Wanting to relax.

He'd spent Friday and Saturday touring Regina about the countryside, seeing the landscape through her eyes, and his love for Hessenberg's rocky shores and high-peaked mountains deepened.

Saturday evening, they dined up by the north bay, at a hundred-and-fifty-year-old pub, Wettin Whistle, named after Wettin Manor.

Like in the atmosphere of the Fence & Anchor, Regina blended in, enjoying the food, talking with the people, joining in the shouting during the final minutes of a rugby match.

She was truly one of them. Tanner couldn't explain it exactly, but heaven above, she felt Hessen to him. Sure, she still spoke like an American Southerner and refused to be called Your Majesty, but she was one of the people.

A mental picture of her laughing, recounting the story of the redheaded man-woman dancing juggler to Jarvis and Serena, flashed across his mind and made him chuckle down in his chest. Her Southern accent grew thick when she was telling a story.

"Tanner thinks he is protecting me from the people getting riled up because Seamus is on TV, talking about the entail and the EU court petition. So we run outside into this minefield of photographers. But did they want to see me? Heck no. They came to see the redheaded he-she dancing juggler." Her laugh rang through Tanner's memory. "The waitress must have tipped them off."

After that, Regina moseyed into the kitchen to tell the chef and the maid like they were . . . family. *Y'all, listen to this . . .*

Tanner didn't have to inquire of Jarvis how it was going with the princess. He could see it written all over the man's face. He adored her. They all did.

But today his thoughts were not on Regina—he appreciated the emotional distance—but on the party about to commence up at Estes Estates.

Should he go? No! How could he? He and Trude had a deal.

Focusing on the sports presenter, Tanner tried to care more about rugby scores than blonde, ten-year-old twins, but with each tick-tock of the clock, his heart wrestled with his decision.

Tanner upped the volume on the telly. *Blimey.* He had to get the party off his mind. He paced to the window and peered down to the street. What did he see? A large bouquet of party balloons floating past.

Well, he was not going to that blasted birthday party.

The clock tick-tocked.

Fine. Fine. He'd go. Tanner fired down the hall to change.

His life was fine. Steady. Manageable. His sins forgiven and stuffed into a very dark closet.

Then his king sent him on a journey. And somehow the buried and hidden became exposed and confronted his solitude, his shallow substitute for living.

In his closet, Tanner yanked a pair of tan slacks from a hanger and selected a blue shirt. What was it Regina said about him Thursday? He was a zero-to-sixty sort of bloke? At the moment, he certainly felt like something akin to a zero-to-sixty g-force was squeezing his heart.

Changing before he could consider what he was actually about to do, Tanner slipped on his loafers, grabbed his keys, and left his flat with the lights on and telly still blaring.

Halfway down the street he realized he had no gift. What did one bring to ten-year-old twin girls?

At the moment, he could think of nothing. Well, nothing he could purchase on a Sunday afternoon.

Sunday afternoons in Hessenberg clung to the old ways. Quiet, restful, most if not all of the shops closed, dozing in the afternoon sun.

In truth, Britta and Bella would have more presents than they could enjoy for the day, or the year for that matter. Why pile on one more from the derelict father they'd not remember anyway?

Driving north toward Estes Estates, a fifteenth-century manor in the highlands, Tanner absorbed the light and sounds of the afternoon, calming his anxieties, studying the bank of white clouds drifting across a crisp, clear river of blue as the edge of the sun crested the mountaintops.

What a perfect party day.

Tanner rehearsed what he'd say to Trude, to her parents. To the girls. Should he have a chance to speak to them. But his words sounded thin and hollow.

The road bent around the mountain, then flattened, cutting through the plains toward the estate. Downshifting, Tanner slowed at the entrance. He parked on the lawn, the last car in a row of many. Frankly, he was surprised the Esteses didn't hire valet service for the day.

He stared at the stone house with its pitched and peaked rooftop, multiple chimneys, and turrets, wondering what waited for him beyond the door. There was only one way to find out. Tanner hauled in a deep breath and moved toward the manor.

The butler answered the door, wearing a pink party hat. "Welcome. Do come in." He offered Tanner a hat, but he passed.

"You'll find the family out on the lawn. Do you need me to show you the way?"

"No, thank you. I remember." Trude lived here, with her parents, when she was pregnant.

Adjusting his jacket, Tanner started down the hall, working his way toward the back of the house through side rooms and short passageways. The lawn was dotted with white-linen-covered tables centered with bursting bouquets of flowers, colorful tea sets, and a gaggle of girls sipping tea, wearing pastel-colored dresses and matching gloves. An equal number of adults clustered on the party perimeter, teacups and saucers in hand, bent together in conversation. Tanner spotted his parents talking to the Trusdales—old and good friends from Dad's first parish. A stage sat on the far end of the party with a banner flying overhead. Meant2Be.

Good grief, Trude. They're ten.

Meant2Be was a very popular boy band on the cusp of gaining international fame. How did she wrangle booking them? And how was the place not mobbed with paparazzi and screaming teens?

Scanning the group of girls for the twins, Tanner's eyes landed on Trude. Beautiful as ever in a cut-out-of-a-magazine way. Perfect hair. Perfect dress with matching shoes. She was lively and charming, impeccably stylish.

He followed her as she moved through the tables, then knelt beside two girls. Since he could only see the backs of their heads, he could only guess they were Bella and Britta. His throat constricted. His heart raced, drawing his chest tight. He wanted to leave, get in his car, and race down the hill for home.

But he'd miraculously mustered the courage to get this far, so he might as well see it through.

Trude was on the move again, meeting a man in the middle of the thoroughfare between the tables, slipping her arm through his as she tossed back her head with a laugh.

Strange, Tanner didn't know the man to be her husband, Reese.

He bent to kiss her and she most assuredly kissed him back. It was then Tanner had a hint as to why Trude invited him here today. She had a new man in her life.

Leaving his preview spot, Tanner stepped outside to the porch.

Trude glanced toward the house, caught sight of him, and waved, smiling.

"You came," she said, stepping onto the porch, taking his hands in hers and kissed his cheek. "I was nervous you'd not show."

The man she'd been with trailed behind her and introduced himself.

"Evan Downy."

"Tanner Burkhardt."

"Tanner,"—Trude glanced at Evan—"we're engaged."

"How does your husband feel about that?"

She chortled. "Oh, Tanner, very droll. But, shh, lower your voice." Trude steered him inside with an over-the-shoulder comment to Evan. "We've not told the girls. Darling, we'll be in the library."

Tanner walked beside her in silence. *Can't wait to hear* this *story.*

In the library, the sunlight streamed in through the high, arched windows, warming the room and making the ancient walls seem youthful.

Tanner chose a chair, intending to sit back and listen, let Trude tell her story. But when she closed the library doors, he fired the first question. "What's this rubbish? Engaged? Where's Reese?"

"I meant to call you, let you know, we divorced last year." Trude hovered on the edge of the library, by the doors.

"Divorced?" He fired up from his chair and crossed over to her. "What happened to the happy, cohesive family? The stable environment in which to raise the girls?"

"That's part of why you're here, Tanner." She moved around him, choosing a chair.

"Trude, you begged me to step out of their lives because you wanted Reese to be their dad. You said I was confusing them. Not you. Not Reese. But me. The part-time dad. The Wednesday and every-other-weekend dad."

"Yes, I know that's what I said." She shot him an exasperated look.

"You brought in your parents, Reese's parents, a child psychologist, all to tell me how unstable it was for them to be jerked around from my place to yours. How they had one mum but two dads."

"I'm fully aware of what I said, Tanner."

"Are you? Because divorce doesn't seem to be the so-called stable environment you begged me to give the girls. If I'd bow out of their lives and let Reese be the dad they so dearly loved and deserved, how grand their lives would be. So emotionally stable."

"I still say I was right. The girls were confused when they returned from being with you."

"They were two. Of course they were confused. And it didn't help that you insisted they call Reese 'Da-da.' You contributed to their troubles, Trude." There, he'd finally said it. Only took eight years.

"I was young . . . Tanner. Reese wanted to be their dad."

"But I was, am, their dad! And you were not that young. Twenty-six is plenty mature." Tanner moved toward her in one hard stride, his feelings, his long-buried words fighting to reach the surface. "Now you tell me Reese is out and Evan is in?"

"Tanner, Reese and I tried counseling, but we weren't working. We were so young when we got married—"

"Stop with the excuses."

"I'm not making excuses. I'm trying to explain. We weren't happy, you see. We were miserable."

"Pardon me if I have no sympathy when I sacrificed my happiness for the girls. You and Reese couldn't see your way through to do the same?" He turned around to the window, the sunlight fueling his anger.

"Don't lecture me, Tanner Burkhardt. Reese and I limped along for several years, but the marriage was over. To be honest, I don't care to go round about this with you. I invited you today so you could see the girls and, yes, to tell you I am marrying Evan. We're moving to America for a few years."

"America? Blimey, Trude, what does any of this have to do with me? Why do I need to know what you're doing with the girls? I'm out of their lives." He gestured in the direction of the party. "I've not seen them in eight years. So tell me why I'm really here."

"I thought you had a right to know. About Reese and, well, everything." She stood, smoothing the skirt of her dress and moving toward her father's desk. "Don't make a case out of it, Tanner. People divorce. Life goes on."

"What do the girls think? How are they getting on?"

"They are typical preteens, Tanner. Innocent and giddy one moment, crying over a trivial squabble the next." She flipped her hand in the air as if it was all so, so droll and ordinary. "They adore Evan, by the way. And he them."

"Naturally. What about Reese? Where's he in all of this?" Tanner covered the space between them and lightly gripped her arms, not caring if it startled her a bit. "I let you take them from me, Trude, endured the scorn of my parents, my family, and my friends because you and *your* cohorts convinced me, dare I say manipulated me, into believing the twins would fare much better with one set of parents. You and Reese. You swore to me he was the love of your life, that you'd never divorce him. Because that was the only way I'd agree. You promised me he adored the girls as if they were his own. So I walked away. Much to my own regret. And now you take this tone with me when I want to know what's going on?"

She jerked her arms free. "It's not like they're children, Tanner."

"They *are* children. Ten is still a child."

"They are mature enough to understand relationships change. It's not like they were born into a perfect situation, a perfect family." She rolled her eyes at him. "We were never even in love. We didn't start dating until after I was pregnant."

"But we were making our role as parents work."

Despite his rebuttal, Tanner knew she was right. The girls' introduction to this world was fractured from the get-go.

Their parents were a couple of fools who let a weekend holiday take them where they never intended to go.

In truth, if he turned the mirror of accusation he held up to Trude toward himself, Tanner bore the same amount of guilt as she. Maybe more.

As much as he loved his girls, there was a small part of him that wanted relief from single parenting, from the pain of missing them when he dropped them off at Trude's. Knowing that every day he wasn't with them, he missed some beautiful part of their lives and who they were becoming.

First words? He missed them. Trude regaled him with the tale of how they said "Mum-Mum" when he came to pick them up for his weekend. By then, they'd been talking for several days.

First steps? Happened while they were on vacation with her parents in Italy. By the time Tanner picked them up for his holiday with them, they were practically marathon runners.

"... so you see," Trude was saying, "it's all for the best. Evan is a good man. I'm so much wiser now than when I married Reese."

Tanner released a bit of his anger and untangled his emotions from the stale, old guilt. "What do the girls say of this marriage and move to America?"

"We're waiting until after the party to tell them. Evan found out about the job last week. It was then that he proposed and I said yes."

"What does Reese say about you hopping over the pond with his girls?" The words *his girls* tasted like bitter herbs.

"Here's the thing, Tanner." Trude slipped her hand in her pocket and retrieved a pack of cigarettes, popping one out of the crumpled pack. She gave Tanner a sheepish look. "Can you believe it,"—she held up the cigarette—"after all these years? But I am trying to quit. I am. Well, no matter. Where was I? Right. The girls are set to enter Scarborough next year, my alma mater, as well as my mother's and grandmother's. Their closest friends, the Exleys, Thorndikes, and Hathaways, are also entering Scarborough next year."

"Your point?"

She tapped the end of the cigarette against her hand. "Tanner, when Reese left, he *left*. Me, the girls, everything. He's not seen them in a year and a half." She stared at one of the bookcases. "He said the girls were not really his, and if he was moving on with his life, he didn't need the burden of another man's children."

Her confession hung in the room, absorbing all the light, eating the air. Tanner dropped to the nearest chair. He had no words. No retort. So this was how it felt to be completely broken.

"I should have never asked you to leave their lives, Tanner." Trude sat on the edge of a low table and faced him. "I was idyllic and foolish. Reese was jealous of you. I'm sure you knew. We fought every time you came round. He's the one who started the bit about the girls needing a one-mum, one-dad family, and I fell for it." She looked frail and tattered, beaten. "You do believe me, don't you?"

He fixed on the pattern of the carpet. "I've lost eight years with my girls, Trude. Your confession can never bring them back."

She hardened, collecting her defenses. "I'm not so sure you didn't count it as a relief, Tanner. Letting someone else do your job. I daresay it's how you let us finally convince you."

"Stop." He wouldn't let her put any of her own burden on him. "I struggled, but I never wanted another man to raise my girls. You convinced me that letting go would make their lives easier. More emotionally healthy."

Trude finally lit the cigarette. "Don't tell my father." She held up the cigarette, fanning away the small tendrils of smoke drifting through the swath of sunlight. "He'd kill me for smoking in his precious library. Here's the thing, Tanner. Not what we did in the past but what we can do now, for the future, and the matter of Scarborough."

"What of it? You said the girls were set."

"Well, yes, but not if we're in America. Evan's assignment is for a minimum of three years. Scarborough is a day school until the girls are fourteen, then they can board, but until then, they need to live with someone."

Ah. The picture was becoming clear.

"Evan leaves for America in January, so we thought we'd marry over Christmas." She smiled at him, dashing out her cigarette after only a few puffs. "If the girls go with us, they'll miss their final semester at Trinity. Which is fine, I suppose, but they do need to be prepared to enter Scarborough next fall."

"Trude, what are you suggesting?"

"There's no easy way to say this, so I'll just be out with it. Tanner, will you take the girls?"

"Excuse me?" he fired away from his perch. "Take them where?"

"To live with you, of course." Her smile reflected her polished charm. "I know it's a lot to ask, enormous really. But it would mean so much to Evan and me."

"What happened to taking them with you? Being a cohesive family?"

"I know, I know. But the girls deserve to stay in school with their friends. I don't want to give them a new stepdad and a new life in a foreign country all at once."

"Then don't. Stay here. You don't have to go to America, Trude."

"Oh, you and your simplicity." She went around the polished desk with intricate carvings on the corners and legs. "Evan has waited five years for this job. If he doesn't take it, his career is stalled. He cannot turn it down just because he's fallen in love with me."

"Why not? Am I the only one required to sacrifice my heart for someone else's happiness?" He sounded a bit bitter, and he didn't care. "You get what you want all the time, but I get to be sacrificed."

"You just said yourself—"

"I gave up my daughters, Trude." He leaned toward her, tapping his chest. "And it killed me. I've lived with the guilt and shame ever since."

"Then why in heaven's name did you do it?"

"For their *happiness* and *stability.* Or so I believed." He jammed his hands in his pockets. How could he have been such a fool? "If anyone was young and unwise, it was me. To let you talk me into giving up the girls. Now you tell me it was because Reese was jealous?"

"Tanner, darling, Evan adores Bella and Britta. But they aren't his daughters, you see, and I can't ask him to turn down his dream job because my girls need to go to Scarborough."

"Why not? I gave up my dream of going to seminary because of you and the girls. And by the way, Britta and Bella don't have to go to Scarborough."

"Don't blame me about seminary. You chose to resign all on your own. And yes, the girls do havē to go to Scarborough."

"I had to resign, Trude. How could I start my life as a minister of the gospel as a single dad?"

"Listen, bloke, you are just as much to blame for what happen—"

"I'm not blaming anyone." Tanner collected his frayed emotions and lowered his voice. "I simply mean to remind you when two people have children out of wedlock, plans and dreams are altered."

"Don't you see? I'm trying to right a wrong here. Let you have the girls. Why are you resisting me?"

"Because it feels to me like you're trying to make your life and your new relationship work while putting me and the girls on the line. Once again. This is more about your happiness than anyone else's, Trude."

She swore in a high, lilting tone. "It is about *all* of us. All of our happiness."

"Tell me, do they even remember me? What are they going to think of you leaving them with a virtual stranger? And what of your parents? Why can't they take the girls?"

"I've not asked them. They're leaving for Barcelona in the new year for four months. Besides, they've raised a family and don't care to do it again. The girls will be fine with you. You're their dad. It's time they got to know you and your family. Don't you think? They can visit me on holidays and summers. I'll come over once a quarter. They'll hardly miss me."

"Do they even know I exist?"

"I've started talking to them about you. Asking if they remember you."

"And?"

"Tanner, not everything about this is perfect or ideal."

"Do they, Trude?"

"Yes, in an absent-uncle kind of manner." She gripped his arm. "Don't you want to get to know them? Now's your chance."

"They're ten." He gestured toward the door. "I know nothing about being a dad to ten-year-old girls."

"No worry, darling. They are perfect at being ten. They'll be more than happy to educate you." Her quick laugh wavered and fell short.

"I work sixty hours a week." He pressed his fingers to his forehead, bringing his cold, stark life into view. "My refrigerator is empty save for week-old carry-out and sour milk."

"I'm sure your mum would be more than willing to help. And mine, when she is here."

This whole proposition set him on edge. Turned him upside down. The fact that he was even considering it . . .

"What is your plan if I say no?"

She shook another cigarette from the packet. "I don't have one."

"I'll have to think about it. But, Trude, if they come to live with me, that's it. No going back and forth. I'll be their primary, *deciding* parent. If I say they enroll in Highlands, then they enroll in Highlands."

"What? Because you get a few years with them? They've been slated for Scarborough since they were two years old."

"Little did you know, I enlisted them for Highlands when they were two years old."

"You cannot be serious. Tanner, I refuse to be held hostage to you simply because I'm asking you to care for your own daughters."

"After what you did to me, I daresay I can make some demands. Not to mention you invite me here to ask me to relieve you of your parenting duties so you can run off to America all carefree with a new husband. You say Reese left over a year ago? Why am I just now hearing about it?"

"Semantics, Tanner. Always semantics with you. Do you think it was easy for me to invite you here for this?"

"Yes, because here I stand." He leaned into her, gaining her full attention. "If I take the girls, I want full custody."

"You can't cut me out of their lives."

"I'd never cut you out. But you're asking me to be their dad and that's exactly what I intend to be." He had driven up to the highlands with trepidation, not a thought of getting a second chance with his daughters. Praying if he met them they'd not kick him in the knee and run screaming. "I'll see to their education, their friends, their social diary. I'll be delighted to comply with your schedule as well as your parents'. But if this is your request and the reason you invited me here today, then these are my conditions."

"My word, Tanner." She pressed her hand over her middle. "Fifteen minutes ago you weren't in their lives at all and countering my request to take them, saying you knew nothing about ten-year-old girls. Now you're wanting full control."

"Let's just say I'm a zero-to-sixty sort of chap." He walked around the back of the sofa and headed for the door. "Think on it, Trude. I'm off to join the party, say hello to Dad and Mum, and venture a happy birthday to my girls."

TWENTY-ONE

*L*ate Sunday afternoon, Reggie sat in the parlor by the window with two thick law books, one printed in 1890, the other in 1910. Jarvis had hooked her up.

Taking up the first book, she flipped through the ancient pages, scanning a bunch of legalese about crime and punishment, legal cases and precedent, but nothing about Seamus's threat to charge her as an enemy of the state.

Taking up the second volume entitled *Vox Vocis Canonicus*, she scanned it looking for the word on lords, earls, and enemies of the state.

If any member of the royal family, house of lords, or nobility are found conspiring to dissolve, overthrow, put down, or destroy the government of Hessenberg, Grand Duchy, they shall be stripped of title and authority, all lands and accounts, and banned from the nation as an enemy of the state.

Reggie closed the book and placed it on a table. Seemed to her Seamus had a case against ole Prince Francis but not her.

But how *did* she have a right to Hessenberg's throne? Shoving aside the law books, Reggie pulled the entail from the attaché case.

... in due course, at the end of the entail, should an heir be found, he or she shall inherit the throne of the House of Augustine-Saxon, the legal rights, titles, authority, and land therein ... granted by the King or Queen of Brighton.

Well, that's where King Nathaniel II came in.

Reggie ran her finger over a very bold signature of Brighton's first King Nathaniel I. She could almost feel his confidence in the flair of his pen. Underneath his signature was the Grand Duke's. Prince Francis's signature was a weak and wobbly script, the ink skipping, leaving gaps where pen left paper.

Oh, what he must have been feeling.

Shuffling through some other official-looking papers, Reggie felt nudged to reread the entail. Was there a clue in there about her future? Was the entail enough to grant her the throne her great-grandmother's uncle abandoned? If so, how could she help, truly help, the Hessen people?

Reggie scanned the entail opening, the words becoming familiar. *Lord, if you want me to do this, help me search out this matter. Find the hidden treasures.* She read each line of the simple entail slowly, carefully.

The ordinary words communicated an astounding message. She was the heir. As she reread the last paragraph, the word *inheritance* lifted from the page and pinged around her heart.

Reggie leaned closer to the lamplight.

... shall use the inheritance of bonds to restore and rebuild the House of Augustine-Saxon.

Bonds? What bonds? Savings? War? Bearer? She worked with some bearer bonds at Backlund & Backlund. They could be lucrative if the purchase was right. Or was the mention of inheritance bonds more altruistic? Bonds of love. Bonds of friendship. Of loyalty? Of time?

Reggie returned to the documents sent from King Nathaniel II, looking for a mention of bonds but found none.

Standing, stretching, rubbing the blur from her eyes, she returned the documents to the attaché case, then leaned against the windowsill.

The scene beyond the glass was beautiful. A stand of Princess Alice trees flaming in the last gold of the day. For early October, the lawn remained green and full.

"Lord, how about a sign. Huh?" She laughed softly, her breath powdering the pane, and thought of Gram. She was a sign. A living, talking, breathing sign. But she'd said nothing. Only to cloak the truth in a mysterious, prophetic fairy tale, and to play princess with construction paper crowns and fire-poker scepters.

She smoothed the dash of perspiration from her forehead, feeling homesick, missing Daddy and Sadie, who were most likely at lunch with a large after-church crowd.

Reaching for her phone, she texted Daddy.

Miss u. Call when u can. XO

But he was worse at texting than phone calls and voice messages.

Reggie slipped her phone into her pocket and offered one last prayer. "Lord, I don't ask for signs very often, but if you can see your way clear this time . . ." She pressed her hand over her heart. "Consider my weak, blind, dark heart. I need your light. Show me your light."

The parlor door opened on the fading whisper of her prayer.

"Miss." Serena's dark hair and porcelain face peeked around the door. "Chef sent me to see what you might want for dinner."

"Whatever he's making is fine."

"He said he'd make an American hamburger with chips if you want."

"Yum. Sounds good." The idea of eating alone made her all the more homesick.

"Do you need anything else, miss?"

Yes, some sort of sign, a confirmation. "No, I'm good. I think I'll . . ." Do what? Go to her suite? A flickering thought about Tanner crossed her mind. She kind of missed him. What was he doing this fine Sunday evening?

"Miss, have you seen the grand ballroom?" Serena gave a shy smile. "It's my favorite room in the whole palace. They shined it up quite nice. Waiting for you to come."

"Grand ballroom? I didn't know there was a grand ballroom." In truth, she knew next to nothing about the palace except her suite, the parlor, the dining room, and the kitchen.

She found it difficult to explore what her heart had not yet possessed.

"Want to see?" Serena motioned for Reggie to follow, opening the door wide.

"Let's go." Reggie scooted into the hall and waited for Serena to lead the way.

But the sweet lady's maid wouldn't step in front of Reggie. "Up that-a-way." She pointed down the hall. "Then across the formal library and down the western corridor."

"You lead, I'll follow."

"No, miss, I cannot walk in front of you. Mr. Jarvis would have my job if I did."

"Ah, I see. Decorum." Reggie linked her arm through Serena's. "Come on, we'll walk together. Does that work?"

Serena hesitated, her eyes on Reggie's, then the bend of their arms. "I don't think Mr. Jarvis would care for us to walk like schoolgirls either."

"Just this once." Serena couldn't be much younger than Reggie. Five years maybe. In another place, they might have been friends. "Our secret."

"All right, but just this once." She smiled shyly and started down the hall, through the formal library with the twenty-foot, glass-and-iron windows, rich purple walls, and shelves upon shelves of gilded, leather-bound books, onto the red-carpeted western corridors.

Reggie nearly tripped Serena when she pulled up short, trying to take in the beauty of the hall with ornate gold molding, carved and crafted moldings around the windows, and a row of crystal lights marching down the high, arched ceiling.

"I feel like I'm in a dream."

"Oh miss, this is just the slumber. The dream is to come."

Around the corner, Serena stopped at a set of enormous double doors nearly the width of the entire wall. "Aren't they grand?"

"Very." They were encased with carved molding and coated with a bronze so polished Reggie could plainly see her reflection.

"They say Prince Francis proposed to the love of his life in this ballroom on his coronation day." Serena twisted open the right door for Reggie to slip inside, then closed the door behind her. "But she turned him down flat. Didn't want to be married to a Grand Duke. Said she'd never have a day to call her own for the rest of her life."

Serena opened a panel on the wall and like magic, the center chandelier burst to life. Prisms of colorful light dripped from crystal teardrops to the glossy hardwood floor.

"Oh, Serena." The light seemed to twirl and float, rising and falling, gathering under the arching ceiling. "This is incredible."

"Told you, miss. My favorite room in the palace."

The walls were a rich red and supported by a marble colonnade alternating with floor-to-ceiling windows in every other panel. Mini-chandeliers swung from their own mini-domes directly above each window.

On the far wall, a balcony hovered high above the floor, hosting a giant gold pipe organ. A mezzanine with curved stairs on either side was on her left.

The orchestra pit sat in the front of the room under a fresco painting of a Victorian couple dancing, their gazes locked with love.

"When was the last ball, Serena?"

"Don't know. But I don't believe there's been one since the last Grand Duke. Maybe more than a hundred years. Oh me, look at the time . . . and Chef is waiting. I must run. Do you want to stay? I'll come for you when dinner is served."

"Yes, I want to stay. No hurry on dinner."

When Reggie was alone, she stood under the grand center chandelier in the shower of the crystal light.

Well, she asked the Lord for a light. And *this* was a light.

She walked up the stairs to the mezzanine, running her hand along the smooth, gilded banister, pausing in the middle to peer out at the room, trying to hear the music, trying to see the dancers in all their splendor.

The fanciest dance she'd ever attended was her senior prom, where she danced with friends to the tunes of DJ Yo Sway.

Against the back wall of the mezzanine was a dais with two large chairs, like thrones, made of carved polished wood and plush, rich-red upholstery. Reggie made her way up the dais's low, wide steps, pausing by the chair on the left.

Was this a throne? She'd seen pictures in books, and these chairs matched the images in her mind. For a split, pulsing second, she had the urge to sit in the seat on her left, but instead of taking a step forward, she backed down the steps. What if sitting meant "I'm the princess. For real. And I'm here to stay"?

Breathing out, shifting the emotional weight of the room

from her heart to her head, Reggie descended the other side of the mezzanine stairs.

What the room must have looked like filled with dancers twirling and swaying to the music. Women in elegant gowns. Men dressed in dark tuxedos. The orchestra sending stringed sounds to the top of the domed ceiling, each note lingering in the air, then at last raining down on their hearts.

In all her days, Reggie never, ever imagined she'd experience the splendor of a grand and regal ballroom, but as she stepped off the bottom stair, she waltzed her way to the middle of the floor, arms raised, eyes closed, chin lifted, her body swaying to the melody in her soul.

"May I have this dance?"

She jerked around with a small yelp, her startled heart churning, quelling the sound of violins in her imagination. "Tanner—"

"Sorry, I didn't mean to startle you." He made his way in from the door, wearing jeans and a pullover sweater, his long blond hair loose about his face, looking as if he'd walked out of an L. L. Bean catalog.

"What are you doing here?" His gaze ignited a flicker of yearning in her soul, a longing to be in his arms, to lean against his chest and hear his heartbeat.

"Looking for you." His tone fanned her flickering flame.

"And you found me." Reggie locked her hands behind her back, watching him move toward her. Dang if her heart wasn't rumbling like a big block engine.

"I ran into Serena. She said I'd find you here."

"Remind me to have a talk with her about—"

Without a word, Tanner had swept her into his embrace and began a gentle, perfect waltz about the room, humming to the exact melody in her own head.

"Wh—what are you doing?"

"Dancing." When he smiled, she felt weak. "I do believe it's the same in America." He tightened his hand at her waist. Reggie tripped a little when he turned her to the right, but he held on to her. "Back, right, front, left, turn. Stay on your toes. Keep your arm taut and raised, your hand pressed into mine . . . good . . . good. No, Regina, don't look down. Look at me."

Look at him? Sir Blue Eyes? She was sure if she did, she'd have no command of her limbs whatsoever. Already she was trembling with an annoying surge of adrenaline.

Say something. Get your mind off of his hand at your waist.

"Wh–what brings you,"—she coughed, clearing her throat—"h–here on a Sunday evening?"

"The king." *Oh.* Disappointment smacked down a bit of her giddiness. *He's only here on business.* "He wants to know if you're available tomorrow."

"Tomorrow? Ooh, I don't know. What for?" *Lighten up, Reg!* "I'm kind of busy. I have this palace to run." Her heartbeat slowed. The trembling eased. "Staff to manage, and oh, you should see the dust on all the chandelier crystals. Tsk, tsk." She pressed the back of her hand to her forehead with a heavy, accenting sigh. "Then there's the gang down at the Fence & Anchor."

He laughed. "Regina, don't look now, love, but I think you're starting to like it here."

Love? Why did he have to use that word? The very sound made her yearn for something she'd never had. "I don't know what I think or feel, to be honest."

"Well, you should decide. The king would like to discuss moving forward with the Oath of the Throne. Seamus's presser Thursday evening stirred up anti-royal rumblings, and the Sunday news presenters picked up on it. 'The Grand Duke abdicated. Why does his heir get the throne?' kind of business."

"It's a fair question. I've asked myself the same thing."

"Fair isn't part of the equation, Regina." As they talked, they continued to dance. One, two, three—turn—one, two, three—turn. "The entail law stipulates that the heir of Prince Francis inherits the throne."

"Unless the EU court decides otherwise."

He shook his head. "Brighton has enlisted Britain's support with the court in case Germany does become a vocal component of Hessenberg's sovereign state petition outside the terms of the entail." His gaze drifted slowly over her face. "A hundred years after World War I, Brighton and Britain are allied against Germany with Hessenberg at stake."

"Maybe I should . . . should just go home. Simplify the problem." She hated the sound of her own suggestion. Because in her heart, she wanted to see Tanner again. And again.

"Your leaving doesn't simplify the problem." He raised his hand from her waist and touched her chin. "Regina—"

The tone of his voice, the way it caressed her name . . .

Reggie's legs had the strength of soft pudding. And her heart was melting, puddling between her ribs. *Say it . . . Tell him.*

Tanner brushed his hand over her cheek and lowered his face to hers, consuming her with a fiery sensation. All of her chaff—along with her fears, doubt, disappointment, and hurt—seemed to burn away at his touch.

"I want to kiss you."

"Tanner,"—she lowered her forehead to his chest, inhaling deep, exhaling shallow—"I've never been kissed. Never been in love."

"What?" He raised her chin with a light touch, his warm breath brushing her face. "Never?"

"Never."

He smiled, slow and easy. "I've lost faith in my American brethren."

She laughed softly, popping his shoulder with her hand. "Don't blame them. It's me." Reggie raised her gaze to his. "I had this wild idea I wanted my first kiss to be with my own . . ." She hesitated to speak the word that had been rattling around in her heart for years—*prince.*

"Prince?" Tanner said.

"Yes, and doesn't that sound ridiculous?" Slowly the dance stopped. "Me, the never-princess girl waiting for some kind of metaphorical prince. I blame Gram, I tell you."

"More girls should wait for their metaphorical prince." Tanner released her, stepping back. "I still want to kiss you, but I understand you've not met your—"

"But, Tanner, I—" Reggie took hold of his arm.

"Your Majesty,"—Jarvis burst into the ballroom through the enormous doors pushing a cart—"dinner is served."

"In here?" Reggie backed away from Tanner, running her hands down the sides of her jeans. Did Jarvis see? Did it matter? Her heart outraced her thoughts, her very breath.

"I thought it'd be fun. I've prepared a plate for Mr. Burkhardt as well." Jarvis pointed to the chandelier. "Dinner under the crystal moon."

Reggie peered at Tanner. "What do you say? You hungry?"

"Can't think of anything I'd rather do than dine with you under the crystal moon."

"Then dinner in the ballroom it is." Jarvis disappeared and returned after a moment with a footman to set up a table for two, complete with linen, the finest silverware, and crystal glasses.

When he left, shutting the big doors behind him, Tanner reached for Reggie and softly kissed her forehead.

She fell against him, inhaling deep and closing her eyes. The moment needed no words.

TWENTY-TWO

"Okay, tell me this." Regina reached for another chip, or as she called them, French fries. "Hardest laugh ever. Like a you-couldn't-breathe laugh."

As they ate, Reggie grilled him with questions about his family, friends, favorite movie, and telly show. Now, his hardest laugh.

"Let's see . . . hardest laugh." He watched her, thinking. The passion between them when he held her had faded, but in its wake an emotional door stood wide open. Cautiously, Tanner stepped through. "I guess it'd have to be when I was in school, messing about with my mates, getting into business we ought not."

Really, it was hard to think with her sitting in a chair not two feet from him, paralyzing him with her blue eyes and *unkissed* but oh so kissable lips.

"Did you attend boarding school?"

He focused on her words, not her lips. "What? Oh yes, boarding school. Naturally. I'm European, after all." Then he remembered a funny moment. "When I was first at university, I ran on the track team and one of my mates, Will, thought if he lost a few pounds, he'd run faster. He all but starved himself up to the day of the race. Lost the last five pounds he had to spare. Reed thin. Weak as a babe."

"He must have really wanted to win." She dipped another fry in a crystal bowl of ketchup.

"He was a competitive chap, no doubt, and had been studying aerodynamics. He shaved his head, his entire body . . . he looked like a billiard ball stuck on a cue." He laughed as the mental memory surfaced. "His shorts wouldn't stay on. He's five minutes from his race and he's gripping them, like this,"—he made a fist at his waist—"and when the gun goes off, he fires out of the blocks like a madman, but he can't hold on to his shorts anymore, so down they go. He's trying to stride long, but the shorts are slipping lower and lower"—Tanner laughed—"along about his knees, and he trips and rolls down the track, hops up, sans his short trousers, mind you, and keeps on running."

"You're kidding." Regina dipped another chip in her ketchup.

"But here's the kicker. In his effort to be as light as possible, Will didn't bother to slip on his knickers too, you see."

Regina's eyes popped wide and she laughed behind her hand, a soft pink tint on her cheeks. "Oh mercy, Tanner." Then she made a face, fanning the air with her fingers. "I'm trying not to picture it."

"I suppose it is a rather tawdry story. But 'twas the hardest I ever laughed. I thought I might be sick."

"Did he win?"

"No. He came in second, quit the team, grew his hair down to his shoulders, and became a café singer. Which he claims was what he wanted to do in the first place. So now you know my hardest giggle. What about you?"

She sobered, taking a sip of her Diet Coke. "Mama was a great laugher. Always telling Daddy a funny story. If there was no laughter in the house, she'd get something going. Make up a game or something. When she died we didn't laugh for about a year. Poor Gram. Her final months had very little laughter. But when we started going to Al and Miriam's most nights for dinner,

Al started every meal with a story. Lots of times about being best friends with Daddy in the '60s in a segregated South.

"But hardest laugh?" She took another drink, eyeing him over the rim of her glass. "I don't know. Seeing you walk the streets of Hessenberg dressed like Sonny Bono was pretty hilarious."

Merriment sparkled in her eyes and Tanner's heart knocked on his head. *Let's fall in love, mate.*

Blast it all if he wasn't one pulse away from drawing her to her feet and kissing those blessed, delicious, *laughing* lips. "It didn't feel so funny at the time but now . . ." He grinned. "It was quite a giggle, was it not?"

"Yeah, it was fun." Her gaze met his for one long, glorious moment. "So,"—she cleared her throat, shifting her gaze, wiping her hand on her napkin—"I've done all the talking. Wh–what was it you said the king needed from me? Take the Oath of the Throne?"

"Yes." Tanner reached for his soft drink, drowning his sizzling image of kissing her. *Don't go there, ole chap. It'll only lead to heartache.* "He wants you to go ahead, get on with the swearing in, as it were, style you Princess of Hessenberg, and establish the House of Augustine-Saxon. Then in six months to a year, whenever you're ready, when the government is more established, we'll hold the coronation for you to be Grand Duchess. He and the prime minister believe it's a strong countermeasure to the muck Seamus is stirring. We'll organize some good press."

"But I've not even been here a week."

"I know. We wanted to give you time. But showing strong support for the entail, for your uncle's wishes, for the king and current government, will stabilize the people."

"Tanner, what would you do if you were me?"

He leaned forward, propping his arms on his knees. "I don't know really. I'd like to think I'd take the oath. But I'm not even remotely in your shoes, Regina. If you choose not to take the oath, then we must believe, hope, something good will come about for our dear duchy." He smiled at her. "On the other hand, we found you and that was a very good thing."

"Tanner,"—she sobered—"I was going over the entail earlier—"

"Were you now?" She proved her worth more every day.

"Do you know anything about bonds associated with the entail?"

"What kind of bonds? Savings? War? Bearer?"

"The text didn't say." She hesitated, thinking. "Do you know if there's money to help out the duchy as it comes into its own?"

"Nothing more than the regular avenues of an economy. However, the duke's holdings were held in trust by the Brighton royal family. You'll receive his accounts when you and King Nathaniel II sign the entail, ending the agreement. It's a sizable fortune."

"Are there bonds in the holdings?"

Tanner reached for his phone. "Not that I'm aware. But I've not looked closely." He tapped a note to himself. *Bonds.* "I'll have Louis collect the data on the duke's assets."

"If you were me, you'd take the oath." Stated. Not asked. As if she were trying to understand her own heart and mind.

"I would. And I'd not fear Seamus. I'd move to Hessenberg and live happily ever after."

She made a face. "Now you're mocking me."

"Am I? The farthest thing from it, Regina. I don't want you to leave. There. I said it."

She shifted in her seat, shoving her remaining fries toward the center of her plate. "Why don't you want me to go?"

"Because I'd miss you." He slipped from his chair and moved to her, pulling her into his arms. Slowly, he rocked from side to side.

"I'd miss you too."

Releasing her, he stepped back. "Regina, I should tell you something." Tanner tucked his hands into his pockets, his heart sounding a full retreat. "This afternoon I went to a birthday party."

"Gasp! I can't believe it. A *birthday* party!" She laughed. "You look so grim."

"I'm not the man you think I am." He paced a few steps, then circled back. "I've done a horrid thing and to be honest, I'm not sure you'll feel anything but disdain for me once I tell you the story."

"Tanner, don't predict my feelings. It's annoying. I can't imagine you'd hurt a fly, let alone do something horrid to anyone. Except maybe to yourself."

"Trust me, I did something horrid. Now that I have a few years of wisdom and the advantage of hindsight, I can't imagine what possessed me to abandon my post as a dad."

"Your post as a dad?"

There, he'd said it. Not as he'd intended, but thanks to his rambling heart he spewed the truth.

"I've twin daughters, Regina." Her eyes widened. But her lack of a visceral reaction urged him to go on. "Bella and Britta. Identical ten-year-olds."

"Tanner, that's great. But I don't get why I should feel disdain for you over twin daughters."

"Because this afternoon when I went to their birthday party, it was the first time I'd seen them in eight years. They did not even know me."

"Eight years?" She tapped his arm. "What happened?"

"Their mother, Trude, and I were college mates, friends. Nothing serious. We got on well, ran with the same crowd. After we graduated, the lot of us booked a holiday on the Mediterranean. Near the end of our stay, after a day of boating and swimming, we were all jolly, drinking too much, which I rarely did—drink, that is—and Trude looked tan and lovely. We'd been flirty with one another all holiday and next thing we knew—"

"She got pregnant."

"One night. One time." He peeked sheepishly at her but inhaled without the constant dull pain that had been in his chest since he agreed to Trude's proposition. Confession to Regina was good for his soul. "First for both of us."

Tanner had purposefully not thought about that holiday in years. Or the night Trude told him in between violent sobs that she was pregnant. He never reminisced about the day he stopped by Dad's cathedral office to tell him he'd left seminary.

But there was a moment in every day, whether in his conscious or subconscious, he remembered leaving Trude's flat with the girls tucked in bed, never to return.

"I asked her to marry me. She said no. We didn't love each other. So I was a W and W dad. Wednesdays and weekends."

"How did you end up not seeing them for eight years?"

"She'd met a chap. Reese." Tanner cut his way through the mental weeds and overgrowth of his past. "They got married, and Trude began chatting me up on how the girls would be better off with one mum and one dad. She thought being with me confused and upset them. Then she brought in the force of an army to convince me I should back off and let Reese be the girls' dad."

"Now *that's* despicable and horrid. You believed her?"

"She hammered me and hammered me. The girls were two and had begun to cling to me, crying, when I dropped them off. I could see it was upsetting to Trude. To all of us. So, yes, I gave in, Regina. Then today she tells me she's divorced Reese, marrying a bloke named Evan and moving to America. And would I mind taking the girls for a while so she can pop over the pond with her new husband for a few years?"

"Is everything in your life zero to sixty? I think it's the way you roll." She laughed, laying hold of his forearm with a gentle squeeze. "Tanner, isn't this good news? You get to establish a relationship with your daughters."

"It is good news, indeed." He smiled at her support. But did she intend to skirt around how he abandoned his daughters? Not call it out, as Dad had done so unabashedly for years after Tanner made his decision? Even Mum reminded him of it every holiday until he told her, *enough.*

"But if I take them, I told her I'd be in charge of their diaries, their education, the lot. Trude didn't take well to the notion, so she's thinking."

"Tanner, you'd have to be in charge if Trude's in America."

"I might have told her that I'd not give them back. They'd be with me until graduation."

"Zero to sixty." She lowered her head, smiling. "All girls need their daddies, but they need their mamas too. Trust me."

"Let me ask you. What would you do if you were me?"

"Ah, turning the tables on me, I see." Reggie propped her chin in her hand. "All I can tell you is I was a ten-year-old girl once, and I remember two things. I adored my daddy, and I wanted him to adore me."

"But I'm a stranger to them."

"Maybe here." She tapped the corner of her eye. "But not here." Regina reached up, pressing her hand over his heart.

"Regina . . ." He collected her in his arms.

"Tanner . . ." She stepped back, shaking out her hands. A move that endeared her to him each time she did it. "We both have a lot on our plates. Me with this princess biz and you with becoming a full-time dad—"

"Possibly."

"No, probably. Maybe we shouldn't complicate and confuse things."

"Complicate? Regina, I was a content, neat, solitary man until I met you. Then all of a sudden, I'm restless, unsatisfied, yearning for things I thought belonged to other chaps. What kind of man sits in his knickers at night watching the telly alone? That was me a week ago and now . . . for the first time in eight years I realize how much I want to be the twins' dad. And I want . . . to fall . . .

in love." He held her gaze for a moment, then laughed softly, staring at the floor. "Zero to sixty."

"You want to fall in love? With me?" Regina's tone harmonized with the beat of his heart.

"I might."

She whipped around, started gathering up their dishes. "Jarvis is probably wondering if we're going to spend the night in here." She skirted around him, heading for the ballroom exit. "I'll go tell him we're done. Wait, I can just push the cart—"

"Regina." Tanner touched her arm. "It's okay if you don't feel the same way."

"How can I explore a love that may not be mine a week from now?" Her voice faltered, weak and watery.

"I'm telling you my heart is yours." He peered into her eyes, sinking deeper and deeper into the truth. "Now. Next week, next year."

"What if I move home? Then what?"

"Why can't you just admit you're our princess, Regina? Hessenberg is home. I need you here, with me." Raw. Real. Rooted in emotion.

"Tanner, excuse me, but I'm not making a decision about my future because you think you love me. Think you need me."

"Are you saying you don't have feelings for me?"

"Look, I–I,"—she shifted her weight, leaning on the cart— "I'm struggling to find my way through the notion of being a princess, of leaving my home, my friends and family, to live in a foreign country. So, no, I don't know how I feel about you. Exactly." Regina kicked at the ballroom floor. "Hessenberg is strange to me, Tanner. There's no Publix or Kohl's. No Target or Panera Bread. Who knew a princess had to give up so much? And you're asking me to make a decision about love? I just met you."

"And I, you, but I'm fairly certain I'm falling for you."

She reached up and brushed his hair away from his face. "I'm afraid we're Niagara Falls meeting the Grand Canyon."

He captured her hand in his. "Two forces of nature to be reckoned with." He kissed the back of her hand. "I think we can make it work."

"Hey, zero to sixty, I may drive fast, but my heart putts along at a steady thirty miles per hour." She withdrew her hand from his.

"All right." Tanner gripped the cart handle and pushed toward the door. "At least you're moving."

Thirty miles an hour. Straight for his heart.

TWENTY-THREE

*A*t last, a voice message from Daddy.

"Reg, sweet pea, we keep missing each other. Sounds like you're doing good over there. We miss you but are so proud of you. What's that, Sadie? Oh, she sends her love and a friend from the bank brought in a picture of you from a Hessenberg paper. It looked like you showed that photographer who's boss." Daddy yawned into the phone. "Give a buzz tomorrow or something. Love you."

"What's going on?" Louis trapped Tanner on the other side of his desk. "You're humming."

"Nothing's going on." Tanner reached behind his desk to the printer. The archbishop sent over the swearing-in oath and a ceremony script for review. "Slept well last night, 'tis all."

Louis made a face. "You look happy, not rested. You do realize it's Monday morning."

"Are you saying I'm usually unhappy on Monday mornings?" Tanner eyed his aide.

"I think my phone is ringing." Louis turned on his heel and

made for the door. "And there's a gentleman to see you. He apologizes for coming unscheduled."

"Who is it?" Tanner glanced at his watch. Dickenson was on his way with Regina.

"Sir Thomas Blakely."

"Of Blakely Oil?" One of the few remaining family-owned oil companies in the North Sea region. "Did he say why he is here?" Sir Blakely was the senior member of the company's board of directors. The president and CEO. Tanner couldn't imagine what sort of errand Old Man Blakely would see to himself.

"No, but he seems to have something on his mind."

"Send him in, please." Tanner slipped on his suit jacket and squared away his tie. Sir Thomas Blakely. Had he come to give a donation? Set up an arts or education trust? The museum had recently petitioned patrons for donations.

Tanner greeted Sir Blakely as he entered, wearing a fine-tweed suit and leaning on a brass-handled cane. "My apologies for coming unannounced, but I was driving past the manor when I had a revelation. So I asked my driver to turn in." His hazel eyes sparkled with a youthful vibrancy, and his voice sounded strong and clear. "I'll have a seat, if you don't mind. My assistant is sending over documents for you to see."

"Please, make yourself at home. Do you care for a spot of tea?"

"Just had mine, thank you." Blakely sat on the couch, favoring his right hip, then folded his hands on top of his cane. "You see, I'm preparing to retire in a year." He pointed at Tanner. "I'll be eighty-one next year, thank you kindly, and I've been at the helm of Blakely Oil since I was twenty-five when my father dropped dead from a sudden heart attack."

"You've had quite a career, Sir Blakely." Tanner took a seat across from the oil magnate. "I studied your international commerce work at the law college."

"Did you now, my boy? Indeed, indeed." For a moment, his

stare seemed to fix on something only seen in his mind's eye, then he gazed at Tanner. "Well now, why I am here? You see, I ordered an audit on all financial records dating back to when my grandfather founded this company with little more than a dream. I want to make sure things are spit-spot before I hand the reins to my son and grandson.

"In doing so, the accountant came across our usual odd stockholder who seems to have vanished from the face of the earth. But Grandfather also offered his investors bearer bonds. Most of those have been cashed out, but we've one bond account held in escrow for more than a hundred years. Though curious, we never did much more than speculate about the account owner. But the auditor noticed not one thin shilling had ever been drawn by the bond holder."

"More than a hundred years? Fascinating." Filler conversation, waiting for him to go on. Did Blakely come to sign over the account to Tanner's office? Otherwise, the Minister of Finance resided on the third floor.

"We talked of putting out a search for the bond holder, but then I remembered that Grandfather kept a register of those early investors. I've kept it in my safe at home."

Louis knocked on the door. "These came for you, Sir Blakely."

"Thank you, young chap." He pointed to Tanner with his cane. "Give them to this lad." Louis arched his brow and passed over the single folder. "You see," Sir Blakely went on, "Grandfather and Prince Francis were chums. Both were fascinated with the newfangled automobile. When Grandfather went to find his fortune in oil instead of gold, Prince Francis offered his assistance. I remember my grandfather telling me as much when I was a boy at his knee. He was always saddened over the prince's final lot."

Tanner opened the file to find a piece of paper listing the bond numbers. And three photocopies of handwritten letters.

Two from the senior Blakely, Artimus, to Prince Francis, and one from Prince Francis to Blakely—dictated to Otto Pritchard.

They all contained brief exchanges about life and seeing one another in the spring season, but nothing to indicate a financial partnership.

Tanner studied the bond numbers. Simple, thousand-pound bonds.

"Do you believe these bonds were purchased by Prince Francis?" he said.

"I'd hoped to tell you for certain, but when I checked Grandfather's registry, he'd only marked the bearer bond numbers with initials, not names. You'll see the copy there, in the back." Blakely tapped the back of the papers with his cane.

Handy tool, a cane.

"Any that would match the prince's?"

"Not one that we could make out." He stomped his cane. "But these are the only bonds we believe have never been collected upon. The timing is curious, what with the prince fleeing in the dead of night to never return. Either he left the bonds behind or passed them on to his niece, Princess Alice. Or even Princess Esmé."

Possible, possible. At this stage, Tanner would believe just about anything. A pot of gold at the end of the rainbow? Why jolly well not?

"How much is in escrow?" Tanner worked a few numbers in his head. If Prince Francis invested several thousand, maybe tens of thousands, that was a tidy sum for any man, even a royal man, pre-1914. And the bonds would be worth millions today given the success of Blakely Oil.

"A hundred million dollars."

"A hundred million dollars?" Tanner launched to his feet. "You're joking."

"I am not," Sir Blakely said. "My barrister recommends we possess the account as it's been a hundred years with no activity.

He claims it's a dead account and we should petition the courts to make it legally ours."

"A hundred million seems pretty alive to me."

The old Sir of European Oil chuckled. "I quite agree. But my thinking is if the bonds do belong to Prince Francis's heir, and if we've found the princess . . ."

"We have, sir."

"Then I'd like to honor my grandfather's friendship with the prince and let the money go to his heir. Let the princess reap the reward. Her uncle's trust in my grandfather was the first seed of our success."

"Except we don't know the whereabouts of the bonds."

"Might the princess have them? Among her things in America? Perhaps her grandmother, Princess Alice, left them to her without her realizing it. Children often sneer at old things like bonds and papers left to them by their elders."

"But you're quite sure these bonds belonged to the prince." With a sigh, Tanner sat back. "Sir Blakely, we've lost so many of Prince Francis's records. He kept few diaries, wrote few letters."

"No, I'm not sure, but Grandfather once told me the prince invested in his hunt for oil. So I do believe those bond numbers did belong to him."

"But, sir, in the last one hundred years, cleaning and construction crews have gone over every inch of the palace and this manor. Rebuilding. Remodeling. Repairing. No bonds were ever found. For all we know, the prince took the bonds with him. They could've been destroyed or lost."

"Ask the princess. Perhaps she knows." With a groan, Blakely stood.

"I will." Could those be the bonds she mentioned to him the other day? But she didn't actually have possession of the bonds. Just read about them in the entail. Besides, Tanner doubted a former accountant would disregard old bearer bonds if she found them. Maybe her father had yet another box of secrets in the attic. Or maybe they were in some safe deposit box in an unknown bank in some unknown country. Tanner made a mental note to make sure Louis inquired about bonds when collecting data on the prince's trust.

"In the meantime, our princess is a millionaire a hundred times over if she can find those bonds." Blakely inched his way between the couch and end table, aiming for the door. He peered back at Tanner.

"Well, what's she like?"

"Sh–she's beautiful. Smart. Funny. Kind."

"The one for the job?"

"Very much so."

"Good." He jabbed the air with his cane. "Once it's all sorted out and that blowhard Seamus Fitzsimmons is put in his place, I'll have Her Royal Highness to our cottage for tea."

Tanner smiled. The Blakely *cottage* rivaled the palace in size and opulence. "I'll tell her, sir. I'm sure she'd like that very much."

She'd agreed to take the Oath of the Throne.

King Nathaniel II was eager to make her "official" with her legal and royal status restored, demonstrating to the people that Hessenberg was moving forward.

Court petition or not, Reggie was restoring their sovereign, independent state status. Nathaniel said this move would also dampen the discontentment Seamus Fitzsimmons was inspiring.

But now that Reggie walked beside Tanner toward the Wettin Manor chapel, fear waged war in her soul.

She wore one of the Melinda House dresses but had refused the fancy high heels and wore her boots instead. She needed to walk in her own shoes. Otherwise, she didn't think she'd make it.

Tanner gave her a weird once-over, eyeing her boots when he picked her up. He started to say something, then thought better of it. "Shall we be off?"

But from the moment she got in his car to entering Wettin Manor, Reggie felt odd, out of sorts, as if this commitment might somehow steal her very essence. Not define it.

She felt ill. Weak. Would she ever be Reggie Beswick again?

"Wait, wait." She whirled around and retreated down the hall, her boot heels thudding an anxious *fleeing* resonance against the marble floor. "I can't, Tanner. I can't."

"Regina, love, talk to me."

She ducked into a small work area containing a copier and a coffeemaker. "First, stop calling me *love*. It's too . . . too personal. Second, I can't, I can't." She tried to draw a solid breath, but her lungs refused to function.

"You're panicking."

"No, no, I'm pretty sure I'm not panicking." She lunged at him, arms flailing, eyes bugged. "I'm freaking out."

"So you've changed your mind? You don't want to take the oath?" Tanner held his voice steady, his shoulders square.

"No. Yes. I can't." She held her arms by her side board-stiff, her hands balled into fists, examining her thoughts through the broad lens of her fear.

"If this is about Seamus—"

"Forget Seamus. This is about me." She relaxed, breathing out. Then in. "About losing myself, about never being able to go home again."

"Regina, you can go home anytime you like. Well, almost anytime." Tanner smiled, trying to draw her in. He'd said nothing so far of their conversation in the ballroom and his declaration of love. Which was fine with Reggie. She had enough on her mind. "You'll have your own Royal Air Force One."

"In my heart, Tanner. I'm talking about home in my heart."

She folded both hands over her heart. "You know, when you're down or blue, and you call up friends and say, 'Let's do something.' Or on a crisp spring afternoon, you ride your bike through the old neighborhood with the sun and breeze in your face, remembering how you laughed and ran around with your friends like banshees all summer long. Or you wait in the longest line at the grocery store because you want to check out with your favorite cashier. Or the afternoon you find an old shortcut through town that you'd forgotten.

"How will I do that here? Where will my memories and thoughts go on a quiet Sunday afternoon? Who will call me up and say, 'Come to the house for dinner?'"

"I'd very much like to ring you for dinner."

"Besides all of this, there was no light . . . no *sign*."

"What are you talking about?"

"I'd asked God for a sign. It's silly, I know, but I need some confirmation that I am supposed to be the princess because he wants me to be, not because Prince Francis wanted to restart his royal line long after he'd gone."

"And you didn't get your sign?"

"No." With a sigh, she leaned against the wall. "You'd think the good Lord would indulge me considering this princess business came out of the blue and all. And because I just might end up with my head on the guillotine."

"The guillotine was torn down in the 50s, you'll be happy to know." This time a wink accompanied Tanner's smile.

Reggie sneered at him, then broke into a grin, unable to hang on to her tension. "Fine, then I'll end up on the guillotine of the press."

"Is that what this is about? The press conference this afternoon? We've rehearsed. I've prepared you. You're ready."

"Tanner, you're all about the surface stuff, going through the motions. I'm talking about my heart, my identity. My whole world is changing. I'm surrendering to another way of life, to another country, to giving up friends and forging new relationships."

"Yes, Regina, your whole world is changing. But isn't that what courage to step into your calling is all about? Discovering the truth and doing everything in your power to obtain it? To live it?"

She dropped down to the only chair in the small office space. "You make it sound so noble. Yet I feel so frail and weak." *Unworthy.* "I just ask God for a small sign, a light, or something miraculous."

"Regina,"—Tanner knelt next to her, his tone full of comfort, his manner masculine and confident—"maybe this is a leap of faith. No signs. No safety nets. Just faith."

She breathed in, dabbing her fingers under her eyes, catching her tears. "I can't go forward, but I can't go backward either, no matter how hard I try to work it out in my head. I close my eyes and try to freeze time on the night I was arguing with Urban about the Vet, right before you showed up. But I can't. Bam! There you are in my mind's eye and everything fast-forwards to now."

"Because once you know who you really are, you can't go back to who you thought you were." He slipped his hand into hers. "This is your struggle. You can't go back."

She pulled her hand free. "This habit of telling me how I feel has got to go."

"Am I wrong?"

"Which is even more irritating. No, you're not wrong." She flicked his forehead with her finger. "But you should be."

"So what do you want to do here?" He rubbed the spot on his forehead where her flick landed.

"I feel like I'm betraying myself by even considering this princess gig."

"Wait here, please. I'll be right back." Tanner strode out of the cubbyhole room and down the hall.

"Sure, fine, whatever." Reggie propped her head against the wall. If this decision wrecked her, how was she going to act as proper Head of State?

She was doomed. Hessenberg was doomed.

"Regina?" She gazed toward the door. Tanner entered with a tall *hello!* gorgeous blonde with summer-sky blue eyes. "This is Susanna Truitt, King Nathaniel's fiancée. Susanna, Regina Beswick, Princess of Hessenberg."

"Lovely to meet you." Susanna smiled and curtseyed.

"You too." Reggie curtseyed back.

"You don't curtsey to Susanna, Reg ... oh, never mind." Tanner checked with Susanna. "Bring her down when she's ready?"

"I will. You tell those blokes to be patient, hear me?" Her sweet Southern voice filled the small space, and Reggie scooped Susanna up in a giant hug.

"Oh, thank you, thank you. It's so good to hear your voice, the sound of home."

"Oh, the sweet sound of the South." Susanna returned Reggie's hug, her gentle laughter soothing the edge from Reggie's tension.

"How do you do it?" Reggie released Susanna and leaned against the wall. "Leave it all behind?"

"In my case, falling in love helped." Susanna folded her arms and joined Reggie against the wall. She wore a rich, royal blue dress with a V-neck and long sleeves. "I had months between meeting Nathaniel and getting engaged. By the time he proposed, I missed him so much I'd have lived on a desert island if he'd have asked. Besides, being the wife of the king doesn't have the same pressure as being the heir, Regina. Can I call you Regina?"

"Are you kidding? Regina, Reggie, Reg ... shoot, I'd answer to 'Yo, Bubba' about now." Reggie laughed, exhaling into Susanna's calming presence. "So you fell in love. With a prince."

"And they say it only happens in fairy tales."

"Are you adjusting to royal life?"

"I am. Little by little. The people are lovely and welcoming, though I'm not sure I'll ever get used to the photographers."

"I can deal with the photographers. It's leaving my entire life behind that's wigging me out."

Susanna nodded in understanding. "I hear you, and it's a decision you shouldn't take lightly. When I knew I was falling for Nathaniel, I told him I wouldn't marry him. I didn't want him to have to choose between me and his country. Then he moved heaven and earth, as it were, to marry me. But I still had to decide, 'Can I leave everything behind for love?' I think I'm still deciding sometimes."

"But I'm not in love." She pushed her affection for Tanner aside.

"Can you love this country? The people? Can you appreciate what God has called you to do?"

"But has he? Called me?"

"Oh mercy, now you really sound like Nathaniel. When I met him, he was all wadded up, wondering if he was really called as the heir of Brighton's throne. Doubting every bit as much as you are right now. He wondered if God called him to be king."

"Exactly. So am I to restore the House of Augustine-Saxon just because old Prince Francis wanted it that way or God?"

"You're standing here right now, Reggie. God literally came for you. In the form of Tanner, but still, he came for you. Do you know how long people looked for the heir? Then suddenly one day, there you were. People like you and Nathaniel are in such a rare, treasured position. You can do good for so many. Most people live their whole lives trying to find their destiny, find their place in this world, and here you and Nathaniel have been born into something extraordinary." Susanna smiled. "Of course, he knew who he was from the beginning. And you just got the news last week."

"Bam, out of the blue." Reggie made an exploding motion

with her hands. Yet she saw the picture Susanna had painted. "I just need to decide if I'm going to step into this royal world or not."

"As did Nathaniel. Abdicating wasn't an option for him, so he had to decide, in his heart, that being king was God's will for him."

"Which is why I'm hesitant to walk down that hall and take the oath, Susanna." Reggie pointed in the direction of the chapel. "I need to know for sure. I can't have one foot here and one in Tallahassee."

"So decide. But it's my conviction God has chosen you for such a time as this. Ask yourself if you can leave the truth of who you are—the princess. Can you take a chance, embrace the unknowns, and see what God has for you? Or will you go back to America, dig in where it's familiar, and live the rest of your life wondering what might have been, a big part of your heart chained and closed off?"

A fast tear slipped down Reggie's cheek and she caught it with the back of her hand, fixing her eyes on the opposite wall. She wanted this to be easy and fun, without doubt. But that wasn't faith, was it?

Susanna reached for a napkin behind the coffeemaker and passed it to Reggie. "Look, I'm as green at this as you, but if you want, I'll be here for you. I'll be your friend."

"My Southern-fried friend on these North Sea shores?" Reggie exhaled, the exchange inspiring more tears. "When I took the plunge to open the car shop with Al, it was a big gamble. Not only with my future and finances, but with his. I had no idea if we'd succeed, but I had just enough vision to make me take the leap."

"What about now? Do you have enough vision to take the leap? That's all it requires to start something amazing. A glimpse at the potential."

"My mind is seeing clear, but it's this dang knot in my stomach that seems pretty blind." Reggie exhaled a laugh, wadding up her tear-stained napkin and tossing it in the trash.

"What do you think?" Susanna tipped her head toward the hall. "Have we kept the folks waiting long enough?"

Reggie raised her courage. "Yeah, let's do this."

Susanna caught her by the arm as she passed for the door. "If it's any encouragement, I believe in you. I know you can do this."

Reggie breathed out, her gaze fixed on the door. "Thank you. Now, let's go before I change my mind."

"For Hessenberg?" Susanna said.

"Yes, for Hessenberg. For my mama and my gram."

The moment she walked into Wettin Manor chapel, Reggie sensed the presence of the Lord, like she had when she was young, with his hand resting on her head. Perhaps he'd come down to oversee the proceedings personally.

The small chapel was filled with men and women who rose to their feet as she entered—the king, the prime minister, the archbishop, other government leaders and ministers, members of the press. All waiting for her.

Then there was Tanner. Emanating courage as Reggie made her way forward, cutting through warm and cold silky swirls, like the wind beneath an angel's wing, above her head and around her legs.

The archbishop greeted her at the altar. "Are you ready to take the Oath of the Throne?"

A photographer tucked in behind the pulpit, aimed his camera.

"I am," she said with a confidence not her own.

The archbishop read from his script. "This oath, Regina, is between you and the Almighty, and the witnesses here." His tone was steady and kind. "Then we will prepare for a royal coronation where your pledge is between you and the people."

Reggie drew up straighter, taller. She was going to embrace this, run the race set before her.

"Regina,"—the archbishop took command—"please kneel."

She wobbled forward, legs trembling, and knelt, her heartbeat sounding in her ears.

"Regina Alice Beswick, do you pledge your allegiance to God Almighty and the Lord Jesus Christ to defend the faith and freedom of the Grand Duchy of Hessenberg?"

"I do."

"Do you pledge the same to hold the people in high esteem, serving them, submitting to the laws of the land?"

A smooth, invisible oil poured over her head and slipped down to her temples, releasing the thick fragrance of spices all around her. Chills multiplied and shimmied down her spine.

The archbishop continued with his questions of commitment. Reggie answered with her simple "I do" until her tears overflowed.

"May it be as you have spoken. Let your yes be yes and your no be no." The archbishop walked behind the communion table and returned with a plain brown mantle, which he billowed over her head, shoulders, and back. The coarse brown material settled on her, heavy but fragrant.

"Almighty Lord, clothe her in humility that she may be your servant. Grant her the wisdom of King Solomon, the heart of King David, and the prosperity of heaven."

As the archbishop prayed, reading Scripture, tremors rolled through Reggie, crashing against her mind, shaking her will and realigning her very identity.

Eyes closed. In the moment. Tears streaming.

"Your Majesty, King Nathaniel II, come forward."

Reggie sensed the king standing beside her.

"I style you Her Royal Highness Princess Regina Alice Beswick Augustine-Saxon, and by the laws and grants of the royal House of Stratton of Brighton, restore the House of Augustine-Saxon. May the Lord bless you, keep you, and cause his face to shine upon you."

Murmurs of assent raised in the chapel.

The archbishop returned. "Remember the difference between David and Saul, Your Majesty. It was the posture of their hearts. David sought the favor of the Lord, crying out, 'Remember your servant, Lord.' While Saul sought the favor of the people, crying out, 'Remember me before the people.' Regina, be like David. Seek the Lord *your* God. Let us pray."

Reggie lowered her head and fixed her gaze on God.

When the archbishop said amen, he followed with, "Long live Princess Regina of Hessenberg."

The witnesses chorused after him. "Long live Princess Regina of Hessenberg."

TWENTY-FOUR

eamus peered out his office window down to the street, watching the media flow into the building. He jumped to his phone when it rang.

"Well?" Seamus barked. It was about time Brogan rang up. *Incompetent ingrate.*

"She took the Oath of the Throne five minutes ago, sir."

"In the manor chapel?"

"Yes, sir."

He swore. "Under our noses. How did we not know this?" His invitation omission said more than words.

"The press conference is about to commence."

"Get down there. See what's going on." Seamus rang off, boiling and reeling. Arrogant Burkhardt. No respect. No gratitude. After all Seamus had done for him—saving him out of the mess he'd created with Trude, advising him after he left seminary.

Snatching up his phone again, Seamus rang Morris Alderman over at the *LibP.* "Morris? Seamus. I'm fine, fine . . . How about helping me take my fight to the next level?"

It was late when they returned to the palace. The press conference went well. Reporters packed the media room and asked cordial questions about Reggie's life and thoughts on becoming a princess.

She'd anticipated questions about the governor's petition and braced for wisecracks about being a redneck royal. But Tanner had orchestrated the question-and-answer portion, limiting the time, then escorting Reggie out of the Wettin Manor media room after ten minutes.

And she was grateful.

Once they arrived at Meadowbluff, Jarvis led Reggie and Tanner into the palace parlor, where he'd set an arrangement of flowers, cakes, and two flutes of champagne.

"H–how'd I do?" Reggie faced Tanner, lost in a swirl of emotions.

"Splendid, Regina. Most splendid. The oath ceremony was most moving. Sincere. The presser went well. How do you feel?"

"I feel . . . I don't know how I feel." She reached for the nearest chair, her legs suddenly weak. "Different."

Tanner knelt next to her, touching her chin gently with the tip of his finger. "Give it a moment to sink in, Regina. You don't have to grasp it all right now."

He was right. Reggie exhaled, pressing her hand to her middle. "I feel peace." She peered at Tanner and slipped her hand into his. "Thank you."

"For what?"

"Putting up with me. For bringing Susanna into the coffee room. For believing in me when I didn't believe in myself."

"I do believe in you, Regina." His gaze lingered on her face for a moment, then he stood, releasing her hand. "As for the other thing . . . in the ballroom, I—"

"Tanner, there's a glow in the trees." Reggie moved around him toward the window and pressed her forehead against the cold pane.

"I don't see a glow in the trees." Tanner cupped his hands around his eyes and peered out the window.

"Straight ahead. In the woods."

Otherwise, the night scene appeared normal. The palace grounds were lit with blue and gold luminaries strategically stationed to paint the palace walls with light. But beyond the palace grounds a silky, twinkling glow bloomed from the heart of the dark forest.

"Where? There's nothing out there." Tanner stepped back from the window.

"I'm sure I saw something." Reggie squinted toward the thin line between light and dark. It must be a reflection. Or some anomaly. "Tanner, is there a celebration because I took the oath?" There it was again, swelling up from the ground, billowing, then fading, but never dying.

"We didn't want to make a big to-do just yet." Tanner turned back to the room. "Let the people get used to the idea of a Hessenberg royal. Get through the end of the entail and all. We'll celebrate in a grand way for your coronation. Regina, remember when you spoke to me of bonds?"

She turned away from the window. "The ones mentioned in the entail." She tapped the windowpane. "Tanner, seriously, you didn't see a glow in the woods?"

"Could your father have discovered bearer bonds among your gram's things? And no, I saw no glow." He grinned at his rhyme.

"Bonds? Not that I'm aware. All he had of Gram's was that one box. The one with the fairy tale. Then why do I see a glow? Look, there it is, billowing." Reggie tapped the top left of the pane. "Like a star fallen to earth."

Tanner angled left to see beyond the glass. "Maybe it's your sign. The one you asked of God." He reached for a napkin and one of the cakes. "What about jewels? Did you ever see a tiara or any diamond necklaces or earrings?"

"Tiara and diamonds. No, never. Gram was very simple. She wore a plain gold wedding band and nothing more. What do you mean bearer bonds?" Reggie joined Tanner by the cakes and champagne, but kept one eye on the window.

"Ever hear of Blakely Oil?"

"Um, yes. I'm from Florida, not east outer Mars. One of my clients at Backlund invested in Blakely Oil. Made a killing." The little chocolate cakes looked yummy. Reggie reached for a napkin, then chose a cake. She wasn't all that hungry but she felt she should celebrate today in some way. Like with chocolate.

"The old man, Sir Blakely, came to see me Monday. His company was doing an audit and came across an escrow account that has never been touched. The money is tied to bearer bonds, and he believes the bonds were purchased by Prince Francis."

"Why does he think that?"

"Because his grandfather, founder of Blakely Oil, was chums with your great-great-great-uncle. Old Man Blakely is pretty sure this escrow money belongs to you, the heir of Prince Francis."

"But I don't have any bearer bonds." On the edge of the window, the glow bloomed again, causing a swirling anticipation in Reggie's gut. She shoved the last of her cake in her mouth. "I'm going out there."

"Out where?" Tanner tossed his napkin to the table and heeled after her as she fired out of the parlor.

"Out there." She pointed in the direction of the glow. "Treasure hunting." Down the hall, through the kitchen, and out the back door, her boots thudding, her skirt swaying, Reggie wondered if she finally had her sign.

Tanner ducked under a branch as he chased Regina through the blackness toward... *nothing.*

Until now, he'd found Regina sane and strong, a spark of life, reasonable, educated, and uncompromisingly beautiful. At least in his eyes. But this? Seeing a light that was not there . . . running through a pitch-black forest on a cold night was lunacy.

Was that rain he sensed in the wind?

Tanner had caught just Regina as she fired out the kitchen door, making her pause long enough for Jarvis to get a couple of torches.

"Regina, this is ludicrous." Tanner yelped when his hair caught in a low-swung limb.

"Are you okay?" She ran back to him, breathless, her burnished tresses blustering about her face.

Tanner aimed his torchlight at his own head. "I'm caught." He inhaled and jerked free, wincing. "That branch robbed me of my hair."

"Simmer down, Samson. I think you can carry on."

"Har-har. You're such a funny woman."

She shined her light on him. "Sorry, but you scared the wits out of me. You scream like a girl." She whirled around, pressing forward through the darkness.

"Excuse me, I do not scream like a *girl*." He intoned her accent. "I have a very manly scream." He belted out his best scream just to prove it.

"Yeah, but that's not what I heard, Tanner."

"Must have been the wind . . . distorting my voice." He fixed his torchlight on the path ahead, then up at the trees. "Regina, we should go back. It's going to rain."

"Tanner, you really don't see anything? Glowing about right over there?" She fired her beam through the trees on her right.

"No, love, I don't. I'm sorry."

"Then why do I?"

He sighed, then laughed. "Maybe it's the sign you asked from God."

"Yeah, maybe. Or . . . a television or film studio making a movie? Or some weird glow from a river or stream?"

"There's no television or film studio out there, and the stream runs south of here."

She fell against the nearest tree. "Why give me a sign *after* I've taken the oath? I needed it before."

"Who knows the Lord's mysterious ways?" Tanner settled against the tree, next to Regina.

"Your dad did a good job at the oath ceremony," she said, low and soft, more to herself than Tanner.

"He did." Tanner raised his torch to the trees. Did he feel raindrops?

"You still at odds with him?"

"We're never at odds, Regina. We simply don't see things the same."

"What did he say about your tryst with Trude?"

"Not 'Well done, my boy,' I'll grant you."

"Ah, so that's it." She stopped hacking through the brush. "You're at odds over what happened with Trude."

"We're not at odds." Tanner exhaled, rubbed his new bald spot on top of his head. "I was following in his footsteps to serve in the church, but I resigned my spot at the seminary when Trude told me she was pregnant."

"I'm sure that was a hard conversation."

"Excruciating. I'd failed him, the family, God. Believe it or not, Seamus Fitzsimmons came along and sort of rescued me. Set me on to law school. Kept the scandal of the archbishop's son having children out of wedlock from the press."

"And look where you are now, Tanner. The Minister of Culture."

"The irony is not lost on me. The Minister of Culture instead of a minister of the gospel."

"Hey, my pastor back home is always preaching that we don't have to be in full-time ministry to share the good news."

"Perhaps, but the Lord can find a better candidate than me to share his news."

"And he could find a better candidate than me for princess, but here I am." She shrugged. "What're you going to do?"

"You *are* the perfect princess." The wind shuffled through the branches, and in the distance an owl's hoot celebrated the night. "The Lord knew what he was doing."

"I see, but with you he's all wet and out of touch."

"Let's just say God and I have a deal. I leave him alone and he returns the favor."

"How refreshing. You get to stay in your pain and shame."

"Regina, don't try sarcastic trickery with me." He raised his torch to her face. "And don't try to tell me tales of God's grace and goodness or how I can return to a relationship with him. Can we go? I'm cold and hungry."

"You do realize this prison you're in is self-imposed?"

Blimey. "God disciplines a man, or the man disciplines himself. I chose the latter."

"Too bad,"—she started around him—"because God would've been kinder, more generous, and definitely more loving."

"Never mind," he said. How did she sneak into his heart and find all of his secrets? "What's going on with your *glow*?"

Regina pushed away from the tree and stepped through a bit of brush and brambles, stirring a dewy scent from the earth's floor. "Gone. I can't see it anymore."

"I'm sorry, Regina. Maybe if I hadn't stopped to talk . . ."

"You really do love playing the martyr, don't you? Taking the blame for everything isn't going to make God or your dad or your girls love you any more. Or less." She ducked past him, the scent of her hair blending with the raw fragrance of forest.

Her pointed words blew hard against his carefully constructed emotional barriers and shook his resolve to view the world his way.

A low, threatening thunder rumbled above the treetops and the dewy, cold breeze kicked up, tugging weak leaves from their limbs. Lightning flickered from the east to west.

"Was that it?" Regina turned back. "Lightning? The glow was lightning?"

"Couldn't have been. Because I saw the lightning." Tanner reached for her arm, and when she looked at him, his heart sank further into love.

"Tanner, I just want you to know—"

"I love you, Regina. I have to say it. I love you madly."

"Love me?" The wind swooped down from the treetops and swirled between them.

"I'm sorry the timing is all wrong. But I love you. If I don't tell you now my heart will burst. I don't care if you return my feelings."

Her soft laugh drummed against his pulsing heart. "I think I love you back. It's just happening so fast. Everything is happening so fast."

The wind shifted again, bringing the first drops of rain. "Regina,"—Tanner brushed her wild, beautiful red tresses out of her eyes and pulled her into his arms—"Just hearing you feel the same is enough for now. Ah, you're shivering. The wind is a bit chilled."

"It's not the wind, Tanner." She giggled and trembled as she brushed her hands over his chest. "You make me nervous."

"Because I love you?" He raised her chin. "And want to kiss you?"

"Yes, and I'm scared to death. Falling in love and becoming a princess all in one fell swoop."

He smoothed his hands over her hair and down her back. "Then we'll wait. Take things at thirty miles per hour."

"But it's a dark and stormy night. The wind is blustery, we're about to get soaked, and all I can think about is that scene in *Sweet Home Alabama* where Melanie kisses Jake in the rain . . ." She roped her arms around his neck. "Tanner Burkhardt, if you don't kiss me . . ."

"While you're thinking of Melanie and Jake? Whoever they are . . ."

She rose up on her toes and pressed her forehead to his. "I'm not thinking of anyone but you on this stormy, romantic night. Can't you feel my heart beating?"

"Not for the horse race going on in my own chest." He fell against the tree, drawing her to him. "I do love you, Regina. Most ardently."

"I love you back, Tanner. Most ardently."

His lowered his lips to hers, brushing over them with a light, feathery touch. She smiled, her breath warm on his face. "Tickles."

"Yeah, tickles . . ." Tanner circled his arms tighter as she wound her fingers into his hair, making her his with the passion of his kiss, a fire igniting in his heart, burning away every hindrance to love.

She was melting, floating, drowning in the taste of him. Warm, masculine, sweet. Her senses tingled with awakening love, breaking free from fear. And she was never going back.

This moment was worth the wait. "I love you," she whispered as his kiss faded.

"I love you too." Tanner raised his head for a quick breath, then kissed her cheek, her nose, her forehead.

She nestled against his chest, inhaling the scent of the rain, filling her entire being with the pure pleasure of the moment.

"That was fun." She rose up and tipped his head toward hers, kissing him, her lips already at home on his.

Tanner's embrace locked her against him so she couldn't tell if she stood on her own strength or his.

As their kiss lingered, another splatter of rain soaked through the back of her dress and the cold wind whistled about her legs. Nevertheless she was warmed by the fire of his touch.

When he lifted his head, Tanner picked her up and whirled her around, laughing, nuzzling her neck. Reggie joined his joy just as the heavens broke open, rain pouring from the clouds.

"We're getting drenched." Tanner set her down and held the sides of her head, brushing back her wet hair. "I love you, Regina, and we'll take this as fast or as slow as you want."

She threw her arms around his neck and kissed him again and again. "I can do this anytime I want?"

"Anytime you want. It is my pleasure to serve the Princess of Hessenberg." He stepped back, hand to his chest, and took a sweeping bow, making her laugh as the rain fell faster.

"I love you, Tanner. I never thought I'd fall in love so fast, but I do. I really do."

He kissed her, whispering in her ear. "I loved you the moment I saw you." Then he cupped her hand in his and together they darted out of the woods, running across the lawn, screaming and shouting.

At the palace, the kitchen door stood open with Jarvis's silhouette in the door frame.

"Your Majesty." He stood aside as Reggie ran into the warmth and the sweet cinnamon fragrance of the kitchen. "You'll catch your death . . ."

Serena waited with two towels. "I've a fire in the parlor. Chef made tea and cakes."

"Can we have hot chocolate?" Reggie took the towel her lady's maid offered, holding it to her chest. "I love hot chocolate on a cold fall night."

"Certainly," Jarvis said, giving Tanner a look. *What were you doing out there with her?*

"I saw a light, Jarvis," Reggie answered the man's expression, defending her man. *Her man.* She had a man. "In the forest, but I don't know, maybe it was nothing. Tanner said he didn't see anything." She laughed. *Ha, ha, I'm so weird, right?*

In truth, she wondered if Jarvis would ask about what had to be her goofy expression and why she couldn't stop smiling.

"Probably lightning, Your Majesty," he said, shifting his glance between Reggie and Tanner.

"You know, that's what I said. Lightning."

Tanner remained quiet, drying his hair, wiping down his arms. "Regina, you should get out of those wet clothes."

"What about you? You're soaked. Let's go sit by the fire."

Tanner cut a side glance toward Jarvis. "It's late. I think I'll head on to my flat. Work comes early."

"Right. Okay." Her heart plummeted faster than she could catch it. "I'll see you out."

Reggie walked with him to the main foyer, her hand brushing his, sending crazy sensations all through her. She wanted to curl up with him by the fire and talk about life, and kissing, life and more kissing. Her heart was alive. Her eyes were opened. The whole world glowed with a glow she'd never noticed before. She wanted to love more, give more, serve more . . .

Tanner paused at the door and gave her a curt bow. "We are being watched," he whispered.

"Why can't we just tell him?" Reggie motioned toward the corner from where Jarvis probably hovered.

"Do you really want to tell him?" His smile was intimate, only for her. "I like this between us for now."

"I'm in love. I want to shout it from the palace rooftops."

He sighed, pressing his hand over his middle. "Me too, but maybe we should keep this between us until we finish this business with the entail and Seamus, and I get through my negotiations with Trude and the girls."

"What?" His words stung, piercing her joy. "That was me a few days ago. Now *you* want to back off?"

"That's not what I said. I just don't want a horde of people knowing. I like keeping our feelings to ourselves. You've got enough controversy ahead of you without adding a romance with the opportunistic Minister of Culture."

"Opportunistic? That's what they'll call you?" She folded her arms, but really she wanted to sit and cry. "Are you?"

"Blimey, Regina, no." He tugged open the door. "I love you, and nothing is going to change that fact. But if we want a chance at this relationship, I think we best keep it quiet for now."

Her disappointment clouded her reasoning, but she understood, even felt the sincerity of his heart. Nonetheless, it ticked her off. "So now I *can't* kiss you whenever I want?" She reached for his collar, releasing the heady scent of his wet skin.

"When we're alone, kiss me all you want." He swallowed his passion. "This might be close to impossible to keep quiet, Regina, but don't you want to give us a chance to know each other without the press or the staff looking in?"

"I suppose so." She stepped toward him, brushing her hand over his chest. "Will you always be the reasonable one?"

"Trust me, this does not *feel* reasonable to me." He traced his finger along the base of her chin. "But I've watched enough—"

"Miss, miss,"—Reggie jumped away from Tanner's warm touch, turning to see Serena coming toward her with hand extended, holding Reggie's phone—"you've received several calls while I fixed the fire, so I answered this one."

"Thank you, Serena." Reggie took her phone. "Hello?"

"Reg, it's me, Al. How are you?"

"Al, hey, I'm fine." The sound of his voice made her weepy for home. "So, what's going on?" She sat on the bottom step of the wide, gilded staircase. "Did we get the Duesenberg?"

Tanner leaned against the door, arms folded, waiting and watching.

"No, no, Reg." His guttural laugh buzzed in her belly. "We didn't get the Duesenberg."

"Really? Rats. He said no? Why?"

"Reg, I told him no. And by the way, I sent the Vet home with Urban."

"You what?" She jerked to her feet, stumbling down the bottom step.

"I wanted to tell you all of this in person, but I saw on the news you took some kind of oath . . . So you're the Princess of Hessenberg? I'm proud, Reg, right proud."

"Al, forget the news. Why'd you send the Corvette home? What's going on?"

"I'm closing the shop, Reg."

"Closing the shop? No, no, no." She paced the wide width of the foyer. "You can't just close the shop. I'm part owner and, Al, I want the shop open."

"Reg, sweet girl, look around. You're living in a palace. You're a royal princess."

"Temporary, Al." She flung her arm out to her side, a creeping fear slinking up her legs and into her heart, warping her reasoning. "Temporary."

"How can you be a temporary princess?"

"Because I'll be back in a month. Six weeks tops. Don't think I left you high and dry. Listen, you call Urban and tell him to bring back the Vet. Gee, Al, what were you thinking? Urban will ruin that beautiful car."

"Reg, listen. I know this is a bit of a shock, and not what we planned when we threw in together to open this place, but—"

"Al, you can't close the shop." Reggie pressed her hand to her throbbing forehead. "You can't." *Everything can't change at once. It can't.*

"Al Jr. and his wife are moving to Texas in a few weeks, and Miriam wants to help them drive out."

"That's great, Al. Good for AJ and Lily. Give them my love. Wally and Rafe can watch the shop. You know Rafe's dying to be in charge. You go on to Texas. Shoot, I might just make it back home by then anyway. 'And in for Al Love, Reggie Beswick. Ding.'" Reggie tapped an invisible boxing bell.

"Reggie—"

"Al, forget it. I know what you're doing, giving me an out, but

I went into business with you fair and square. I'm not letting you give up our dream."

"Don't look now, Reg, but the dream has changed."

"I'm coming home. You stay put." She raced up the stairs two at a time, barely aware of Tanner's heavy footsteps resounding behind her. "See you tomorrow, Al. See you tomorrow."

TWENTY-FIVE

*D*espite the cordial press conference, Friday morning dawned with mixed headlines.

Yee Haw, We Got Us a Redneck Royal

Minister of Culture Burkhardt a Derelict Dad

Governor Fitzsimmons: "Hessenberg Needs True Leaders"

American Regina Beswick Takes Oath of the Throne. Hessenberg on Her Way to Independence

Tanner slammed his office door and dropped to his chair, slapping down the papers, muttering to himself.

Gone fifteen minutes and he felt her absence. He missed her. He'd have climbed on Royal Air Force One himself if she'd so much as nodded in his direction.

But she waved good-bye without a hint of anything more. Without a good-bye kiss. Or a confirmation of love. He'd raised heaven and earth to clear her departure with the King's Office and get her on a royal jet by 10:00 a.m., with a security detail.

All overtures of love had died an excruciating death, rendering their first kiss in the rain to the dark recesses of his mind.

Tanner reminded her right up to when the pilot fired the jet's engine that she had to return to sign the entail. On 22 October Nathaniel would no longer be king. Henry Montgomery would no longer be Hessenberg's prime minister. It would be up to Regina to pick a leader to form a government . . .

She'd assured him she'd return in time but doubt lingered where hope once lived. The look in her eyes when she told him Al was closing the shop . . . fear mixed with sorrow.

At this point, Tanner had half a mind to suggest Seamus run things. Let the old blowhard have the duchy. It'd give Tanner a good excuse to immigrate to America. Take Bella and Britta with him. Raise a couple of Southern girls.

Blast but he'd wanted to kiss Regina good-bye. But they never had a moment alone. At this very moment she was winging her way to America with Clarence, and their last exchange was terse and tense, filled with details of her trip home.

He'd slept not a wink last night. Not a wink. Missing her before she even took off. Did she regret their kisses? Had he taken advantage? The whole thing nearly brought him to his knees. But he'd made a promise to the Lord and he was bound to keep it.

I'll not bother you if you'll not bother me.

The light rap on his door did not wait for an answer. Seamus entered with a pompous grin.

"Good day to you, my boy." He pointed to the stack of newspapers. "You've seen the headlines."

"I have. What's the big idea bringing me into this, Seamus?"

"Discredit you, of course." He tapped his unlit pipe against his palm, releasing the subtle whiff of burnt tobacco. "Make the people wonder who advises the princess."

"You're not going to get rid of her that easily. And be advised, you can hurt me all you want, but don't you dare bring my girls into this."

"My boy, my boy, I am a statesman. Did you not read the article? I left Trude and the girls out by name. I merely wanted to tinge your character in the public's eye. I hear the princess fled the country this morning. Winging her way home, is she?"

"She needed to see a friend." So Seamus tossed Tanner's

name in the media mud. It was long overdue, well deserved. Nevertheless... "You need to tread lightly here, Seamus. Whether or not you like it, I have sway with the princess."

"Just as I thought I had sway with you." His gaze darkened. "I believed you to be my ally."

"I am your ally, but not against Regina."

"Tanner, I'll not back down. My lawyers are working hard to convince the court to take our case and rule in our favor. Hessenberg will be a self-governing state sans a monarchy."

"You need to know I support the princess." Tanner sighed, his patience thin and brittle. "Seamus, why are you doing this?"

The governor patted his wide gut. "Because I've been around long enough to recognize opportunity when it comes knocking. Have you seen our new ad? Ran it on the morning show, getting people awake and ready to become a true democracy. In the twenty-first century, no country intentionally forms a monarchy. We've been given a window to loosen the bonds of our ancestors and become a modern country."

"So I can expect more controversy? More negative press?"

"You can expect a well-planned offensive."

With those words hanging in the air, Dad entered Tanner's office, glancing between Tanner and the governor.

"Archbishop, good to see you." Seamus offered his hand.

"Governor, good to see you. I just came by to see—"

"Well, I'm off. Tanner, you know where to find me if you need me."

Yes, he knew where to find him. In the mire. Tanner slipped behind his desk, taking a seat. "How can I help you, Dad?"

"I saw the headlines."

Tanner shuffled through the papers. "Seamus is launching an offensive to build political favor for his agenda."

"He leaked your story to the press?" Dad took the seat next to Tanner's desk. "I thought more of the man."

"It took thirty years, but he finally showed his true colors."

"What do you make of it?"

"What can I make of it? It's out there. I'm grateful he left off Trude's name and the girls'."

"I heard from Trude's father she's marrying again and moving to America."

"Yes, and she's asked me to take the girls." Tanner went to the window and gazed down on the hustle and bustle, wishing for a moment he could disconnect from his emotional turbulence and get lost in the conversations and activity below.

"Well, isn't this a divine twist in things?"

"Divine? I don't know but a twist I'll grant you. I told her I'd take the girls but added my own conditions. Which she's considering."

"Does your mother know?"

Tanner shook his head. "I've not told her. Wait until we get it all sorted out. Trude may turn down my deal just to spite me."

"I'll add this to my prayers."

"That would be appreciated." Tanner and God had brokered no deal about others praying on his behalf.

"Tanner, I want you to know . . ." Dad cleared his throat. "I'm proud of you."

The confession stirred Tanner's stale, stored tears. He bent to pick lint from the carpet, his eyes hot and burning. "Is there anything else?"

"No, I guess not." The air in the room hung heavy between them, as if exhausted by their short exchange. "Ring when you know more."

"Will do." As Dad reached for the knob, emotional tremors shook Tanner to the center of his being. If he didn't say it now, he'd never say it. Or it would be ten times harder when he did. "Th-thank you, Dad. Thank you."

Dad's eyes glistened. "Anytime."

Battling back a rare wash of tears, Tanner cleared his head

and heart with deep breaths. He was just gathering himself when his phone pinged. A text from Trude.

This is how U plan 2 take care of my daughters? In the headlines?

Tanner sat down hard, read her text again, and heaven help him, he started laughing.

As the dawn's sunrise crested over the sleepy, north Florida skyline, Regina urged her little old Datsun around Capital Circle, heading for the shop.

Al and the boys would be there by now, and she buzzed with anticipation. *Surprise! I'm home.*

First thing in the morning, Al always sat down with his chocolate milk and box-o-donuts. "Stuff like this will make you never want to leave home."

Know what? He was right. What in the world ever made her want to leave home? To be a princess. *Pffbbt.* What was her life anyway? A movie? A soap opera?

Gram was right. Being a princess wasn't a job, or a title. It was a way of life. One she could live right here in Tallahassee.

Wasn't that what Gram did? Lived the life of a princess by her actions, not her title?

Gripping the wheel, Reggie slowed for a light, excitement buzzing in her middle. She was home. Where she belonged. *This* was her kingdom. The light switched to green and she was off, heading for the shop, turning down the driveway a few minutes later.

The Datsun's door creaked as she stepped out, and it took both hands to reset the hinges and close it. Reggie ran across the grass and gravel parking lot toward the dark, quiet shop, calling for

Al, Rafe, or Wally, stopping short when she spied the sad empty space that once housed the Corvette.

"Al?" She stepped back outside. His truck wasn't here. In fact, her car was the only car on the grounds. "Al? Rafe? Wally?"

Back in the shop, Reggie peeked around the short kitchenette wall, expecting to be assaulted by the aroma of coffee. But the space was also dark and quiet.

She ducked into the office, slipping her keys in her pocket. The desk was a mess of invoices and bills scattered over the opened checkbook. Al had been writing checks.

The sound of a door slam drew Reggie out of the office. Finally. A face she knew and loved. Al headed her way with his milk and donuts.

"Hey, what gives?" Reggie greeted him smiling, hands on her hips. "I go out of town for a few days and everyone slacks off?"

"Reg! You said you were on your way but I didn't think you could get here so fast." Al swung his big arm around her shoulders, careful not to bop her with the milk carton. "Ha, ha, girl. It's good to see you. What'd you do, hop on the next plane as soon as we hung up?"

"Almost, yes. Look, Al, I know it's Saturday, but why is everything so dark?" She followed him back into the office.

"What'd you do with my invoices, Reg? I had them all arranged."

"Arranged? They were strewn all over the desk." She sat in the rickety old office chair, a dark sadness tainting her previous excitement. Everything was changing. Everything.

"You organize in file folders; I organize by strewing." He set down his milk and donuts.

"Why are you doing the invoices? The books are my job." Maybe if she acted as if nothing had changed, things could get back to normal.

"You aren't the only one who can pay a bill and balance the

books. I ran a side business the entire time I was in the Marines." He pulled down two glasses, setting one in front of Reggie. "Have a glass of chocolate with me, Your Majesty?"

"Stop . . . and it'd be my honor."

Al poured and set out the donuts before taking a seat. All the while, Reggie sat under the stark fluorescent light, realizing more and more she'd not returned home to save the shop but to close it.

Al capped the milk carton and raised his glass. "To you and all the good Lord has called you to do."

She took a small sip. "So, it's true. You're closing the shop."

"Reg, look around. It's a leaning old red barn. We've got no jobs."

"We had a job until you gave back the Corvette."

"It's time. We had a good six months. Had a fun run with the Challenger. But life is moving on, Reg. You're a princess, for pity sakes." Al motioned toward the shop. "Wally and Rafe cleared out their tools already."

"Cleared out their tools?" Reggie set down her milk glass and peered into the shop. Sure enough, the walls and workbenches were all but empty.

"Rafe's got a job interview with a shop over in Pensacola. It's been around for thirty years. Good pay, good business. Wally told me last week, if it was all the same to me, he was finally ready to retire."

"Hmm . . . well,"—she shoved up the sleeves of her shirt— "we were bound to lose Wally sooner or later. But Rafe? Why can't he stay here and run things?" She couldn't give up without some kind of fight.

"Reg, I turned Rafe onto the job. He's young, probably going to get married soon if things keep going like they are with Carrie. Rafe needs more than we—I—can give him right now."

"But we're going to build the business." Reggie turned back to the office. "Grow this up so we can pay talent like Rafe."

"Reginator," Al said, low and sweet, "you're not coming back."

"But I am." She hammered her fist against her palm, proclaiming words her heart did not believe. "Sure, I won't be here all the time, but I'll be here enough. Think of what great publicity we can get by me being a princess. We can make it our brand, you know. Get your classic car refurbed by Princess Regina and Marine Master Sergeant Al Love."

"Reg, girl, I love you. You're about the most generous person I know. But I reckon I should be honest with you. I never wanted a big business. Never wanted much more than we had. I loved the idea of working on a Duesy, but at night I about sweated through my pajamas thinking about working on such a rare, expensive car. We're good, but we didn't have the wherewithal to take on that project."

"We did, we do—"

"See that right there?" Al pointed at her. "That determination and belief in yourself is not for a girl restoring cars but for a princess. For a girl fighting for her people, for the downtrodden, and the ones without a voice. You're in a position to do something extraordinary."

His words echoed Susanna Truitt's.

Al took a donut out of the box. "I only opened this shop 'cause I knew you were miserable at Backlund & Backlund. But deep down, I suspected greater things were coming for you, Reg."

"No, you opened the shop because we love what we do." Protesting came easy when the truth cut deep.

Al rocked back and bit into his donut. "Know what I did Tuesday? Hit the golf course with Urban. Had myself a blast."

"You can still golf. Sure, take a day now and then." She just couldn't let go. She needed this old shop if for no other reason than to ground her when the world went crazy around her.

"Reg, come on. Seriously? You can't give up being a princess to rat around in this place. I won't let you. When you got on the plane to Hessenberg, I knew you were heading for something great."

"What about the warehouse?"

"Mark found a renter for it. He called me, asking if it was okay to back out of our deal. I think he felt what we all knew. You're not coming home to work on cars anymore."

Tears filled her eyes, Reggie strolled out of the office toward the wide barn doors. A brilliant morning light filled the yard with golden orbs dripping through the fall magnolia leaves.

She fell against the door frame and kicked at the dirt, breathing in the scents of the Tallahassee day, of an old barn turned auto shop. Of the sweet dew on the morning grass.

"Reg, girl." Al's voice slipped over her shoulder. "Seems to me this is the most classic, most important restoration job of your life. Restoring a nation. Restoring your family's name and inheritance. Are you going to cling to who you thought you were and miss this incredible opportunity?" Her friend and mentor aligned his toes with the edge of the barn floor. "Got to tell you, I'll be disappointed if you choose this old barn over a palace. There's not a thing holding you here except your fears. Maybe your own stubbornness. You can keep the shop open if you want, but I'm retiring."

Reggie lost the battle with her tears. "You bet I'm scared. Everything is changing so fast, Al." She brushed her hand over her cheeks, wiping away the first emotional streams.

From her pocket, her phone buzzed. She pulled it out and read the screen. "It's Clarence, wanting to know where I am."

"Who's Clarence?"

Reggie grinned. "My security detail."

"Well now, lookey here." Al folded his arms, angling away from Reggie. "Our girl comes with a bodyguard."

"Tanner wouldn't let me come otherwise."

"Don't say as I blame him," Al said, facing the barnyard. "How is the old *chap*?"

"Fine." Her skin flushed hot, and she knew her feelings displayed on her cheeks.

"Very fine, I see." Al popped his hands together, laughing. "Oh, Reginator, can't you see for looking? The Lord is blessing you. Do you know the best way to embrace change? Dive in and hold on. When I went off to the Marines, a Southern black boy just a few years outside of Jim Crow law, I was terrified. But I went. Best decision I ever made. Fear is a blinder, Reg. A cruel taskmaster. Don't let it rule you. You've graduated to your real calling." Al gripped her shoulders. "Embrace it."

TWENTY-SIX

anner arrived home Sunday night, tired and irritated. A couple of his mates rang up, invited him to dinner, and he thought, why not? He'd not spent an evening with friends in a good while.

Besides, it would distract him from thinking about Regina.

But the boy-talk was coarse and ribald about the women the lads were bedding or wanting to bed. The longer Tanner sat there, the more slimed he felt. When Fin began sharing details about an encounter with a lass he'd met in the south of France, Tanner took his leave.

Three months ago, he'd have gone along with the conversation, laughed, maybe even envied. But he'd encountered something beautiful and pure in Regina, and he didn't want that image sullied.

Flipping on the light in his flat as he entered, he stared at his stark surroundings. Regina or no Regina, he must bring life to this place. If Bella and Britta were to walk in right now, they'd run screaming, accusing their mum of sentencing them to a prison cell. Well, perhaps it wasn't a prison cell, but it had about as much warmth.

After a quick shower, he fixed a sandwich—his dinner portions were expensive and slight—and searched the telly for something entertaining and distracting.

He'd settled on a rerun of *Doc Martin* when his phone buzzed from the end table. Snatching it up, Tanner glanced at the screen, hoping to see Regina's name.

Trude. He gathered his courage and answered.

"Tanner, I'm sorry to call so late on a Sunday, but I remembered you never went anywhere—"

"Trude, what can I do for you?" He didn't need a rehash from her about his desperate existence.

"Evan and I just had a horrible row with the girls." Her voice quavered with emotion. "I told them the whole truth. About you, me, and Reese—"

"The whole truth?"

"Minus some intimate details, of course. Anyway, we told them tonight about the wedding and moving to America."

"Fired the whole cannon on them, did you?" He walked around the kitchen island, setting his sandwich plate on the bare countertop.

"I hadn't intended to, but one thing led to another"—*been there, done that*—"and I found myself spilling it all. I wouldn't wish such a thing on my worst enemy. Thank heaven for Evan. He remained calm and levelheaded."

"So why are you calling me, Trude?"

"The girls want to see you."

The bursting beat of his heart shot fire brands across his chest. "Now?" He glanced round the flat. Dull. Boring. Flat.

"Tomorrow, after school. They want to see your place."

"They want to come here?" Tanner walked back to the living room. "Tomorrow?" Did he have time to book a decorator by then?

"How about four thirty? Tanner?"

"Four thirty?"

"Are you agreeing or merely repeating everything I say?" she both snapped and sobbed. "What a mess I've made of everything. They hate me, and I don't blame them."

"They don't hate you."

"Then they should. I deserve it."

"Stop. That's my line. Four thirty is fine. Ring me at three thirty to make sure nothing urgent has come up."

"Thank you, Tanner. Thank you."

After she confirmed his address, Trude asked, "Is it true? We really have a princess again?"

"It's true."

"What's she like, Tanner? The girls would love to meet her."

"She's a good sport."

"A good sport?" Trude laughed. "She's not a chap at the rugby club, Tanner. Or is she?"

"She is a good sport. Took the news of being our long-lost princess like a champ. She'll do splendidly." If she returned to Hessenberg. "Is there anything else? Besides tomorrow at four thirty?"

"No. Right o. See you then." And Trude rang off.

For a moment, Tanner felt stunned. His girls were coming to his flat. Then he smiled, a giddy sense of satisfaction cleansing away the slime of spending an evening with his mates.

His girls wanted to see him.

Now that he'd made contact with them, now that he had a chance to be their dad, he couldn't go back to being all-business, no-fun, stoical Tanner Burkhardt.

Looks like Regina isn't the only one stepping into a new destiny.

He stared at his phone, thinking he might ring her and share his news. But he reconsidered. Give her space. This is her time with family and friends.

Returning to the kitchen, Tanner stood at the counter and

finished his sandwich, thinking he should inspect the guest bedroom.

It was a large space with a stellar view of the city, but used mostly for storage.

Back in the room, Tanner flipped on the light, surveying the storage bins and the heavy boxing bag swinging from the corner.

Then he broke his cardinal rule. "Lord, thank you for giving me a second chance. It's unmerited and undeserved."

He left his prayer without an amen, without pausing for a holy response, and dug into the room's mess, sorting through the bins.

He was halfway through the second boxes, finding most of it rubbish, when his phone rang.

Regina. His heart palpitated.

"Hey," she said. "It's me."

"And what do you know? It is also me." She laughed and he felt completely renewed. "How are you?" Tanner perched on the nearest solid-looking bin.

"I'm good."

Silence.

"Say,"—he ran his fingers through his hair, shoving the curls from his forehead—"the girls are coming by tomorrow after school. They want to see me . . . see the flat."

"Yea, Tanner! That's amazing." Her Southern lilt made him smile and yearn for her. "So Trude is letting them move in?"

"It seems this is our trial run. See how we get on. But my place looks a bit like a grumpy bachelor hovel. The décor is black, white, and boring."

"Go to Target, or whatever we have over there that's like a Target"—he liked her plural pronoun we—"and get some colorful beanbag chairs and throw pillows, maybe a corner floor lamp to warm up the lighting."

Tanner scampered for a pen and paper. "Brilliant, brilliant."

"Go on Pinterest and look for decorating ideas for preteen girls. Print out the stuff you like and tape it on the wall of their room. Tell them they can decorate any way they like. I'm sure there are even creative ideas for twins on there. Then have some fun snack for them like M&M's or ice cream."

"Mum can make her famous cinnamon cake. I loved that as a lad." Oh, wait, then he'd have to tell Mum about the girls possibly moving in, though Dad may have already told her. No bother, desperate times call for desperate measures.

"Perfect. That should be enough to give them a taste of what life could be like with you."

Tanner set down his pen, sobering. "What of you, Regina? Will you be coming home? To see what life with me might be like?"

"I wasn't sure when I left," she said in a hushed tone. "I knew I had to come back for the entail and all that government stuff."

"Yes, all that government stuff."

"But this life is over, Tanner." Her voice quavered. "Al's closing the shop. Rafe is probably moving. Wally is retiring." She sighed. "Al said there's no way I can give up being a princess to dink around in an old car garage."

"Did I ever tell you how brilliant I found Al when we met?"

"Hush. You're just glad he's on your side."

"I won't lie. I am. But this is your decision."

"We're having a barbecue at Daddy and Sadie's tonight."

"And?"

"I'm going to say good-bye to everyone."

Tanner grinned, his heart fluttering. Wasn't this his lucky, er, blessed night?

"I'm coming home, Tanner. Tomorrow, I'm coming home."

Home. Such a sweet word.

"I'm glad, Regina. So very, very glad."

TWENTY-SEVEN

A bonfire crackled and blazed, the flames high and hot, on the back acre of Daddy's property. Reggie sat in a folding chair between Sadie and Carrie, listening to Jeb Cartwright's bluegrass band, watching the gathering crowd.

"Thanks for doing this, Sadie."

"Reg, please. We can't let you go without some sort of send-off. I wish we had time to do more." Sadie reached through the darkness and squeezed her hand. "Going to miss you around here, girl."

"I'm going to miss being here."

"But we'll come over for Christmas," Sadie said, popping her hands together. "Won't it be beautiful?"

Clarence made his way toward her, looking casual in jeans and a sweater, not like a royal security officer. Every so often he made a sweep of the party, making sure everyone was safe.

"Clarence, sit down," Sadie said. "You're in the South. Reg is more than safe. I guarantee you every man here and most of the women have a gun tucked up in their car or truck." She stood, scanning the crowd. "There are no less than three police officers here."

"Thank you, ma'am, but it's my job to keep watch over her.

Those officers won't be the one answering to the king or the people of Hessenberg." Clarence pulled his folding chair around behind Reggie.

As odd as it sounded to hear a man say it was his job to "watch over her," Reggie felt cocooned in Clarence's attentiveness.

"Well, please tell me you got something to eat," Sadie the banker-baker said.

"Yes, ma'am. I never had barbecue before, and it was quite lovely."

"Land sakes, I'll send you home with a good recipe. Reg can help you make it. Then you can invite a lady friend over and . . ." Sadie looked back at him. "Are you married?"

"No, ma'am." Clarence's broad cheeks flushed pink.

"All right, well, this stuff will do the trick. See those two over there?" Sadie pointed to Richard and Kathy Fox. "Fell in love over a plate of my sweet barbecue chicken."

"Sadie,"—Reggie reached out and lowered Sadie's hand— "just give him the recipe." She smiled back at the big man. "But let him find his wife his own way."

"Just saying, a good dinner never hurt."

"If Rafe gets the job in Pensacola, I think he's going to pro-pose," Carrie said out of the blue, more to herself than Reggie or Sadie. Or Clarence.

Reggie swerved to face her. "And what will you say to this proposal?"

"Big honking yes. Are you crazy? Though I can't imagine you not being around for all the planning, Reg." Carrie stretched her arms toward her friend, drawing her into a soft hug. "Are you sure you need to leave and be a princess?"

"Yes." Sadie cut the air with a side swipe of her hand, her tone flat and unwavering. "She does. So don't start, Carrie."

Yes, yes, she did. Reggie squeezed Sadie's hand, blinking away a sting of tears. Sadie sniffed and wiped her eyes. "Oh, there's

RACHEL HAUCK

LeeAnn Burnett . . ." She shot out of her chair. "LeeAnn, I need to talk to you about this year's Christmas gift drive . . ."

"She's a good mom," Carrie said.

"The best." Reggie sat back in her chair, but then saw Mark crossing the yard. "Clarence," she said, getting up. "I'll be right over there."

She met Mark at the soda cooler.

"So, you're leaving. Off to be a princess." He dug a soda from the ice and popped the top. "I thought Al was joking when he said you were a real princess. Then your dad confirmed it."

"I'm sorry I left without talking to you. It all happened so fast."

A couple of Sadie's friends came up, asking for a photo, but Clarence appeared out of nowhere and blocked the shot.

"No posts on Twitter or Facebook." He stepped up on the picnic table bench, shedding his stoic reserve. "Do not post pictures of Her Majesty. Do not tweet or Facebook about her. It is a matter of security. If you have posted photographs, kindly take them down."

When Clarence hopped off the table, Mark scoffed. "Your own security detail?"

"Comes with the job." Reggie stooped to retrieve a soda from the ice. "One of the perks." She laughed. "Lighten up. Clarence is just being super cautious."

"I'll say."

"Mark, hey, we're friends, right? We'll always be friends." She popped the tab of her root beer as the cold dew from the can dripped to her flip-flopped foot.

"You know, Reg, when I said we'd be a great power couple, I didn't mean for you to run off and inherit a kingdom. Being a partner in a CPA firm suited me just fine."

She laughed and bumped him with her shoulder. "Come see me in Hessenberg?"

"Yeah, maybe. I got a lot of irons in the fire here."

"Some things never change." She bent forward to see his downcast eyes. "Can we be power friends?"

He tipped up his can for a long swig. "Not the same. Not the same."

"Mark, even if I wasn't a princess—"

"I know." He stared straight ahead, toward the fire. "What do you say? Care to go for a drive for old times' sake?"

"I–I think I'd better stay here." Reggie tipped her head toward the party. "Lots of people to talk with yet. Besides, Clarence would never let me go alone. Old times' sake never included personal security."

"All right, then how about a two-step around the dance floor?"

Reggie gave Mark her hand and he led her to the dance floor— a plywood board Daddy stored in the attic above the garage.

They moved around the board with the other dancers, the familiar steps stirring her melancholy. She was going to miss home.

But she yearned to see what lay ahead. Ached to begin the journey of her heart. With Hessenberg. With Tanner.

The melody changed and Daddy tapped Mark on the shoulder. "Pardon me, but I need to step around with my daughter."

As Daddy began scooting with her around the floor, Reggie pressed her cheek against her rock, her daddy, and her tears flowed.

"Going to miss you, Reg."

"I'm going to miss you, Daddy." She dried her wet cheeks with the back of her hand. "Do you think I can do it?"

Daddy stepped back to see her face. "I've no doubt. I just know your mama and gram are up in heaven cheering you on. Mama would want you to fly and, princess sweet pea, so do I." He laughed. "Me, a master plumber, father of a princess."

"Ah, but Daddy, I'll always be your sweet pea, the proud daughter of a master plumber."

Arriving at his flat with just enough time to change before his four thirty meeting with his *daughters*, Tanner changed into jeans and a jumper, going for the hip dad appearance.

In the kitchen, he arranged Mum's cake so it could be seen, even fanned his hand over it trying to fill the house with the scent of cinnamon.

The doorbell chimed, and he wiped the dew from his palms as he opened the door.

Dressed in their school uniforms, the girls stood to Trude's shoulders, their silky blonde hair falling over their shoulders in soft, wide curls. Their perfectly matched blue eyes studied him, and as he had at their birthday party, he caught a hint of his mum in their smiles and stubborn chins.

"Come in, please. Welcome." He stood aside, exchanging a glance with Trude, hoping for a clue as to the girls' moods. She made a face, rolling her eyes.

What did that mean?

"Tanner, you remember Bella,"—she put her hand on the girl's head to her right—"and Britta"—then on the daughter on her left.

"I–I remember. We spoke at your party." He did remember them. When they were little he could tell them apart by their . . . aura? Was that the right word? Bella had a fiery spark in her eye that had started when she was a baby. Britta, the serious one, emanated a certain embracing sensitivity.

The girls greeted him as they moved into the living room. And that's about the time it took for all the love he had for them as babies and toddlers to spring to life and saturate his soul. He'd been tentative with them at the party, but now he realized eight years of silence had not dulled his heart at all.

"The place is kind of bare."

"Bella"—Trude thumped her on the back of the head—"mind your manners."

"You're right, it is kind of bare," Tanner said. "I–I'm not here very much."

"Do you work a lot?" Britta asked in a soft voice.

"I do but I can work from home if you decided to live here."

"We're not children," Bella said. "We don't need supervision."

"Tanner, we've a car that takes the girls to and from school. By the time they complete their after-school activities it's well into teatime."

"What kind of activities?"

"I play lacrosse." Britta tapped her hand to her chest, then pointed her thumb at her sister. "She's a choir *bird*."

Tanner tried not to laugh. He'd have guessed the opposite activities based on personality. Back into parenting for less than a minute and he was already being schooled.

"They look alike, but that's where the similarities end," Trude said. "Britta loves the roller coasters, but Bella is afraid of heights."

"I love the haunted house," Bella said. "*She's* afraid of her own shadow."

"Mum, tell her to stop saying that."

"Are you going to fight in front of Tanner? Ensure he won't want to live with either one of you?"

"We didn't say we wanted to live with him." Bella moved to the windows and peeked out.

"You don't have to live here," Trude said. "We've discussed it. Evan and I are fine for you to come to America."

"What about Scarborough?" Trude cauterized Tanner's question with a single glance. Ah, seems she had a strategy and he was mussing it up.

"But I'm going to be captain of the team next year." Britta turned to her mother.

"And I'm trying out for senior choir." Bella looked at Tanner as if to garner his support.

"Girls, that's a whole year away," Trude said with a wink at Tanner.

"But if we move to America, we lose our spots."

"Isn't that why we are here, then? To see if you want to live with your father?"

Father. The word sounded so foreign. But so sweet.

Britta grabbed his arm. "Do you know the princess?"

"Yes, I do." Very well, thank you.

"Can we meet her?"

"Oh please," Bella joined her sister's petition. "Please, can we?"

"I believe it can be arranged."

"Is she nice? For an American?"

"She's very nice."

The girls squealed and huddled together. "Mary Margaret will just be green with envy when we tell her."

"Girls, don't go flaunting this to your friends. Be nice." Trude looked at Tanner with a shrug and a grin. "I'd like to meet her myself."

"I'll arrange a tea for the family. Mum hasn't met her yet." Tanner lightly tapped the girls on the head. "But she'd like to meet you two the most."

The dialog went supersonic, the girls talking so fast Tanner wasn't sure they were actually speaking real words. Trude was right in there with them. Oh no, how was he ever going to navigate the life and times of ten-year-old twins?

At last they paused to breathe and he jumped into the verbal action break. "Would you like to see your room?"

And the rapid-fire dialog ignited again.

He'd enlisted the aid of his staffer, Marissa, to help with the beanbag chairs and throw pillows. And Tanner worked with Louis to print out his Pinterest finds—what a smashing site—all morning.

Tanner led the girls down the short hall and lit the floor

lamp, giving the normally austere room a warm, inviting change. Lights just coming on from the city dotted the dark picture window and, even to Tanner, the scene felt magical.

"Wow, Mum, look. We can see the whole city." The twins pressed their faces to the window.

"My, Tanner, this is extraordinary."

"I thought you could decorate any way you want. I printed out some ideas." Tanner motioned to the images on the wall, nervous if not a bit slaphappy. "Here's one where the twins divided the room down the middle."

"Look, Bella, isn't it marvelous?" Britta leaned into the images, asking Tanner if they could do any one they wanted, squealing when he answered in the affirmative.

Trude went to the kitchen and returned with plates, forks, and the cinnamon cake.

"Shall we dine in your new room? Bella, look, a purple beanbag. Your favorite color."

Tanner listened as the girls talked, trying to enter their world. When he sat on the floor with his cake, wondering if indeed, after the excitement, this would ever really work, he looked up to see Britta moving her beanbag closer to him.

She smiled when their eyes met. His mouth went dry and his heart tapped out *D-a-d-l-o-v-e*.

"I think I'm going to like living here."

"Me too," Bella said.

"It won't be easy, girls." Trude exchanged a glance with Tanner. "Your dad's been single a long time." *Your dad, your dad . . .* no sweeter words except *I love you.* "And we'll be apart. Think about this now . . ."

Britta stared at Tanner, then leaned toward him with a serene expression. "I remember you," she whispered.

He choked on his cake, the crumbs sticking to his dry throat. "Y–you remember me? From the party?"

"No, from when I was little." With a shy smile, she looked back at her plate, her golden hair falling against her cheek.

"If we're here, Mum," Bella said, "Tanner—Dad—won't be a lonely bachelor. He needs us."

"Now, girls, don't go getting ideas in your head about—"

"She's right, Trude." Tanner reached out, placing his hand on her shoulder. "I do need them." And he hoped they needed him. "But it's not going to be smooth sailing."

"So?" Bella shrugged. "We can learn together."

Tanner tried to finish his cake, but he'd lost all taste for its sweetness. Having his girls in his flat overwhelmed all of his senses. For the first time in a very long time, he felt like he was really living his life. Really home.

He listened while the girls talked with Trude, interjecting where he could, but he loved the sound of their chatter. The old flat had suffered with his silence too long.

The girls were in the middle of discussing the Pinterest printouts when Tanner's phone pinged. He retrieved it from his pocket. A message from King Nathaniel.

EU Court agreed to hear the petition. Arguments begin in the morning.

Tanner excused himself for a moment. Thank goodness Regina was returning. Hessenberg needed her.

As he left the room, intending to call Louis, he caught his reflection in the dark windowpane and paused, touching the top of his hair, the chatter of the girls floating around him.

His life was changing. He was changing. And the need for his long, stubborn locks was finally over.

On a mid-October Friday evening, dusk settled over Strauberg as Reggie rode with Tanner toward the Fence & Anchor.

Slowing for a red light, he leaned toward her. "Regina, love, look this way. You've something in your eye."

"I do?" Reggie swatted at her bangs, blowing a breath up, fluttering the ends. Tomorrow morning she had an appointment at a stylist Melinda recommended. Thank goodness.

"Yes, see, right here . . ." Tanner brushed her bangs aside and kissed her right eye, then her left, moving to the tip of her nose. At last—oh, at last—her tingling lips.

She slipped her hand around his neck, returning his affection. She'd been home four days and had yet to fill her kisses quotient. It seemed every time they were alone, for just a moment, someone came along. Louis. Jarvis. Serena. An aide. A photographer.

So they kissed at red lights like a couple of teens.

When he greeted her at the airport, she didn't recognize him with his styled, short hair, but oh, now she saw every angle and contour of his fine face, the face of the man she wanted next to her in this life.

A green hue fell against the windshield, and a car horn blasted.

Tanner's kisses softened into a laugh. "Some blokes have no romance."

"The shame of it all."

Tanner wove his fingers with Reggie's and headed past the light. "Are you sure you want to go to the Fence & Anchor? We can go to a nicer place."

"The Fence & Anchor, please, sir. The patrons are my kind of people. The ones who work hard all week, then get with friends on the weekend for fellowship, blow off a bit of steam." She pulled her hand from his, sitting forward, peering out the front window, watching the storm clouds gather, screening the last tendrils of twilight. "I didn't have one bite of my stew the last time, and I've been getting memory whiffs ever since."

"The F & A will be thrilled to have you."

"So, Tanner, the girls . . . ," Reggie said. "Moving in the day after Christmas. Are you excited?"

"I'm terrified." He laughed, a low melody that played well on his lips and sparked a glint in his blue eyes. "But they're going to start coming on the weekends."

"I'll be there for you. I will." She squeezed her hand over his. "As you need me. I don't want to interfere."

"Are you joking, Regina? They love you."

"They are fascinated with Princess Regina, whom they've met yesterday for a few minutes. Wait until they run into Tallahassee Reggie Beswick. They'll beg you to get rid of me."

"This I must see."

"Come on, it won't be pretty." She made a face, and he laughed.

Her favorite thing, besides kissing him, was laughing with him. She loved how joy morphed him into a gentle, easy, confident soul instead of the somber, rigid, closed-off man she'd met in Tally.

Tanner took the next left and maneuvered a narrow lane to park on the side of the Fence & Anchor. Nigel and Jace, the second-team security, parked next to them.

Stepping out, Reggie inhaled the fragrance of the city and saline-dew drifting up from the bay. Already the scent was becoming familiar. In the distance, a steamer horn blasted. And for a split moment, Reggie was in another era, another life altogether.

Tanner came up behind her, lightly touching her shoulder, giving her a wink.

"You think they saw us?" she whispered, tipping her head toward the dark-suited, broad-chested security men.

"Why do you think I skirted away from them and cut in front of that truck?"

She bumped him with her hip. "Clever chap."

Across the street, a couple of women slowed, pointing, then raised their phones in their direction. Reggie stepped to the curb, smiled, and waved. They bumped into each other, giggled, and aimed for more snapshots.

But Nigel came around and ended the spontaneous photo shoot, directing Reggie inside the pub. "Safer in here," he said.

The atmosphere of the crowded, noisy Fence & Anchor embraced her as Gemma hurried through the chairs and tables to greet them. "Your Majesty, welcome, welcome. We've got a booth in the back all reserved."

She started down the length of the booths, but Tanner held her arm. "Gemma, we won't find a bank of photographers outside when we leave, will we?"

Her expression darkened. "No, sir." She jerked her arm free. "What sort of girl do you take me for?"

"Exactly as I thought," Tanner said. "One we can depend upon."

She harrumphed, tugged on her skirt, and led them to the booth, chin raised.

Reggie loved the atmosphere and pressed into the hubbub, the voices, the blaring announcer on the TV . . .

"Gemma," Reggie said, "can't we sit out here with everyone?"

"I have the booth in the back . . . like last time." Gemma shot Tanner a nervous glance.

"Regina,"—he leaned into her—"there's more security in the back."

"Tanner, I'm not going to live afraid. If we're going to do this, let's do it. Nigel and Jace are here. What can happen?"

"I've got two tables right here," Gemma said. "Stan, Pip, shoo, shoo." She shoved on the shoulder of a young working man.

"Gemma, no, please don't kick them out of their table. Those tables over there will do." Reggie moved around Stan and Pip to a set of tables by the bar, drawing them together herself.

By now, the pub was buzzing. The atmosphere changing.

"The princess . . ."

"Where?"

"There . . . ."

"Pretty . . . looks like one of us . . ."

Maybe that was her advantage. She was one of them.

"Are you her?" A young woman with purple hair and a lip ring stepped forward. "The princess?"

"I am, yes."

"Please, we just came in for dinner." Tanner tried to block the woman. "Go back to your table."

"Wait, Tanner. It's all right." Reggie offered the woman her hand. "What's your name?"

"Jayel Carmichael. I work around the corner at Gilden's."

Other patrons started to gather around. Nigel's low "Keep clear . . . don't press in too close" went completely ignored.

Reggie drew a mental path to the door if need be, but she saw or felt no threat here.

"What do you think of Hessenberg having a princess, Jayel?"

"Why not, I say. A royal family can do a country a lot of good. Especially a small duchy like us."

"The governor thinks differently," came a strong voice behind Reggie.

"Yeah, that blooming governor can get over hisself. He wants to be the one in charge."

Voices in the pub rose, rumbled, and blended.

"That's what I say."

"Well, what of it?" This from a female patron. "He's a fine man who's served and loved his country—"

"Was Princess Alice really your grandmother?" Another soft voice interrupted the woman.

"—and knows our culture and laws. I trust the governor."

"Yes, my great-grandmother was Princess Alice." Reggie rose up on her toes. "And I do agree with the woman saying the governor has served this country. He does know the laws and culture."

"So what are you doing here, getting in the blooming way?"

"See there now,"—Jayel stood on a chair, patting down the noise with her hands—"she saved us from being a province to Brighton for the rest of our lives. That's what she's doing here."

"Did you know your great-grammy?" another asked.

"I did." Reggie turned, trying to line up voices with faces. "She died when I was twelve."

"She's real, just like us," Jayel said with a campaign trail tone. "Got family and hurts, I suspect."

"Here now, what's all of this?" A booming voice parted the crowd. "I come for some grub and here's the princess clogging up the works."

Keeton Lombard III. "Hello, Mr. Lombard." Reggie smiled at the older man.

"Your Majesty." He removed his cap as he bowed. "At your service." The lines around his eyes appeared deeper than when she met him, but there was a light and vigor in his eyes. "Move aside, chaps, let the princess have a seat." He reached for a chair behind a man at another table. "You don't mind, Pembrook, do you?"

"Please, Keeton. Let Mr. Pembrook eat his dinner."

"Listen to her. Let me have my tea in peace, Lombard." Mr. Pembrook glared up at her. "I for one agree with the governor. The time for royals has passed."

Rumblings from the crowd rolled forward.

"Royals are a bother. Drain on state finances—"

"Drain? They *provide* finances. Tourism and—"

"Tourism?" The man laughed, swearing. "The people have to pay rent to the crown on the very grounds the tourists walk. Tourism? Malarkey!"

"We can make reforms." Tanner finally joined the conversation. "In the land holdings, how the crown's property is managed."

"How about giving it back to the earls who lost their land with the blasted entail?"

"Agreed. We don't need aristocracy. We're all equal here, and we have a chance for a fresh start with a fresh government."

The crowd stirred. Voices of dissension fired between the pub patrons.

"I think having a princess is fabulous." Jayel pumped her arms as if it might help her emotionally charged argument. "She's good for us. She comes straight from Prince Francis, the Grand Duke. That should mean something."

"Here's what I want to know." An older man, dressed in a fine-weave suit and a neatly tied tie, appeared between the shoulders of two women. "How are you, an American, going to help us find our identity again? Help us rediscover who we are?"

"Tobias," Keeton addressed him. "Give the girl some room. She just found out she is a long-lost princess herself."

"I–I don't know," Reggie said. "We can learn together."

Laughter rippled around the group. She winced. She did sound a bit *Sesame Street.*

"We're doing all we can to bring out archives, Mr. . . ." Tanner offered his hand but the man didn't take it.

"Horowitz. Tobias Horowitz. Archives don't answer my question. Can the princess help us find our *identity*,"—he patted his hand over his heart—"who we are in here? Or will Seamus Fitzsimmons be the better one?"

"What do you mean, find our identity?" Tanner released the button on his jacket and loosened his tie. His blue eyes sparked and a red hue covered the high contours of his cheeks. Reggie loved it when his passion tinged his face. The creeping hue was a sure sign he was engaged in the moment. She noticed it when he met her at the airport when she came home, kissing her before he even said hello.

"How is this young bird—" Tobias glanced at Reggie. "No offense."

"None taken."

"—going to resurrect what it means to be a Hessen? Remind us of our days of old? Of our pride. Of our history. Of how our parents and grandparents *felt*."

"Identity?" Pembrook said. "Horowitz, have you lost your blooming mind? What about our economy?"

And so the room debated—her side, his side, their side, all sides. Even the waitstaff and the barkeepers leaned in to have a say. A tightness in Reggie's chest twisted around her heart, her lungs, and for a moment she had to work to breathe. See, this was why she hated politics. Everyone had a side and valid reasons for what they believed and why.

Then the first note of a song fluttered across her heart. She tipped her head to one side, trying to listen. Two more notes fluttered past. An old song, from deep in her mind. Three notes played across her mind.

Where had she heard it before? Her first day here? On the radio?

She felt a soft, invisible drop on her head. The same oily sensation she felt in the chapel when she took the Oath of the Throne. It was as if the Lord was saying, "I'm here. Ask me."

Okay, what do I do? What do I say?

The melody began to flow, faster until she heard the entire song. Gram's song. Of course. She used to sing it to her when she was a girl, afraid of the night. Closing her eyes, she pictured herself on Gram's lap, leaning against her breast, weaving her little fingers through Gram's soft, weathered ones.

Da-da-da-dum . . . Reggie searched for the lyrics that went with the melody.

She waved at the barkeeper. "Can we turn down the TV?"

"Ian, cut it!" Gemma called across the bar, making a slicing motion at her throat. "Miss, are you all right?"

"Yeah, I'm trying to remember something." She could almost

317

see the words as the melody drifted in and about her heart, her mind.

La-da-da. Moonlight, sunshine, waves upon the shore, all for the homeland, pick up your oar.

Reggie lifted her head and sang out. "Moonlight, sunshine, waves upon the shore..."

A rough, gravelly voice joined hers, and when she looked around, Keeton wedged in next to her, his hand on her shoulder. "All for the homeland, pick up your oar." His rich bass rose and fell with the melody. They sang together, "Man and woman, boy and girl, we're all meeting down on the Hessen shores."

She peered at the hovering patrons, urging them to join in, but they stared back with stunned expressions. Pembrook's and Horowitz's eyes were slick with tears as Reggie and Keeton finished the song.

"La, la, la, la we're going to the shore. La, la, la, la to dance once more. No more worries, no more cares, we'll sleep in peace tonight under stars so fair."

"I say, laddies," Mr. Horowitz said, clearing the emotion from his voice. "I've not heard this song since me own granny rocked me to sleep."

"I've never heard it." Jayel still stood in the chair, hands on her hips. "Sing it again."

Mr. Horowitz came around the table, shoving folks aside to join Reggie. "It's an old Hessenberg evening song called 'Sleep Tonight.'" He held out his hand to her. "Join me, Your Majesty?" And he stepped up on a free chair.

She took his hand and stood on the chair next to his. When she lowered her hand, Horowitz still held on.

She smiled, her heart overflowing.

If the EU court decided she had to go, fine. But she'd have this moment with these Fence & Anchor patrons forever, when she helped restore some piece of their past, their culture, to their hearts.

"Here we go now." Mr. Horowitz counted the beat with a conductor's expertise.

"Moonlight, sunshine, waves upon the shore..."

When the song ended, pub patrons erupted with cheers. Keeton Lombard immediately started another round, teaching it to the younger Hessens.

Reggie felt a light hand on her leg. Tanner. "How am I doing?"

He pressed his hand to his chest. "Stealing every heart in this room."

The pub patrons were about to go another round with the evening song when the pub doors burst open, a mob surging inside, a blend of workers in uniforms, men and women in suits, and policemen trying to control the chaos.

"The EU has delivered their ruling. They sided with the princess and the entail. We'll be an autocracy in five days with the stroke of her royal pen."

TWENTY-EIGHT

From the peace of an evening song to mob-riot pandemonium in the span of one breath.

The news of the ruling hit the pub like a tidal wave, exploding over them, knocking them back, then flowing out of the pub with such force, taking the patrons with it. The court's ruling touched the festering debate in the Hessen people. Even those with no previous opinion were suddenly rabid and vocal.

For Tanner, panic. He'd lost Regina. One moment, he was standing by her, his hand resting gently on her leg. The next, he was pinned against a booth, unable to move. And he could no longer see her in the melee.

"Regina!"

The wave knocked him forward and sucked him out of the pub into the streets, and he was running with the stampede. He didn't have eyes on Nigel or Jace either, and he prayed one of them had the princess.

"Regina!" The noise shoved his call back to his lips.

He searched for her red head among the crowd, the hot, sticky air pocketing between the rioters, making it hard to breathe. Then he saw her burnished tresses not far ahead.

Calling for her over and over, he jammed, cut, shoved, and

pushed his way forward. When he reached her, he cupped his hand on her shoulder. "This way. Come with me."

The woman screamed, spinning round, jack-hammering Tanner with her fist, dragging a sharp ring across the top of his eye.

"Get off of me."

Falling back, Tanner pressed his hand to his face, a slithering pain shooting from his eye to the back of his head. He buckled forward, reaching blindly for something, anything, to grab on to. But his feet were caught ... stumbling ... tripping.

Floating white orbs flashed and popped in his eye. Finally, his palm landed flat against a streetlamp and he pulled himself upright.

The street noise was deafening. The voices, the horns, the shouts. When he heard an explosion, his heart nearly stopped.

He *had* to find Regina.

Warm blood oozed down his cheek. He yanked his handker-chief from his breast pocket and pressed it to his wound. A breeze freshened the air from the stench of terror, the sweat and smoke swirling around him. He jumped onto the base of a lamppost.

Lord, help me find her. Not for me. For her. For Hessenberg. Please. Keep her safe.

If he were Regina, where would he go? *Think, think* ... Peace began to whisper through his thoughts.

To the car? No, she'd not be able to push against the riot, which was moving with tidal force toward the park.

Melinda House was between here and the park, as was St. John's and Loudermilk's Bakery. Places she knew.

Still clinging to the lamppost, Tanner yanked his phone from his pocket, trying to dial Nigel while the mob slammed against his legs and back.

But the security officer didn't answer. He tried Jace to no avail, then Clarence, who also did not answer.

Tanner left a harried message for Clarence to rouse the entire security team and search for the princess among the rioters, throughout the downtown to the bay to the edges of the city.

Then, jumping down from the lamppost, he ran along the edge of the riot, weaving in and out of the fray, making his way toward St. John's.

He launched up the portico steps two at a time and burst into the church foyer.

"Regina!"

Through the nave doors and down the thick, carpeted aisle, his footsteps like muffled thunder.

"Regina!" His voice boomeranged around the arched, trumpeted rafters.

At the altar, he stopped running, stopped flitting and panicking, stooping forward with his hands on his knees, filling his lungs. A small drop of blood dotted his shoe.

"Come on, Lord, come on." The pressure of his prayer intensified the pain around his eye and sent a burning sear over his scalp. "Please . . ."

Tanner wiped the blood from around his eye with his coat sleeve as his phone buzzed in his pocket.

"Louis. Louis, please tell me Regina is with you."

"I was hoping she was with you. Nigel and Jace rang the office. Said she got swept up in the riot and they lost the princess."

Tanner exhaled, angry, frustrated. "She's out there, Louis. Alone and exposed."

"It's not good, Tanner. There was an explosion. The details are sketchy, but there's at least two fatalities."

Tanner dropped to his knees at the altar as he hung up, breaking the last cords of his deal with God, pleading with him for help. Regina needed him.

Above all, Tanner needed him.

The crowd moved whitewater fast, roaring, swollen with the rains of passion. Terrified, Reggie went limp and flowed with the force of the riot, bodies smashing against bodies, and tried to stay on her feet.

If she tripped or stumbled, or landed on the cobblestone street, she'd never get up. She'd be trampled.

Loud. The throng was so loud. She couldn't think. Or breathe. Her pulsing adrenaline was beginning to wane, and her legs had become like soft rubber. She felt weak and helpless to keep from eventually falling headlong onto the ground.

Someone smashed into her from behind. Stumbling, tripping, she grabbed at air, searching for something, someone to hold on to. But there was nothing. *Tanner.*

A broad, strong hand caught hers, snatching her to her feet. Reggie inhaled the fragrance of flour and vanilla instead of Tanner's scent of rustic floral and spices.

"Hang on to me, miss. You fall, you'll never get up." A young man, dressed in white, with a chocolate-stained apron wrapped around his narrow body, anchored her against him.

She tried to work her legs. Weak, so weak. Next to her a woman stumbled and went down.

"Help her . . ." Reggie leaned away from the man. "We . . . have to . . ."

"Keep running. If we stop, we'll be lost." The baker manhandled someone crossing in front of them, a foghorn in his hand. "Looks like we're heading to the park."

The park grass muffled the stampede and, for the first time, Reggie heard the shrill call of police whistles. There was another explosion, and the rioters ducked with a collective awe, smoke billowing over them. Then they rose up and resumed the shouting and running and general frothing of the soul.

The baker tripped but Reggie steadied him. "Come on, we're in this together."

SWAT teams with shields and helmets were now running with the riot, surging through people. Flares rocketed, piercing the coming night with fire. Voices rose in a cacophony of spiking and heated sounds with no one message piercing through.

The baker paused with a pinched expression. "I can't find a way out."

Reggie glanced back, into the dark face of the mounting riot, her heart a tight fist in her chest. A scream billowed between her ribs and Reggie felt certain that in the next breath, she'd begin flailing, slamming her fists into guts and faces.

Anything to get out of here.

A princess is defined not by her title alone but by how she lives her life.

Another push from behind. A foot smashed down on hers.

Do something, Reggie. *Lord, peace! We need your peace.*

Sing the song.

The idea hit fast, almost desperate, then settled in her mind.

A smoke bomb exploded in the middle of the park, polluting the air, stinging Reggie's lungs.

But instead of diffusing the rioters, the tactic only infused them with energy.

Sing the song.

Reggie spotted a park bench and cut a path through the crowd, dragging the baker along with her, Gram's melody louder and louder in her soul. "Help me up."

"Stand on the bench? Are you out of your mind, miss?"

"Probably." Trembling with the ebb and flow of adrenaline, Reggie pressed her hand on his shoulder and launched up onto the bench, facing the riot gathering in the park.

This was crazy. How were they going to hear her? One weak, thin voice against the noise?

Sing the song.

Then, drawing a deep breath, remembering her choir

teacher's admonition to sing from her diaphragm, she sang with her very last breath of courage.

"Moonlight, sunshine, waves against... upon... the shore..."

Her voice warbled, but in her ears, the riot frenzy shifted down a notch.

"La, la, la, la we're going to the shore.

"La, la, la, la to dance once more.

"No more worries, no more cares.

"We'll sleep in peace tonight under the stars so fair."

If the craziness ebbed at all, it flowed again the moment she stopped singing. So Reggie took a breath and began again. In faith.

"Moonlight, sunshine, waves upon the shore..."

TWENTY-NINE

At Wettin Manor, Tanner charged through the second-floor corridors toward Seamus's office, his shirt collar and coat sleeve stained with blood.

"Tanner—" The governor's aide, Brogan, chased after him. "He's in a meeting."

But Tanner kept stride, shoving through the governor's heavy, carved door. "If anything happens to her . . ." He pointed at Seamus, walking around the board table where several of his staff sat, tapping on their e-tablets. "I will hold you personally responsible."

"My good man,"—Seamus stood—"what happened to your face?"

"This is your doing . . . this *riot*." Tanner pointed to the dark window. "She's out there in it."

"The princess?" Seamus scoffed. "Are you admitting you lost the princess in the riot? I daresay, this will not make the king happy."

Tanner lunged at Seamus but caught himself before grabbing the man by the collar. "I meant what I said. If anything happens to her . . ."

"Tanner, need I remind you to whom you are speaking? Where are your loyalties, my boy?"

Their gazes locked, man against man, will against will. "Need I remind you of your failed plan to steal the country from Regina?"

"No need. The authority canon will do my bidding."

Tanner had enough. As he turned to go, he addressed the men at the table. "This is what you want? A country ruled by this man who's manipulating the law for his own gain? Look at the lot of you. It's Friday night at seven o'clock, chaps. There's a riot in the middle of the city. Go home to your wives and children." He shot Seamus a look. "Don't lose your souls to another man's selfish ambition."

Gathering himself, still fuming, Tanner made his way to his office, lightly touching his healing cut, checking his phone for news updates.

Louis met him outside his office. "We've got the entire security team looking for her. And the king is in your office along with the archbishop."

"Fan-blooming-tastic." Tanner exhaled, steadying his nerves. He'd have to face this music sooner or later. "Your Majesty," he said as he entered his office. "I'm terribly sorry—"

"Tanner, any word?" The king wore jeans and a pullover, clearly not intending to work on a Friday night. "Your face . . . are you all right?"

"I'm fine." Tanner went to his window and peered out. *Regina, where are you?* "No word on the princess." He looked toward the park, but his view was obscured by buildings and the coming night. *Lord, I have to trust you for her safety.*

"She strikes me as a resourceful, brave woman, Tanner," Dad said.

"She is." He glanced at his father. "But she's in a riot. Not a Festivus parade." He turned to the window again. "Do you remember an old Hessen evening song?"

"Hmm, not sure," Dad said. "Your grandmother used to sing an old song."

"See here, Burkhardt." Seamus burst into Tanner's office. "Oh, Your Majesty, begging your pardon, I didn't know you'd arrived." He clipped his pipe between his teeth and settled his feathers.

"Seamus." Nathaniel, ever calm, full of diplomacy.

But Tanner remained focused on the song. He must remember the song. Humming part of the melody, he tried to piece the lyrics with the melody. "Something . . . moonlight, sunlight, waves upon the shore . . ." He tapped the beat in the air with his finger.

"I'm afraid I don't know it," Nathaniel said.

"Regina sang it in the pub tonight, and I tell you, it captured the people. Their hearts. Sour old men battled tears." Tanner felt more than words swelling in his heart. He felt the warm power of love. He pressed his sleeve to his wound, catching the last ooze of blood. "There was a man in the pub, Tobias Horowitz, who asked Regina, 'Who will help us find our identity?' Then out of the blue she sings an old Hessenberg song the last three generations have forgotten."

He turned to his dad, then to the king, and last to Seamus. "Don't you see? She carries Princess Alice and the duke within her. Does she know how we celebrate our Thanksgiving? Or Festivus? No, but she carries within her our very essence. I daresay she *is* our essence."

"Pardon the interruption, but you must see this." Louis shuffled the piles of paper on Tanner's desk for the telly remote. The riot in the park filled the screen. An on-site reporter said, "It's believed the princess, Her Royal Highness Princess Regina, is among the riot crowd . . ."

Tanner's pulse drummed thick in his ears, searching for her as cameramen moved through the crowd.

" . . . and we've a report of singing."

There were several quick-changing camera shots, then Regina popped onto the screen, standing on a stone bench, her red hair blowing across her eyes.

"Louis,"—Tanner tapped his assistant on the arm—"raise the volume."

The image shimmied as the cameraman jostled through the crowd for a closer angle.

Eyes closed, voice loud and clear, Regina sang the evening song with passion and heart.

On his left stood the king. On his right, his father. Even Seamus had taken a step toward the telly, captured by Regina and her song.

"The old evening song," Dad whispered. "I've not heard that since my grandmother was alive."

"Nor I," Seamus muttered.

"Louis, which end of the park? Can you tell?" Tanner backed toward the door.

"East end. Off Market."

Down the manor stairs, Tanner burst into the night and ran the ten city blocks to the park, expecting to run into a wall of warm, frenzied bodies. Instead he found a thin, quiet, dissipating crowd.

"Regina!" He raced against the light, crossing Market Avenue, toward the park. "Regina!"

Tanner jumped up on the bench, scanning the park grounds as the rioters headed home. Surely she wasn't still here.

He jumped off the bench. Where could she be? His cell phone rang as he tripped over empty Starbucks coffee cups. It was Jarvis.

"Is she there with you?" Tanner said.

"No, we saw her on the telly. Is she all right?"

"I don't know. I can't find her."

"You can't find her? How did you lose the princess?"

There was a riot, for pity's sake. "Never mind, Jarvis. If she arrives at the palace, please call me." Tanner rang off and dashed across Market Avenue, then turned onto Gilden, running past the eponymous department store toward Loudermilk's Bakery.

Through the front glass, he caught sight of a woman with full, red hair and nearly tripped over his own feet trying to get through the bakery door. "Regina!"

The woman turned round and his heart failed.

"Sorry." He backed away. "I thought you were someone else. My apologies. I'm just looking for—"

"The princess?" A lanky chap dressed in white and tied up in an oversized apron came from behind the counter. "Who might you be?"

"Tanner Burkhardt, Minister of Culture. Friend of the princess."

"She was brilliant in the park, was she not?"

"Then you saw her?"

"Saw her? I escorted her. Didn't know she was the princess when I saved her from stumbling under the rioters' feet, but sure enough, that's who she was. Once the riot died out, we came back here. I gave her a whole box of cinnamon puffs."

Tanner grabbed the man's arms. "Where is she now?"

"I'm not sure. She simply said she had to go."

"You don't know where?"

"She didn't say."

"Thank you, mate." Tanner dashed out of Loudermilk's, skipped left, no, right, then turning in a circle. The church. Aim for St. John's.

He slowed his pace and gathered his wind and allowed the baker's news to set in. She was all right. She was all right. Thanks be to the Almighty.

As he made his way to the church, his heart told him this was no longer about finding a princess, but the one his heart loved.

He'd left his comfort zones for her, given his heart. He wasn't going to give up finding her—the beautiful Regina with sun-kissed hair and radiant blue eyes.

He took the church steps toward the center doors two at a time, and inside yanked on the sanctuary door. Locked.

No, no ... He tugged on the next door, and the next, hammering the last with his fist.

"Regina!"

The door on the far end swung open, and a man dressed in priest's robes appeared.

"Can I help you, Tanner? Is everything all right, son?"

"Bishop, sir. Have you seen Regina?"

"The princess? Yes ..." He tapped his hand over his heart, and his piercing eyes were vibrant and radiant. "I've not heard that evening song in decades."

"Yes, it's ... a ... wonderful ... song." Tanner locked his gaze with the holy man's and the anxiety in his chest began to fade, being replaced by a fiery presence. "Do I know you?"

"You do." The bishop leveled his gaze straight at Tanner. "We met years ago."

"At my father's church? Or parsonage?"

"In my Father's house."

Tanner's heart burned and pulsed. His thoughts went silent. And in an instant, he felt as if a decade's worth of guilt and shame had crumbled at his feet.

"Forgive me, I've been away too long." The words came from a depth he did not know, but they washed him, cleansed him.

"And now you've returned." The bishop smiled. "I see you've been wounded."

Tanner touched the cut above his eye. "Yes, the riot." The bishop's simple, gentle voice somehow spurred tears in Tanner's eyes and pinned him where he stood. For a long moment, he just breathed, the weight on his soul feeling lighter and lighter.

"The princess is not here but she's fine, Tanner. Do not worry. Do not worry." The bishop turned to go inside. "When you find her, give her my regards."

"Yes, sir, I will." The arching, hardwood door clicked closed as Tanner realized he never got the bishop's name. "Sir, wait a minute." Tanner hammered the thick door with his fist. "From whom should I give her regards?" He jerked on the handle, but the door would not budge. Locked. Impossible. How could the bishop have disappeared so quickly behind a locked door? "Hello?"

But the bishop did not return.

Tanner skipped down the steps with a final look over his shoulder at the chapel. He raised his fingers to the cut to find it'd stopped bleeding.

As Tanner turned down the dark, quiet avenue, heading for the Fence & Anchor, his spirit rumbled, quite certain that he'd just now encountered the Divine.

She could've been trampled. Wounded. Killed. Maybe even kidnapped. But she'd stepped out in faith and sung a song. And in Daddy's vernacular, "God backed her up."

The taxi had let Reggie out at the palace, and now she stood at the iron gate pressing buttons. What was the security number Tanner dictated to her? "It's me, let me in," she hollered into the speaker, hoping someone inside would answer.

Or come outside and see her standing there with her face between the iron bars.

"Hey, Jarvis. Chef. Serena. It's me, Reg. Your Majesty. The princess."

Her voice wobbled. Her body shivered. What had she done? It wasn't until she'd left the bakery with a box of fresh puffs that she realized she'd faced a raging mob fueled by fury against her and started singing. She could've been dragged through the streets. Hung from a tree. Tarred and feathered.

Somewhere along the way she'd lost her phone so she couldn't call Tanner. Didn't know his number by heart yet. Then she spied and hailed a passing cab, telling the driver up front that she didn't have any money but would compensate him later.

The kind, older man assured her money was not on his mind today. He'd been giving free rides since the riot suddenly ended.

"Were you in that blooming mess?" he'd asked.

In it? She was part of the cause. "Unfortunately."

He'd peered at her through his rearview mirror. "You're not from around here. You sound American. From the South, maybe."

"Sure enough." Reggie slid down against the seat. Where was Tanner? Did he survive the stampede? Nigel and Jace? What of old Keeton Lombard and Tobias Horowitz?

"Where to, miss?"

"Meadowbluff Palace."

The driver glanced at her again via the rearview mirror. Regina was grateful for the Plexiglas barrier.

"Welcome to Hessenberg, Your Majesty."

"Bit of a rough start, don't you think?"

He laughed and nodded. "Bunch of hullabaloo. It'll blow over."

So that's how she came to stand on the other side of the earth-to-heaven wrought iron gate guarding Meadowbluff Palace.

"Jarvis? Serena?" She mashed down on the Call button. "Anyone?" She stepped back to wave at the surveillance camera. "Yo in there, it's me. Can I come in?"

The gate clicked and slowly—very slowly—eased open. Jarvis's frantic voice came from the box. "Your Majesty, you're safe. Thank the Lord."

"You ain't kidding." She squeezed through the gate and started up the long drive to the palace, exercising the panic and anxiety from her body. From her mind and soul.

Jarvis met her halfway down the drive with a flashlight and all but hugged her. "Your Majesty." His eyes misted. "I was so worried."

She fell against the older man, resting her head on his shoulder. His tone, his glistening gaze reminded her of Daddy. "It all happened so fast."

The last of her tension broke and she sobbed.

"There, there, miss." Jarvis stiffly patted her back. "It's all over now."

"Jarvis?"

"Yes, miss?"

"If you're going to be in my life,"—she sniffed, gripping her puffs bag a bit tighter—"you're going to have to do better than this."

"But I'm staff. Propriety and all, you know."

"Y–you're also . . . one of my only friends."

It took a moment, but his arms encircled her. "You're home, safe and sound. The evening song was lovely. So very lovely."

Regina shuddered through her last sob. "We don't have to tell the others about this. Our moment."

"It's our secret, Your Majesty." He stepped aside, waiting for her to start forward. "The entire security force is out looking for you," he said. "I'll ring Mr. Burkhardt. Let him know you've arrived home."

"Thank you." Up the steps, she was suddenly exhausted, hungry—and cold.

"Chef has a hearty wild-pheasant-and-rice soup simmering on the stove. I'll send it up to your room. Are those puffs from Loudermilk's?" He pointed to her bag.

"Yes, the baker, Ben Loudermilk, saved me, Jarvis. He really did."

"Shall I arrange to have him to tea?"

"Oh please, that would be awesome."

Jarvis opened the door for her, but Regina paused on the stoop. "Why were you so kind to me? I came here a stranger, an American, an interloper into your world, your government. Half this country hates me. But you've treated me like a princess from the first day."

"Because it's what I do. Serve the princess." He glanced away, toward the garden lights. "You remind me and all of us who we are as a people." His eyes shone when he faced her. "I've a renewed appreciation and love for my country, for my own heritage. I'm grateful."

"Guess we're all getting a refreshed glimpse of our destiny."

"Of that I have no doubt." Jarvis touched his hand to his chin, lowering his gaze. "What you did today in the midst of chaos showed true courage and wisdom. I knew then. You are a true princess."

In her suite, a fire flickered in the fireplace. Reggie removed the coat she'd never even had a chance to take off at the Fence & Anchor. But her bones were aching for a hot bath. Her stomach grumbled for a bowl of Chef's wild-pheasant-and-rice soup.

But as she passed the window, she caught a glow among the dark forest trees.

"What?" She pressed her face to the window. There it was, in the exact same spot as before.

Snapping up her coat, Reggie headed out, running into Serena. "I'll be back."

Daggum, she was going to find out what was hidden in the woods if it was the last thing she did. And if the woods contained anything like in a '70s slasher movie, it might be the last thing she'd ever do.

Through the kitchen, she fired out the back door, then backtracked for a flashlight before making tracks for the trees.

What kind of trick or hologram lurked in her woods? Her panic in the midst of the riot had somehow morphed into I-dare-you courage.

Ducking into the forest, slapping aside limbs and vines, Reggie kicked through the brambles, squinting through the darkness toward the swirling light. The air about her face was warm while cold air circulated around her legs. Contrast. Everything around her shouted contrast. Shouted impossible.

But with God, all things are possible.

Suddenly, she was free of the brambles, bursting into a grass-carpet clearing with a red-and-gold-leaves path, leading her to a glow and an old red stable.

Gram's stable.

Reggie gasped as she moved through the dancing, twirling light particles. The same thick, oily fragrance from her oath ceremony, from the Fence & Anchor, permeated the atmosphere.

God is here.

"This is incredible."

Cutting off her flashlight and tucking it into her pocket, she swirled in the beams with both hands. They jumped and bounced, as if aware she stood among them.

At the stable door, Reggie raised the latch with a surge of anticipation and shoved the door open. The light from outside swooshed in, filling the low structure and stirring another kind of fragrance.

The fragrance of life. Of hay and barley, as if a stable hand had just finished his chores.

Reggie moved down the wide center aisle, peeking into the stalls, her boot heels thudding. There were three stalls on either side, and a work space with something large under a faded green canvas was at the far end.

As she grabbed the canvas, the old material crunched in her hands. She jerked it to the ground, and a cloud of dust puffed from the coarse threads.

The glow she loved but could not explain had begun to fade, so Reggie retrieved her flashlight from her hip pocket.

The first glimpse of a chrome headlight nearly sank her to the ground. It couldn't be. It just *couldn't*.

"Oh my word. No, no, no. I can't believe it."

"Regina! Regina!"

She whirled around to see Tanner skidding through the stable door, his shirttail out, his tie askew at half-mast, and his normally neat, clipped hair going in every wild direction.

"Tanner, look, look. The Starfire #89. From the fairy— What happened to your eye?"

He snatched her into his arms and kissed her, gripping her so tight, pulling her into his heart, loving the star fire right out of her. Reggie swooned against him.

"I'm so sorry, so sorry. I tried to find you. I tried."

"It's okay, Tanner, it's okay . . . Are *you* okay?" She brushed her fingers over his cut. "It's not bleeding. Did this happen today? It looks almost healed."

"Some lady caught me with her ring. Regina, you were brilliant, singing that song. We saw it on the telly." He touched his forehead to hers. "Oh, love, when I'd lost you in the crowd . . . I thought I'd go crazy. I looked everywhere for you. But mostly I realized how madly I love you, Reggie."

He kissed her cheek down to the curve of her neck until she thought she might decompose into a love puddle right there on the stable floor.

"Hey, wait a minute." She gathered herself and pushed out of his arms. "How did you find me? Here, in the stable?"

He jerked his thumb over his shoulder. "I followed the light."

"The light?" She squinted at him. "You saw the light? The swirling stardust?"

He grinned, his blue eyes snapping. "Yes, Reggie, I saw the light."

She held his face, careful of his injury, and pulled him close for a kiss. "You called me Reggie."

"Because that's who I fell in love with. The girl chatting up the lawyer with motor oil running down her face. The girl with the song in the pub. The girl who quelled a riot with her voice."

"What about the princess?" She fiddled with his collar, running her hands over the muscled curves of his shoulders. "Do you love her?"

"Very much." He twirled her around. "I love Her Majesty too."

"It is going to be complicated, isn't it?"

"Very."

"That's okay with you?"

"Is it okay with *you*?"

"Wouldn't have it any other way," she said.

He kissed her forehead. "Now, what's this about a Starfire #89?" With his arm about her, he turned to the car.

"It's the car in the fairy tale. It has to be Prince Francis's Starfire #89." She aimed her light over the sports car with its giant, exposed coils and single-seat chassis. "The original. Number one."

"Hold on now." Tanner walked around the car. "If this stable existed in 1914, how was it and the car not discovered?" He shined his light on the red, gleaming car.

For a moment, Regina couldn't think. Only feel. This was what Gram was trying to tell her. Find the stable and the car. Then it will all make sense.

"Don't you see? God hid it until the right time." Reggie spun around, pumping her fist in the air, then rammed Tanner with an engulfing hug. The last chain of doubt broke from her heart.

Reggie chatted at top speed, explaining to Tanner about the car's design, how the low, single-seat racer was modeled after Ford's race car #999, built on a wood chassis with a whopping 50 horsepower engine.

Tanner inspected the smooth curve of the chassis, lowering his flashlight to inspect the paint. "It's in incredible shape for sitting a hundred years."

"The tarp saved it, I'm sure." She glanced toward the rafters. "And I don't see any leaks."

But it was more than solid roofs and thick tarps that had saved the Starfire—that had saved the kingdom. It was the hand of God. This was his fun way of saying, "See? I got this," and Reggie felt it to her core.

Tanner inspected the open, big coil, eight-cylinder engine.

"Lev Goldstein broke Ford's racing record by point one second in 1910." She bent to inspect the engine next to him. "He blew the engine but not before wowing the racing industry with a speed of 102 miles an hour. Unheard of in its day. It would be years before any other racer came close."

He brushed his hand over her shoulder. "I love your passion."

"Tanner,"—she stood—"I've been thinking."

"About . . ." He leaned to inspect the leather interior.

"I have to ask someone to form a government, right?"

"Yes, according to our old laws."

"I want to ask Seamus."

Tanner snapped upright. "What? No, Reggie, no. I forbid it." He stormed around the back of the car toward her, tripping over the tarp. "He's a slime. I blame him for the riot today, what with all his meddling and media futzing. No, you can't."

"First of all, I don't think you can forbid me. Can you?"

"As one of your advisors—"

"Second of all, Tanner, he knows this country, he knows the structure and the people. They like him. The half that hates me likes him. The half that hates him likes me. Together, we make a whole team."

"He will stab you in the back, Reggie."

"More than he's already tried?"

"Yes! He's only shown us the tip of the iceberg. He's a weasel and the people deserve better. You deserve better."

"Look around you." She motioned to the stable. "We just found a magical, unexplained glow in the woods hovering over a never-seen-before red stable in which we find probably the original Starfire #89, and who knows what all is in here. If I can't have faith that God has my back in being Princess of Hessenberg, if I can't trust my heart telling me to make peace with Seamus—and yes, I'll pray about it—then let's just call it quits and go home."

She reached for him. "Tanner, I was a car restoration girl in Tallahassee, Florida. And God, in his mercy, saw fit to make me—weak, broken me—a princess. How can I not afford some of the same kindness and faith toward Seamus? What if God wants me to be as generous to him as he's been to me? Besides, what's the old adage? Keep your friends close and your enemies closer."

He sighed, a funny look crossing his face. "I went to St. John's to look for you this afternoon." He braced his hands on his hips. "And this bishop came out to tell me you were all right. Then he said something to me that made my chest feel on fire . . . like he might have been the Lord himself. He said to tell you hi, by the way."

"Tanner, our whole world has been flipped inside out. Yours. Mine. The duchy's. Seamus's." She touched his arm, knowing more than ever she was right about the governor. "I at least want to talk to him. Before he has me arrested."

He regarded her for a long second, then nodded. "Fine, but I want to be there."

"I'd have it no other way." She kissed his cheek. "I love you, Tanner."

He drew her into a warm, cocooning hug. "Love you back, Princess."

So, the car. Reggie slipped from Tanner's embrace and walked around the car. "I can't believe it . . . I just . . . it's a miracle. Say,"— she held out her hand, wiggling her fingers at him—"I lost my phone in the riot. Can I borrow yours?"

"You lost your phone?" He took out his mobile and pressed it to his ear. "Louis, contact Mr. Beswick in America and have him cancel Regina's phone plan. Get her a new one." He made a face at her as he hung up and passed over his cell. "How did you lose your phone?"

"The riot. Now, shh, this is a sacred moment. I'm taking a picture to send to Al. He's going to die, just die." Her heart fluttered just imagining Al's face when he got this text. But wait . . . Reggie lowered the phone.

"I should just ship him the car. Let him restore it. He'd be so surprised. He was always saying to me, 'No Starfire #89 is ever going to find its way down to Dixie.' Well, ha!"

"But he closed the shop."

"Yeah, but that doesn't mean he's not going to tinker around. I know him. And he'd move heaven and earth to work on the Starfire #89."

"If you're sure, I'll see what we can do about moving it." Tanner moved to the back of the car, tipping his flashlight. "Didn't the fairy tale have the princess stashing something in the boot? There's a small one back here."

"Yeah, it did. And, Tanner, you don't have to do everything for me. Just point me in the right direction and I can see about shipping the car." Reggie bent down to feel for the release. The small door bounced open and she aimed her flashlight inside. "There's a leather bag in here." She reached for it. "Feels like books. Wouldn't it be like my ancestors to leave me books? Not that I mind, but personal effects would've been nice."

Kneeling down on the canvas with Tanner next to her, Reggie passed him her flashlight and unbuckled the straps.

"A scarf . . . a blue scarf . . ." She pulled it free. "Tanner, I think it's the one Gram wore in her portrait. There's something wrapped up in it." Reggie brushed the dust from the tarp before peeling away the scarf.

The beam of their flashlights caught and captured the brilliant sparkle of a diamond tiara.

"Oh my word—" Reggie gasped, pressing her hand to her chest as flashlight beams shoved light through the gems, fanning glorious prisms across the stable.

"So this is where you've been hiding, you naughty tiara," Tanner said. "I looked high and low for the Princess Alice tiara."

"I've never seen anything so beautiful." She peeked around

Tanner at the racer. "Except maybe the Starfire . . . No, no, the tiara wins. It's a tie. Yes, a tie. I can wear the tiara when I drive the car." Raising the crown, Reggie inspected the platinum and diamond piece from all sides. "Astounding."

"I found coronets, the royal crowns, and the tiara your gram inherited from the last Grand Duchess, but never this beauty. I thought it was lost. Like so many other archives."

Reggie faced him. "What's the story with this one? Do you know?"

"It's a diamond garland tiara made by Cartier in 1913 for your gram's sixteenth birthday. It was a gift from Prince Francis."

"Along with the Princess Alice tree?"

"Ah, you learned of the tree." Tanner pointed to the top of the tiara. "See these arching laurel wreaths with the sapphire leaves? Your uncle's design just for her. It's one of a kind." Tanner motioned to the satchel with the edge of his flashlight beam. "I bet there's a matching diamond-and-sapphire drop necklace and earrings inside."

Reggie dug in and retrieved a yellow silk scarf, unwinding it to discover the necklace and earrings. The stones radiated against the golden threads.

Reggie propped against the car. "The more I discover of Gram's world, the more I don't understand her silence. She talked about how she came to America, her second husband, and her daughter, my grandma. She reminisced about her lovely childhood in Hessenberg. But never, ever did she say, 'For my sixteenth birthday, my uncle, the Grand Duke, commissioned a diamond-and-sapphire tiara for me made by Cartier.'"

"Perhaps it was her way of dealing with the pain." Tanner eased down to sit next to her. "When I gave up the girls, I basically stopped talking about them. If I did, it kept my pain alive. Like your gram, I thought I was never getting them back. I'd never see them again."

"Makes sense, but I still wish she'd said something."

"She did, love. In the fairy tale."

"And we're back to that." Reggie held the crown against her Kohl's Vera Wang top. "What do you think? Goes great, doesn't it?"

"Yes, with the woman, not the clothes." Tanner exchanged his flashlight for the tiara and gently set it on her head. "Beautiful."

A soft blush covered her cheeks.

Tanner held up his phone. "For me? Please. To remember this moment."

"Okay. But only you." She smiled as Tanner snapped the photo.

Feeling shy, she slipped the tiara from her head. "How ridiculous do I look?"

"You look stunning. The tiara becomes you." He brushed his finger along her cheek. "You truly are a restorer. Of lost history. Of lost relationships. Of lost dreams. You stepped into my life and everything changed. It will be the same for Hessenberg."

"Maybe. But, Tanner, it all started with you." She stared at the tiara, holding it delicately in her hand. "I'm a little bit scared."

"Me too." He scooted in next to her. "I don't know anything about raising girls. But you'll help me. You don't know much about being a princess or politics, but I'll be with you." He clasped her hand. "One for one, one for all."

She peered into his eyes. "One for all." Then she leaned in for a kiss. "Still loving I can do that *almost* anytime I want."

"What say we film some of this car? I can have the media team jazz it up a bit." Tanner aimed his phone at the car, then Reggie. "What else is in the bag?"

Digging in, she retrieved two leather books, a photograph, a small wooden jewel box, and a pair of cream kid-leather gloves.

She thumbed through the first book, a compact leather-bound piece, worn around the edges as if carried often.

"Tanner,"—Regina rose up on her knees—"aim the flashlight over here. Oh my, oh my!" She sighed with a small laugh. "It's

Gram's journal." She flipped to the first page. "Look . . . 1913,"—
she fanned to the last page—"to October 1914. Tanner, she left
her journals behind."

"Regina, she left her story behind."

"The fairy tale," they said in unison, eyes meeting.

"She was telling me to find the car and look in the trunk."

"I told you she was speaking to you in that book." Tanner
tucked away his filming, his phone, and every outside intrusion
to the moment.

"With pictures and symbols rather than straight-up truth."

Regina glanced down at the page and read aloud.

"Mamá just entered my room tonight by candlelight, grim
and grieving. I am to pack my things and prepare to leave, rather
flee our beloved Hessenberg. How can this be? . . . The palace is
dark and I was admonished not to turn on my light or light a
candle. Uncle, she said, signed over all rights and rule to Cousin
Nathaniel. He surrendered to Brighton."

A reverence fell over her heart. "I changed my mind about
the car and the tiara." Reggie held the journal to her chest. "This
is my most treasured possession."

"Hear, hear," Tanner whispered.

"I'm so glad I followed the light." Reggie raised the leather
bag to peer in one last time. "There's an envelope." She pulled it
out, handing it to Tanner.

When he looked inside, he laughed. "My dear Reggie, I'm a
believer. I *am* a believer."

"What is it?" She hooked her hand over his, trying to see the
contents inside. "What converted you?"

"Bonds. Lovely, beautiful, bearer bonds."

"The bonds. Mentioned in the entail."

"Your Majesty," Tanner said. "You are a very wealthy woman."

She peered at him through her tears. "Now I can *really* restore
the kingdom."

THIRTY

She'd found bliss—*and* true love—between the shores of a small gem of a nation, restored to royal, sovereign perfection. A past she'd never known came to life, roared into her present, and redefined who she was and all her future days.

As strange as it still felt to be a royal princess, Reggie was confident *this* was what she'd been born to do—restore Gram's ancient, beloved Hessenberg to its original, classic beauty.

And it only took her twenty-nine years to find out. Her heart understood more every day that this was where she belonged.

For now, however, she was late. For her first official Princess of Hessenberg engagement. October twenty-second, the official signing of the entail and ending Brighton's hundred-year rule over Hessenberg.

She only had a few minutes to dress. Reggie hurried to her suite, yanking off her boots, squirming out of her jeans. She was excited to find a crew to extract the Starfire #89 from the stable and have it shipped to Daddy. That chore had consumed her the last few days but the antique gem was on its way.

Wouldn't Al be surprised when he returned home from Texas?

She might just have to fly home for the big reveal. Even Daddy didn't know exactly what she was shipping him other than, "It's huge! Big! Unbelievable!"

Going toward the dressing room, Reggie caught a glimpse of herself in the mirror.

Mop of red hair, blue eyes, and the curves of the Beswick women . . . all very familiar. But the glint in her eye was new, a symbol of her growing confidence that she was exactly where God wanted her to be.

The warm drops of oil continued to hit her head, mostly when she was about some royal duty. Like the day she asked Seamus to form a government. He blustered and pontificated, got red-nosed, and accepted her invitation in the end, pledging to drop his plan to charge Reggie as an enemy of the state.

So, the oil drops? The occasional hand on her head? Odd, but she was convinced it was God's world breaking into hers. All in all, this was his journey, and she was just holding on for the ride.

In her dressing room, Serena had selected dresses from three designers who were already sketching ideas that would define Reggie's style—wide skirts and cowboy boots.

Choosing the Melinda House silky rich green dress with the front buttons, Reggie slipped it over her head, the fabric flowing down her arms, swishing about her knees. If she'd known dresses like this existed, she might have gone this way long ago.

Tugging on a pair of cream-colored soft calfskin dress boots— hey, she was just reinforcing her style—she headed out.

"Miss, you look beautiful. Redneck royal, my blooming eye," Serena said, coming in the room. "Shall I do your hair? Mr. Burkhardt sent word to wear your tiara."

"Wear the tiara? For signing the entail?" She'd embraced the notion she'd have to change some of her ways. Don a fancy dress more often than she'd like. But the tiara and diamond-drop earrings made her feel like a lipstick-wearing, diamond-encrusted poser.

"But this is a formal ceremony, miss. You're the royal princess. If ever there was a time to wear your gram's tiara, 'tis now." Serena unwrapped the delicate crown from the silk pouch Tanner had commissioned for it.

"I feel so silly. Like I'm putting on airs."

"Come. Sit." Serena patted the vanity chair. "Let me do your hair and settle on the tiara. You won't even know it's there."

Reggie hesitated. Couldn't she just tell Serena no? After all, she was the princess. "Okay, but kind of puff up my hair to hide it."

Serena proceeded to do the exact opposite, taming Reggie's hair and pulling it back into a twist before settling the tiara on her head.

"Your Majesty, it's beautiful. You are beautiful." She met Reggie's gaze through the mirror. "Like I said, redneck royal, my blooming eye."

"Serena, this is not what I asked for." Reggie winced at her appearance and the lush array of sparkling diamonds on top of her head.

"But it's perfect for you."

"Are you sure?"

Jarvis's gentle voice came over the room intercom. "Mr. Burkhardt is here, miss."

Reggie stood with a glance at Serena. "I'm trusting you with this updo."

"You're going to pop his eyes out, miss."

"Pop his eyes out? Who, Mr. Burkhardt?" Serena caught Reggie kissing Tanner once. Okay, maybe twice. But it was on the cheek both times.

"Oh, go on." Serena waved off her comment with a shy giggle. "We all know, miss."

"Well, pretend you don't." Reggie smiled at her lady's maid.

As she came down the stairs, Tanner glanced up, his heart molding his expression. Love.

He won her all over again.

With a low whistle, he propped his elbow on the banister, watching her descend, soaking her with his adoration and desire.

"You know you're never getting rid of me," he said, reaching for her when she arrived at the bottom of the staircase.

"Because I wore this tiara?" She raised her chin and tapped the very tip of the crown with her hand.

"No." He kissed her forehead. "Because you wore those boots."

She laughed, electric shivers firing through her. *So this is love . . .*

"Regina,"—Tanner breathed out, slowly bending to one knee—"I love you and—"

"Mercy above and all the angels." Serena bent over the landing banister, eyes like saucers, her mouth dangling open.

"Serena," Tanner said, "give us a moment."

The lady's maid shook the palace with her fleeing footsteps.

"Tanner, what are you doing?" Reggie sat on the bottom step, facing him.

"I thought about it all night. Why wait when we know we love each other?"

"But I'm a new princess and you're a new dad."

"And we're going to need each other to learn our jobs. For support."

She brushed her hand over his cheek, his blue eyes intense with a determined spark.

"It's going to be complicated."

"Yes, but it's going to get fun too." He wiggled his eyebrows, making her laugh.

"So," she said, looking down and fluffing her skirt, "what exactly are you asking me, Tanner Burkhardt?"

"Regina Alice Beswick Augustine-Saxon, will you—"

"You forgot to say princess."

"Pardon me, Your Majesty. Princess Regina Alice Beswick Augustine-Saxon, will you—"

"Tanner,"—she pressed her hand over his heart—"all teasing aside, ask me from here."

He smiled, raised up off his knee, and scooted onto the step next to her. "Reggie, I've loved you since you crawled out from under a Corvette with leaves in your hair and oil on your face. I want to share my life with you. I want you to share yours with me. I can't imagine another day going by without you promising to marry me. Will you do me the honor of being my wife? Please." He dug into his pocket and produced a diamond solitaire in a simple platinum band.

Tears welled in her eyes. He knew her well. "Oh, Tanner, it's perfect." She cupped her hand over his and met his gaze. "I think I fell for you when you told me who I really was . . . the long-lost princess of Hessenberg. I've loved you more every day, and I can't imagine my life without you. So yes, Tanner Burkhardt, I will marry you."

He slipped the cool, smooth ring onto her finger and gathered her in his arms, sealing their pledge with a kiss. And then she knew. Regina Beswick was finally *all* the way home.

THIRTY-ONE

One Year Later

At one o'clock in the afternoon, the cathedral bells pealed, chiming glorious sounds through the streets of Hessenberg. Tell the whole world! Princess Regina Alice Beswick Augustine-Saxon has married Tanner Wingate Burkhardt.

And next month, after the honeymoon, she'd press on to the coronation, becoming Princess Regina, Grand Duchess of Hessenberg.

As she walked the long aisle of St. John's nave with Tanner in a fitted white gown wearing Gram's tiara and jewels, Reggie never felt more like a princess.

Love had a way of crowning every woman's heart.

Tanner whispered, "Happy?"

"More than."

Bridesmaids Carrie, who married Rafe last year, and Bella and Britta wore cream dresses with burgundy sashes. The twins were beautiful, fun, exasperating, and fully taking up residence in Reggie's heart.

Emerging from the church into the October sunshine, she

and Tanner stepped into the thunderous cheers and shouts of the Hessenberg people.

"I can barely hear myself think," she shouted toward him, waving to the crowd, leaning against her man.

At the bottom of the steps, Reggie caught the eye of Hessenberg's stately Prime Minister Seamus Fitzsimmons, without his pipe between his teeth, looking dapper in a top hat and tails.

"Reggie, look." Tanner pointed to the Brightonian World War I biplanes flying over, releasing a rainbow shower of confetti.

The throng oohed and aahed, trying to collect the colorful paper marked with Princess Regina's cipher and the wedding date.

Moments later, a World War II fighter plane passed over, waving its wings and followed by the raucous, stupendous roar of United States F18s flying in formation. A gift to Her Royal Highness from the United States on her wedding day.

Reggie tipped back her head, letting loose her own rebel yell. Such a thrilling sight and sound.

"That's fantastic," Tanner yelled.

A row of trumpeters in red knee pants, braided blue coats, and tri-fold hats raised their instruments and blasted a royal declaration.

Taking hold of her hand, Tanner ran Reggie down the steps toward their waiting carriage. But when the security team parted, she found a gleaming red, restored Starfire #89 pulling the carriage instead of matched white horses.

And their chauffeur? Al, standing by the car in his Marine uniform, straight and proud.

"Al!" Forgetting decorum, Reggie broke from Tanner and ran into the man's embrace. "You came, you came."

"Ha-ha, my girl, you done good. I hated lying, telling you Miriam and I couldn't come, but we wanted to surprise you."

Today was full of joy. And for tears.

On the other side of the car, Bella and Britta gathered with Daddy, who beamed, all sharp and handsome in his tuxedo. "We surprised you, Reg."

"You sure did, Daddy."

Sadie wept, wiping her eyes, wearing one of the craziest hats Reggie had ever seen. But she was already Mimi to the twins and Mum to Tanner.

Archbishop and Mrs. Burkhardt beamed standing next to Sadie. Tanner finally came to understand how much his dad loved him and had a standing lunch with him every Thursday.

It had been a busy but incredible year.

"This is unbelievable." Reggie stepped back to inspect the car while Carrie gathered the hem of her gown to keep it from dragging on the ground. "Does it run?"

"Girl, don't be talking smack to me when I came all the way over here to drive you on your wedding day." Chuckling, Al motioned to Tanner. "It was his idea to use the car. He made sure we got it done on time. Helped us find parts, experts, labor, you name it."

"Happy wedding day." Tanner slipped his arm around her, kissing her cheek.

"This is the best day ever!" She shot her arms in the air over her head. Come on, now, she couldn't completely give up her Southern roots.

Tanner helped Reggie into the carriage as Al fired up the Starfire #89. The engine rumbled as the ancient car moved through the cheering crowd, the noise level rising and rising, never letting up.

Photographers raced alongside of the carriage, aiming to capture the photo of the century—a royal Hessenberg wedding.

Reggie slipped her hand into Tanner's. "Thank you for all of this, Mr. Burkhardt."

"Couldn't have done it without you, Mrs. Burkhardt." He

slipped his arm around her and lowered his lips to hers, kissing her long and sweet.

Reggie Beswick found love by saying yes to her destiny and began her very own once upon a time and happily ever after.

READING GROUP GUIDE

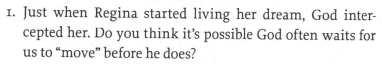

1. Just when Regina started living her dream, God intercepted her. Do you think it's possible God often waits for us to "move" before he does?

2. Tanner is burdened by his past mistakes and alters his life course. Is there an area of your life you've "quit" living because you thought you'd ruined your call?

3. Through Prince Francis, we see how one man's failures can destroy the destiny of future generations. Yet through another person's obedience, Regina's, we see how that destiny is restored. Is there an inheritance in your family or life you need to ask the Lord to restore?

4. Regina has a great life in Tallahassee. One she's designed for herself. But God sends her on a journey for which she feels ill prepared. Yet he's made all the provision she needs. Is God asking you to step out in an area in which you feel ill prepared? Can you believe he'll make a way?

5. So many times in our life, we are comfortable with the familiar—our families, even the dysfunctional ones, our jobs, our churches, and we can resist God's call to a "higher life." How does Regina's journey to follow God inspire you?

6. Tanner has to find courage to face his twin daughters

again. Discuss his dilemma. Do you know someone who walked away from children or family because the pain of the past was too great? Do you see how his willingness to serve Regina ultimately restored his children to him?

7. Princess Alice never told her granddaughter she was a princess. Why do you think she hid the truth? Was the fairy tale really her way of telling Regina her true identity? Is reading the Bible a way to see God's "story" for us? His personal letter to our hearts?

8. What do you make of the glowing light around the stable in the woods? Is there some "glowing stable" in your life where God is directing your attention?

9. Regina's ability to restore Hessenberg to its "essence" is demonstrated when she sings the evening song. Discuss times in your life when music or worship has restored your heart to peace or some element of truth.

10. Because of Tanner's view of himself through the lens of his past mistakes, he believes God, his father, and others see him as a failure. But when he meets the bishop at St. John's Chapel, he realizes he's forgiven. It's a symbolic scene to show God's forgiveness toward all of us. Can you "see" how Jesus sees you rather than how you see yourself?

11. Regina loves to wear jeans and T-shirts, then cowboy boots with her dresses. She's unique. What is your favorite type of clothes to wear?

12. Do you think Regina and Tanner will live happily ever after?

Susie Warren, friend and teacher, brainstormer, writing partner. I wouldn't be where I am in my writing journey without your wisdom and inspiration. Love you, friend!

Beth Vogt for brainstorming last-minute ideas and cheering me on. Appreciate and love you!

My agent, Chip MacGregor, for your support and wisdom.

My husband, my own prince, my rock, and best friend. You demonstrate amazing grace as you roll with the writer's life.

Thanks to the entire staff of HarperCollins Christian Fiction: Daisy Hutton, it's an honor to work with you. Katie Bond, so thrilled we get to keep working together. Ruthie Dean, you bless me so much! Becky Monds for your hard work. Kristen Vasgaard for great cover designs and the rest of the fiction team for *all* you do!

Thanks to Kimberly Buckner for lending me the line about Reggie looking like a lit match. I look forward to holding your book in my hand one day!

Thanks to Darren Plumber for helping me keep Al Lovett real.

And to my neighbors for lending me the cool name Beswick.

Big thanks to all of you readers! Put your name in here: _____. You make this journey worthwhile. Especially on the hardest days. Just when doubt is grabbing hold and I wonder, "Why do I do this?" one of you will post on Facebook or send e-mail with encouraging words, and I realize I'm not alone and that writing a book is about more than me! From the bottom of my heart, thank you!

Worship leaders Jeremy Riddle and Steffany Frizzell Gretzinger. Thanks for demonstrating your love for Jesus through your songs. I worshiped almost nonstop to the YouTube worship set of "Our God" while finishing this book. At times, the Lord's abiding presence was so evident I raced toward the deadline knowing He was my inspiration and help.

Jesus the Christ, my life, writing, everything I do is for You and Your name because it's all meaningless without You. I'm so humbled to call You my Lord and my friend! For Your glory!

ACKNOWLEDGMENTS

J love this part of writing a book—saying thanks to everyone who encouraged, blessed, and helped me along the way.

Hessenberg and Brighton Kingdom history, people, and dialog are entirely of my imagination.

Big royal thanks to:

The authors and historians who documented royalty and European history.

My editor, Susan Brower, who took my raw manuscript and gave me wise direction on how to fix it. I love your enthusiasm for this series. Thank you!

Line editor, Jean Bloom. Thank you.

My brother, Danny Hayes, for classic car help and for the idea of the Duesenberg. Any and all mistakes are mine.

Author Davis Bunn, for ideas on how to simplify Hessenberg's independence issue, and financial planner Sarah Burnett, for help with the financial story thread. Any and ALL mistakes are mine as they relate to the real world. But as they relate to the fiction world, they are all true.

Cheryl Hyatt Smith for once again coming through with a key contact at a key time in the book! You rock, sister!

Moyer Fuel Tank Renu in Greensburg, Pennsylvania, for giving me tips on restoring a fuel tank!